KU-008-060

Praise for *No Good Brother*:

'Keevil's writing is unmissable . . . quite simply
a brilliant writer'
Viv Groskop, author of *The Anna Karenina Fix*

'*No Good Brother* is a paean to brotherly loyalty and a
meditation on the things we can change and the things we
must learn to love regardless. It is also the funniest and
most exciting book I've read in years. A grand adventure
in the spirit of Mark Twain, it is reckless and wild and
beautiful, like something dreamed up by Cormac McCarthy
and Hunter S Thompson on a drunken camping trip.
It's as big and as perfect as the prairie sky'
D.D. Johnston, author of *Peace, Love & Petrol Bombs*

'A tender and at turns thrilling novel about grief and
the way it seeps unshakably into the lives of the living.
Keevil's storytelling is both elegant and meaty and his
prose stunning as per; I could almost taste the
bitter sea air of Vancouver's North Shore'
Rachel Trezise, author of *Fresh Apples*

'Quite a story. Keevil's prose proceeds with
the laconic madness of a patient horse,
and the same ability to buck and kick'
Cynan Jones, author of *The Dig*

70004411790X

Also by Tyler Keevil

Fireball
Burrard Inlet
The Drive

NO GOOD BROTHER

Tyler Keevil

THE BOROUGH PRESS

The Borough Press
An imprint of HarperCollins*Publishers*
1 London Bridge Street
London SE1 9GF

www.harpercollins.co.uk

This paperback edition 2019
1

First published by HarperCollins*Publishers* 2018

Copyright © Tyler Keevil 2018

Tyler Keevil asserts the moral right to
be identified as the author of this work

A catalogue record for this book
is available from the British Library

Excerpt from 'Highway Patrolman' by Bruce Springsteen.
Copyright © 1982 Bruce Springsteen (Global Music Rights).
Reprinted by permission. International copyright secured.
All rights reserved.

ISBN: 978-0-00-822891-0

This novel is entirely a work of fiction.
The names, characters and incidents portrayed in it are the
work of the author's imagination. Any resemblances to actual
persons, living or dead, events or localities is entirely coincidental.

Set in Simoncini Garamond Std by Palimpsest Book Production
Limited, Falkirk, Stirlingshire

Printed and bound in Great Britain by
CPI Group (UK) Ltd, Croydon, CR0 4YY

All rights reserved. No part of this publication may be
reproduced, stored in a retrieval system, or transmitted,
in any form or by any means, electronic, mechanical,
photocopying, recording or otherwise, without the prior
permission of the publishers.

MIX
Paper from
responsible sources
FSC™ C007454

This book is produced from independently certified FSC™ paper
to ensure responsible forest management.

For more information visit: **www.harpercollins.co.uk/green**

For my brother

'For I know that in me, that is,
in my flesh, dwelleth no good thing.'

Romans 7:18a

'Man turns his back on his family,
well he just ain't no good.'

Bruce Springsteen

Chapter One

THE END OF THIS STORY is pretty well known, since people wound up getting killed and the trials were in the news. My brother Jake was portrayed in a lot of different ways. Some said he was just a patsy who had gotten caught up in the scheme of these upstart gangsters. Others said he did it for the money. Then there were the ones who actually believed he was an activist of some sort, or a gentleman robber, and I suppose it was easy to sympathize with that on account of what happened to him. But none of those versions is true, or entirely true. I intend to tell it straight and lay out how it all happened, and how I became involved.

It started when Jake showed up at the Westco plant and boatyard, the day we got back from herring season. That was the end
of February, last year. A Monday. I was standing at the stern of
the *Western Lady* across from Sugar, this giant Haida guy who
shares the licence with Albert, the skipper. Sugar and I were the
ones working the hold, but we had to wait around in the drizzling
cold for the plant workers to get the hose and Transvac pump
in place and line up the sorting bins. They were union guys and
on the clock and in no hurry. Albert was up top, directing them
from the wheelhouse.

'Holy Mary,' he yelled at them, which is about as close to
swearing as he gets. 'You fellows gonna *move* that thing or just
hope it wanders down here by itself?'

'Yeah, yeah,' they said.

But they moved a little faster. Albert has that effect on people.

I rubbed my bad hand with my good one. The hand that got
crushed hurts something fierce in the cold, even now, years after
the accident. Sugar held the water hose with the steel nozzle
cradled against his hip, casual as a gunfighter. While we waited,
he directed it into the hold and let out a jet-blast of water,
churning the fish. The herring, all belly-wet and slickly silver,
were packed together in a soupy mix of blood and brine, still
flecked with flakes of ice. It was a perfect-looking hold (Albert
doesn't over-fish and only ever takes his quota) but it still made
me sad as hell to see. The herring had been in there for forty-
eight hours and a lot of them were still half alive, still twitching.
They gazed up from the depths of the hull with dull and desperate
eyes that had no real understanding of their place or fate. Some
of them were so ready to spawn they were already leaking roe:
little yellow globules that glistened like fool's gold.

I heard a vehicle pulling into the lot across the water from where we were moored. I looked over and saw Jake's truck: a beat-up orange Toyota, twenty years old, with a muffler all shot to hell. I hadn't seen my brother since Christmas. That hadn't gone so well. We'd gotten in a fight – first with each other, then with some other guys – and he'd taken off for a while because one of them had been hurt pretty bad. Jake had a record and was worried that the guy might report it, maybe lay an assault charge on him. But nothing ever came of it. I'd talked to Jake on the phone before I headed out for herring season, and he'd gotten some new job that he claimed was legitimate. A cleaning job, was what he'd said.

Jake climbed out of the truck. He was wearing torn jeans and a bomber jacket and his red bandana. He came to the fence that separates the lot from the docks and leaned on it, his fingers hooked like talons between the chain-links. He spotted me and deliberately rattled the fence, like an ape in a cage. He was grinning like an ape, too.

Sugar asked, 'He your friend?'

'My brother.'

By then the union guys had manoeuvred the Transvac along our port side, but were still fiddling with the controls. I waved to get Albert's attention.

'Give me a minute, Albert?'

'A minute is all you got.'

I vaulted the gunnel and landed clumsily on the dock, turning my right ankle but not badly. I made my way around the boatyard and up the gangway that connects the docks to the wharf. The water beneath reflected the cannery, but the image was all broken up by the dribbles of rain riddling the surface.

Jake waited for me at his truck, leaning back against the side, smoking a cigarette. As I came up he smiled. He'd lost one tooth when he was in jail, and still hadn't bothered to get a cap. His hair was long and greasy and held back by the bandana. The bandana was faded and tatty as hell but it was the one Sandy had given him, years ago, so he would never replace it.

'You look like a real fisherman, Poncho,' he said.

'And you look like an ex-con, Lefty.'

I removed my left work glove and we clasped hands, pulling each other into a hug. Jake and I always shake hands like that – with our left – because he's left-handed and my right hand is the bad one. Two of the fingers are gone and the other three are all mangled, like the legs of a crab crushed under a rock. Whenever I shake hands with anyone else it's always awkward, because even left-handed guys have learned to shake with their right.

'You forgiven me for sucker punching you?' he asked.

'Let's forget it.'

'Close enough for me.'

'How'd you know to come?'

'Stopped by the cannery last week. They said your boat was due back this morning.'

I looked over at the boat. Albert was watching us from the wheelhouse, arms folded over his chest like a sentry. The union guys were passing the Transvac hose to Sugar.

'We're just about to empty the holds,' I said.

'What time do you get off tonight?'

'We don't get shore leave until the weekend.'

'I need to talk to you before then.'

'About what?'

He flicked his cigarette to the ground, between us, and twisted it out with his boot. 'I just need to talk to you is all. Can't you get away tonight?'

'It's boat policy. Nobody leaves till the boat's stripped down. If Albert lets me go, the other guys will be choked.'

'So sneak away.'

'I share a cabin with the other deckhands.'

'Ah, shit.' He exhaled his last drag, which he'd been holding in. 'Well, damn – I'll be gone by this weekend.'

'Where you going?'

'That's what I want to talk to you about.'

From the boat, Albert hollered to me across the water: 'Timothy!'

He held out his hands, palm up, as if to ask what was going on. I waved.

'Timothy?' Jake said. 'What is he, your dad?'

'I got to go, man.'

'Ask him. Tell him it's important. You got wheels?'

'Not any more.'

'Walk down to the Firehall and meet me there, then.'

'What the hell for?'

Jake just looked at me. He looked at me for a long time.

'Oh,' is all I said.

'You forgot.'

'No I didn't.'

'Goddamn liar.'

I started backing away. 'Look, I'll try to come, okay?'

'Whatever. I'll be there tonight, with or without you.'

He opened the door to his truck, and slid back behind the wheel.

I said, 'If I can't make it, I'll call you.'

'If you can't make it, don't bother.'

He slammed the door and gunned the engine. As I turned back towards the gangway I heard him peeling out, spinning his wheels as he left the lot.

On the *Western Lady*, Albert had come down from the

wheelhouse and was helping Sugar lower the Transvac hose into the hold. I hopped onto a bollard and used that as a stepladder to clamber back over the gunnel of the *Lady*.

'I got this, Albert,' I said.

'You sure? Because I can take over if you want to play with your friend.'

'No, no – it's all good.'

He grunted and stepped aside. The hose was about a foot in diameter and made of ribbed plastic. I positioned it so that the mouth dipped six inches into the soup of herring, then nodded at Sugar. He began blasting away with the water and we signalled for the dock workers to fire up the pump. The hose started to buck in my arms, wiggling amid the herring and snorting them up like the long nose of an anteater. The dark bodies flashed through the funnel, on their way to the sorter and the bins and a better place.

At around five we clocked off. Sugar went to clean himself up in the cannery washrooms, but I needed to talk to Albert. I took off my slicker and gloves and moseyed on into the galley. Evelyn, Albert's wife, was standing at the stove, stirring something in a steel pot. She was a big lady, low-built and wide-hipped, and when we set our nets she directed us on deck while Albert navigated. She was pretty much the second-in-command on the *Lady*. Albert, he liked to joke that she was actually the head honcho, the big chief.

'Smells good, Evelyn.'

'You don't.'

'I know it.' Even without the slicker, I still stank of herring. 'What you got on there?'

'Beef stew, and an apple pie.'

'Hot damn.'

'You mean hot darn.' She pointed at me with her spoon. 'Tracy's coming for dinner.'

Tracy was their youngest daughter. She'd worked on the boat when I first started but had taken this season off to train for her sea captain's certificate.

I said, 'She mentioned something about that.'

'She say anything else?'

'What else might she have said?'

Evelyn smiled, and shook her head. 'Just something we been talking about.'

She sounded sly, secretive, and raised a spoon of stew to give it a taste. She smacked her tongue theatrically, making it clear she intended to leave me wondering.

'Say,' I said, as if it had just occurred to me. 'Is Albert about?'

'Down in the engine room.'

'Still at it.'

'Always.'

I kicked off my boots and headed that way, down the short hall between the two cabins where we slept – one for Albert and Evelyn, one for us grunts – and down a short stepladder. The engine room was divided from the rest of the boat by a hatch, which was ajar. I pushed it open. Inside it was cramped and low and you had to hunch over as you walked to avoid cracking your head. Albert was lying on his back, shining a flashlight at the underside of some pipework.

'Problems, Captain?'

'Nothing that ain't fixable. Leaking a bit of coolant.'

I hunkered down beside him, squatting on my haunches, and watched him work for a bit. He reached for a wrench lying next to him, fitted it to a nut on one of the pipes, and gave it a twist.

He held his palm beneath the joint, waiting to see if that had done the trick.

'Need a hand?' I asked.

'I'll tell you when you get around to asking whatever it is you want to ask.'

'Okay, then.' I sat for a time, staring at the joint rather than Albert. 'That fellow in the truck today – that was my brother.'

'The troublemaker.'

'He ain't all that bad.'

'Thought he did time in Ferndale.'

'That was a while back.'

'And?'

There was an oil rag on the floor at my feet. I picked that up and began wrapping it around my bad hand, for no real reason.

'He's only in town for a day, and wants to see me tonight.'

'You don't get shore leave till Saturday.'

'I know that.'

'Nobody leaves the boat until she's in shape.'

'I know that too.'

Albert shook his head and made a sound, sort of disgusted. At first I thought it was a reaction to what I'd asked, but he held up his hand, showing me the greenish glisten of coolant.

'Washer must be shot.'

He went to work with his wrench again.

He said, 'If I let you go, what do I tell the other guys?'

I didn't have an answer to that, so I didn't try.

'Can't very well let you go and keep them here.'

'No sir. Reckon not.'

'But you want me to make an exception, so you can meet your no-good brother.'

'I told you – it ain't that he's no good.'

I said it sharper than I normally would have. It registered. I could tell by the way Albert paused, just for a second, in twisting that nut. Then he kept working it until it came loose, and with his forefinger fished out the old washer. He gave it to me. 'Pass me another, will you? Should be in the top of the toolbox, front-left compartment.'

I found a new one and handed it over and waited while he fitted it. There was no use negotiating or haggling with him.

He said, 'We're having Tracy over for tea and pie.'

'Evelyn told me.'

'Did she now?'

'She was acting pretty mysterious about something.'

He looked at me, and I could tell by the look that he was in on it, whatever it was.

'It's important to Evelyn. I suppose you want to skip that, too.'

'Tracy is working the night shift, so won't stay late. I could go after.'

He was twisting the nut back on, turning the wrench in swift rotations. On his upper forearm he had this tattoo of a heart, pink and sun-faded, which shifted with each movement.

'I can't give you permission to do that, Tim.'

I stared at the oil rag, at my bad hand.

'I figured that would be the case,' I said.

'But if you slip away – say after we're all down – I might look the other way.'

'Thanks, Albert. Thanks for that.'

'I ain't doing you no favours. If you get caught, or they see you, I'll come down hard on you just the same.'

He tightened the nut the last few turns, snugging it into place. On the last twist the wrench trembled with tension and the muscles in his forearm flexed. When it was done he nodded, satisfied, as if that had decided it.

Chapter Two

BEFORE DINNER, WHILE WE WAITED for Tracy, I hopped on dish duty. I wanted to get a head start, and I suppose make amends in advance for what I intended to do later. So I stood at the sink and scrubbed away at Evelyn's pots and pans. In the window above the sink I could see the reflection of the others sitting at the galley table behind me, their images transparent and ghost-like. There was Sugar and Albert and Evelyn and Big Ben, Sugar's nephew: a quiet kid with a buzz cut and a scar across his nose, who'd joined the crew the same season as me. The four of them were talking about hockey and listening to Gram Parsons. It was one of Albert's scratchy old cassettes, and the ragged vocals always reminded me of Jake, the way Jake used to sing.

Evelyn still hadn't said any more about her little secret. She'd told me I had to wait till Tracy got there. Since I was at the window I spotted her first: clambering over the port-side gunnel. Like her mother she was strong and solidly built and at ease on the boats and water. When she straightened up she saw me and smiled, her cheeks burnished red from the cold.

'Company's here,' I said.

Albert got up and hurried to open the door for his daughter, reaching it just as she did.

'Should have called out,' he said. 'Would have helped you aboard.'

'I'm training to run this boat, Dad. Reckon I can board it myself.'

Big Ben shook her hand and Sugar told him that was no way to greet a lady, then demonstrated by wrapping Tracy up in a bear hug and lifting her right off the ground. He'd known her since she was six years old and could make that kind of thing seem completely natural. I shuffled over to join them, and when it came my turn to greet Tracy I hugged her as well, though with me it was different. I hugged her cautiously, as if she were a cousin or a formal acquaintance. I always worried, hugging her, that it would seem improper in front of Albert.

'Let's all sit down,' Evelyn said.

'I just got the pots to finish.'

'Oh, leave the dishes, Tim. We have company.'

We sat around the galley table, pulling up a pair of extra chairs for Tracy and me. Evelyn put on her oven mitts – these mitts in the shape of flippers we got her two seasons back – and brought the stew over to the table, along with homemade buns and a bowl of salad. This was all dished out, plate by plate, and the plates were handed around the table to the person on the end: Sugar, in this case. That was how we did it. Everything we did on the boat had its own ritual, and eating dinner was no different.

As we ate we chatted about the herring season. Tracy had already heard from Evelyn that we'd made our quota, and that the rest of the company had, too. Sugar and Albert shared the licence but operated through Westco in a collective. We told her about where we'd cast our nets that year and some of the stories we'd brought back: the skiff that had run aground and the yahoos on the *Western Rider* who'd gotten gooned and overslept and nearly missed the fisheries window. We moaned a little about the weather and how hard Albert worked us.

'Your dad sure gets his money's worth out of his poor crew,' Sugar said.

'Don't I know it,' Tracy said.

'These fellows,' Albert said, shaking his head, 'would sleep through a hurricane if I let them. They would sleep through the End of Days.'

After the stew came the pie, and when that was done we got out the cards and played High Chicago for pennies, which was another ritual. Sugar lost quickly, and after declaring bankruptcy he palmed the table-top to push himself up. He's six-four and two-twenty, and in the close confines of the deckhouse he moved slowly, carefully.

'You coming for a walk?' he asked his nephew.

The way he said it wasn't a question. Big Ben folded his hand and followed his uncle outside. We played a few more rounds and Evelyn made a pot of coffee and we got to talking about payday and the cheques we all had coming our way. Albert was going to install a new furnace in their place out in New West, and Evelyn, she was putting some of her share away for a trip to Palm Springs. But even then I had the feeling that it was all preamble. I was still waiting for whatever it was they were going to spring on me.

'What about you, Tim?' Tracy asked. 'You got any big plans once this taskmaster sets you loose?'

'Ah, you know me. I ain't got much imagination.'

'No raising Cain?' She elbowed me. 'No lady friend to buy pretty things for?'

'Well, there is one.' Evelyn stopped sipping her tea. They all looked at me, waiting. 'Old woman by the name of Evelyn,' I said. 'Might need a new dishwasher.'

Evelyn got up and slapped me with her flipper mitt.

'No sir,' Albert said, playing along. 'Nobody buys my woman a dishwasher but me!'

The joke ran its course, and as Evelyn settled back down she said, 'Albert – why don't you tell Tim. Tell him what we were talking about.'

'Oh no,' Tracy said.

Albert frowned at her, and cleared his throat, and then spread out one hand to stare at the fingernails. The cuticles were rimmed with black: a lifetime's worth of engine oil and grease. He ran his thumbnail beneath the nail on his forefinger, as if removing some. Then he said, 'You know we normally head up to our cabin in Squamish for a week at the end of season. Well, we'll be heading up this Saturday, after we finish, and wondered if you wanted to come.'

'Wow,' I said, which was all I could think to say. 'That's real kind of you.'

'Our boy Rick will be there, with his kids, and Tracy.'

Tracy was staring into her teacup, as if trying to read the leaves.

'That would be really something,' I said.

'Of course,' Albert added, 'if you got other things going on . . .'

'No. No I don't got anything else. The only thing keeping me here would be my mother. If she needs me, I mean. Seeing as I've already been away for a while.'

'Of course, Timothy,' Evelyn said. 'You've got to look after your family, too.'

'It would only be for a few days,' Albert said.

'That sounds real nice.'

'Think about it, anyway,' Evelyn added.

'I will. I really will.'

She stood up and began to clear the cups, even though mine was only half-finished.

'Well,' Tracy said, 'I better get back. Shift starts in an hour.'

She was working security at a local college, while undertaking her training.

'I'll walk you out, if you like.'

The docks were quiet, aside from a few old-timers on one of the boats, drinking to celebrate the end of season, their voices and laughter echoing across the water. Tracy and I walked in silence until we crossed the gangway. Then she said, 'I'm sorry about that. They like to play matchmaker.'

'It's a nice idea.'

'Nice is an easy word.'

'I mean it would be fun.'

'Well, maybe it would be.'

We reached her vehicle: a classic Jeep that she'd salvaged from the scrap heap, and fixed up. She'd parked in the same spot that Jake had earlier. She unlocked the driver's door and before she got in I hugged her again. In the dark, away from the others, I could have held onto her longer, and maybe I should have. But it was funny. I still acted the same way.

That night, it wasn't hard to slip away. I just waited until Sugar and Big Ben were asleep (this was easy to determine because they both snore like bears) and then crept out of the cabin, eased open the galley door, and lowered myself down to the dock. Sneaking off felt shady and dishonest but those were feelings I generally associated with my brother, and any plan of his which involved me.

The Firehall, where we were meeting, is on the corner of Gore and Cordova, just a few blocks away from the Westco plant. It isn't a firehall any more. It's an arts centre and performance space now – a fairly well-known one. They produce shows of their own and also put on work by touring theatre and dance companies. The outside still looks like a firehall: worn brownstone walls, glossy red doors, and those high-arched windows.

The night I met Jake, a company called The Dance Collective was performing. The name was spelled in block capitals across the marquee, and on the A-frame board out front a series of posters listed the various dancers and their pieces. I walked cautiously up the wheelchair ramp and stood for a time outside the doors, peering in through the glass.

The place hadn't changed much. On the left was the box office, and on the right was the bar – a classy-looking affair, with a marble bar top, chrome beer taps, and leather stools. On some of the tables platters of appetizers and hors d'oeuvres had been laid out: smoked salmon and pastries and little vegetable rolls. In the foyer thirty or forty guests – a mix of well-dressed artists, hipsters, and bohemian types – stood chatting and milling about.

All of it looked so eerily familiar I felt like a ghost, lurking in the cold and haunting my old life.

I have to admit: I just about turned and walked away.

But my brother was in there, waiting for me. So I went ahead, passing through the glass doors and falling backwards into memory. I knew exactly where to find Jake too: hunched at the bar, ignoring the room and world.

I sat down next to him and he said, 'So the old man let you loose.'

There were three empty bottles of Molson in front of him and he was already looking a bit belligerent.

'He said he wouldn't stop me, if I snuck off.'

'Better make the most of it.' He motioned to the bartender, signalling for service. 'Two more Molson and two shots of Wiser's.'

'Only beer, for me,' I said.

'Forget that. You just got back from sea, sailor.'

'I'll be scrubbing holds at six thirty.'

The bartender – a slim, trim guy with a stud earring – looked at us in a way that made it clear he'd rather be serving anybody else.

'Do you want the whisky or not?' he asked.

'I ordered it, didn't I?' Jake said. Then, to me: 'Get this bartender. I been tipping him big and behaving myself and he still treats me like a dishrag.'

Jake folded a twenty in half and flicked it towards the guy. The bill fluttered in the air like a demented butterfly, before coming to settle in front of the bar taps. The bartender took it reluctantly and smoothed it out before slipping it into his till and pouring the drinks. When the whiskies landed in front of Jake, he nudged one towards me.

'Drink up,' he said.

'I ain't playing, Jake.'

He shrugged and scooped it up to knock back himself.

'You been drinking here all night?' I asked Jake.

'Hell no. I saw the show.'

I looked towards the stage doors. A few of the dancers were coming out, now. You could tell by the way they dressed – track-suits or tights and leggings – and also by how they held themselves: that particular upright posture, chins outthrust, heads perfectly level.

'You watched the whole dance show on your own?'

'Why not? I know more about it than most of these posers.'

The bartender, bringing over the beers, frowned when he heard that. Jake waggled his head and stuck out his tongue at him, as if to imply some kind of uncontrollable insanity.

'Was it any good?' I asked him.

'It was hit and miss.'

'Any unarmed turnips?'

Jake snorted and sprayed beer on the bar top.

Before one of our sister's performances, we'd seen this guy do a modern dance in the nude. He'd swaggered up to the front of the stage, swinging his pecker like a little lasso, and announced that he was an unarmed turnip. That had been the benchmark, from then on, and the kind of thing that Sandy had to rise above: the legions of unarmed and untalented turnips.

'No – no turnips, thank God,' Jake said, wiping his mouth with his hand. 'But hardly any of them were classically trained. You can tell. They just don't have the range, like her.'

'Nobody did.'

That wasn't really true, but it was true enough, in our minds. My beer was still sitting there – I'd been eyeing it but hadn't touched it yet. Now I reached for it, in a way that felt momentous.

It tasted smooth and cold and nice as ice cream. I swivelled around on my stool and leant back against the bar to watch the crowd.

'I ain't been back here since,' I said.

'That's because you're trying to forget.'

'I haven't forgotten anything.'

'Except the anniversary.'

'I was at sea. The season was late, this year.'

'On your boat with your little fishing family.'

'They're good people.'

'They ain't kin.'

'I'm here, aren't I?'

'Your body is.'

A dancer came up to the bar beside Jake and ordered a vodka lemonade. Her hair was pulled back into a tight bun, so you could see where the roots tugged at her scalp, and she still had sparkles and stage make-up on her face.

Jake glanced sidelong at her, then down at her feet.

'This is one of the real dancers,' he said to me. 'She's done ballet.'

She looked at him, startled, still holding a ten up for the bartender.

'How'd you know that?'

'You're standing in third position. Only ballet dancers do that.'

Jake said all that without looking at her. He said it in a calm and certain way that is difficult to describe and unlike how anybody else talks – at least unlike how they would talk to a stranger, off-the-cuff. She might not have liked it, but he had her attention, all right.

'Did you enjoy the show?' she asked.

'I liked your dance, and a few of the others. But you want some advice? You need to work on your arabesques. You bend your back leg too much.'

She turned to face him more fully, almost as if she were squaring up to him.

'It's not ballet. Modern isn't as strict as that.'

'An arabesque is an arabesque.'

'I can do a proper arabesque if I want.'

'That's what I'm saying.'

Her drink was ready, and she took it without thanking the bartender, as if it was an inconvenience or a distraction. She looked about ready to dash the vodka in Jake's face.

'You sure know a lot about it,' she said.

'Our sister used to dance. She used to dance here.'

The dancer put her drink down. She looked hard at Jake's face, and then over to me.

'Oh my God,' she said. 'You're Sandra's brothers, aren't you?'

'That's right. Jake and Tim.'

'I've met you. I danced with her. It's Denise, remember?'

Without waiting for a reply, she hugged Jake, and then me. She started tearing up, so I patted her forearm, in a way that felt awkward, even to me.

'It's so good to see you. It's been so long.'

'Ten years,' Jake said, tonelessly.

'I still think about her.' She was wiping at her eyes, now. All her mascara had run down her cheeks in black streaks and it was hard as hell, seeing that. I don't know. It was as if she were crying for all three of us. 'I was younger than her. She was the one we all looked up to. She was the dancer we all wanted to be.'

'Me too,' I said.

'Oh – you wanted to be a dancer, too?'

Jake started laughing, and I had to explain that no – I meant I'd looked up to Sandy.

'Of course. Everybody did.'

Denise took the straw out of her drink and threw it on the bar top and drank most of her vodka lemonade straight from the glass, knocking it back. When she finished, a little breathless, she asked, 'What are you guys doing here, anyway?'

'Just came down to see the place, again.'

'Are you coming to the after-party? We're going to the Alibi Room, I think.'

Jake said, 'I got to take my brother somewhere. But we should meet up later.'

'For sure.'

She pulled a pen from her purse, jotted down a number, handed it to him. Then she hugged Jake again, and me, longer this time – really squeezing the breath out of me. I could feel the strength in her body, thin and lithe as a wire cable, and she still smelled of sweat and activity, of a body in motion. All of that was so familiar, like hugging a memory or a dream.

'I should mingle,' she said. 'But I'll see you later.'

She took another look at us, not quite believing it, and moved off. We swivelled back to the bar and drank our beers in silence and after about five or six seconds Jake said, 'Jesus.'

'I know.'

I motioned to the bartender: two more whiskies. When he brought them this time he treated us with a kind of deference, his eyes downcast. He'd overheard some of it, I guess. I gave him another twenty and waved away the change and Jake and I knocked back the shots. I felt the belly-burn, that old familiar smoulder.

I said, 'You said you wanted to take me somewhere.'

Two months before Sandy died, she auditioned for a dancing job in Paris with the Compagnie Cléo de Mérode, and landed it. At first I didn't understand the significance of that. I just knew it meant she would be living in Europe for a while. But the full extent of her achievement was made clear to us at the celebration party. It was held at the house of one of Sandy's dancer friends and all the people there were either dancers or choreographers or artistic types of one sort or another, aside from me and Jake and Maria, who he was still with at the time, and who has her own part in this story.

Jake and I were working the bar, mixing cocktails and pouring drinks and generally acting like jackasses. It was magical and heavenly to be surrounded by, and serving, all of these lean-limbed, long-necked women with perfect posture, who seemed to float from room to room and every so often stopped to order from us and teasingly flirt with us because we were Sandy's little brothers and in that way were little brothers to them all.

At one point Sandy and Maria came up together, and Maria ordered them both a Bloody Mary. This was a unique opportunity because Sandy hardly ever drank, due to the demands of being a dancer, and even when she did it was seemingly impossible to get her drunk. Our sister was always focused, severe, in complete control – both of herself and us. She was the only one who could keep Jake reined in, seeing as our old man was no longer around, and our ma, well, she'd had it tough for a while. And since Sandy took care of all of us, she never relented in what I would call her vigilance.

That night we made a good go of it. Jake mixed the Bloody Marys and dumped a good splash of vodka in both. He served them the real way – over ice, with salt around the rims – and Maria scooped hers up and raised it high to toast and passed on what some local hotshot choreographer had just told her: he'd said that Sandy getting in with the Compagnie Cléo de Mérode was the same as if she'd won the gold medal of modern dance.

'Gold medal winner,' Maria repeated.

'Solid gold sister,' Jake said, and kissed her on the cheek.

Sandy laughed it off, but the phrase stuck with me, and the memory of the night. Sandy had two more Bloody Marys and sat Jake and I down, very solemnly, and laid out her plans for moving the whole family to Europe so we could stay together. Jake could make his music and I'd apprentice to be a carpenter and Ma would sit on our balcony and have coffee and croissants every morning. Maria claimed she wanted to come too and Sandy said that was fine, but she – Maria – would have to marry Jake and when they had kids Sandy would be the godmother. Then once Sandy hit thirty she would retire and marry a French plumber and start a family of her own and we would all move back home and buy an acreage in the Okanagan, and I could build houses for each of us and her husband would fit the plumbing and together we would set up polytunnels and vegetable fields and start our own farm.

She had all these plans, crazy but brilliant enough to believe in. At the time, we had an unquestioning faith that Sandy could shape our future through her force of will, and even now it doesn't seem to me as if that faith was naïve.

Later in the night, when Jake and I had abandoned our posts at the bar, we built this makeshift sedan out of broomsticks and a kitchen chair. We put Sandy in that and hoisted her up on our shoulders and carried her around the party, with Maria clearing the way in front of us. When we passed everybody cheered and applauded, and Sandy played her part perfectly: sitting upright, looking stern and commanding as Cleopatra, our golden queen and champion.

Chapter Three

JAKE HAD HIS TRUCK AT the Firehall but he was too far gone to
drive (he was very particular about that, on account of what
happened) and instead we took a cab down Granville and west
on Marine Drive towards the Southlands area. There are some
huge spreads out that way: big rancher-style houses with sprawling
yards, which might have been smallholdings or farmsteads back
in the old days. We cruised past those and I had no idea what
we were doing, or why, but something in me – my brotherly
pride, I suppose – refused to pester him about it.

Jake told the cabbie to drop us at a place called Castle Meadow

Stables and Country Club. The sign out front was small and discreet: just a brass plaque mounted on a gateway beside a curving drive. We walked up the drive in the dark, crunching gravel beneath our bootheels. At the end of the drive was a parking lot, and the clubhouse. Over to the left were the stables, still and quiet at this time, and beyond them a field or paddock or what have you.

As we approached the front doors, I finally gave in and asked, 'You going to tell me what we're doing way the hell out here?'

'Just getting a drink,' Jake said, and pushed through the doors.

They opened into a foyer, leading on to the clubhouse and bar: a big room with low ceilings and hardwood floors. The walls were lined with wainscot panelling, and above the wainscot hung black-and-white pictures of old racehorses, presumably famous ones. The place felt like an old-time golf club, crossed with a western-style saloon. In one corner a cluster of video poker machines bleeped forlornly.

It was getting on near ten o'clock and the only other customers were a bunch of good old boys wearing plaid shirts and cowboy boots and, sitting a little apart, two younger guys in suits. At the bar Jake ordered us two more Molsons and two shots of Crown and asked the bartender to put it on his tab. The woman smiled at him and punched it into her screen, and I figured this was partly why we'd come out here – just for me to witness Jake order on a tab.

We sat down and knocked back our shots, which were tasting better and better. After being dry for so long it was going to my head and I felt very tender towards my little brother.

I said, 'How'd you get membership in a place like this?'

'I ain't a member.'

'How'd you get a tab, then?'

'This is where I work.'

'I thought you had a cleaning job.'

'I do – cleaning stables.'

It took me some time to get my head around the notion of Jake cleaning stables, or being associated with that realm in any way. It just seemed so peculiar. But then, no more peculiar than delivering brake parts or laying paving slabs or working on a seiner or any of the other jobs we'd both done over the years.

'So you're like a stable boy?' I asked.

'Hell no. Stable boys actually look after the horses. They groom them and feed them and dress their injuries and crap. I'm not even really supposed to go in the stalls. I just clean the alleyways between the stalls, hose down the drainage troughs, carry loads of horseshit out back to the bin. Make sure the stable boys and trainers have everything they need.'

'How in the hell'd you land a job like that?'

'Connections I made inside. A lot of the gangsters are into horses.'

He nodded significantly at the two guys in suits. They were eating chicken wings and talking earnestly about something and didn't appear drunk at all. If Jake hadn't pointed them out I would have assumed they were businessmen.

'What – they *ride* them?' I said.

'They ride them and breed them and race them. This is one of the places you can keep them, if you don't have a ranch of your own. And I clean up their shit. Literally.'

'I guess hard work is honest work,' I said, 'as Albert would say.'

'Work sucks. But it's something. And I get a tab.'

'A tab you've got to pay.'

'Not tonight I don't.'

He looked up at the TV above us. There were half a dozen spread around the room. The screens were all the same size – thirty inches or so – and they were all showing the same image: a long shot of a racetrack in some exotic location, where the skies were dreamily blue and where everybody wore white linen clothing and wide-brimmed hats and carried parasols. It made me think of Monte Carlo or Casablanca. Some place that we'd never see, anyway.

'Mostly it's a farce,' Jake said. 'Hardly any of their horses get into real races, let alone win.'

'But the bigshots need something to do with all that money, eh?'

'You got it.'

We touched glasses and drained what remained of our beers. It was warm and flat and tasted almost soapy, like watered-down dish detergent. As I finished I heard a buzzer going off, and the TV screen images changed to a close-up of the starting gates, springing open. In the faraway country the horses were racing now. At a nearby table, this beefy guy with a mullet started shouting at one of the horses, telling it to come on, come on. But even before the home stretch he'd given up on that and sat watching morosely. He was all on his own.

'How's Ma?' Jake asked.

'No worse, but no better, either.'

'I was thinking of going over there this weekend, if you want to come.'

'I usually do, when I'm not on the boat.'

'The model son.'

Jake picked up a bar coaster and drummed it repeatedly on the table, tapping out a rhythm that I recognized but couldn't quite place. I knew he was holding something back.

I said, 'Down at the plant you said you needed to talk to me.'

'I'm going on a little trip and I just wanted to see you and Ma before I go.'

'What kind of trip?'

'Don't worry about it.'

'I'm not worrying.'

'Worry about your other family, and your little fishing girl-friend.'

'Her name's Tracy. And she ain't my girlfriend.'

'Sure – she's your mermaid.'

'I don't know what you got against them.'

'Forget it. Tonight, I just want to have a good time with my big brother.'

Hearing that, more than anything else, made me start worrying in earnest. Jake hopped up and took our empties back to the bar and returned with another round of whisky and beer. This time when he knocked back his shot I left mine standing there.

'Lefty,' I said. 'Are you in some sort of jam or what?'

'I'm always in a jam, Poncho.'

'How bad a jam?'

He folded his hands and rested them on the table. He looked at them for a long time and then he looked up at me. Greasy strands of hair hung out the sides of his bandana, and his jawline was shadowed with stubble. Then there was that gap tooth. But he still had this innocent look about him, somehow, which he hadn't lost since childhood.

He said, 'We never talked about my time inside.'

'I wanted to.'

'I'm not laying a guilt trip on you. I'm just trying to explain.'

Jake jerked his head at the mullet-haired race fan, as if implying he didn't want the guy to overhear. Jake got up and I followed him out. He led me through the clubhouse to a set of glass doors that opened onto a patio overlooking the training grounds. They had tables and chairs out there, but no heaters or lights. Nobody was sitting in the cold.

We smoked in the darkness next to the paddock and Jake explained what he could. It was as if he needed the shelter of the shadows to let some of it out. He said that a lot of what you saw on TV and in films about being in jail was bullshit. But not all of it. It was true that sooner or later you ended up needing protection, and when you accepted that protection you were expected to repay the favour some other time.

'Do you understand what I'm saying?' he said.

I said I did, or thought I did. At the same time, I didn't understand at all.

'What do they want you to do?'

'Just one thing.'

'A big thing.'

'Not so big I can't handle it.'

'And then?'

'That's it. I get paid and that's it.'

I said, 'It's not legal, though.'

'That goes without saying.'

I leaned my elbows on the railing, and stared at the empty field. It was mostly hard-packed dirt and on the far side a few show jumping obstacles seemed to hover in the dark.

I said, 'I just don't get it.'

'It's not complicated.'

'I mean how this is happening. How this has happened to you. We're not bad guys. We had a decent family. A pretty nice house, even. Hell, we had a fucking vegetable patch.'

'That's all gone and you know it. It's as gone as that hand of yours.'

I flexed my broken fingers, feeling the sting of the cold. Sometimes, I almost get used to the injury. Other times it catches me off-guard and I see it for the first time, or I see how people react to it. Then I wonder: what the hell is this mangled thing at the end of my arm? But Jake was right. It had all happened and this was where we were at, him and me.

I tucked the hand in the pouch of my hoody, warming it.

I asked, 'What exactly are you supposed to do?'

'That's hard to say, at this stage.'

'Well, when will you know?'

'By the weekend. Saturday. It's happening Saturday.'

'Why Saturday?'

'It just has to be Saturday.'

'I hope you don't expect help from me.'

'I don't expect anything from you.'

'I'm working till Saturday, and then I'm heading up to Albert's cabin, with Tracy.'

'I know you got your other life, now. I just wanted to let you know what's going on in mine.' He patted me, a little too hard, on the shoulder. 'Come on. Let's have another shot and play the slots.'

Chapter Four

BY THE TIME THE CLUBHOUSE closed we'd lost about fifty bucks – most of it mine – playing video poker and since we didn't have enough cash left to pay for another cab we had to ride the night buses back across town, by a route that seemed circuitous and convoluted to me in my drunkenness but which I now suspect was deliberate. Jake's bartender friend had sold us a mickey of Seagram's for the road and we passed that back and forth between us as we rattled along Victoria. We were sitting side-by-side and I could see our reflections in the window across from us. We looked pretty haggard: just a couple of bums, beat-up and worn-out.

'Can you believe,' Jake said, 'that these places are worth a million bucks?'

He was looking beyond our reflections at the passing houses: one-storey clapboard or stucco boxes, with rusty fences and overgrown yards. But Jake was right about their value.

I said, 'Every house in Vancouver is worth a million bucks or more.'

'That's what I'm saying.'

'No way we'd ever be able to afford a place.'

'You make decent money.'

'It's seasonal. And there's Ma.'

We got out near Hastings and instead of waiting for another bus just started walking. By then it was past midnight and everything was closed except a few late-night pho noodle houses. A car tore down the strip and the passenger lobbed a half-empty can of beer in our direction. It skittered across the sidewalk at my feet.

'We could go see Ma next weekend instead,' I said. 'After I'm back from the cabin and you're all done with your "little trip".'

Jake made a vague sound in his throat. 'I might be gone for a while, with this thing.'

'Where the hell you going?'

He took a long pull on his smoke, the flare illuminating his jaw and cheekbones. He exhaled using an old trick of his: blowing smoke through his gap tooth, which makes this eerie whistling sound, high and long and lonesome.

'It don't matter,' he said.

'Then it don't matter if you tell me.'

'You got any cash you can front me?'

'I knew you wanted something,' I said.

'That's me. Always mooching. I'm the mooch and you're the Scrooge.'

'I give you plenty.'

'Like all the money you gave me to help me get back on my feet.'

'You still sore about that?'

'I know you had some.'

'That was for Ma's care.'

I pulled up my hood and cinched it tight, using it like blinders to block him out. I walked with my head down and my fists tucked in the pouch of my hoody, cradling my bad hand with my good one. We passed a rundown apartment block and a couple of empty lots and in time came to an intersection, where Jake stopped. I looked up. I hadn't been paying attention and I couldn't understand why we were waiting there when the walk light was green. On our right was a used car lot and on the corner across from us was an auto repair shop. I knew those places. I knew that intersection. Hastings and Clark.

'Oh,' I said. Just that.

Tied to a directional sign on the meridian, on our side of the intersection, was a bouquet of lilies in cellophane wrapping. Some of the petals had fallen off and lay on the concrete divider. I removed my hands from the pouch and stared at the street and the asphalt, which the rain had left all slickly glistening, like the surface of a dark pool. I figured this final stop had been part of the night's plan – just as much as the Firehall, and the stables.

'You put those flowers there?' I said.

'You sure as hell didn't.'

He walked to the centre of the crossroads and uncapped our

mickey and poured what remained of it out on the pavement, the liquor glinting gold in the light of the streetlamps and spattering into a small puddle. It was a melodramatic gesture and no doubt partly staged for my benefit. When he was done with the ritual Jake went over to the meridian and laid the empty bottle at the base of the sign, beneath the flowers. He picked up one of the petals.

'Fucking cheap bouquet,' he said, which struck me as a very Jake thing to say. 'I spent fifteen bucks on these shitty flowers and the goddamn petals are already falling off.'

He tried to throw the petal, and of course it didn't go anywhere. It just fluttered to the ground and landed in a puddle.

Before moving to France Sandy had several more shows to perform with her old company at the Firehall. On that night, the last night, I didn't see her dance because I was working as a dishwasher at an Italian restaurant downtown. It was my day off but I'd offered to pick up a shift and of course that's one of the things I can't help thinking about, and hating myself for, because if I'd been at the show I would have waited for her and we would have driven home together, probably along a different route and definitely at a different time. Jake did see the show – we always saw her shows when we were free, even if we'd seen them a dozen times before – but he had Maria with him so didn't wait around to say hello to Sandy afterwards, which I know is something that haunts him even more than my absence haunts me.

Since neither of her brothers was there after the show that night, Sandy changed and showered and had a glass of soda and lime with her friends and then left the Firehall at five past ten. She had a small white Nissan hatchback at the time and that was the car she was driving. She drove east on Hastings with her windows down, which she always did after a performance, even in winter, because it took hours for her core body temperature to fully cool down. She was going forty-five kilometres an hour, five klicks under the speed limit. I often think of those moments, of that drive with the open windows and the cold coastal air and the sea-brine stench of the city. In my mind and memory, I elongate that stretch, grant her just a little more time. I know she would have been filled with the feeling she always got after dancing, a feeling that she'd never been able to fully describe and which I can only partway imagine: riding that updraught of endorphins, gliding along like a hawk, the world all in focus, clear and sharp as cut glass. I let that elation last for as long as possible.

In reality she only made it ten blocks. At the Hastings and Clark intersection her car was hit broadside by a black Mercedes going a hundred and eight kilometres an hour. The whole front of her car was sheared away and the rest went spinning into the meridian. There is no doubt about any of this because it was not so late that there were no witnesses.

At that point she was alive but unconscious.

At eleven twenty-nine the emergency crew arrived. They examined the car and found that the driver's footwell had collapsed inwards, crushing Sandy's legs. The steering wheel was up against her sternum and most of her ribs were broken and her collar bone and breastplate and a lot of other bones, too. They had to use the jaws of life to cut her out. There was blood, of course. Her legs were mangled. They put a tourniquet on each, above the knee, and got her onto a stretcher and gave her blood and oxygen, and that was when she came to, waking into the nightmare of what remained of her life, and started to scream in pain and fear and shock.

Jake and I squatted together on the kerb and stared at the spot where all that had happened. There was nothing to say about any of it and so we didn't, but simply sat with our elbows on our knees, hands clasped in front of us like two men praying to a saint. I thought vaguely about whether Sandy's blood had reached the pavement, mingling with the oil and coolant from the destroyed car. If that had happened it had long since been washed into the gutter and down the drain and out through the sewers to the sea. There was no trace here of the sister we'd once had and that fact was brutal and eternal and unalterable.

Eventually Jake stood up and I did too. We crossed against the light and plodded on in a mute and morose daze. Jake was staying at the Woodland – this dive hotel further along Hastings – but instead of heading in that direction he walked with me towards the waterfront. Off to our right was the DP World shipping terminal, where industrial cranes loomed up like monstrous mechanical insects, soulless and indifferent. At Main Street we crossed over the railway tracks and circled back to the Westco plant parking lot. I could see the *Western Lady* in her berth, the windows dark.

Jake held out his left hand and I took it, and we shook formally, like strangers.

'I'll be seeing you, Poncho.'

'Just tell me what you're up to.'

'I'm up to no good – what else?'

'Seriously.'

He considered it, and said, 'It's better I don't tell you if you're not going to help.'

'Do you *need* my help?'

He put his hands in his coat pockets and kicked the ground. He looked at the water, and at the sky, and then he looked back at me. His features were softened by shadow and in that one moment it was as if he'd aged backwards, losing some of the edge and hardness that prison had given him. Back before Sandy's death, and all that came after. Back before what Jake had done and what he had become. And when he spoke, it was in the voice of that boy.

'You're my brother,' he said. 'I've always needed your help.'

He turned and walked away from me and then – maybe realizing that was a bit much, a bit too over the top – he flipped me the finger and called back: 'Stay gold, Poncho.'

'Nothing gold can stay.'

I watched until he merged with the darkness and faded out of sight.

Chapter Five

ONE OF THE LAST JOBS we did each year was to offload the supplies that Albert and Evelyn had brought from their house and didn't leave on the boat during the off-season. It included a mix of cutlery and crockery, pots and pans, sheets and bedding, dry goods and perishables, and also Albert's power tools, which were top-of-the-line and worth a pretty penny, as he liked to say. Security at the boatyard wasn't great and there had been a couple of break-ins over the years.

Thursday Tracy came to help with the unloading. She drove Albert's truck down to the plant: a big Ford Ranger with a tonneau cover. With Albert and Evelyn, she and I began loading all the supplies into a wheeled skip alongside the *Western Lady*. Evelyn and Albert carried the boxes onto the deck and I lowered them over the gunnel to Tracy, who arranged them in the skip. She did this in a practised and specific way, so that all the different items fitted together, snug and intricate as a jigsaw.

'You haven't forgotten,' I said.

'Heck,' she said, dropping a box of frozen fish into place, 'it ain't been that long.'

'You miss it?'

'I'll be back, once I'm qualified.'

Evelyn, who was coming on deck with a sack of flour, overheard and said, 'She'll be skipper some day, if I can ever convince that man of mine to retire.'

'Hope there'll still be room for me,' I said, and took the flour from her.

'There'll always be a place here for you, Timothy.'

'Glad to hear it,' I said. 'Don't know what I'd do without your cooking.'

'Lose some pounds, I reckon,' Tracy said.

I patted my belly, which was getting substantial. 'It's all muscle.'

Albert emerged from the galley, his boots clomping loud on the deck, a box of pots and pans in his arms. He must have overheard us, because he added, 'Boy's still a rake, compared to me.'

We laughed at that, politely, and continued handing boxes and bags to one another, like a game of pass-the-parcel. There was a familiar rhythm to it all, and to the dialogue, too.

The morning air carried a frosty, refreshing sting, and behind the clouds the sun glowed like an opal, and everything felt just fine while the four of us worked together. But eventually Evelyn stepped out of the galley and made a criss-cross motion with her hands: no more.

Tracy said, 'I'll wheel the skip up to the truck.'

'Leave that to me and the greenhorn, princess,' Albert said.

'I been with you for years,' I said, 'and I'm still a greenhorn.'

'You'll always be a greenhorn,' he said. 'Leastways till you grow up.'

He stepped down from the boat, moving heavy, and we both leaned into the skip, pushing it on rusty wheels down the dock, up the gangplank, and then along the wharf.

'You thought any about coming up to the cabin?'

'I thought plenty about it. It sounds real nice.'

In two days they would be locking up the boat and heading out to Squamish. I still hadn't given any clear indication one way or the other whether I'd be going with them.

'I could use some help up there. Got a copse of spruce to cut down.'

'It's just my mother is the only thing.'

'Your mother or your brother?'

I didn't answer immediately, and I guess that was answer enough.

'You two had a good time the other night, I gather.'

We'd reached the parking lot, and turned the skip towards his Ranger. We positioned the skip at the back, and then Albert locked its wheel brakes and dropped the truck's tailgate.

I said, 'He's a hard fellow to say no to.'

'His type often are.'

'He ain't a type.'

'I know that.'

Albert shielded his eyes, gazing back down at the boat. Tracy was on the aft deck, waving to get his attention. She held an imaginary phone to her ear, and motioned for him.

'I'll send Tracy up,' he said, 'to help you load.'

He headed back. He moved slowly – Albert never rushed – but each stride was solid, deliberate, purposeful. As I waited I massaged the fingers of my bad hand, feeling the little nubs that had healed over. A few minutes later Tracy came down the wharf. She clambered into the back of the truck, hunching beneath the tonneau, and I lifted boxes up to her, one by one. As we worked we chatted about her night job, and the training she was doing.

'It's just a piece of paper. I know all I need to know about boats.'

'I'll say.'

'But it's got to be done, if I'm gonna take over.'

'You ready for a life at sea?'

'For two fisheries a year, anyway.'

'I can think of worse ways to earn a living.'

I said it the way Albert might have, which got her laughing. When we finished with the unloading we stood leaning against the truck, jawing for a time. She asked – as casually as possible – about the cabin. I looked down at a coil of rope in the skip, really considering it. I mentioned my brother, and him maybe needing my help. It sounded about as vague and suspect as it no doubt was.

'But I'm not sure yet,' I said. 'I haven't heard from him since the other night. If I do have to stay around here, though, I could always come meet you up there a couple days later.'

She nodded, but I couldn't really tell what she thought, of any of it.

'You don't talk much about your brother.'

I pushed away from the truck, and picked up the rope. I started knotting a bowline – just to be doing something. 'You remember how bad off I was, when I first started working with your dad?'

'No shame in that. You'd lost your sister.'

'Well, Jake took it even harder than me. He was younger. Our pa died when we were kids and our ma didn't always have it together. Sandy, well, she was like a parent to the both of us. And after what happened, Jake just got on the wrong track, if you know what I mean.'

'He went to jail.'

I nodded.

'Is he getting back on track, now?'

I grunted, snugging up the bowline, and then held it at eye level, checking my work. Through the loop, I could see gulls circling above the cannery, lured by the stench of roe. They went around and around, white scraps in a whirlpool, slowly going down.

'No,' I said, 'I don't reckon so.'

The night Sandy died Jake got to the hospital first. I don't remember much of my own drive over there, or finding the emergency room where they were operating on her. It's all just impressions, really. The glare of those fluorescent tube lights. A hallway lined with white tiles, shiny as a sheet of ice. At that time I didn't know much. Just that she had been in an accident and had been rushed to Vancouver General, which was the closest hospital to the scene of the crash. They hadn't told me it was bad or that she was not likely to survive, and I suppose those are the kinds of things they don't tell you over the phone. She had both our numbers and the home phone number in her emergency contact details on her cellphone and that was how they reached me at work, and Jake, who was with Maria. Our mother had her phone off – she was at a movie with a friend – and so they couldn't get a hold of her. She had a few more hours before she found out, and in a way I envy her that extra time.

When I got to Emergency, Jake was standing alone and staring hard at a glass window that was covered by venetian blinds. He was staring at the blinds as if he could see through them. Looking back now, the intensity of his expression – the tightness in his jaw, the hard look in his eyes – seemed to signify the beginning of the change that occurred in him. I grabbed him by the shoulder and asked him what the hell was going on and he told me that she'd been T-boned by a drunk driver, and I asked him if it was bad and he said that it was – he said that it was very bad and after that we didn't say anything.

I went over to a coffee machine in the corner and stared at it. I suppose I went over to it because I'd seen people do that, in TV and films, but I didn't want coffee or anything else. I went back to Jake and we took up the vigil together, staring at those blinds. Everything that happened to Sandy happened out of sight and out of our realm of knowledge and understanding. I didn't know what the regulations were at the time about relatives being in the emergency room, but in retrospect I wish we'd forced our way in there to at least be by her side. As it stood we were excluded, relegated to the role of bystanders during those final and definitive moments.

People passed us and at some point a nurse asked us if there was anybody else we should contact and we both looked at her, dazed. I had to think of the question again, going over the words in my head, before I mentioned our mother and that she ought to be called but that one of us could do it. The woman moved away and Jake said he'd already tried Ma. I was fiddling with my phone, thinking I ought to try again, when the door to the operating theatre opened and a doctor came out. He had taken off his gloves and cap and mask but still had his scrubs on and the front was spattered with blood. I knew that it was Sandy's blood and knew, too, by his expression that she was dead even before he came over and opened his mouth and said words to that effect. For a few minutes I shut down and was vaguely aware of Jake talking to the doctor in intense, terse tones, and when I tuned back in Jake was asking if we could go in and see her. The doctor said it would be okay but asked us to wait while they cleaned up the operating room. He stepped away from us gently, cautiously, moving backwards and keeping his eyes on us, as if he had a feeling that in our grief we posed a potential problem.

The door shut for a few minutes and opened again and the doctor came back out, and the rest of the trauma team came with him this time. They looked at us with sympathy and timidity and the doctor said we could now go in to see our sister if we wanted. He also said something about needing us to come talk to him afterwards but I don't think we ever did.

The room was smaller than it had looked from the outside and darker than I expected. They had left the overheads off and turned out the surgical lights and the only illumination now came from a bedside lamp that cast a grim yellow glow. Jake closed the door behind us, shutting out the noise of the ward. Any surgical tools and instruments had been removed, and the machinery all around her that had presumably been working to keep her alive, or monitor her life, was still and quiet. The dim silence had a dense and murky underwater quality to it, as if we had locked ourselves in a submersible and were slowly floating down, away from the world of light and warmth that we had always known, towards some place else.

Sandy lay on the operating table in the middle of the room. Her lower half had been covered by a sheet. The sides of the sheet were bloodied. We went to stand on either side of her and we each took one of her hands and the one I held felt as warm as my own, as warm as it always had. Her face was bruised and one cheek swollen into a grotesque bulge but she was still recognizable as her, or what had once been her. Jake reached down for the sheet. When I saw that he was going to raise it I looked up and away, at him, so I never saw what happened to her legs. But I sometimes think that seeing the reaction on his face was worse, in a way.

After that I did something odd. I walked over to the corner of the room and sat down and sort of curled up, like a child or a wounded dog. Jake, he stayed beside her. I could hear him talking to her in low and tender tones and even though I couldn't make out the words I knew what he was saying and just wished she could have heard it. Through all of this I've never been tempted by any notion of comfort in another life and have no doubts that what was lying on the table was no longer our sister, and in that state had meaning only to us.

The door opened. I thought it would be the doctor coming back, but when I rolled over I saw it was somebody else – a younger woman about our age. She wasn't in the OR scrubs and instead wore some kind of blue uniform. She stopped and made a startled sound and put her hand to her mouth. I couldn't stand but managed to sit up, facing towards her.

She said she hadn't known anybody was in there and I explained that we were family, that we were her brothers. Then she started talking, a bit too fast, and it took me a moment to work out that she was saying she had been part of the paramedic team that arrived at the crash site. She said she'd wanted to see Sandy, to check up on her. She said she probably wasn't supposed to and apologized and then she said she'd never seen anything like that and she put her hand to her mouth again and started to cry. Seeing those tears made me wonder why neither of us was crying and I remember being hazily aware that I was probably still in shock. Jake stood looking curiously at the girl and then went to shut the door behind her and said he wanted to ask her about something. She wiped at her eyes and said that would be okay. First he got her to describe the crash site: what it had looked like when she arrived. She told us about the demolished vehicle and how her supervisor had known right away that they needed the fire department and the jaws of life to cut out the driver. Sandy was unconscious at that time and the girl had stayed next to her, just talking to her gently through the broken window, in the ten minutes it took the crew to arrive. I did not think to thank her for that at the time, but I have thanked her often since, in looking back on it, offering up my silent gratitude like a futile and hollow prayer.

The girl – who was staring at the floor, remembering – said that Sandy had come around when they cut her out of the car. Jake asked her if Sandy had been lucid at that time, which confused the girl and she said something about them giving Sandy morphine for the pain, but that wasn't what Jake was getting at. He put his hands on the girl's shoulders, not roughly, but as if he needed to make sure she understood what he was asking. He asked if Sandy had been aware and understood what had happened to her legs. The girl had to think. Possibly she was thinking about lying to us. But eventually she admitted that Sandy had been crying out about her legs as they loaded her into the ambulance and after that the girl didn't know any more.

When Jake heard that he sat on the edge of Sandy's bed and put his hands to his face, as you might if you were splashing yourself with water, only in this case he held them there for a long time. The girl said she was sorry again and I expected her to leave, but she didn't. Her presence didn't seem out of place in any way, though, and she stayed with us until Jake stood up and headed for the door and shoved it open and left. I went after him. I came out of that dim murk into the blazing lights of the ward and the noise and the people. I spotted Jake down one of the hallways, moving away from me, hunched forward and cradling his guts as if he were physically hurt or wounded. I called out his name and started to hurry. He reached the end of the hall where there was a big plate-glass window overlooking Oak Street. In front of the window was a gurney, an empty gurney, and Jake picked that up and hurled it at the window. Only the window didn't break. They must have safety glass in those places, in case of all the things that might happen, things like that. The window didn't break but the gurney did. It bounced off and landed in a tangled mess, upside down, like a dead mantis.

I reached Jake at the same time as two orderlies. They held him – gently – by both arms, but he didn't struggle or react to them in any way. It was as if they weren't even there. He looked at me and his face was teary and boyish-looking and filled with a terrible hatred. Keep me away from that guy, he said, or I'm going to kill him. It sounded like a vow. At that time we didn't even know the name of the driver, but I told Jake I would and that was just one of the many ways in which I failed him, one of the many ways in which I'm just as responsible as him for all the no-good things that he's done.

Chapter Six

ON THE BOAT THAT NIGHT my sleep was as fretful and uneasy as the first night I'd spent at sea. I had dreams and Sandy was in them, regarding me with what you might call a reproachful expression – which was just like her – and though I do not believe in such things as visitations I knew damn well why she'd appeared. By four thirty I was already awake, alert, waiting. I could hear Big Ben snoring in the bunk opposite. I lay there listening to that. It was a very human sound. After a few minutes I reached for my phone and texted Jake: *if you really have to do this you won't be doing it alone. I'll see you tomorrow.* Then I

put the phone away. The only thing left was to break it to Albert.
Evelyn and Tracy, too. But especially Albert.

It seemed as if most of the day was spent looking for that
chance. But I needed to get him alone and the opportunity didn't
present itself. We all had our end-of-season jobs, and moved
about the boat in an orchestrated routine: passing to and fro,
working around each other. Evelyn was wiping down all the
surfaces in the galley and Sugar was inside cleaning our cabin
and bunks. Big Ben was gathering any excess gear – ropes, buoys,
life jackets – and loading those in the storage locker. Albert was
down in his engine room, making a few final adjustments: as
pernickety and mysterious as a piano tuner. The urgency of the
past week was now gone. We had worked hard up until the last
day, and had plenty of time to perform these tasks and we did
so with a melancholy sort of reverence. The end was in sight and
when it is there's no longer such a rush to get there.

In the morning, Albert gave me a job I'd done every other
season: repainting the boat's name across the transom. I tied a
floating dock off the stern and crouched down there with the
brush and bucket of marine paint. I had to use my left hand for
the job, since my right was no longer good for delicate tasks. My
forefinger and middle finger are the ones that are missing, making
it impossible to hold a brush properly. But I've gotten pretty
good with my left.

I dipped the tip in the pot of white paint and gently stroked
the letters, coaxing them to lustre. The boatyard was still and
quiet and echoed with emptiness. Some of the other crews, skip-
pered by captains less thorough than ours, had already battened
down the hatches and locked up the cabins and headed back to
their respective houses or trailers or apartments or whatever
abodes they each had waiting.

Around mid-morning my cellphone rang. I fished it out of the pocket of my coveralls. I could see by the number it was Jake.

'Poncho,' he said, right off. 'I need you tonight.'

Just that. He didn't thank me for agreeing to help. I guess my involvement had been a given, for him. I put down the paint brush, balancing it precariously on the edge of the pot.

I said, 'You said Saturday.'

'The job is Saturday. But I'm meeting them tonight.'

'You're meeting these guys?'

'And they want to meet you, too.'

I stood and stared at the water. It was lapping at my little dock, spilling over the edge nearest me, where my weight had lowered it.

'But you said Saturday. I said I'd come Saturday.'

'And I'm telling you, I need you tonight.'

'Albert won't let me go.'

I could hear voices in the distance. He told me to hold on and I heard him swearing at somebody. Then he was back. He said that if I wanted to sell out there was still time and he didn't care, but if I was going to help him I had to come tonight. That was it.

'I can't do it, Lefty.'

'Whatever, then.'

'I can still come tomorrow.'

'That's no good. It's tonight or you're not part of tomorrow.' Again I heard the voices, and again he swore back at them. Then, to me: 'Look, I got to go. Some horse is shitting all over itself or something. Forget about it, okay? Just forget the whole thing and forget I even asked you.'

'Jake –'

And of course he hung up. I stood and stared at the phone. I was still staring like that when Albert leaned over the stern to check up on the work I was doing. I tucked the phone away but not before he'd seen it. He didn't ask about it, though. He eyed up the work and told me it looked good. I thanked him and he didn't leave right away, and if there was a time to tell him it would have been then. But after Jake's call I didn't know what to say, so I just said I'd be done soon and up for lunch when it was ready. And then Albert was gone.

I bent to pick up my brush but my bad hand betrayed me and I knocked the brush off the side of the pot. It bounced on the dock, splattering paint, and rolled clumsily off the edge. I lunged for it – swiping my paw through the water – and missed. I watched helplessly as it sank, slow-turning through the murk, until it vanished. I hadn't finished the job. The 'Y' was fainter than the rest of the letters, and stood out.

That night, I got up and left.

I waited till Sugar and Big Ben were out, which didn't take long, and from beneath the bunk pulled the duffel bag that I had filled with my belongings. Packing hadn't seemed odd or conspicuous because all of us were doing the same, and we were due to depart the next day, anyway. There wasn't much work left to be done but it wasn't about the work or the hours so much as the act of leaving early and abandoning ship. Albert always said he couldn't abide a man who shirked his responsibilities and I guess I was about to prove I was that type of man.

In the galley I stepped into my work boots and picked my jacket off the hook. I had a letter addressed to Albert and Evelyn that explained some and I left that folded on the table. I took a final look around and eased open the door and crept out onto the deck and shut the door behind me – turning the handle before I closed it so as not to make any noise.

'Sneaking off like a thief, eh?'

Albert was up in the wheelhouse. I don't know if he'd been waiting for me or just standing up there, on watch, like he did at sea sometimes. I stood, tense and hesitant as a jackrabbit, as he came down the stairs to deck, his big boots ringing on the metal.

'I didn't know how to tell you.'

'So you did the cowardly thing, instead of the right thing.'

'I guess so. I guess I did.'

He had his arms crossed and his face looked hard and unforgiving as granite. Just this big carved figure of a man. He said, 'And you'd also decided not to come to Squamish.'

'I was thinking I could come meet you, later.'

'You can forget about that, now.'

The strap of the duffel bag was burning my collar bone. I shifted it a bit.

'I'm sorry, Albert. I'm sorry as hell.'

'Tell Tracy, why don't you.'

'I want to do right by her.'

'She doesn't need you to do anything for her. She's fine. Only trouble is she likes you.' He nodded, once, as if affirming the truth of that. 'We all do. But you're making a bad choice here. I know it and I think you know it too.'

'He's my brother, Albert. He's in a bind.'

'That doesn't surprise me.'

'What if it was your family?'

'I'm done jawing about it. Go and do what you got to do, or think you got to do. But don't expect us all to be waiting here for you when you finish being loyal. Don't expect a job to be here, either.'

'Ah, hell, Albert.'

'Get off my boat, I said.'

His tone was furious and fearsome, and if I hadn't gone he'd have thrown me off. So I went. I'd seen him when he got like that and all I could hope was that time would cool his rage, and that maybe my letter would help some, too. It was a simple letter but it was honest and Evelyn would have his ear. And Tracy, as well. That might be enough. If it wasn't, I'd just given up the only home I'd had for five years.

Chapter Seven

WHEN I REACHED THE WOODLAND Hotel I stood outside in the dribble of rain, with the duffel bag slung over my shoulder. It was a four-storey beige brick building, with two shops built into the ground floor: a paint and hardware store, all shuttered up for the night, and some kind of Christian mission with pictures of Jesus and a crooked cross in the window display. Above that the hotel sign jutted out on an awning, green-on-white, only half illuminated. I had a notion Jake had chosen the Woodland deliberately, to accentuate his sense of hardship and destitution. Or maybe he really was that down on his luck. With him it was hard to tell.

A black security gate barred the entrance, but somebody had left the gate ajar, so I could walk right in. The hotel had no lobby or reception, and no employees on duty, and in that way it wasn't really a hotel at all, but more of a flophouse. I pressed the button for the elevator (Jake's room was on the second floor) but when no elevator appeared I took the fire stairs, which stank of piss and beer. Up there some of the doors had numbers on them, in the form of black stickers, and others didn't. Jake's did: twenty-two. I stopped in front of it and considered knocking but then I just reached for the handle and pushed it open.

Jake was sitting on his bed with his elbows resting on his knees, dressed in jeans and a tank top. His hair was wet and stringy as if he'd just come in from the rain. Something about his expression really got to me. A lot of his performance had been planned, I'm sure, and put on – but not that look: a look of surprise and relief and gratitude. He stood and came over to me and pulled me into a hug, holding me fiercely and clapping my back with his palm.

'I thought you wouldn't come,' he said, 'I thought you'd cut me loose.'

What do you say to that – when your brother tells you something like that? I stepped into his room and dropped my duffel bag on the floor, like an anchor I was laying down.

'What about the boat?' he asked.

'I left the boat.'

'You mean you *left* it?'

'I mean I left it.'

'Ah, hell.'

He reached into his back pocket and fished out a rumpled pack of Du Mauriers and withdrew a bent cigarette. He lit it and took a drag and held in the smoke as he crossed to the window, which was open: an old sash window with rotten wooden trim. I could feel the cold wind blowing in. He exhaled in a thin stream and stood for a time looking out. I don't know what he was looking at. Nothing, maybe. Then he nodded, as if I had said something else.

'I appreciate it, Poncho,' he said, 'I really do.'

The room was a ten-by-ten-foot box, not much bigger than a prison cell. It didn't have a toilet or shower but it had a sink. Above the sink was a mirror with a jagged crack running diagonally across the centre. I could see a divided version of myself in there, and he looked like a damned fool. Next to the mirror an old medicine cabinet stuck out from the wall at a lopsided angle. Then there was the bed: a steel cot with a thin foam mattress. At the foot of the bed lay Jake's battered leather suitcase, open and overflowing with dirty clothes.

Draped atop the pile was a white sports bra. I nodded at it.

'You cross-dressing now?'

He grinned, both sly and shy, and I understood.

'You and your dancers.'

'I can't help it.'

'You know who you're really after.'

'Don't say that.'

He went over and modestly tucked the bra behind the suitcase. Next to it, his old guitar stood propped against the wall. He picked it up and sat on the bed, resting the guitar across his lap. The body was battered and chipped and one of the strings was missing but I was glad to see it. If he still had his guitar it meant something. He plucked the E-string and let it quiver, resonating.

I said, 'You going to tell me?'

'I don't know all of it.'

'Do you know any of it?'

He squinted through the cigarette smoke. 'I know we got to make a delivery.'

'Something stolen.'

'Probably.'

'Then what?'

'We'll find out more tonight.'

'And then it's done?'

'Then it's done. And we get paid, too.'

'I don't want any money. I'm not doing it for money.'

On the top shelf of his medicine cabinet were two teacups and a twixer of Black Velvet. I got down the teacups and rinsed them in the sink. The water smelled brackish and a ring of rust encircled the sinkhole. I dried the cups on the inside of my shirt and poured us each a few ounces. I took one over to Jake and he accepted it and we each pinched our cup by the handle, very genteel, like a pair of elderly gentlemen having afternoon tea.

We clicked the cups together and drank.

'Was the old man choked at you?' Jake asked.

'Said he wouldn't take me back.'

'Damn, man. What about your girl?'

'Tracy ain't my girl.'

'She's something to you.'

I said I hadn't even had the chance to break it to her. I didn't know how she'd react.

'But maybe she'll see my side of it,' I said.

We looked out the window together. Directly opposite was the Paradise, this dive bar and hotel where hipsters go to drink. Compared to the Woodland, the place might as well have been paradise. Out on the patio, a handful of customers stood in a herd, smoking and laughing. Every so often cars hummed along

Hastings Street. A few blocks down somebody shouted, though whether in anger or merriment it was hard to say. Either way, things were in motion. Time hadn't stopped. Already the boat and my chaste relationship with Tracy seemed very distant, like some other life. A better life, maybe. But not my life.

'So where the hell are we going tonight?' I asked.

Chapter Eight

IN JAKE'S TRUCK WE HEADED east on Powell, then merged with McGill and got onto the Second Narrows Bridge, which connects Vancouver to the North Shore, where we grew up. Beneath us Burrard Inlet shimmered and rippled, a dark swathe of water burnished by city lights, and up ahead the mountains stood out blackly against the night sky. On the far side of the bridge we kept going along the Upper Levels and the Cut – this long stretch of highway hacked into the hillside. Drizzling rain smeared the windscreen and one of Jake's wipers was busted, so the blade flopped around all crazily, like a snake having conniptions.

Along the way, Jake forgot to act grave and compassionate about the loss of my job. My presence had cheered him up some and as he drove he whistled through his gap tooth – some little ditty that was irritating as all hell.

'It's good to have you along, bro.' He leaned over, punched me in the shoulder. 'Good old Poncho. The handsome old buck, with a busted hand.'

He was smiling reminiscently.

'What are you grinning at?'

'Just thinking. Having you involved always made my schemes seem more legitimate, somehow. You were the respectable one. If you were part of it then Sandy and Ma figured it had to be okay.'

'Even when you were up to no good.'

'I was always up to no good.'

'What are we getting into, man?'

'You remember the Delaney brothers? Mark and Patrick?'

'From back in the day? Sure.'

They had grown up on the North Shore and gone to a rival high school, around the same time as us. I'd come across them a few times. Back then they'd had a reputation as badasses but there were a lot of posers around who dealt a bit of weed and pretended to be gangsters and most of the time it didn't amount to anything.

Jake said, 'They've been busy since then.'

'I heard something about that.'

'They're making a name for themselves.'

He told me that two years ago they'd formed this new gang that was causing quite a stir. Most of the gangs in the Lower Mainland were one ethnicity or another, but theirs – the World Legion, they called it – had done away with that, and they were muscling in (that was the term Jake used) on the turf of the older gangs: the Triads and the Hells Angels.

I said, 'Equality among criminals, eh?'

'They're the ones who helped me out inside.'

'Because you're North Shore?'

'An old friend vouched for me, and Mark Delaney remembered me.'

'So that's why you owe them.'

'Now you're getting it, Poncho.'

We'd followed the highway past the Lynn Valley turn-off and took the exit at Upper Lonsdale. We swung north, going up the hill towards the mountains, past the Queen's Cross pub and the squat apartment buildings near there. The area beyond was leafy, suburban, and pleasant-looking.

'This is where we're meeting them?' I asked.

'They use their house as a base,' Jake said. 'Their mom's house, actually.'

He laughed, and snapped his fingers, as if that was the punch-line to a joke.

Of all the outrageous parts of this story – and I admit there are many – the one I find hardest to get a handle on is the existence of the Delaney brothers. For the same reason, they were a source of fascination during the trials: people wanted to know how two guys from a white-collar background (their father was an accountant, their mother a legal secretary) could get it in their heads that they wanted to be gangsters, and then go about it in a way that forced the actual and established gangsters to take them seriously, at least for a little while.

But a lot has been written about that, from all kinds of angles, by people who have far more direct knowledge than me. All I can do, really, is relate our own experiences in dealing with the Delaneys, which – it goes without saying – did not end very well at all. Looking back, most of those troubles were set up in that first meeting, played out on a small scale.

The Delaney family lived on a cul-de-sac in a new real estate development, with tree-lined boulevards and big sprawling lawns. Their house was built in the style of all the others: two storeys, faux-brick façade, cream siding, double-garage. There was nothing to set it apart except, I suppose, for the vehicle parked on one side of the driveway: a black Cadillac Escalade, as blatant as a tank, with tinted windows and jacked-up suspension.

Afterwards, Jake told me there had been brawls, showdowns, police raids, and a drive-by at the place: the hazards of their gangland aspirations spilling over into suburbia.

At the porch we rang the bell, and while we waited I asked Jake what he wanted me to do, how he wanted me to act in there. He said it would be best if I kept quiet and let him talk it over with them, which of course was fine by me.

The door opened and an elderly woman peeked out at us. She had her hair done up in an old-fashioned perm, and was wearing an apron around her waist. The entranceway smelled of baking and perfume. The woman, who I assumed to be Mrs Delaney, welcomed us in and said it was very nice to see us. I felt as if I was back in high school, having come to a friend's house to hang out. But Jake, he just took it all in stride. He commented on the smell of her cooking and she patted her perm and said that the cake wasn't ready yet, but when it was she would send some up.

'Mark's in the office,' she said, pointing to a stairwell on the right.

It ran straight up to a small landing and door. I could hear odd sounds – clanking and grunting – in the room beyond. Jake knocked and after a second somebody shouted for us to come on in and so Jake pushed open the door. Directly opposite, facing us as we entered, a guy sat at one of those personal gyms (the elaborate kind with complex pulley systems) doing reps on the fly press. That explained the clanking. The peculiar thing – or the more peculiar thing – was his outfit: he was wearing jeans and a sport coat, rather than anything resembling gym gear. The rest of the office looked relatively normal: desk, chairs, filing cabinet, card table.

The guy grimaced at us and said, 'Just got to finish this set.'

And Jake said, 'Sure thing, Mark.'

We waited and watched, respectfully. As we did, the door shut behind us. I looked back, startled. Some other guy had been back there the whole time: I hadn't even seen him. He had sunken, angular cheeks pitted with acne scars. He didn't smile or greet us in any way. He just stared, clinically, and my overall impression of him was not a congenial one.

Mark finished with the fly press, hopped up, and patted his belly.

'Trying to get rid of this goddamn jiggle-ball,' he said.

'Ladies like a man with a little padding,' Jake said.

Mark laughed. 'Fucking Jake Harding. Come here, man.'

He met Jake halfway and gripped Jake's hand and they did a shake and punch. Mark started talking right away about how glad he was to see Jake, and have him on board.

'How are things at the stables?' he asked Jake.

'I'm getting on all right.'

'See, Novak?' Mark said, looking beyond us at the other guy. 'I told you Jake would make it work. Novak here thinks you're gonna screw this job up. He thinks it's a bad idea.'

Novak just smiled, or seemed to. His teeth were not nice to

look at: yellowish and square and standing out from the gums. Skeleton teeth.

'Nobody's gonna screw anything up,' Jake said.

He sounded very confident, very convincing. At the time, even I believed him.

'That's my boy. Send those fuckers a message. Pull some Coppola-type shit on them.' Mark snapped his fingers. 'Hey Novak – why don't you see if that cake is ready?'

'Cake,' Novak said, as if considering it. 'Yes, I will get the cake.'

He slipped out the door, eel-like, and shut it silently behind him.

'Don't mind Novak,' Mark said. 'He's a crazy Slav. But useful.'

He led Jake and I over to the card table. It had four chairs around it and on top, in the middle, was a crokinole board. The board was carved from mahogany and so were the discs. I'd never seen a board like that. Mark noticed me studying it and rapped on the edge.

'We just got into this. Crokinole. My bro's obsessed with it.'

'We used to play as kids.'

'Oh yeah?' He sort of perched sideways on the edge of the table, in a way that didn't look particularly cool or comfortable, and eyed me up and down. 'Jesus, Jake. You didn't tell me you were bringing the Angels in on this deal. What chapter are you with, buddy?'

I told him I wasn't with any chapter. I wasn't with the Angels. I sort of got that he was making fun of me but I still didn't understand it. Then Mark laughed. His laugh was really something: a high-pitched, squeaky giggle, like a teenager before his voice breaks.

'Shit – I'm just messing with you. I meant the outfit.'

I was wearing my watchcap and goose-down jacket and work boots.

'He's on the boats,' Jake said, clapping my back. 'Fishing and shit.'

'At the docks? We got some guys down there.'

Mark rattled off a list of names, but I didn't recognize any of them, since I didn't actually work at the docks he had in mind. This seemed to disappoint him momentarily, and he looked at me anew, as if I might not be a fisherman at all but a guy posing as one.

'So this is your brother?' he asked Jake.

Jake introduced me, and Mark held out his hand to shake mine. As we did, he noticed my fingers and turned my hand up so he could get a better look. He bent over it as if he were going to kiss it.

'Jesus Christ. You get bit by a shark or what?'

'No – I got bit by your mom.'

I do that, sometimes, when I'm nervous. I say something completely inappropriate and out of line. Mark let my hand drop. For a second it seemed as if it could go either way, but Mark laughed again – that squeak of a laugh – and said something about me having balls, to make a crack like that. Then he stopped laughing, and gave his earlobe a gentle pinch.

'Just don't say anything like that around my brother, okay?'

'Where is your brother?' Jake asked.

'He'll be here. We got a few minutes to kill.'

He took a seat and we did the same. While we waited he wanted to see our crokinole skills. We divided up the rocks and took turns shooting twenties. Mark wasn't that good but he was very enthusiastic. We did that for ten or fifteen minutes, until headlights flooded the office. A vehicle had turned into the drive: another SUV, a big Durango. As it pulled into the garage beneath us the thump-thump of heavy bass beats made the whole room vibrate. Then the music cut out, and a few moments later Patrick Delaney made his entrance.

'What's the fucking dilly, yo?' he said.

Pat had Mark's features but he was heftier, all muscled up, with a crew cut and the kind of wide-shouldered, swaggering walk tough guys develop. It should have been comical but there was undeniably something intimidating about him. Jake and I both stood up, since the situation seemed to call for it. Pat ignored us. He had a duffel bag slung over his shoulder and he went right to the desk and dropped it. It landed heavily.

Mark said, 'You got them.'

'Check it,' Pat said, and unzipped the bag.

There were black vests inside. They were puffy and heavy and when Pat pulled one out I realized it was a bullet-proof vest like cops wear. Mark held it up to his chest, checking the size, then undid the Velcro and strapped it on, over his sport coat.

'Yeah, motherfucker,' he said, and thumped his chest.

'You're invincible.'

They played around with the vests a while longer, and I got the sense that this was largely, or partly, for our benefit: they were showing off their toys. Then Pat deigned to notice us. Or notice Jake. He came over to the crokinole table and stood in front of him.

'We ready to roll on this, Jake?' he asked.

'We're rolling like dough,' Jake said.

Mark patted Jake's back. 'Jake's got full run of the place.'

The four of us sat down and Pat didn't mess around with preamble. He reached into his jacket pocket and brought out a white envelope and placed that on the table, beside the crokinole board.

'There might be a key in that envelope. If there is, it might fit a vehicle that will be parked in a particular location tomorrow night.'

'What kind of vehicle?' Jake asked.

'I don't know. I don't even know what's in that envelope – get me? But whatever it is, it'll be what you need. Once it's there, ready to be picked up, you'll get a call on this.'

He slid a cellphone across the board. It spun and came to a stop near us: a black clamshell Nokia. Jake took the phone and envelope and tucked them in his jacket pocket.

'You drive it over,' Pat said, 'and when you get there, and everything's a go, you give us a call just to let us know. We'll make sure the next phase is in place.'

At that point, I assumed it was money. Or dope. That was what I'd been expecting all along: some kind of drug run or delivery with us acting as mules or couriers or whatnot.

Pat asked, 'You sure you can gain access?'

'I got clearance.'

'If you screw any of it up, you're fucked, and we don't know you. You take the fall. That's how it works. Can you handle that?'

'We can handle it.'

Pat looked at me. I'd been frowning, trying to follow it all, but when he looked at me I smiled instead. I smiled in what must have been a weird and extremely unconvincing way.

He said, 'Your brother doesn't seem so sure.'

I said, 'It all sounds pretty vague.'

'That's called being smart. That's called deniability.'

'Deniability,' his brother repeated, and giggled. He was still wearing his vest.

'We can handle it,' Jake said.

'Good. Maria said you'd get it done. She said you were reliable.'

'Maria?' I asked.

I couldn't help it. It just popped out. They all looked at me, expectantly.

'Like Maria O'Connell?'

'That's her,' Mark said. 'That a problem, Relic?'

'I just didn't know she was involved.'

Pat jerked a thumb at me, and asked Jake, 'He gonna be all right?'

'He's fine.'

Mark was giggling again. He started telling a confusing anecdote, the overall point of which seemed to be that Maria had set fire to his brother's Hummer, after an argument.

'She was always a firebrand,' Jake said.

'She's turning into a goddamn liability,' Pat said to him. 'You're gonna see her and her brat down there. Do me a favour and make sure she's not too strung out, will you?'

'I'll look after her.'

There was an edge to how Jake said it. Pat didn't miss that. He jerked his chin.

'You two used to have a thing, didn't you?'

'Years ago.'

'You're lucky the bitch dropped you.'

The door opened and that guy, Novak, came back in. He'd brought the cake and four plates. He laid the cake in the centre of the board and from his pocket slid out a slim blade, a stiletto, which he used to slice four pieces, getting the sizes exactly the same. With the flat of the knife he lifted each piece onto a plate, then went to take up his position by the door again.

'Our mom makes the best fucking cake,' Mark said. 'Try this shit.'

Pat took his piece and stuffed the whole thing in his mouth.

I ate mine more slowly, pretending to really appreciate it. I have to admit: it was good cake – lemon and poppy seed.

'Golden,' Jake said.

Pat grunted. Then his phone buzzed, and he checked the screen.

'I got shit on,' he said. 'We good here?'

'What about our money?' Jake asked.

'You'll get your money on delivery.'

'And then Jake's square with you, right?' I said.

Pat held out his hand, palm up, as if to say, 'Who the fuck is this guy?' and they all laughed. When the laughter settled, Pat reached over and thumbed a crumb off his plate.

'Sure,' he said, popping it in his mouth, 'and then Jake's square with us.'

Chapter Nine

ONCE WE HAD LEFT THE Delaneys' and were alone in Jake's truck, cruising back along the Upper Levels towards the bridge, I didn't say a damned thing. Not at first. I sat with my arms crossed and stared out my window at the concrete barricade that divided the highway from the houses and yards and normal lives that lay on the other side. I was trying to demonstrate my rage and general ire at the mess my brother had once again gotten himself into, and me along with him. In addition, I was trying to work out the whole thing in my head, but didn't have much success. A lot of what I'd heard in there hadn't made any kind of sense. But one thing had stood out.

'Maria,' I said. 'Your Maria.'

'She ain't mine any more.'

'Why didn't you tell me she was part of this?'

'She isn't, really.'

'That's not what it sounded like.'

'She's with him now. Big slick.'

'When did that happen?'

'Few years back. You know Maria. She's got her needs.'

When it all went haywire after Sandy's death, he and Maria had both gotten into a lot of different shit. Jake went clean, eventually, but Maria didn't. And apparently still hadn't.

'I knew she was rolling with some shitty people,' I said. 'But that boner?'

He flicked his cigarette out the window. 'Why do you care, anyway?'

'I care because you told me this was about you paying your debts.'

'It is.'

'Now it turns out Maria's involved, and brought you into it, and that we happen to be working for her boyfriend, who's a total fucking Carlito. Don't tell me that's a coincidence.'

'Of course it's not, you turnip. You heard him: she suggested me.'

'Why would she do that?'

'Maybe because she knows I need a chance to pay them back.'

'Or maybe because her boyfriend needed a patsy, and she knew you'd do it.'

We were on that section of the Cut with a wide shoulder. I told Jake to pull over and, after a second's hesitation, he swung in and shoved the stick into park and killed the engine. The rain spattering the roof and hood seemed to crescendo, like the roar of applause, or laughter.

I said, 'Are we doing this for her or for you?'

'It's not that simple, man.'

'It's simple enough.'

'It's not like it was all laid out. It's not like they called me up and said, "If you don't do this you're dead." She recommended me and they asked me and I said yes because these are not people you say no to, and because I owe them, okay?' He paused, and shifted in his seat, as if he'd sat on a pinecone or prickly pear. 'And I owe her, too.'

'You don't owe her anything.'

'You weren't even here.'

'Weren't here when?'

'When do you think? Some brother.'

I couldn't talk to him like that, all twisted sideways in the cab. So I got out. I got out and he got out and we started shouting at each other across the hood of the truck in the rain. I pointed at him and demanded he take it back, but he said it was the truth and that at the time I hadn't been much of a brother, and I told him that was a cheap and low-down thing to say.

He said, 'Sandy dies and you skulk off like a total shrew, and go tree planting for God's sake. You were up there for like three months, having your little blue-collar bonanza. What the hell do you think was happening back here, aside from Ma having a stroke?'

'I know what was happening. You and Maria were playing Sid and Nancy.'

'Fuck you we were. We were looking after Ma, getting her treatment.'

'That sure worked. Did you inject heroin directly into her brain?'

Then something shifted in his face and I understood we were

going to fight, right there at the side of the highway. And it came as a relief, that realization. It was inevitable and probably had been since he'd first arrived at the boatyard.

Jake walked around the truck and started trotting towards me and I stepped into him and we sort of crashed together like that, like a couple of rams or bucks, both of us hard-headed and bone-stubborn, and both of us just as dense and senseless as the other.

I know exactly what my brother will do in a fight and he knows the same about me. He has a penchant for chokeholds and grappling and I prefer to punch him repeatedly in the ribs and torso. We rarely hit each other in the face unless we're drunk or insane with rage, which sometimes happens – so perhaps by rarely I mean less often than not. He tends to get my head under his arm and squeeze down so my chin touches my chest and my windpipe gets cut off, and now the tendons at the back of my neck click repeatedly from having suffered this technique so often. But I also know how to wriggle out of it, just as he knows to cover his sides with his elbows to avoid the body-blows with which I aim to hammer him. It's worth noting that my punches are much less effective than before the accident with my hand but in truth even before that I wasn't much of a puncher. My hands are too small.

This makes our fights strangely futile. Neither of us can get the advantage because neither of us really wants to win. What we want, I suppose, is to annihilate the other and at the same time absorb or become him. We're like conjoined twins, frustrated at being yoked together, grasping and punching and flailing both at our brother-double, and ourselves.

We scuffled like that for several minutes, flopping about in the wet gravel, caught in the glare of headlights as cars swept past.

Some of the drivers honked (either disapprovingly or enthusiastically) and others slowed down to heckle us or just rubber-neck and have a look. Eventually one of the cars pulled over and an old-timer got out. By then we were spent and gasping and lying on the shoulder of the road like a couple of wounded raccoons.

'Cops are on the way,' he said, tipping back his cap. 'You two better move along.'

'You called the cops?' Jake said.

'My wife did.'

'Damn.'

Jake picked himself up and sort of brushed his jeans off extravagantly. I sat there for a moment longer, still panting. I'd skinned the knuckles of my good hand on the asphalt and they were bleeding and Jake's face was bleeding too. He held out an open palm to me, and after staring bitterly at it for a moment I took it. He tried to haul me to my feet, but I was too heavy, or he was too weary, and so instead I ended up pulling him back down beside me.

Jake wanted to buy me a drink to make up, but no bar would let us in looking like that so we took his Black Velvet up to the roof of the Woodland, where we sat on a vent in the cold and gazed over the alley to the inlet. The darkly shimmering water reflected back a broken version of our city, and we stared at that and drank miserably from his little teacups and nursed our wounds and didn't speak. I must have smacked my head during the fight because my skull seemed to be buzzing, irksomely, as if there was a small insect inside it.

It was true what Jake had said, about me sneaking off after Sandy's death. I signed on with a tree planting company based out of Quesnel and bought a Greyhound bus ticket for sixty-eight dollars and change and that was enough to leave behind what remained of my family. In the mornings we were assigned plots and given sacks of yearlings – baby trees – and I would take my sack and go to my plot and stab my shovel into the ground and make a hole with the shovel and put a yearling in the hole. Then I did that again, and again and again. And at the end of the day I would have blistered hands and a face swollen with bug bites and the arch of my right foot would ache from stomping the shovel. It tired me out enough to sleep and then morning would come and it would start again. All the days merged into one, or maybe the same day enacted repeatedly. A kind of penance. It was what I had needed, but when I came back things had changed, and my brother had changed, too.

'I'm sorry, man,' I said.

'I started it.'

'I mean for bailing like that.'

He leaned back and blew a slow whistle of smoke upwards, like a steam train.

'I appreciate that.'

'But you got to be straight with me about this.'

'Who says I'm not?'

I sipped my whisky, by habit sipping from the teacup as if the liquid was hot and might burn my tongue. 'You should have told me Maria was involved.'

'Her involvement doesn't change things.'

'Like hell. I know what she means to you.'

'But not to you, right? She's just my crummy ex – some troublesome chick.'

'Hell, Jake.' I stared at my hands. They were all grimy and cut up from scrapping in the dirt with him. 'You know that ain't true. I cared for her, too. She was like family to me.'

'And to Sandy.'

'But she drifted away, man. That junk meant more to her than us, in the end.'

'The end hasn't happened yet.'

He stood up and went to peer down at the alley. The wind caught his bandana and blew it sideways and he seemed to sway with the motion. I had this terrible image in my head of him leaning forward, letting himself go over the edge. A long fall into the dark.

'What else haven't you told me?' I said.

'What else is there?'

'What the hell we're stealing, for one thing.'

He tipped back his teacup, draining it. When he finished he backed away from the ledge, took a few running steps, and threw the cup in a long lobbing arc, over the roof of the next building. A few seconds later I heard the distant shatter-pop, delicate and irreparable.

'A horse,' he said. 'We're going to steal a racehorse from Castle Meadow.'

I didn't even answer. I couldn't. I just lay back on the roof and stared at the stars. The concrete was hard and cold beneath me and those stars looked impossibly far away.

Chapter Ten

THE NEXT MORNING JAKE ANNOUNCED we were going to see her, this horse we were meant to steal. I'd already told him that I didn't want any part of it but no doubt he'd expected this kind of resistance: it was why he'd held off telling me for so long. So he cooked me a fried egg on his hotplate – just an egg, no toast or bun or anything – and convinced me to at least come out to the stables with him, as if that would somehow bring me around to the scheme. I also had a brutal hangover, and when I went to take a shower I stumbled across an old lady in a housecoat smoking crack in the bathroom on Jake's floor. When I walked in she smiled at me, bashfully, and offered me a toke. Overall it was a terrible way to start the day.

We took Jake's Mustang to Castle Meadow. During the drive Jake assured me he'd 'scoped out' the situation (he was already talking like that) and claimed it wasn't as bad as it sounded. Security at the stables was minimal, he said. A night watchman, a couple of CCTV cameras – that was all. It wasn't like at the racetrack, where they were paranoid about people tampering with the animals. At Castle Meadow they didn't worry about horses getting stolen because it just wasn't something anybody had ever done.

'Yeah,' I said, 'and there's a reason for that.'

When we arrived, we wheeled past the clubhouse – where we'd had a drink the other night – and parked closer to the stables. They were long clapboard structures with corrugated tin roofing. Nothing fancy.

'This isn't going to change anything,' I said.

'Just come check it out.'

He whistled idly through his gap tooth as we crossed the yard. We entered the stables through a garage door, big enough for vehicle access, and walked along a concrete alley between the stalls where they kept the horses. The air smelled of manure, hay, and animals. At that time – mid-morning – a lot seemed to be going on. We passed stable hands mucking out the stalls, and grooms measuring scoops of feed, and riders saddling up their horses. A few of the riders looked small enough to be professional jockeys, although they weren't dressed in their full get-up like you see at the track. Some of the workers nodded at Jake, but for the most part we were ignored.

Jake stopped at a stall, with a tin nameplate nailed next to it: *Shenzao*. It was empty.

'She must be out for a run,' he said.

He took me through another door that opened onto the training grounds. I hadn't been able to see much the night we came out. The main enclosure was about the size of a lacrosse box, the turf mucky from recent rain and cratered with the impressions of horseshoes. At the far end a set of bleachers rose up, but the seats were empty. A few spectators sat at tables on the clubhouse patio, and others leaned up against the perimeter fence, observing the grounds. A dozen horses were prancing around out there, doing laps or jumping over obstacles. Their hoofbeats thudded dully across the big space. As we watched, one barrelled towards us: a big dappled grey. It snorted and steamed as it ran, bearing down on us before peeling away along the fence-line, kicking up clumps of turf in its wake.

'How do you like that?' Jake said.

'That's the horse?'

'No. I don't see her yet.'

We leaned against the wooden rail. The morning was misty and dreary. I stared sullenly into the middle distance, across that pit of mud, and tried to find a way to say it.

'I'm out, man,' I said. 'I can't do this.'

'This isn't the kind of thing you back out of, brother.'

'You didn't tell me what we were doing.'

'Sure I did. Pick-up and delivery.'

'I thought it would be drugs or money or stolen goods. Not a *horse*.'

'Would you keep it down?'

About twenty yards away, an elderly woman – tiny and grey-haired, possibly Asian – was watching the horses through a set of opera binoculars. At her side stood a man in a grey overcoat and dark sunglasses, even though the sun wasn't out. They made for an odd pair.

'They can't hear us,' I said.

Jake got out his crumpled pack of Du Mauriers and tapped one free. Lighting it, he blew a plume of smoke into the morning cold, and nodded slowly, as if in understanding.

'I get it,' he said. 'You've got cold feet.'

'I've got cold everything. It's madness, man.'

'It'll feel a lot better once we're dancing.'

It was something Sandy used to say to us, as a joke, when one of us – usually Jake – had gotten into trouble or screwed something up. But it was a cheap trick to use under these circumstances, and I just shook my head.

'I'll come see Ma with you,' I told him. 'Then you're on your own.'

He reached over and grabbed my bicep. 'Here she is,' he said.

He pointed to the far side of the enclosure. It's a moment I remember well, and not just because of all that came after. She seemed to emerge from the mist, on account of her being entirely white. Even her mane was white. She had a long stride and drifted over the ground towards us, swift and effortless. The guy atop was just along for the ride. She flew down the straightaway and soared past, her head straining at the reins. Then she was gone.

'Hell,' I said.

I knew nothing about horses, but I could tell she was really something.

'Morning spirit, or spirit of morning,' Jake said. When I looked at him curiously, he explained: 'That's what her name means. Shenzao.'

'And she's valuable.'

'She's rare,' Jake said. 'There aren't any white racehorses.'

'I've seen white racehorses before.'

'No you haven't.'

'How do you know what I've seen?'

He held out his hands, as if gripping an imaginary box, and moved it up and down. It was a gesture he used when explaining something that he thought was very simple.

'You've seen grey horses that look white. She's actually white.'

'Like an albino.'

'It's called Dominant White. And a potential winner – unlike most of these nags.'

She was across the paddock now, floating like a phantom through the mist. Just beautiful. The elderly woman was slow-tracking her progress through the binoculars.

'What the hell do the Delaneys want her for, anyway?'

'Ah hell,' he said, and kicked the bottom rung of the fence with his boot. The timber reverberated ominously.

'You said you'd be straight with me.'

'They honestly didn't tell me.'

'But you have an idea.'

He dropped his smoke in the dirt, and checked his watch. 'We better get a move on. I told Ma we'd swing by at eleven. You know how she is.'

'Jake.'

'I'll tell you after, okay?'

'No more bullshit.'

The horse was coming back. This time the jockey had slowed her to a canter. In passing the elderly woman, he tipped his cap, and she clapped vigorously, almost comically, the sound echoing across the enclosure. Shenzao carried on, high-stepping and tossing her mane. As she got closer she tilted her head to look at us sidelong, and snorted dismissively – as if she already suspected that we were up to something, and that it involved her, and that the result would be no good for any of us.

Chapter Eleven

OUR MOTHER OPENED THE DOOR to her apartment and smiled, or partially smiled. Half of her face still drooped, lopsided and permanently saddened, but the effect was no longer so strange or disconcerting. We'd grown accustomed to it. It had been like that since the day Jake found her, sitting at the kitchen table in our old house in Lynn Valley. She had been glass-eyed and slack-jawed, with a dribble of milk and Rice Krispies leaking from the corner of her mouth. At first he'd thought she might be dead but when he came into her field of vision her eyes reacted and seemed to register his presence, though on a distant and dimmer level.

She had recovered a lot of mobility and some awareness but still needed assistance, so we'd sold the house in the Valley and paid off the mortgage and with the remaining money rented her a one-bedroom apartment on Lower Lonsdale, four blocks up from the Quay and Sea Bus terminal. We paid a local company – Helping Hands – to send somebody for an hour each day to check in on her and bring her a hot meal and do her chores. She had a microwave and an electric kettle but not a stove. A stove, we'd been told, was a bad idea. Our mother was not quite herself, or not quite the mother we'd known, but she was still our mother.

'Boys,' she said, slurring the word slightly. 'Come here, boys.'

She got up to hug us fiercely – me first, then Jake. Physically she was still pretty good, pretty strong.

'We brought Timmy Ho's,' Jake said, shaking the bag of dough-nuts.

'Oh,' she said, and clapped her hands. 'That's wonderful. Let me put on the kettle.'

She shuffled through to her kitchen, walking with a slight limp. It was one o'clock and she was still wearing her bathrobe. She was also wearing a shower cap. Not because she had just gotten out of the shower, but because this was something she had taken to doing. It kept the bugs out, she said. It made her look a little like a prep cook at a fancy restaurant.

Jake and I sat down to wait at the dining table. The table was from our old house, as was the majority of her furniture and deco-rations. She'd wanted to keep as much as possible. The items were familiar but the arrangement was bewildering and of course the space was diminished, cramped. It felt like entering a museum, filled with the paraphernalia of our past. She had put up so many paintings and old photos that they completely obliterated the walls, in an overwhelming collage. Most of the paintings depicted the prairies, where she had grown up, and the photos were of us: family shots of when our father was still alive, and later ones with just the four of us. After Sandy, there were no more photos.

Our mother filled the kettle and set it to boil and while she did this she chattered to us excitedly. She was having a good day and remembered I'd been on the boat and asked about the herring season, and also asked about Tracy, who she called such a nice girl. She hadn't seen Jake for months but she didn't question his absence, just as she hadn't fully registered the time he'd been in jail. She asked him about his own work and he explained he had a new job down at the stables. That impressed her. She had spent portions of her youth on a farm, where they kept dairy cows and some horses. The stroke hadn't dimmed those memories at all, and instead had made them clearer by wiping away some of the intervening years.

She asked Jake, 'How did you get that job?'

'I had some connections down there.'

'That's wonderful. How convenient.'

'Yes,' I said. 'Very convenient.'

Jake frowned and shook his head, as if my comment was too stupid and obvious to warrant a reply. He began laying out the doughnuts on a plate in the centre of the dining table. Our mother went on talking about his new job until the kettle started shrieking and she said, 'Oh!' and rushed over there. As she poured the water – slopping some down the sides of the cups – she asked him, 'And do you get to work with the horses?'

'Mostly I clean up after them.'

'That's a start, though.'

'I could bring you down there some time.'

'I'd love that. I miss horses so much.'

'They're amazing animals.'

'Amazing,' I said. 'Priceless. And worth stealing, no doubt.'

He whipped a doughnut hole at me, sideways. It was dusted with icing sugar and left a starburst of white in the centre of my shirt. I calmly picked it up and put it on the plate next to the others. He'd grown more and more surly since I'd started talking about backing out.

'You're a goddamn clown,' he said quietly.

Our mother brought the cups in one at a time, gripping each with her good hand, her right. I adjusted my chair in case I had to move quickly, to catch her or rescue a cup, but she managed okay. Then came the milk and the sugar, again separately, and she joined us at the table and beamed.

'And what about Sandy?' she asked. 'How's Sandy?'

'She's good, Ma,' I said, before Jake could answer. 'Wherever she is.'

'It must be so cold there. She sent me a postcard, you know.'

'That's right. I remember.'

Sandy had sent her one from Paris, when she went out for the audition that got her the job. The postcard was on our mother's fridge: a photo of the Sacré-Cœur, all lit up at night.

'I'm so proud of her.'

'She blew them away, over there.'

Jake shook his head and sort of sneered. I spread out my hands, as if implying, what do you want me to do? He popped a doughnut hole into his mouth and chewed it loudly, deliberately smacking his lips, and then made a loud comment about the terrible weather.

'Yes,' our mother said. 'It is rather dreary.'

In the aftermath of the stroke both Jake and I had tried to explain the truth to her in our own way and each time our mother had either perceived the revelation as a terrible joke or expressed horror and dismay – as if she was finding out for the first time, all over again, that her daughter was dead. The blood vessel that had ruptured in her brain had wiped away that era of her life. That was all it had taken to obliterate the tragedy. Possibly it was also psychological but that didn't matter to me. I envied her the magic and the blissful ease of it.

Sandy didn't come up again while we sat and drank our coffee and ate our doughnuts. When the doughnuts were done Ma fumbled for her pack of Craven A, which she kept in the pocket of her bathrobe. It was a fresh pack, probably her second of the day. She slid open the top and peeled back the foil with her fingers, stained that strange yellow-brown from years of tar. Jake asked for a cigarette and she said, 'Don't be silly, Jake – you don't smoke.' But when he reached across for one she didn't try to stop him.

'I've been a bad influence on you boys,' was what she said.

Jake grunted – neither in acknowledgement nor disagreement.

Both our parents had smoked when we were kids, until our dad had died of cancer – not lung cancer but another cancer, pancreatic, which had most likely been brought on by his smoking. After that our mother had quit, due in large part to Sandy's vigilance. Sandy had patrolled the house and found hidden packs of smokes like a detective uncovering clues, and destroyed any she found. She had stopped Ma from smoking for fifteen years, but when what happened had happened, Ma started up again and there was nothing to be done about that.

While they smoked I got up and opened the sliding door that led to the balcony. It was barely a balcony at all, and felt as confined as a coffin. Just a few feet deep and about six feet across. All she had out there was a single chair and two potted plants – both dead. They were so withered I wouldn't have even known what they were, except that I had bought them for her: a gardenia and a magnolia.

I stood at the rail. The balcony overlooked the alley behind Keith, and the back of another apartment block. In the alley three storeys below I saw greasy puddles of rainwater, overflowing Dumpsters, and the rusted remains of a bicycle. That view, and her little apartment, was all our mother had, and all she would have until we moved her to a care home, if we could afford to move her to a care home. Standing there in the dreary cold on my mother's balcony, for the first time I felt the allure of Jake's plan, of receiving a big pay-out, a windfall. He hadn't told me how much the Delaneys were offering but it had to be a lot, considering the risk.

I turned and went back inside and slid closed the door, shutting those thoughts out. Our mother had lit a second cigarette and was talking fondly about Sandy again. Jake was gazing vacantly at the photos on the wall, tolerating her but not really listening. When I sat back down, he seemed to rouse himself. He said to her, 'Ma – I have to go away.'

She smiled uncertainly. 'For how long?'

'A little while.'

'Not to jail again? You're not going to jail, are you Jake?'

Her voice peaked a little as she said his name. I was surprised she'd remembered.

'No, no – on a little trip, is all.'

'So long as you're careful.'

'You know me.'

She frowned, sceptically, in a way that reminded me of her old self. 'Is Tim going with you?'

'No,' he said. 'He was going to but now he's not.'

'Oh, Tim,' she said. She reached over to pat my hand. Against mine, hers looked very small and withered. A mummified hand. 'I'd feel better about it if you were going.'

'I might, Ma. I guess I might.'

'That's a relief. You take care of your brother, won't you Tim?'

'I do,' I said. 'I will.'

Jake and I gazed at each other, through the haze of smoke they'd created. I guess I knew then that I was going to be part of it, and that all my talk about backing out had been just that: talk. The truth is, my loyalty to my brother was so strong that I would have gone along with pretty much any plan, no matter how dumb or foolhardy or crazy, no matter what.

Our mother asked, 'Where are you boys going?'

I raised my eyebrows at him, but he pretended not to notice.

'Just on a drive,' he said, distantly. 'A sort of road trip.'

'Will you see Sandy?'

'You can't drive to France,' Jake said.

'But she might meet us,' I said.

'Oh – how wonderful.'

'Ma,' Jake said.

But she was up. Charged with nicotine and caffeine. She went into the kitchen and started opening and closing cupboards, mumbling about us taking Sandy something. But it wasn't clear what she had in mind. Then she seemed to remember and opened the bottom door of her fridge – the freezer compartment – and got out a microwaveable burrito. We'd eaten them all the time as kids. She brought it over and deposited it on Jake's lap.

'That's for her,' she said, triumphantly. 'Bean and cheese. Her favourite.'

Jake held it up, helpless. He said, 'Ma – we're not going to see Sandy.' And then he said, 'Ma – Sandy's gone. I can't give her some frozen burrito, for God's sake.'

He said it quietly, but not so quietly she didn't hear. She laughed, high and terrified. 'What are you talking about? Timothy – what on *earth* is your brother talking about?'

'Nothing, Ma. He's just messing around.'

'It isn't very funny.'

'I know. I know it isn't.' I took the burrito from Jake. He let it go but his hands retained its shape, as if he were still holding it – as if he were now holding an invisible burrito. 'We'll give this to her. Sure we can give this to her. Sandy loves these things.'

'I know she does. And they don't have them in France.'

'No – that's good thinking. That's real considerate.'

She collapsed in her chair and reached for her cigarettes, even though she'd left one smouldering in the ashtray. She lit another and dragged on it desperately, sucking the smoke in as if it was saving her, not killing her: inhaling as if her life depended on it.

Chapter Twelve

OUTSIDE, AS WE WALKED BACK down Lonsdale towards the Quay, Jake asked if I meant what I'd said about helping, and I told him I did but that any money we earned from this fool's errand would go towards Ma's care. He agreed, and though in many other ways I suspected he was stringing me along I believed him about that. It cheered him mightily, having me on board.

'We're going whole hog on this, Poncho,' he said, tossing me the frozen burrito.

'Hell no,' I said, and flipped it back. 'We're going whole horse.'

The first thing we did was withdraw the remainder of my pay

from herring season, which amounted to just under six hundred dollars. We needed the money to buy tools and supplies for the job. That was how Jake now referred to it: the job. As if we were seasoned thieves, a couple of old pros.

We went to buy our tools at Canadian Tire.

This, too, was a familiar tradition. In the past, whenever Jake had concocted one of his schemes, which were always on the cusp of legality, we'd go stock up on supplies and I generally ended up paying because he was always broke. The previous times this happened it had been comical and even vaguely innocent: our attempt to break into a defunct bakery – of all places – to steal a bread-making oven for Sandy's birthday, or his plan to salvage a haul of copper piping from a building site, or the minor scam he'd run that involved sneaking people, for a small charge, into rock concerts at the Coliseum, where he'd been working at the time.

We wandered around Canadian Tire, between endless aisles and shelves laden with power tools and gardening equipment and painting supplies. Jake held a basket hooked over one elbow and every so often he tossed something into it: leather driving gloves, balaclavas, nylon cord. Then he announced we needed bolt-cutters, and started peering down various aisles, searching for the tool section.

I asked, 'Why bolt-cutters?'

'At night the horses are locked in their stalls.'

'I thought you had keys.'

'I have keys for the stables, not the stalls. The stalls are locked by the owners.'

In passing through the kids' section, Jake picked up a backpack – a Ninja Turtle backpack, adding to the general sense of juvenilia and ridiculousness.

I said, 'I'd feel better if I knew a little more about the plan.'

'You heard Pat. We get the call tonight, and we pick up the vehicle.'

'That much is easy. What's next?'

'Next we head out to Castle Meadow, park up, and wait till the security guard goes to make his cash drop. He's off-site for half an hour, sometimes more if he stops for a coffee.'

'That doesn't sound like much time.'

'It's time enough to go on in and steal her.'

'What about the security gate?'

'I know the code.'

'You said there's CCTV.'

'We'll have these.'

He lifted up one of the balaclavas. It was meant for skiing, and had a little colourful bobble on the top. He waggled it on his hand like a puppet, making the bobble dance. Still doing that, he led me down the next aisle, having stumbled on the cutting tools.

I said, 'You still haven't told me why the Delaneys want the horse in the first place.'

'Ah, hell,' Jake said, and dropped the balaclava. 'They've got some beef with the owners. They want to send a message. They're going to take her and hold her for ransom or use her for leverage.'

We'd reached the bolt-cutters, hanging with their handles open and jaws spread wide like steel traps. Jake picked up the biggest set and hefted it, checking the weight.

'And these owners,' I said. 'They're gangsters too.'

He pretended to be focused on the cutters, and their action: opening and closing them.

'Reckon so,' he said.

'Shenzao,' I said, trying out the word for the first time. 'Is that Mandarin?'

'Cantonese, actually.'

I swore and cursed him something fierce and said I didn't want to hear any more. I got out my wallet and threw that in the basket next to all the supplies we'd picked up for our ludicrous endeavour. I walked away and left him practising with his damned bolt-cutters.

'They weren't gonna be stealing her from Daisy Duck,' he called after me.

I pushed through the doors and sat on the kerb out front, feeling the coolness of the concrete through my jeans. A pigeon with a damaged wing was limping around nearby, looking for scraps in the gutter. It waddled up and pecked at my boot and, apparently deciding I had nothing to offer, cooed irately.

'You and me both,' I said.

As I sat there my cellphone rang. I thought it might be Ma's care company phoning – I'd left a message about her bills – but it turned out to be Tracy. I stared at the display for a time, debating, and eventually accepted it.

'It's good to hear from you,' I said.

'I hope you're okay.'

'I messed up pretty bad.'

She didn't disagree, and I guess that was a form of agreement.

'Is your dad still mad at me?' I asked.

'He's not happy. But he's mellowed a bit. You know his temper.'

'I sure do.'

'He said you just upped and left.'

'I feel terrible about that. I really do. But . . .'

'I know. Your brother.'

I kept adjusting my grip on the phone, and shifting its position against my ear, as if I could get it to work better, or communicate what I wanted to say, if I put it in the right place.

I said, 'Guess you know the cabin is all off, too.'

'Goes without saying. But he might take you back.'

'You think?'

'My dad will listen to me.'

'You call the shots, eh?'

'In our family the women have the last word.'

'That was the same in our family.'

'You never told me much about your family.'

'No. I never did.'

I heard a voice in the background. Maybe Evelyn.

'I better go,' Tracy said. 'We're leaving for Squamish, soon.'

'I left a note,' I said. 'Ask him to read the note, will you?'

She told me to take care of myself, that she'd try me when they got back. Then she hung up.

Jake came out shortly after. I still had my phone in hand, gazing at it emptily. He asked me who I'd been talking to and I said Tracy and he asked if I'd smoothed it over with her and I just shook my head and said, 'There ain't no smoothing this over.' Then he stood beside me for a time, and I didn't get up. He had his bolt-cutters in one hand and the Ninja Turtles backpack in the other, filled with our thieves' tools.

'You pay in cash?' I asked finally.

'Sure I did.'

'Give me back the damn wallet.' He flipped it in the air, so I had to snatch at it, but my bad hand betrayed me and it flopped out on the concrete like a dead bat. That wounded pigeon sidled over and pecked at it once, as if to check whether there was still any life in it.

I said, 'What do you figure the Triads will do when they find out we took their horse?'

'They won't know it was us.'

'Let's hope so.'

I stood up, then. I stood up slowly, purposefully, as if I was hefting a five-hundred-pound weight. I stood and put my hands on my brother's shoulders. I looked him square in the face. He was smiling faintly, mockingly, his straggly bangs dangling in his eyes.

'Is there anything else?' I said. 'Anything you haven't told me?'

'Not that I can think of.'

'If there is, you tell me now.'

'Except maybe where we're taking her.'

I just waited, my nerves humming.

'Across the border,' he said. 'We're taking her to the United States.'

He stooped to scoop up the wallet, and held it out to me.

'You dropped this,' he said.

The pigeon squawked at us, with what seemed to me derision.

You wouldn't have thought we'd be able to fall asleep on the night we were planning to steal a racehorse. But that's what we did, after eating takeaway from the Pink Pearl and drinking a few cans of Molson. When I awoke it was dark in the room and I could hear the boot-stomp of honkey-tonk over at the Paradise. It had to be near closing time, around midnight. Every so often a car cruised along Hastings Street and the headlight beams swept across the ceiling, steady and repetitive as a lighthouse beacon. The effect gave me a kind of comfort, at least.

Jake was awake, too. I could tell because as kids the two of us had shared a room, so I had an almost instinctive feel for it: the rhythms of his breathing, the rustles of restlessness.

'Lefty,' I said.

'Poncho.'

'What time is it?'

He sat up and switched on the bedside light, casting a dirty yellow glow over things. He squinted at his watch, a battered Timex that had belonged to our pa. That was all we had, when it came to him. An old watch, and a few memories: his smile and his smoky smell and the way he picked you up, burly as a bear. We were both pretty young when he went.

'About eleven,' Jake said.

'I ain't gonna sleep no more.'

He stood and from the bedside table picked up the phone Mark Delaney had given us. He snapped it open to check the display. Nothing. He put it back down and stood there for a minute with his hands on his hips, staring at the floor.

He said, 'We should get our shit together, so we're ready.'

He unbuckled the clasps on his suitcase and flipped it open. Into it, he tossed various supplies and possessions: dirty clothes, the half-drunk bottle of Black Velvet, some veterinary gels and medicines (which he'd apparently stolen) and a few keepsakes, including a photo of us three as kids down in Stanley Park. Lastly, he added two passports. One was old and well-worn and the other still looked new and crisp and uncreased. I picked it up from the top of the pile and opened it. It was Sandy's. She gazed up at me from the page, her face solemn in the way you had to be for passport photos. She had a hard, angular face, all chin and cheekbones, and dirty-blonde hair, like us. In the picture it was pulled back in a ponytail.

'I forgot you had this,' I said.

She'd applied for a new passport and work visa just before leaving. Then she'd died and never left and the passport had arrived in the mail a month or so later. That was a terrible thing

I recalled from the time of her death: how mail kept arriving, the phone kept ringing, people kept asking after her. And we kept having to explain what had happened.

'I was supposed to mail it to Ottawa, to cancel it.'

I checked the dates. It hadn't expired yet.

'These things last forever,' I said.

'Ten years, but it might as well be.'

I closed it gently, and handed it to him. He put it back in the suitcase with the photo and keepsakes. Then he sat on the bed with his guitar and started fitting a new B-string. I was pretty much packed (I hadn't really unpacked) so I just lay on the floor and watched.

He affixed the string to the bridge and ran it over the fretboard and up to the neck, where he twisted it around the peg. With that in place, he hunched over the guitar and set to tuning it: strumming it once and adjusting the first peg, then strumming it again. These were motions I had watched him perform many times, and as on those other occasions it struck me as a rarity to see Jake so tranquil, and unencumbered by the fierce and bitter tensions that had been humming through him ever since our sister's death.

'Are you going to bring that?' I asked him.

'I sure ain't leaving it.'

He motioned with the neck of his guitar around the room. Now that his stuff was all packed up, the only things left were empty beer cans and the chipped teacups and an old toothbrush on the sink. Other than the backpack loaded with tools for the job, all we had was that battered suitcase, his guitar, and my duffel bag from the boat.

'Funny to think this is all we've got,' I said. 'Two bags and a guitar.'

He frowned, plucking repeatedly at the new string, and made an adjustment.

'That ain't all.'

'What else, then?'

'We got each other, asshole.'

'I wasn't talking about that.'

'Just remember it.'

'I ain't likely to forget.'

He was still working on the guitar when the call came. As the phone rang, it also vibrated and shuddered atop the table, creeping towards Jake like a black cockroach. Jake looked at me and there was nothing to say or do, so he leaned forward over his guitar to pick it up and answer. He said, 'Yeah?' and then listened and said, 'Okay,' and then hung up and tossed it to me and kept tuning his guitar. It was reassuring to see him treat it so lightly, and even though I knew it was largely put on I appreciated it all the same. When he finally finished with the guitar he strummed it once and patted the body like a drum. All set.

He said, 'It's down at Burrard View Park.'

Chapter Thirteen

BURRARD VIEW PARK IS THIS public park near Penticton and
Wall Street, in a residential district that comes right down to the
railway yard, overlooking the inlet. We drove there in Jake's truck,
with me riding shotgun and all of our gear in the flatbed: duffel
bag, suitcase, guitar, backpack, and of course the bolt-cutters.
We had no trouble finding the vehicle, since at that time of night
it was the only one in the parking lot: an extended transit van,
a Ram ProMaster, with no windows in the back. It didn't necessarily look like the kind of vehicle you would transport a horse
in, and I guess that was the point.

'That's it,' Jake said, pulling up beside it.

We got out and walked twice around the van, inspecting it in the dark. I don't know what we were looking for. I guess we were inspecting its very reality – as if it might not even be a real van, as if the whole escapade would be revealed as a charade.

'What about your truck?' I asked.

'I'll park it up the street.'

While he did that, I unlocked the back doors. The interior was empty except for a few pieces of rope, and straps with come-alongs. It looked as if it might have been a moving van at one time. A loading ramp lay flat on the floor, near the bumper. I shut the doors and put our luggage and Jake's guitar up front, under the seats.

A few minutes later, Jake came back, smoking and whistling. From across the lot he lobbed the keys to me. They flashed in the streetlights and hit me in the chest, hard, landing at my feet. I scooped them up.

'Why do I have to drive?' I asked.

'Because if we get pulled over, it won't be an ex-con at the wheel.'

I couldn't really argue with that.

The van's steering alignment was off (it dragged to the right) and the shocks were shot to hell, so that the chassis continually bounced and shuddered. Years previously, I'd driven a similar van with those same flaws, when I'd worked for an auto-supply company, delivering car parts. Jake and I had both done that job, actually. I'd put in a good word for him and at first we'd even done some of the early morning deliveries together. But after Jake was given his own van, he started driving around idly, hanging out with Maria, and ignoring his duties. So they fired him, and then they fired me, for vouching for him. I got fired by association.

My memories of that job made the drive we had to do in a similar van seem more normal than it was. It felt as if we'd done something like this before: Jake yawning beside me, the two of us weary and surly, the radio tuned to a late-night sports station. We could have been heading down to load up a supply of brake pads and disks, not steal a racehorse.

It was about half an hour to Castle Meadow from there. We trundled along Oak Street, hung a left on Marine Drive, and followed Macdonald Street down to the entrance. Instead of turning in we drove past the gates, which were shut, and carried on another fifty yards, towards what looked to be a golf course. I spun the van around and pulled over onto the gravel at the roadside. From there we had a good view of the stables and clubhouse.

'Kill the engine,' he told me.

I did, and we sat in the dark and the quiet and the cold. Jake checked his watch and said it would probably be another half hour. He rolled down his window to smoke. I had parked next to a willow tree and you could hear it swishing in the breeze and – beyond it – the sound of traffic over on the highway, faint and steady as a river. The air smelled of fertilizer and manure and nothing felt out of the ordinary to me.

When Jake was done smoking he unzipped the bag and got out our balaclavas. We both tried to put them on, but they didn't fit: we couldn't even pull them over our foreheads.

'Damn,' Jake said. 'I must have grabbed kids' sizes.'

'You're joking.'

'Don't panic, Poncho.'

He reached under the seat, to open his suitcase. After rooting around in it for a bit, he came up with Sandy's red bandana, and a second one, a blue one, for me. We tied these over our faces, just below the eyes, so that they hung down in a triangle that covered our features.

'How do I look?' he asked.

'Like a real horse thief. Like a goddamned desperado.'

Jake guffawed, making his bandana flap, and punched my shoulder.

'Poncho and Lefty ride again.'

'Jesus Christ, Jake,' I said.

Wearing our bandanas, we sat and watched the clubhouse. A few vehicles were still parked out front, and Jake explained they belonged to the cleaners and bar staff. After ten minutes, a little red hatchback started up and pulled out, followed shortly after by a maroon sedan. Neither had been the guard's vehicle. Jake said it was a Jeep, and would be next. But then nothing happened. A screech owl shrieked, way off, and a plane slid across the sky, and we were still waiting.

I said, 'Goddamn stupid, trying to get her across the border.'

'The Delaneys have a ranch down there, near Olympia.'

It was maybe two hundred miles, and a straightforward drive. It would have been fine, as a destination, aside from it being in a completely different country.

'If the border guards search the van, we're done.'

'They won't search it.'

'I'd sure search a vehicle like this, driven by two suspicious characters.'

'The Delaneys have a guard on the payroll. For their drug runs.'

'At what border crossing?'

'Aldergrove. But don't worry about that – worry about the job in hand.'

'One of us better do some worrying, or we ain't gonna make it further than Langley.'

As it turned out, that was pretty much true.

In the parking lot, an engine started up and headlights came on.

'That'll be him,' Jake said, and pulled on his gloves. I did the same. We watched the vehicle come down the drive: a Jeep, like Jake had said. He got that much right. The driver waited for the security gate to swing inward, and then turned out and away from us, towards the city. The taillights dwindled to dots, and I started our engine.

'How do you feel?' I asked him.

'Surprisingly optimistic,' he said.

I suppose that was part of it: why he thought the plan would actually work. Jake, despite his record, was inherently innocent. And because of that – because he didn't feel guilty, or like a criminal – he figured we would get away with it. It's always been like that, with him.

By the time we reached the drive, the security gates had closed. Jake slipped out and punched in the key-code. The gates swung inward again, smooth and silent, and we passed through. We rolled down the gravel drive, as we'd done the other day, but instead of parking in front of the stables we circled around behind. Jake directed me over to a big garage door, then told me to turn the van around and back it up – so that our rear bumper was towards the door.

Beside the garage door was a regular door and that was how we gained access, using the keys Jake had for doing his morning cleaning work. The stables felt completely different at night: no grooms or stable hands, no movement or activity, no light or noise, aside from the faint rustle of nervous horses, disturbed by our presence. Jake flipped a switch to the left of the door, turning on a series of lights strung from the ceiling beams. The bulbs were bare and clear and the curled elements within seemed to hang suspended in mid-air, like glow-worms. A pungent animal stench filled the space, coalescing in the cold like mist, almost tangible.

The alley between the stalls looked empty and exposed. We walked down it, our footsteps muffled by the covering of hay on the floor. Each of the stalls had a sliding door with a box-sash window built into the upper half. From one of them a horse's snout emerged, the nostrils flaring – as if trying to smell us. We walked past, and Jake led us back to the stall we'd visited that morning. Inside it was dark, but through the window I could see a large white shape, faint but distinct, hovering amid the shadows. The horse stood very still and must have been asleep though at the time I didn't know that. I've been reading up on horses since and most of the time they sleep on their feet, because they're prey animals and don't feel comfortable lying down.

Jake made a clicking sound with his tongue, and the horse shook her head. She came forward and put her nose up to the bars. Her nostrils and mouth were pale pink, and I could smell her breath: oaty and somewhat sweet.

'Atta girl,' Jake said. 'It's just me.'

He stroked her nose and she seemed to tolerate that.

'She knows you.'

'I've been making nice with her.'

He opened his backpack. In addition to the cutting tools he'd brought a bunch of bananas. One of them was already loaded up with Sedaline, a horse sedative that comes in a gel paste. Not enough to knock the old girl out, but enough to relax her a little.

He removed the peel and held the banana between the bars. Her nostrils flared – testing its scent – and then her lips pushed out and puckered and enveloped the fruit. She munched it lazily.

'How long before it takes effect?'

'A few minutes.'

'So long as she doesn't pass out.'

'I asked around and measured the dose.'

The stall door was held shut by a sliding deadbolt, secured with a hefty brass padlock. It was quite the lock: the kind of thing you'd see on a pirate chest. Jake dropped the bag and held out a hand for the bolt-cutters and I passed them to him. Pulling the handles wide, he aligned the jaws and scissor-pinched down on the lock. His upper body trembled with effort for a moment, and then the handles of the bolt-cutters came together: he'd sliced clean through. He twisted the lock and tugged it out of the deadbolt.

'That was easy,' I said.

'Told you.'

Before opening the door to the stall, we checked on the horse again. She had backed into the corner. He clicked and made soothing sounds but this time she didn't come forward. Our bolt-cutting shenanigans must have spooked her. Jake started talking to her as he slid the deadbolt across. He repeated her name a few times and told her what we were doing.

'I'm just going to open this here door now,' he said. 'We're gonna get you on out of here.'

He said it as if we were saving her from a life of imprisonment.

When he slid open the stall door, I tensed up: I half expected the horse to charge out, like you see at the rodeo, kicking and neighing and bucking. But none of that happened. She just stood very still, looking as spooky and beautiful as an alabaster sculpture. Yet alive, and real: you could see the steam of her breath. I got the sense that she didn't know what to make of any of this and in that respect she and I were in the same boat. On a peg next to the door hung a leather halter and lead rope. Jake gathered those up and we stepped inside the stall.

I suppose it wasn't entirely farfetched to believe we could walk in there and halter the horse and guide her down to the van without any trouble – though in retrospect it seems more than a little naïve. At the time I knew so little about horses that I was trusting Jake to handle that part of it. He seemed competent in that regard. Or confident, at least.

But then, Jake's never lacked for confidence.

Before that moment, I had never been close to a horse. I could feel this great animal warmth radiating from her. Her coat was sleek as mink and in the dark I couldn't see the individual hairs: it looked as if she'd been dipped in white paint. She seemed placid, but that was deception on her part, for when Jake tried to fit the halter she simply flicked her head – knocking it aside – and trotted past us into the alleyway. She didn't bolt. Rather, she cantered in a frisky circle, her hooves thumping the hay-covered concrete. Upon finishing this, she stopped and eyeballed us, sidelong, as if to imply: like hell I'm going to let you two fools halter me.

'Well,' Jake said.

'We should have shut the gate.'

'I thought she might panic. I didn't want to be stuck in here if she started kicking us.'

'I didn't know she could kick us.'

'She's a horse, idiot.'

'*I'm* the idiot.'

'Just shut up a minute, will you? I'm thinking.'

'Now you're thinking.'

The horse stamped impatiently, as if daring us to try again.

'You got the bag?' Jake asked.

'I got the bag.'

'Dig out another banana, will you?'

'You reckon she'll fall for that?'

'You got any better ideas?'

'I don't have any ideas.'

'Then get out a banana.'

I did. I peeled it halfway, and ventured into the alley, holding the banana out like a pistol, sort of waggling it in a way that I hoped was tempting. But my hand was trembling. My nerves were starting to show. Containing your nerves is easy when things are running fine as cream gravy. Not so when it's all turning into a bag of nails. I didn't know how long we had before the guard came back, or somebody else showed up, and our preposterous plot was revealed as the shambolic and desperate and ill-conceived act that it undoubtedly was.

'Here girl,' I said, and made kissing sounds.

Jake crept up beside me, holding the halter ready, like a cape he intended to drape over her. She cocked her head, bird-like, to observe our next move. That was the first time I got a real sense of her personality. She looked at the banana, and the halter, and us, and then snorted and skipped off down the alley. She was in no real hurry but she definitely wasn't dawdling, either. Her hoofbeats sounded loud and incriminating in the confined space, echoing off the walls and ceiling, like a whole herd of horses instead of just one.

'Come on,' Jake said.

We both sprinted after her. Seeing that, she slowed her pace to let us catch up, but once we got within a few feet she took off again – just playing with us. She ran all the way to the end of the alley, stopped, and turned around. She stared at us and we stared at her. She shook her head, as if to scatter away flies. That could have been the Sedaline kicking in.

'You stay here,' Jake said. 'I'll drive her around.'

The alleys formed a rough rectangle, around the perimeter of the stable.

'What do I do when she comes at me?'

'Just get in her way.' He dug a rope out of the bag. It had a loop on one end, but the knot was already loose and slipping apart. 'Toss this around her neck if you can.'

'What kind of bowline is that?'

'Tie a better one then, Tonto.'

I traded the banana for the rope and hefted it up, to show him I would. Jake headed down the alley. As he got near Shenzao, she whinnied and took off again, around the corner. I lost sight of them, then. I tied a proper bowline – a running bowline – and held the rest of the rope coiled in my left hand, with the lasso dangling in my right, feeling the roughness of the nylon through my glove. I stood with my legs apart. At the end of the hall I could see one of the CCTV cameras. Jake had said nobody monitored them: they recorded the footage as a precaution. But when they found Shenzao gone they'd be checking the footage all right, and I figured they'd have a real show to see, now. I just didn't know how much of a show.

I heard her coming, and saw her dance around the corner, shaking her mane and high-stepping like a real show-stopper. Jake was jogging behind her – no longer trying to catch or calm her but just herding her towards me. When she caught sight of me she drew up, about twenty yards away. She pivoted and saw

Jake behind her and spun back to face me again. I stood up real
tall. I thought maybe it was like when you confront a bear in the
woods. You have to show them dominance. I had to show that
animal who was boss.

'All right, girl,' I said. 'Bring it.'

And she did. She came cantering towards me, veering to one
side in a bid to barge past me. I held out the rope and draped
it around her neck, light as a lei. I remember feeling proud of
that. And then she just jerked me clean off my feet. It happened
sharp and sudden, like doing a dock-start on water-skis. I
floated along behind her and came down hard on the concrete
and got dragged through the hay and mud and horse manure.
I would have let go but I actually couldn't: the rope was
wrapped around my wrist, burning the skin. I started hollering
and kicking, calling out for help. This went on for some time
and was more than a little mortifying.

Eventually she slowed to a trot, stopped, and looked back,
no doubt confused by my idiocy. I lay there, still tangled up in
the rope, clinging to it like a lifeline. She wheeled her big body
around and lowered her snout, so that the nostrils were hovering
directly above me. She snorted in disdain, spraying snot across
my face. And she sat down, just like that, which isn't the kind
of behaviour you normally see in a horse, but by that point she
must have been feeling the effects of the Sedaline, and had
probably decided all the fun had gone out of her little game,
and that we, in our ineptitude, weren't worth any further expend-
iture of energy.

Chapter Fourteen

IN LOOKING BACK ON IT, our antics in the stable marked us out as fools and amateurs rather than actual felons, and possibly that aspect of the story was what made it catch on. That and the CCTV footage: drop-frame black-and-white action, and us chasing around after the animal, wearing those comical bandanas. Then my dive and manure slide, like some Buster Keaton stunt. Luckily the cameras didn't have audio or my hollering would have been picked up, too. As things stood the clip still went viral, after one of the stable hands got hold of it and posted it online: me getting jerked along by that horse, just like I'd been getting jerked along by my brother since the start of the whole affair.

At the time, of course, it all felt serious and grave and frightening. We thought we were wasting time, which we were, and that the security guard might come back any moment. We had no way of knowing that the plan – at least the initial plan – was not going to work, and that a few extra minutes bumbling about in the stables would have no impact whatsoever.

As I lay face down on the concrete, smeared in mud and silage, I heard Jake's footsteps. He ignored me – he leapt right over me, actually – and began fitting the halter onto Shenzao's snout. I watched from where I lay, stunned and dazed. He seemed to know how to go about it. Possibly he'd been practising. The horse shook her head once, as if to clear it, but didn't resist much. She seemed resigned to the ordeal, now.

Jake looked down at me.

'Help me, man,' he said. 'Get up. Can you get up?'

'I don't know.'

'We need to get her in the van before she blacks out. I think I gave her too much.'

'I thought you measured the dose.'

'I eyeballed it.'

'My brother, the vet.'

'Get off your ass and help.'

'My brother, the master criminal veterinarian.'

But I moved. First I untangled my arm from the rope. I had a brutal burn that coiled around my forearm like a snake tattoo, the skin raw and torn and speckled with broken blood vessels. I cradled it as I got up, moving painfully. My shoulder joint twinged. It was an old injury – I'd once separated it playing hockey – and it came back at inopportune times. Like when I was trying to steal a horse. I had to adjust my bandana, which was all askew.

Jake had put the halter on Shenzao, now. He cinched the strap tight across her chest, and took up the lead. The horse seemed content to let him do this, but she didn't look all that interested in moving. She was sitting very still and acting more like the statue of a horse than an actual horse. Jake walked forward with the lead, and pulled on it to get her moving.

'Come on, girl,' he said. 'Come on.' Then, to me: 'Use the rope, will you?'

My lasso still hung from her neck, too. I took hold of the loose end with my bad hand. My good hand was the one with the rope burn. So in that way, my bad hand was now my good hand, and vice versa. Or, to put it in plain terms, both my hands were now bad.

With Jake hauling on the lead, and me reefing on the rope, we made some sluggish progress. Shenzao shuffled forward reluctantly, without actually standing up. She looked like a dog dragging its butt along, like they do when they have worms.

'Give it a bit more,' he said.

'My arm is screwed, man.'

'Try pushing, then.'

'Pushing what?'

'Her ass. But don't get behind her. I don't want her to kick your damned head in.'

'I don't want that either.'

I stood off to one side, but right close to her, and put my shoulder against her haunch. I leaned in, like a prop in a rugby scrum, and Jake pulled, and the horse's legs unfolded and lifted her body up off the concrete. She was moving.

'Keep going,' Jake said. 'Don't stop.'

Working her like that, we managed to get her to walk the length of the alley. She was taking the path of least resistance, and so long as we made it more effort to remain still than move forward she complied. When we reached the door Jake gave me the lead and told me to keep her on her feet. He had to open the garage door – a rolling shutter that rattled upwards – and then the back doors of the van. He positioned the ramp: fitting one end into a slot on the tailgate and lowering the other side to the ground, at about a thirty-degree angle.

'Okay girl,' he said. 'Come on.'

He took the lead back from me and walked up the ramp, guiding her along. When Shenzao saw where she was going, she held her head stiff and turned it sideways – mighty suspicious – and tried to backpedal. Jake pulled on the lead, struggling to hold her. If she had been lucid, and not sedated, that would have been it. But she was too confused to put up a real fight, and eventually made her way up the ramp and into the cargo box.

Jake tied off the lead to a clip at the front of the trailer, and slipped around her, watching closely in case she kicked. She seemed reasonably calm, all things considered.

'Can she just stand like that?' I asked.

'That's how they travel. She'll be fine.'

We pulled down the garage door, and Jake re-locked it from inside. Then we walked out of the access door (Jake locked that, too) and got back in the cab. Once we were in our seats, with me at the wheel, we lowered those bandanas, so they hung around our necks like kerchiefs. We sat there for a time, and Jake laughed, short and sharp – a sort of bark of a laugh. Neither of us could quite believe that we'd done it. We'd made asses of ourselves and we'd made a lot of noise, but we had the horse in the van.

I started the engine. Now we just had to drive her to wherever it was she was going. For the first time, it almost seemed possible: doing it without getting caught. Not the perfect crime but a crime. It happened. People got away with crimes all the time. Bank robbers and car thieves and, in the old days, train robbers and horse thieves. We were now part of a grand tradition: in cahoots with all those other fools like us.

Chapter Fifteen

THAT SENSE OF HOPE AND optimism buoyed us up like hydraulics as we bounded out of Castle Meadow, got onto Marine, and followed that all the way around to the Pattullo Bridge. From there we scooted over to the TransCanada highway, heading southeast. It was two thirty in the morning. The city had settled into that sleepy, late-night state, lazy as an old tomcat, and we had the highway almost to ourselves, aside from a few truckers hauling freight.

'I never thought we'd actually do it,' I said.

'I told you: pick-up and delivery.'

'How much they paying us for this delivery, anyway?'

'A hundred grand.'

'A hundred grand?'

'Yeah – ten for you, ninety for me.'

'My ass.'

'We'll negotiate.'

'If I'd known it was that much, I would have signed up quicker.'

It seems funny, looking back, that there was a brief period in all of this when we really and truly believed we could simply drive across the border with a stolen horse, drop her off, and get paid. We even started talking about what we were going to do with the money. I had this idea about putting a down payment on a boat, and getting my own licence, like Albert.

'You could come out for the fishing seasons, man,' I said.

'Sure. It'll be a family affair.'

'Me, you, and Ma.'

We talked and joked about that for a while, even going so far as to name the boat – *The Sandra Jane*, after Sandy – and then it was Jake's turn.

'Me?' he said. 'I'm gonna buy myself a little place in the interior. You can get a lot of house and a lot of land, with that kind of deposit. Turn one room into a studio. Just live out there and make my music. Fuck this city, and its millionaires.' He waved a hand at the buildings we were passing, as if he could make them disappear. 'I'll get by doing odd jobs.'

'We could have a vegetable farm, like Sandy wanted. Live off the fat of the land.'

'You fucking Lenny.'

'Tell me about them rabbits again.'

'Just remember what happened to Lenny.'

'I always hated that part.'

Thinking of poor Lenny getting shot sobered us up, some.

'Still got a long way to go,' Jake said.

Olympia, where we were headed, was straight down the coast, south of Seattle. I'd been that way before and from what I recalled the journey hadn't taken too long.

I said, 'How close to Olympia is it?'

'A little beyond, out in the hills. But there won't be traffic.'

'You figuring on four hours?'

'Five, tops. We got to cross at Aldergrove.'

The plan was to get the horse down, and then come back in a different vehicle the following day, leaving the van at the ranch with Maria. On Monday Jake would show up for work, as usual. It would be his job to act as surprised and shocked as all the other grooms and stable hands. That was the plan, anyway. It wasn't a particularly good one. But I'm not making any grand claims for our criminal capabilities. I'm just telling it how it was. And it was nice, for a little while, to make believe it was all going to turn out okay.

Near Langley, just before we turned off onto Highway 13, the fuel light came on. This was not a complete and total surprise. When we'd picked up the van, I'd noticed we had about a quarter tank. I'd just clocked it, in the way you do, when you get into any vehicle. It wasn't nearly empty and of course we'd had other things on our mind. And it hadn't been an issue.

Now it was. It meant we only had about eighty klicks before we'd be running on empty. We debated whether to cross the border first and gas up in the States, which was what tourists usually did because it was cheaper down there, or to gas up before we made the crossing. In the end we decided the second option was better. If we hit any delays at the border, there was the risk we'd run down the tank while we waited and get stuck, which of course would have been disastrous. And partly I think we were more comfortable stopping at a Canadian gas station. The familiarity made it seem safer.

We pulled into an all-night Shell station off of Highway 13. It looked innocuous enough: eight pumps, car wash, air and water station, and a till with a little twenty-four-hour shop. I parked the van and Jake got out to fill up, turning his collar up against the cold. An employee was out on the forecourt, wiping down the gas pump opposite. At that point I didn't pay him much attention, other than as a figure at the edge of my vision.

The digits on the pump display cycled upwards. A car whooshed past on the highway. Jake slowed down as the total neared fifty bucks. When he finished he replaced the nozzle on the pump and I asked him to pick me up a coffee for the journey.

'Sure,' he said, but just as he said it, from the back of the van, the horse whinnied, or neighed, or whatever you call it. It made a noise, anyway. Jake and I exchanged a look – both of us understanding that it was time to go, and now – and he fast-stepped across the forecourt to pay at the till inside.

But the guy cleaning the pumps had heard. He shuffled towards the van, carrying his mop like a staff. He was an old-timer with a wisp of white beard, wearing a puffy ski jacket. He sidled up to my window – which was open – and asked what we were transporting.

'Livestock,' I said, which was all I could think to say.

He asked something else, but I didn't catch the question: it was obliterated by a second bout of neighing, which then turned into an ominous stomping. Shenzao was kicking the side of the van. It sounded like a goddamned clap of thunder each time, or somebody belting away on a giant kettle drum. Thrum, thrum, thrum.

The old guy – he looked surprised as hell. I didn't know what to say, and so I reached down and patted the driver's door with my palm and told him, 'Don't worry – this thing is sturdy.' As if to reassure him it could withstand the onslaught.

'Your animal,' the old man said, 'is not happy.'

He pronounced this very solemnly, as if reciting a proverb, or reading my fortune. My animal was not happy, or my karma was out of line, or what have you – which was no doubt true, since I was now a thief and lawbreaker and deserving of all the bad luck I had coming my way.

'She's a live one, all right,' I said.

'What kind of animal?'

'Well,' I said, and stopped.

I didn't want to lie, in case it sounded as if I was lying. But some guilty instinct also wouldn't let me say horse. So I considered it for a few seconds, but was saved from having to answer because that was when Shenzao kicked open the back doors of the cargo box.

Later, Jake told me he saw it all from inside, through the windows. He said he heard this huge crash and him and the woman at the till both looked across the forecourt, and there was Shenzao: stepping out onto the pavement like the queen of goddamn Sheba, looking royally pissed off.

The woman just said, 'Wow.'

Jake threw fifty bucks at her and came sprinting across the lot to help.

I'd got out of the van, but I hadn't approached Shenzao. I simply stood at the ready. I didn't want to spook her, in case she bolted. She took half a dozen steps across the forecourt and then drew up short, as if she'd just noticed she was somewhere completely unfamiliar. She held her head high and sniffed, scenting the air – possibly smelling manure or other animals on nearby farms. Beneath the gas station lights her coat seemed to be glowing, bright and pearlescent. In that setting she looked absolutely surreal.

The cleaner rubbed his eyes with his fists, in this pantomime manner, as if he thought he might be dreaming. He said something wondrous to himself, in another language.

Then Jake got back. He said, 'What the hell, Poncho!'

'She just went crazy.'

'You should have pacified her.'

'You should have tied her up better.'

Clearly, there were a lot of things we should, and shouldn't, have done. We put our heads together and had a quick pow-wow. The funny thing was, the guy – the cleaner guy – came to join us.

'I help you,' he said.

Apparently he was going to help us.

'Okay,' Jake said, accepting the offer without question. 'You both circle around, one on each side. Keep her between the pumps. I'll get a hold of the lead and take her back to the van.'

The two of us followed his instructions, splitting up and getting into position. I was having visions of her bolting, and dragging me like she'd done in the stable.

'I ain't lassoing her again,' I told Jake.

'Just stand your ground, okay?'

I waited there, with my arms out wide, like a rugby player ready to make a tackle. Opposite me, the cleaner got into a crouch and made gentle clicking noises with his tongue, intending to soothe her. We held our positions as Jake sidled up to her, talking all the while. I think the fact she didn't bolt was due less to his horsemanship and more to her own uncertainty and terror at being in such a daunting location, the like of which she'd never known.

She let him take her lead, anyway.

As he led her back to the van, I hustled around to set up the loading ramp. Jake walked her right up and in, but when we tried to shut the doors, they wouldn't latch, let alone lock. Her kick had busted the damned mechanism. We fiddled around with that for a bit, bickering all the while, and the old man observed us doing it. Eventually he patted Jake on the shoulder and went over to his cleaner's cart. He came back with a reel of wire and from it he uncoiled maybe two or three feet. We used that to hold the doors in place by winding it in a figure eight around the door handles. It wouldn't resist one of those thunder-kicks, but so long as she stayed tied up her hooves weren't within striking distance.

'Your animal,' the man said, and smiled wistfully, 'is very beautiful, very strong.'

Jake thanked him, already getting into the van. Just before we pulled away, I looked over at the till. The woman was talking on the phone, peering out at us. Whatever we were doing with that horse in a nondescript van, she'd clearly guessed we were up to no good.

I didn't tell Jake about the clerk until we'd put a few miles behind us, and things seemed to have settled. Shenzao was no longer stomping or kicking, anyway. The rhythms of driving seemed to calm her. It was after we had stopped that she'd lost it. It started to rain – a faint drizzle that hissed across the windscreen – and we came up to the turn-off for Aldergrove.

Then I mentioned the clerk, and what I'd seen.

He said, 'She could have been calling a friend.'

'A friend.'

'Yeah – in a "you won't believe what I'm seeing" type way.'

'Or she could have been reporting it.'

We both had to think about that. Let it sink in, as it were. In the back, Shenzao nickered, as if she was laughing at us.

Jake said, 'It doesn't change anything.'

'Like hell.'

'Worst-case scenario: they'll put two and two together and figure out the horse was stolen by some guys in a shitty white van. They'll know she's gone by the morning, anyway.'

I stayed quiet for a minute, pensive and worried as all hell.

'Were there cameras?' I asked.

'What?'

But you could tell he was only saying that to buy time. We both tried to recall.

'I don't think there were any near the pumps,' I said. 'What about the till?'

'I didn't notice,' Jake said.

The way he said it sounded suspiciously disinterested.

'Say there was,' I said.

'There probably wasn't.'

'If there was,' I said slowly, thinking it through, 'they'll have your face.'

Jake fumbled for his pack of Du Mauriers and thumbed the cigarette lighter. When it popped he pulled the little cylinder out and held the glowing coil up to his cigarette. As he took a first drag he cranked down his window with quick, vigorous jerks. Cold air poured in, smelling of winter, and the Coast Mountains, and potential snow.

'Well,' he said, kicking a foot up on the dash, 'if that's really the case then this might be a one-way trip for me. Instead of a cabin in the interior, it might have to be a ranchhouse down Mexico way. Or Guatemala.'

'This isn't Butch and Sundance.'

'No – it's Poncho and Lefty.'

He exhaled smoke through his gap tooth, making it trill. The smoke disappeared out the window, snatched away in the rush of wind. Partly it was an act – Jake will always strive for a kind of theatrical bravado – but he also seemed genuinely gleeful at the idea.

'Damn,' I said.

'So long as we make it across the border,' he said, 'we'll be fine.'

We had about thirty minutes to go. I drove at exactly the speed limit and the road markings strafed by and alongside us telephone poles flashed past like fence pickets. We passed the turn-off for Vancouver Zoo, and crossed the intersection with the Fraser Highway at Aldergrove. From within the cargo box, every so often I heard Shenzao move – and could feel the van shift under her weight. She was restless, anxious, as if she'd picked up on our mood. We came into that long straightaway leading to the border, where there's nothing but farming fields and a few big greenhouses and plant nurseries. As we were driving by them, the phone rang. The Delaneys' phone. For a while Jake let it ring, vibrating in the glove box. I didn't ask him why.

Eventually, though, he reached in there to open it.

He said, 'What's up, Mark?'

There was a pause, and he said, 'I hope I didn't hear you right. Say that again.'

Then he said, 'I'll call you back.'

He snapped shut the phone and opened the glove box and shoved the phone inside, locking it away out of sight. Then – and this was typical of Jake – he opened the glove box again and very deliberately snapped the door off at the hinges and flung that out his window like a square-shaped Frisbee, and shouted curses into the night with a genuine sense of indignation.

Then he took a drag of his cigarette and said, 'There's an APB out, for a white van. Their man won't get us through the border any more.'

I could actually see the border now, up ahead: just this glimmer of twinkling lights, tantalizing and taunting us. We'd almost made it.

Chapter Sixteen

WE FOUND A HIGHWAY TURN-OFF that led down to a parking lot and rest area beside a stream, surrounded by tall sitka spruce. As we rolled in our headlights panned across tables and benches and grass and the water beyond. It looked real picturesque: the kind of spot Tracy and I might have gone for a little picnic lunch, to eat potato salad and strawberries and these salami sandwiches she was fond of making. Of course, such thoughts of her now seemed all the more dreamlike and beyond reach, in the dark of the deserted lot, with our inept plan unravelling and the stolen horse weighing us down like a curse.

I parked near a barbecue pit and turned off the engine.

Jake told me to hold on: he was going to phone the Delaneys back. He shoved open his door and got out and I got out, too. I stood and leaned with my back against the side of the van, feeling the coolness of the metal through my shirt, and gazed at the stream. The surface roiled and simmered over hidden stones, as if stirred by a mass of herring. I listened to Jake saying things like, 'I thought this was all set up. I thought you had this guy in your pocket. Do you remember saying that?' To me he was illuminated in flashes as he crossed back and forth in front of our headlights, and when he wasn't in a beam he was gone, a shadow.

'You're telling *me*,' Jake said. 'I've got a stolen horse, here.'

As if she'd heard and understood they were discussing her, Shenzao began to neigh and whinny as she had done before. The sounds echoed within the van, and since my head was pressed against the metal, the vibrations seemed to resonate right through my skull.

Jake flapped his free hand at me, signalling that I should deal with her.

I went around to the side door and opened it and when I did the horse went still and quiet, watching to see what I'd do next. I shushed her and said her name repeatedly and tried to touch her, but she nickered and shied away. The van smelled of her piss and sweat and manure and fear. I thought she might be thirsty. The only thing we had that was suitable for holding water was Jake's aluminium frying pan, which he'd brought from his room. I took that down to the stream and crouched and rinsed it several times (it still had fried egg in it) before filling it to the brim. I carried that sloppily back to the van and placed it in front of the horse. She sniffed at the pan, dubious, then lowered her nose and began slurping away.

'Good girl,' I said, and touched her haunch, but she flicked her tail at me, as if to say: I'll accept your water, buddy, but don't expect this to change anything between us.

Behind me, Jake said, 'So what do you want me to do?'

I went over to stand by him. He had one hand out in front of him, gesturing with it as if Mark (I assumed he was talking to Mark) was actually there in front of him.

'Leave her?' Jake said. 'Just set her loose? That's all you've got?'

He listened for a moment and I heard the tinny voice of Mark, and Jake shook his head back and forth. 'No no – just forget it. Let me talk to my brother. I'll call you back.'

He snapped the phone shut and said, 'You heard what that wingnut said?'

'Even if we leave her, you could still be ID'd. We'll still have stolen her.'

'I know. Goddamn. I didn't want to tell him about the gas station, though.'

Together we walked around the side of the van. We stood and watched the horse drink. Her slurping seemed to echo the noise of the stream. Even confined in a cramped van and surrounded by her own excrement she still looked noble and far more digni- fied than us.

'It's only a crime,' I said, 'if the horse is reported stolen.'

He considered that. A bat whipped in a circle above our heads, and vanished.

'You mean take her back?' he said.

'If we can.'

'There's the broken lock.'

'They might not even care about that, if the horse is still there.'

'There's the CCTV footage.'

'If they bother to check the tapes.'

Jake crossed his arms. 'So we give up,' he said.

'We tried. The Delaneys can't blame you for any of this.'

He scuffed the dirt with his heel a few times, and then he said, 'Fine.'

It was past three in the morning by the time we turned back towards the track. At the stables the work generally started early but Jake said he wouldn't normally expect any stable hands to be in with the horses until at least five. So we retraced our route, believing that our new plan was feasible, and even plausible. After all, we'd stolen the horse without too much trouble, so we didn't see any reason why we couldn't sneak her back in using the same methods.

'If this doesn't work,' I said. 'We could go to the cops. Lay it all on the table, and explain the situation.'

'You mean snitch?'

He was still doing that: using the kinds of terms I'd only heard in movies.

I said, 'Whatever you want to call it.'

He just shook his head, a quick jerk, and stared out the window. 'What?'

'The Legion would kill us.'

His tone was flat, monotonous – almost as if he was disinterested. I took hold of the gearstick and downshifted, accelerating to sixty, seventy, eighty. The van shuddered like a shed in a hurricane.

'Don't get all pissy with me,' I said. 'I'm just trying to talk it out.'

'There's no talking it out.'

'No shit. The plan was stupid from the get-go. Bunch of

wannabe gangsters with their penny-ante *Godfather* scheme, and you and me the patsies dumb enough to sign on.'

'It could have worked.'

'How could it ever have worked?'

Jake pawed at his face, running the palm over it. He looked tired, beaten, defeated.

'I'm sorry,' he said.

'You actually said that like you mean it.'

'I do mean it.'

We pulled alongside a big freight truck, slowly overtaking it. It was hauling a trailer laden with chicken cages. Through the wire mesh you could see sad and sodden birds, their feathers tatty, and a few errant beaks poking out into the night.

Four in the morning is probably the deadest time in any city: that hour between the closing of the night clubs and the earliest commuters. It's particularly true of Vancouver, which isn't like New York or Los Angeles or one of those cities that never sleep. As we approached the area on the southside around Castle Meadow, we didn't see any other vehicles on the roads, or any other people out and about. It seemed promising. I started to really believe we could simply drop the horse back off and return to the way things had been: as if my previous life had been left behind like an old jacket, which I could go pick up again and put back on.

In the back of the van, Shenzao had gone completely quiet.

We came off the highway at Marine and swung back down onto Macdonald Street – essentially following the path we'd taken on the way out. As we neared the entrance to the stables I flipped on my blinker and began to slow, and through the gate and perimeter fence I saw the police cars. There were three of them, but only one had its lights still on, glowing cherry-red and lazily rotating, like a hazard beacon, warding us off. There were other vehicles, too, including a CTV news van. And people moving about, some of them with cameras. We'd only been gone a couple of hours or so but of course that had been enough.

I switched my signal off and coasted past. We carried on in a wide circuit, turning right and then right again so that we had eventually doubled back towards Marine.

Neither of us said anything.

I kept going and somehow ended up on Main, heading north, just driving now, not even knowing where I was going or if there was anywhere left to go. It just seemed wise to put some distance between ourselves and the stables. I suppose returning to the scene of the crime is another thing real criminals know not to do.

Main led us down to the waterfront, and I headed over the traffic bridge that loops around to Crab Park, and the Westco plant. I did that mostly on instinct (I was so accustomed to taking that route) but it was also a good stopping point since it's an industrial area sheltered from the city by the railway tracks. The Westco parking lot was empty at that hour and I wheeled in, rolling to a halt in one of the reserved spots overlooking the water.

I turned off the engine and we sat for a spell staring out at the inlet. It was past four now and the sky was smearing to grey in the east, but the water was black and still as a pit, ready to swallow us. Beyond it you could see the lights of the North Shore, our home, and the shapes of the mountains outlined in silhouette against the sky. It looked very far away.

Behind us, Shenzao whinnied, in the way she did whenever we stopped.

Jake said, 'You should get going. They can't ID you.'

'They'll know there were two of us.'

'I'll tell them it was me. Me and Delaney. Take that prick down with me.'

'Nobody's going down.'

'Oh yeah?' he said.

Then Jake started going a bit overboard. He asked me to look after Ma and also Maria. He told me he thought that her suggesting him for this job had probably been a way of asking for help and that she needed help and always had, even if she didn't know it, even if I didn't understand it. He was trying to say all this in what you might call a stoic and resolute fashion but beneath that he sounded frustrated and scared. He sounded like my little brother. He went on like that for a while, as if to convince me and himself he was okay with it all – with impending imprisonment and possible death – until I said, 'Just hold on a second, here.'

I was looking down at the docks. I could see the *Western Lady* in her berth.

I said, 'There might be a way out of this.'

He gazed at me mutely, and for a moment we settled into familiar roles: he having gotten us into trouble, and me, as the older and more responsible one, needing to get us out.

'There's the boat,' I said.

Chapter Seventeen

IT WAS A DESPERATE, RECKLESS, foolish idea – that's a given – and possibly required even worse judgement on our part than stealing the horse in the first place. But though the idea of transporting a horse by boat might seem absurd and faintly ridiculous, in actuality it wasn't totally impractical. And even though it meant adding to our crimes in the eyes of the law, for Jake it was clearly better than the alternative. It was as if we were going double-or-nothing.

It didn't take him long to come around to the idea.

Once it was decided, we became very focused and pragmatic.

Jake laced another banana with Sedaline, and we pulled open the door of the van and fed that to Shenzao, who ate it without any suspicion or reluctance. While we waited for the drug to kick in, I hustled down the wharf to ready the boat. Generally we loaded heavy supplies onto the boat using the crane, which obviously wasn't an option when it came to a horse. So for me the main obstacle was the four-foot rise from the dock to the boat's gunnel. The *Lady* was riding high in the water since the holds were now empty and we'd stripped her down.

But we had the ramp from the van, and on the dock, alongside the boat, there were bollards: wrought-iron posts, fat and squat and black, which we lashed tie-lines around in mooring the boats. My idea was to brace the ramp against a bollard and angle it up to the boat's gunnel, and after inspecting the height and distance I thought this seemed a reasonable proposal.

Albert kept a spare set of keys in the storage locker outside the galley, in case the master set – his keys – ever got lost overboard. I had the combination to the locker, since he of course trusted me, or had trusted me, and could not have imagined I would ever take the keys or the boat without his permission. Up until then, I had been thinking of the boat as partially mine, something I had every right to borrow, but in reaching in to touch those keys I began to feel the import of the decision, and had a premonition of the possible repercussions.

I used the keys to unlock the galley door and propped it open and stepped inside. I tried to imagine a horse in there and I couldn't. I didn't even know if she would fit.

From the storage locker, I pulled out a couple of canvas tarps that we used whenever we were painting or priming, to protect the decking and woodwork. I laid these out across the vinyl floor tiles, and atop them I spread a few sheets of newspaper. It wasn't much – and not nearly enough – but it was all I could think to do by way of preparation.

By then it was light enough to see, and though it was the weekend and all the crews were done for the season, within an hour the first cannery workers would be arriving. The sorters worked seven days a week, once the herring came in, to extract and grade and pack the roe.

Back at the van, Jake had already untied Shenzao and guided her down out of the cargo box. Standing so still, she looked stately and regal in the morning light, but as I got closer I could see her nostrils flaring, and her ears flicking back and forth, all twitchy with anxiety. Seeing me she jerked once on the lead rope, and Jake had to hold firm to keep her steady.

'Did you give her enough of that stuff?' I asked.

'Adrenaline counteracts it, some.'

'She looks a bit skittish.'

'We're all a bit skittish just now.'

'Should we feed her another?'

'Once she's aboard I've got some Xylazine.'

'I don't know what that is.'

'General anaesthetic. For surgery and shit.'

'How in the hell did you get your hands on that?'

'Let's just hope it does the trick.'

I hefted the ramp, which was made from solid aluminium, and must have weighed a good seventy pounds. I carried it across my back, stooping over, and stumbled along like an inept hang glider trying to take off. Jake followed behind with the horse. I had some trouble negotiating the gangway that led from the wharf down to the docks, due to the narrowness of it and the awkward nature of my burden. I got the sense that, behind me, Jake was having troubles of his own in getting Shenzao down, but I couldn't stop or go back up to help. By the time I'd reached the bottom, however, he'd coaxed Shenzao into motion, and the two of them started down the gangway together, her hooves clanging alarmingly on the metal grating. Jake talked to her as they descended. I worried that she'd take fright and end up in the water, but it didn't happen. Partly that was Jake, and partly it must have been the Sedaline. But mostly, I think, it had to do with her temperament. She seemed to have an odd trust in us, despite our conduct, and even if that trust proved to be misplaced.

Once he had her down on the dock, it was only a short walk to the *Western Lady*. The boat was moored with its port side towards shore, and Jake stroked the horse, keeping her relatively docile, as I got the ramp into place: bracing one end on the bollard and hefting the other end, like a weightlifter, to raise it high enough to reach the gunnel.

The ramp was at a steeper angle than when we'd loaded her into the van, but it looked manageable. I held it steady and Jake hopped up, guiding Shenzao with the lead. She came to the start of the ramp and stopped, leaning back. She turned her head sideways, getting a good look at him, as if to ask, 'Do you really expect me to go up there?'

Then a kind of tug-of-war began, with him straining on the lead – though trying not to do this too violently or viciously – and her pulling back, her hooves braced on the dock, and her head held rigid.

'Give me a hand here,' Jake said.

I edged around behind and put my shoulder against her haunch (a trick that was becoming familiar) and I could feel her muscles quivering, either with nerves or strain. Jake and I were both talking to her encouragingly – *come on, girl, come on* – and this went on for at least a few minutes. It felt like trying to roll a boulder. It was clear the horse would only move if she wanted to. Finally, maybe because she'd grown bored, or realized we weren't going to relent, she did move – and once she got going she stepped up quite nimbly, with no trouble: so quickly, actually, that Jake had to jump back to avoid being trampled.

'Take her on inside,' I said.

It would only work if she was inside. It would do no good to pilot around in a stolen boat with the white horse of the apocalypse standing at the prow like some figurehead.

She was less reluctant to enter the galley, I suppose partly because she was somewhat accustomed to going into a stall or confined space. She did have to lower her head to make it through the door, but once inside was able to stand: her ears just brushed the roof.

I sidled in behind them. The galley table was on the left as you entered, the sink and stove and cupboards on the right. Jake was backed right up against the far wall, near the passageway that led to the bunks. The horse dominated the entirety of the space. If the *Lady* had been a modern boat – one of the aluminium new-builds that Albert detested so much – we wouldn't have been able to fit Shenzao inside. But those old wooden seiners are longer and wider, the deckhouses more spacious. Still: it was absolutely absurd, standing in there with that horse. Like something out of a nursery rhyme. Two men and a horse. On a boat.

'Where can I tie her up?' he asked.

'You could use the table.'

The galley table stood on a single steel leg, or pedestal about as thick as a tetherball pole. The pedestal slotted into a base bolted to the floor, and was held in place by a lynch-pin. He guided the horse over that way, so that she was positioned across the width of the boat, her tail hanging right over the sink where I'd been washing dishes the other night. Jake ducked under the table to loop the lead around the base of the pedestal.

Shenzao accepted this, and her eyes had a glassy Sedaline glaze, but she didn't exactly look docile. Her tail swished back and forth, brushing across the taps and counter, and her chest puffed in and out, in and out, with alarming rapidity.

'How do you think she'll handle it?' I asked.

'I don't know, man. Sedaline only goes so far.'

'The engine makes a hell of a noise when it fires up.'

'You think I should use the Xylazine?'

'What will it do?'

'It'll knock her six ways from Sunday. It's intravenous.'

'We don't got time to mess around.'

'It's in my bag.'

He unzipped the main compartment, and withdrew a case about the size of a hardback book, made from black plastic. It contained two vials of clear liquid – the Xylazine – and a hypodermic needle, which looked about four times the size of a normal needle: that is, a needle you might use on humans. He loaded it up and readied it and looked at the horse.

I asked, 'You done this before?'

'I've seen it done.'

'Famous last words.'

'Distract her, will you?'

I went around to the front of the horse. I stood with my head near hers and talked to her, feeling like a cheat or a conman. Over her shoulder I could see Jake approaching with the needle. He lined that up with her haunch and sank it in there. She stiffened and I braced myself for a buck or a kick but neither of those things happened. Maybe she'd been injected before. She exhaled loudly, into my face, and I could feel the damp warmth of her breath.

'That it?' I said.

'Takes about ten minutes to kick in.'

He put the needle in the case, and the case in the bag. I was still standing by the horse's head, holding her halter. Her dopey, sad eyes seemed to be looking at me accusingly. Of all the things we did, it was our treatment of that animal for which we were most guilty.

We agreed that we needed to move the van. Otherwise what we'd done would be fairly obvious. So we unloaded all our gear: the suitcase, the duffel bag, the backpack, Jake's guitar, a few odd items such as his frying pan, and any other bits of equipment that could have identified or implicated us – like those giant bolt-cutters. I began to carry all that down the wharf to the boat while Jake went to park the van.

It took me three trips, or about fifteen minutes. When I was done I went to wait with the horse. She had stretched out on the floor of the galley, with her hindquarters folded under her and to the side, and her forelegs extended in front of her. Her eyes were closed and her head hung bowed towards the floor, in the pose of a knight chess piece. I didn't go inside. I just skulked in the doorway, feeling ineptly apologetic. It had to be closing in on five, by then. Clouds glazed the paling sky, like layers of varnish on an oil painting. The waves rolling through the break-water sloshed against the side of the *Lady*, steady and resonant, drum-like. It evoked a sense of familiarity: morning in the boat-yard.

Jake appeared, jogging across the lot, having to high-step it because of his heeled boots. He continued along the wharf, the raggedy knot of his bandana flouncing along behind him like a ponytail, and descended the gangway to the docks. At the boat he reached for the gunnel and vaulted it with a scissor-kick, landing a little breathless from his jaunt.

He peered into the galley, and said, 'Damn man – she's cosy as a cat in there.'

'Knock on wood.'

He looked around, surveying the boat, as if he couldn't quite believe it. He'd never set foot on the *Lady*, or any fishing boat as far as I knew. He clapped me on the shoulder.

'You may have just saved my life.'

'We're not there yet.'

'We're not in jail yet, either.'

'Where'd you leave the van?'

He gestured vaguely. 'Half a dozen blocks away. I didn't want to hoof it too far.'

'There's enough hoofing going on as it is.'

At that bit of inanity we both laughed – a little maniacally – and once the fit passed Jake shouldered me and asked, 'What next, Captain?'

I had to think about that. I wasn't accustomed to calling the shots, either on the boat or in our relationship. 'Keep an eye on her while I fire up the engine,' I said. 'This thing roars like a sonofabitch.'

'Aye-aye, Captain.'

He went into the galley and I clambered up the ladder to the wheelhouse, the rungs cold and dew-slick beneath my palms. At the top I opened the door and flicked on the light. The wheelhouse was about six by twelve feet: just big enough to house the wheel, captain's chair, controls, a small electric fan heater, and the navigation equipment and radio.

I stood at the helm and gripped the wheel (a classic ship's wheel, with eight spokes radiating out from the axle) and, after feeling the momentousness of it, slotted the key into the ignition. The keychain had a little rubber float on it, in the shape of a duck. Albert loved ducks. I turned the key to the 'on' position. The controls illuminated. I didn't switch on the navigation system, since it was of no use piloting out of the boatyard. We always did that by sight. I adjusted the throttle, sliding it to neutral, and thumbed the start-up button.

The sound of a boat engine, particularly in an old classic like the *Western Lady*, is nothing at all like a car or van. It might be comparable to a sixteen-wheeler, but even that is fairly lightweight in comparison to the din of a twin-diesel 3,600-horsepower marine engine firing up. It erupted like a damn volcano, and in the morning stillness the din sounded loud and incriminating. The exhaust coughed and spewed black smoke before settling into a steadier rumble.

Over the noise, I couldn't hear anything from below. I leaned out the door of the wheelhouse, but from my perch didn't have a view of the galley beneath. I was about to climb on down when Jake poked his head out. He was massaging his shoulder.

'Damn,' he said, 'that startled her.'

'How is she?'

'She tossed me, and kicked a cupboard.'

'Any damage?'

'The cupboard lost a door.'

'Which cupboard?'

'One of the cupboards by the sink.'

'Son of a bitch.'

'She's settled now.'

He limped out onto deck. It felt odd looking down on him.

I'd been up there so often, and driven the boat a fair bit (we had to take turns, when a fisheries window opened, since it sometimes ran for seventy-two hours solid) but Jake looked almost as out of place on it as the horse.

'Do me a favour,' I said. 'Hop down onto the dock and untie them lines, will you?'

He saluted and leapt overboard. It took him a while to loosen the half-hitches but he got there eventually. I told him to toss the lines on deck, which he did. When the bowline was undone, the boat started drifting away from the dock.

'Get aboard,' I called down.

A three-foot gap had opened between him and the boat. He hadn't taken that into account. He shrieked – childishly – and leapt for the gunnel, catching himself and landing awkwardly with his belly astride it. He kicked and wriggled and managed to pull himself over, falling onto the deck with a clownish elegance. Then he popped up, as if all that was perfectly natural: the normal way you might launch a boat.

'Anything else?' he asked.

'Pull in those bumpers.'

Half a dozen fenders dangled off the port side, to protect the hull. As he made his way down the deck, hauling each one in, I fired the stern thrusters to push us further from the dock, and then took hold of the throttle and eased it forward. The tone of the engine altered as the gears shifted and the propellers spun faster. Behind us a billow of whitewash bubbled up in our wake.

Jake had the last buoy in by now.

'Go on and stand look-out!' I hollered at him, pointing to the bow.

'What am I looking for?'

'Deadheads. Logs. Anything.'

It wasn't really necessary, but it gave him something to do.

The docks were laid out in an 'L' shape and I steered us around the bend, then along the north arm – past a dozen other boats, nestled snug and quiet in their berths – before we reached the gap in the breakwater that led to Burrard Inlet.

I saw the shadow of a tanker out there, and a few earlybird trawlers, but no real boat traffic. As we passed through the gap the two sides of the breakwater seemed to pull back, parting before us like curtains, revealing the backdrop of the North Shore, where the snow-capped mountains glowed in the winter dawn. And so much water. I'd seen that view before, of course. But it felt different to be in charge, with nobody to turn to and no Albert watching over me, guiding and chastising.

Jake looked back and held out his arms, as if he was trying to gather it all in one big hug – the whole of the inlet. And then we were through, with the water rolling under us and the sky arched above us, and I pushed the throttle up a gear and for a time we left all that had transpired behind.

Chapter Eighteen

THERE ARE A FEW THINGS I should probably make clear. Despite the accusations and charges that were later brought against me, I never actually intended to steal the *Western Lady*. As has no doubt become evident, our decision to put the horse on the boat wasn't particularly well-planned, or thought-through. If we had thought it through we likely wouldn't have done it. Another way of putting it, I guess, is to say that even though I don't quite know what we were thinking, or doing, I know what we *weren't* doing: we weren't stealing the boat. I would not have done that to Albert and Evelyn and Tracy.

My plans were vague, but I knew that they would be at their cabin in Squamish for a week. I also knew that Albert, who kept his own counsel, most likely hadn't told anybody else at the boatyard about his plans. There wasn't much chance the dock workers would notice the boat was gone, or report it if they did; they would assume he'd taken it to drydock, or up the river to New West, which he sometimes did.

The last thing they would expect was that it was being used to smuggle a horse.

I didn't know the exact length of the ocean journey to Olympia – I'd never been that far south – but I'd been to the San Juan Islands, and estimated that we could make the return journey in a couple of days, including any requisite stops. I'd be able to get the boat back by Monday or Tuesday – several days before Albert and Evelyn and Tracy were due to come back from the cabin. That was the plan, anyway (albeit not a very good one). Just because other circumstances prevented this doesn't mean it wasn't my intent.

The *Lady* had a maximum speed of eleven knots. That morning there was no headwind to speak of, and the inlet was tranquil as a pond. It only ever got that still at dawn, before boat traffic and morning winds whipped it up. We made good time. We skimmed across the darkly glossy water, heading west with the North Shore mountains on our right and the downtown skyline on the left. I wasn't thinking about what lay ahead: the crossing of international waters, the fact that we'd have to stop to declare ourselves and pick up supplies (without letting the horse be seen), how and where we would dock and unload her in Washington. I was aware of all that, but those obstacles seemed distant and removed and somehow abstract. I suppose I was simply too bone-weary and bleary-eyed to care much, and also relieved not to be stuck on shore, or already in jail. I could feel the reverberations of the engine through my arms on the wheel and my feet on the floor, and for a time that was all that mattered.

Within half an hour we'd passed Portside Park, the Seabus terminal, and Canada Place: a massive conference centre on the waterfront, constructed to resemble a series of sails, which always features prominently in postcards of Vancouver. A mile beyond that lay Coal Harbour, a high-end marina in the centre of downtown, where bigwigs and celebrities moor their yachts and powerboats. From up in the wheelhouse I could see the white shapes of the vessels, nestled side-by-side in their slips like bloated geese.

From the bow, Jake shouted up at me. I couldn't hear him over the roar of the engine, and cupped my hand to my ear to signify this. Then I motioned for him to join me – his role as spotter being even less necessary than it had been in leaving the boatyard. When he came into the wheelhouse he brought the cold with him. The thermometer above the bridge console read five above but out there in the inlet the wind-chill had a fair bit of bite.

He said, 'Had a missed call from the Delaneys.'

'What are you going to tell them?'

'Not the truth – that's for sure.' He stared towards the city with a bitterly intense expression, as if he could see the Delaneys from our position. 'What a plan. Bunch of goddamn amateurs.'

'Our stop at the gas station probably didn't help.'

'We don't know that.' He patted down his pockets until he found the right one – in his jacket – and fished out the cellphone. 'As far as everybody's concerned, we did our bit. It was their side that let the whole thing down. That's what I'll tell them, too.'

'Be diplomatic about it.'

'That depends on them.'

He snapped the phone open and held it up, checking for signal. Apparently he found some, because he began thumbing in the number. I suppose I should have expected what was about to happen, Jake being Jake.

He said, 'Mark? The deal's still on.' A pause. 'Yeah, yeah – it is. What? Well, put him on. That's right. I want to talk to Patrick. I want to talk to big-slick Delaney himself.'

A beat, then I heard a different voice on the other end – Patrick.

Jake said, 'Here's the deal. My brother and I are still going to get your horse down there, and you're still going to pay us.' Delaney tried to say something, and Jake cut him off: 'Forget about your man at the border. I don't care that he wet the bed. I got a better way to go about this. Never mind. As far as you're concerned, we're air-lifting her over, okay?'

Delaney said something else. He didn't sound happy.

'Yeah, yeah – I *am* calling the shots,' Jake said. He was pointing at the floor in front of him, adopting an outraged and overly indignant tone, which was very familiar to me, but which must have taken Delaney off-guard. 'Because you clearly showed you are incapable of that. So from here on in it is our show. No, no – *you* listen. I am not doing this for the money. I'm doing this as a favour, since your boys helped me out inside. But I didn't sign on for some two-bit penny-ante operation. I thought you were professionals. Clearly you're not, but luckily we are. So just leave it to us. All you have to do is pay up and shut up.'

I was so appalled by this speech that I actually dropped the throttle into neutral. I could hear Delaney shouting back. It was odd, hearing somebody scream through a phone. His voice sounded tinny and whiny and ineffectual. Jake let him go on for a bit, and then he said: 'Buddy – I don't care how many people you've had killed. All I know is you dropped the ball and we're picking up your fumble and carrying it over the line. You want to kill me for that, wicked. You're sweet.'

Then Delaney said something else, and Jake's face shifted, alarmingly expressionless. He said, 'You touch my brother or any member of my family and I'll kill you with my bare hands. That's what I do to people who fuck with my family.' The tone of his voice had completely changed: he sounded very calm and certain. 'I'll see you in Olympia, at your ranch, with your horse. Bring my money and then we'll be done.'

Then Jake snapped the phone shut and opened the door to the wheelhouse and lobbed the phone way the hell out there. It landed with a little splunk about twenty yards off the port side. And Jake – he took a deep breath, as if savouring the scent of the sea and spray, all that open-water goodness. 'Well,' he said cheerfully, 'that went better than I expected.'

I put the throttle back into gear.

Shortly after Jake made that phone call (which was no doubt a contributing factor to how messy and murderous things became later on) we passed beneath the Lions Gate Bridge. They had built the bridge at the inlet's narrowest point, where Stanley Park stretches out towards the North Shore, and on the other side it opened up, with West Vancouver on the right and English Bay to the left. Each year the mansions of West Van seem to creep higher and higher up the North Shore mountains, matched on the opposite shore by the condos and apartment towers that also get taller and taller, gleaming like big stacks of silver. Jake said that it was funny how our gambit, this big payout we were chasing, was still chump change compared to the money that saturated the city. It was a lame attempt to divert my attention.

'Funny but fitting,' I said.

'How do you figure?'

'Chump change for a couple of chumps.'

Jake shrugged and took up his guitar (we'd stashed our things in the wheelhouse, well away from the horse) and collapsed behind me on what Albert called the Captain's chair: a La-Z-Boy recliner we used for nights on watch during season. Propping the guitar on his knee, Jake stroked the strings once and resumed tuning them. He plucked repeatedly at his new B-string and made some adjustments that were indiscernible to me. But then, I'm pretty much tone-deaf so any adjustment would have been. Jake got the musical ability in our family, and Sandy got the physical coordination. I don't know what I got.

Jake worked on the tuning for a time and I expected him to play a song, but he didn't. He shook his head and made an overly exasperated sound and laid the guitar atop his suitcase. He fiddled with the footrest lever on the chair and reclined it.

'Make yourself comfortable,' I said.

'You need me to do anything?'

'You've done enough for now.'

'You ain't still mad about that phone call?'

'I ain't mad about anything. Not about stealing a horse or stealing a boat or the phone call. Least of all the phone call.'

Jake yawned and stretched – deliberately, just to show how unconcerned he was.

'So long as we're good.'

'We'll pull up later to look at the charts and plan where we'll dock. I want to put some miles behind us.' I adjusted my course, angling a few degrees to port. 'You might as well get some sleep.'

'I'll drive later.'

'You don't drive a boat. You steer it.'

'I'll steer it then.'

I didn't bother to answer. I stood and gazed out the windshield, feeling the thrum of the engine. Ahead of us the inlet, which runs east–west, opened up into Georgia Strait, the body of water that divides Vancouver Island from the mainland. A morning haze veiled the island, but poking up above the layers of fog and cloud you could distinguish the mountains, like fragments of frosted glass. I made some comment on the scenery – some vague comment, meant to patch things up between us – but Jake didn't answer and when I looked behind me I saw that he'd closed his eyes. His head was tilted back and his mouth hung half-open. With each breath his gap tooth whistled mournfully. Even in sleep, his hands clenched the armrests, holding on tight, as if he was in a plane coming in for a rough landing. His hands did not look like musician's hands. They were grimy and the nails were rimmed with black and he'd skinned two knuckles on his left hand during the shenanigans of that night – loading the horse, probably. The blood had dried in dark flakes and started to peel.

His threats to Delaney weren't merely a form of grandstanding, since he had tried to kill with those hands. I know this because I was there and I saw it, and possibly prevented the murder, though I can't be sure about that and I suppose nobody really knows except Jake.

It happened at the Lynwood pub, which is closed now, but which used to be down on Barrow Street, at the base of the Second Narrows Bridge on the North Shore side, among the docks and warehouses. It felt a bit like a warehouse itself: one long room, dimly lit, with a low ceiling, and filled up with any old junk the owner thought to put there: motley table and chair sets, a battered jukebox, and a mix of sports paraphernalia, pin-up girls, and historic photos. Mostly it catered to a blue-collar crowd: longshoremen, labourers, and railyard workers. Jake and I went there to drink regularly, always alone or with Maria. After Sandy's death we began to avoid the bars we used to frequent, and which were still frequented by our old high school friends. We'd been permanently cut off from them by the perennial nature of our grief, which did not dwindle or fade with time but instead seemed to grow and grow, relentless as ivy, slowly overwhelming and stifling us.

With Maria it was different because of her closeness to our family and the fact that she had been with Jake the night we lost Sandy. It had devastated her, too, a fact which should not be lost in all of this. She had always wanted to please and impress our sister, and – like everyone – had looked to her for guidance. Her own home life hadn't been easy, to put it mildly, and I often felt that for Maria we represented a source of stability and normality.

So Maria was still one of us, and with us, the night this all happened.

We were sitting in a corner booth. They had a few of these booths with faux-leather benches, the vinyl all torn and sprouting stuffing. For a time Jake and I took turns dancing with Maria, and afterwards we settled down to share a pitcher of Pilsner. I remember very well the moment Maria reached over and touched Jake's arm and said Jake's name, and also the way his face changed when he turned to look at what she'd seen.

At the bar sat a guy in a pinstripe suit, the face and figure unmistakeable. The suit resembled the suit that he'd worn to the hearing, where he'd been charged with what they call impaired driving causing death. Since he lived in that area, once he got out on parole I knew that we would likely run into him at some point – though it still strikes me as unfortunate (or perhaps fated) that it happened so soon, and under such circumstances.

It was seven months after Sandy died.

His name doesn't matter. He was just a guy. Maybe five ten, and overweight, with a bit of a beer-paunch and a jowelled face. He had thinning hair and was wealthy enough to own that kind of car, and to think he could drive it at that speed, while coked up and half-cut. I suppose there was more to him than that but it was as much as I needed or cared to know.

In the hearing, he said he'd been depressed, that he hadn't known what he was doing.

In the bar, he had a lady friend with him – a brunette in a red dress – and the two of them were drinking, drunk, leaning towards each other to shout over the music. Jake watched them for a while. I repeatedly said that we ought to get out of there, and forget we ever saw him. Jake put his drink aside and ignored me, and ignored Maria too. She'd offered to go get our coats. Jake said he wanted to sit tight. Jake said he wanted to see what the guy did.

I thought I knew what he meant, and in any event he would brook no argument. We pushed aside our drinks and watched, and waited. The guy knocked back two more highballs and then he and his date hit the dance floor, grinding away in a drunken daze. This went on for some time. I felt as if the three of us were on surveillance: clear, focused, professional.

After about half an hour they got their coats, and went outside.

Jake stood up and followed, bulldozing towards the door in a straight line, forcing people out of his way. This part, since I've thought about it so much, plays out dreamily in my memory. Maria was behind him, and then me. Outside, in the parking lot, the guy had his arm around his date and his keys in his other hand, jangling them. When Jake saw that he started to trot. Maria called out to him, and he looked back over his shoulder, and even though his answer was in response to her, in my head I see

it as him talking past her, to me. He said something oddly innocuous, about needing to take care of this.

He was smiling. He looked almost exultant, relieved. I ran
after him, overtaking Maria, but I was about twenty yards back,
and Jake reached the guy before I caught up to them. The guy
had just opened his car door. It was another fancy car – not a
Mercedes, like the one he'd hit Sandy with, but in that league.

From ten yards back, I heard Jake say, 'Let me just give you
a hand, here.' And he shoved the guy down, half in and half out,
and started shutting the door on him repeatedly.

The guy screamed, and his girlfriend started shrieking. She was
shrieking over and over, piercing as an alarm. I ran the last few
steps and caught Jake with a tackle. We both went down together
and I had to hold him and he fought back against me – really
bucking and raging. At the trial the guy's date said Jake shouted
out that he wanted to kill him. I actually don't remember that, but
even if he didn't say it I think it was true. Jake had talked often
about killing him, though of course I never mentioned that to
anybody else. Jake didn't succeed, anyway. The guy had four cracked
ribs, a shattered ulna, and a concussion. But I got there in time.
Jake was still charged and found guilty of attempted murder.

The guy had gotten two years for killing our sister, and served
six months. Jake got seven years, and served five and half. Partly
that was due to the fact that he never showed remorse – not
during the trial or at any of his parole hearings. There was no
real reason to think he wouldn't do the same thing again, given
half a chance.

So there it is. That's what Jake was in for. It's no great mystery.
Anybody could read most of that in the papers. On the one hand,
it has nothing to do with this story, and what happened. On the
other, it has everything to do with it.

Chapter Nineteen

SOONER OR LATER THE HORSE had to figure out she was on a boat, and when she did something outrageously destructive was bound to happen. It occurred at about nine o'clock, three hours after we set out. We'd passed the headland of the Pacific Spirit Regional Park – by the university – and Wreck Beach, which is a nudist beach, though of course at that hour and that time of year there were no nudists on it. The morning clouds had begun to thin and crack apart, revealing lines of blue, like turquoise veins in a cavern of quartz. As we approached Steveston, I heard a terrible and thunderous racket from below deck.

I shouted at Jake, who was still dozing in the recliner. I often think how bewildering it must have been for him – that moment when he awoke. He sat straight up, so the recliner seemed to rocket him forward. His bandana half-covered his eyes and a strand of spit clung to his mouth and he looked like a patient who had been given a jolt of electro-shock therapy: terrified and completely bamboozled. Then, in whatever order, he must have remembered that we had stolen a racehorse, and a boat, and that we were now on our way south towards the United States – a chain of happenings that wasn't just unbelievable, but unthinkable.

Considering all that, he took it surprisingly well.

He adjusted his bandana and said, 'What the goddamn fuck?'

'The horse is going batshit,' I said, and dropped the throttle into neutral. 'That horse of yours is going absolutely ballistic.'

We went out onto the upper deck – the sea spray catching us cold – and slid, one at a time, down the ladder to the lower deck, like a pair of firemen roused by the alarm. Just as I touched down, Jake said something I didn't hear, and the aft window of the galley exploded: bursting outwards as if it had been shot. Pebbles of glass rained down on us, tinkling across the deck. It was safety glass, which was lucky for us and the horse as well.

'Ah, hell,' I said.

We had a clear view of Shenzao through the window. She had either freed or broken her lead and as such was no longer restricted in her movements. She stamped and snorted and kicked. I could see her hind legs flicking out in white flashes, quick as lightning, and where they struck woodwork cracked.

'Albert,' I said. 'I'm sorry, Albert.'

I said it as if he was there, standing with us.

'Christ,' Jake said, 'I hope she doesn't hurt herself.'

That hadn't even occurred to me. Up until then, I had been thinking of her as invincible, which I suppose is what we're prone to do with powerful animals.

'Stop her, man,' I said. 'You've got to stop her.'

'I don't got to do anything.'

'You're the goddamn groomsman.'

'Groomsmen are the guys at weddings.'

'You're the expert – you're supposed to know about this.'

'I know not to go near her in that state.'

'Goddammit, Jake.'

'She'll calm down in a few minutes.'

'We won't have a galley in a few minutes.'

Jake threw up his hands and went off to the stern to have a smoke. I stood and watched the horse. She turned around on the spot – somehow manoeuvring that great muscular bulk of hers in a tight circle, like a dog chasing its own tail. Then she seemed to notice me and stuck her head out the broken window, her eyes wild with wrath.

'Hey girl,' I said.

I cooed to her and coaxed her and held out a hand, acting like I was some damned horse whisperer. She bared her teeth and snorted at me. Then she turned in a circle again and kicked in the two cupboards above the sink. They crumpled like cardboard.

'Sure,' I said. 'Go right ahead.'

I sank down on one of the fenders and held my head with my hands. I couldn't bear to watch. But I heard. I heard her raging and rampaging and rumbling. She sounded like a thunderstorm trapped in a bottle. It went on for a while – long enough for Jake to have his smoke, anyway. When it finally petered out he came back and I stood up and without saying anything we went inside together to assess the damage. I saw the sink first: spouting water straight upwards, like a damned geyser. She had kicked the tap off. Then there was the broken window and the smashed cupboards and the gaping holes in the walls. You could see right through to the bunks. The galley table had been uprooted from its pedestal on the floor and overturned (this was how she'd freed herself) and the vinyl bench seats had tears and teeth marks in them. The tarps I'd laid down were now soaked in urine and dotted with dollops of horse crap. The destruction was complete and total and, in its way, astonishing.

Jake said, 'I'm sorry, man.'

I didn't answer. I just made a feeble, frustrated sound. I was close to sobbing right there in the galley. The thought of Albert and Evelyn and Tracy seeing that, and knowing it was me who had done it, was enough to make my heart shrivel up like a goddamned prune.

'I don't know what to do,' I said.

'You can fix it when we get paid.'

'This'll take a lot of fixing.'

'We'll have a lot of money.'

'I don't want to talk about the money.'

I slumped onto the remains of the bench seat. Jake hunkered down in front of the horse, who had her snout buried in a box of Cheerios. As far as I knew the box was empty, but maybe she could smell the remnants. Jake looked her over.

'I don't think she's hurt.'

'I wouldn't care if she was.'

'Don't talk like that. None of this is her fault.' When I didn't answer, he spoke to her: 'Is it, girl? You're just angry and scared. Tell him, Shenzao.'

At her name, she lifted her head up, and when she did the

cereal box came up too – stuck on her snout. Jake chuckled, and swatted my shoulder, as if to say, 'Come on now – let's look at the light side of this.' Shenzao irritably shook the box loose, stepped on it with her forehoof, and set to gnawing at one of the cardboard flaps.

'She's hungry, too,' Jake said. 'She needs food. No wonder she's all agitated. A hungry horse, trapped on a boat. You'd be mad, too.'

'Well give her some oats or whatever.'

Jake looked at me. I could read it all in that look.

'You don't have any food for her.'

'It was supposed to be a border run – four hours tops.'

The broken tap was still spraying water everywhere.

I filled one of Evelyn's pots from the leaky tap before shutting off the water supply in the engine room. We hadn't had much water when we'd set out, on account of it being the end of the season, and now we were down to a few litres, according to the gauge. Then there was the issue of food – for the horse and for us – and also diesel fuel. Albert always topped up the tank at the end of season, but that wouldn't be enough for a round trip. So there were serious implications to consider.

'We'll have to stop anyway,' I said. 'We'll have to stop when we cross into US waters. We can get food then.'

We were still standing there in the destroyed galley. Shenzao lapped lustily at her water. The storm had run through her and she seemed calm and serene as a rainbow now.

Jake asked, 'Why do we have to stop?'

'To declare ourselves. You got to do that.'

Jake stood with his hands on his hips.

'Where would we stop?'

I got out the charts, which we kept under the bench seats in the galley. We didn't actually use them much in the wheelhouse, since the boat had Satnav and a built-in digital map display, which was far easier to navigate by. But Albert was traditional and still liked to sit down here in the evenings, plotting our courses, and he'd taught me how to do it. He said any seaman worth his salt could plot by a chart and a compass, and even the stars. He said Satnavs and fancy tech could fail, in a storm or for no reason at all, so you had to prepare.

'Should we take these up top?' I asked.

We looked at the horse. She was still slurping at the water.

Jake said, 'Don't reckon she's going to freak again.'

We lifted the table and set it aright: the pedestal had a bit of wobble to it now but held. I found the chart we needed and unrolled it. Jake and I stood over it, looking down. It depicted the northwest seaboard, showing the coastline from Alert Bay, near the northern tip of Vancouver Island, down to Astoria, Washington.

'This is us,' I said to Jake, tapping a point on the map, 'near Steveston, here.'

'I know that much. I know where Steveston is.'

I slid my finger south, over the ferry terminal at Tsawwassen; beyond it was the red dotted line representing the border, which hooked south around the tip of Vancouver Island. On the other side lay a cluster of green patches: the San Juan Islands. I pointed to them.

'Me, Tracy, and Albert went on a fishing trip here, a year or two back.'

'Romantic.'

'Just listen, will you? The ports on the islands are all pretty small: just little marinas, sometimes with a hotel or grocery store or a few restaurants. We could stop in at one of them to declare ourselves, and stock up.'

'How the hell are we going to declare a stolen horse?'

'We don't. But at these little ports, they don't even board your boat. Albert just went up to the harbour master's office with our passports, last time.'

'What about the boat? The boat's stolen, too.'

'It ain't reported stolen, yet. And hopefully never will be.'

'Could we just hotball it all the way? Straight shot.'

'If we get spotted in American waters without declaring ourselves, we're done.' I glanced over at Shenzao, lapping away at her water. 'Plus our girl needs food.'

'How long you reckon it'll be to Olympia?'

'Depends on the currents. But it'll be an overnight trip, for sure.'

The two of us stared intently at the map, like a puzzle we could figure out. As we stood there, I felt warm breath on the back of my neck. Shenzao's snout appeared between us, still dripping water. Jake reached up to stroke the bridge of her nose – the long part that horses like to have scratched. That was the first time she'd allowed it without shying away.

'What do you think, girl?' he asked.

She snorted, spraying spittle over the map and making the corner flap. It was a disdainful sound, as if she were dismissing both our options, our entire plan, and all such human foolishness.

Chapter Twenty

WE HEADED SOUTH, PAST THE long landspit at Richmond and the airport. The planes coming in to land seemed to materialize out of the cloud layer as they descended, and those taking off slow-faded away, turning into phantom shapes before vanishing entirely. We kept five miles offshore. As the day progressed the wind picked up, which often happens around mid-morning. The waves came at us head-on: these hump-backed swells that rolled smoothly beneath the hull.

When we reached the north arm of the Fraser, I reprogrammed the navigation system, plotting a course southwest. I wanted to stay in Canadian waters for as long as possible and the way to do that was to hold close to Vancouver Island. The route I had in mind would also take us towards the west side of San Juan Island, and Roche Harbor. That was where we had docked during our previous trip. It was smaller and quieter than some of the other harbours, and the customs officials were less likely to take an interest in us or our cargo.

I had only crossed into American waters that one time but Albert, being a stickler for protocol, expected you to learn something on the first go, and commit it to memory. So I was confident about the procedures, and I wasn't worried about the officials boarding us (Albert had told me that hardly ever happened), but there was still the issue of passport control.

'What's the deal with your record?' I asked Jake.

He'd pulled his chair over to the heater, and sat huddled in front of it.

'I can enter the States, but they might be suspicious.'

'If I take your passport up with me, will there be a red flag on it?'

'Reckon so. That's how it works, isn't it?'

'That's what I'm worried about.'

'I'll just stay here with the horse. You said they don't search the boat.'

'Just looks odd. Guy on a boat, all on his own.'

'So maybe you're going to pick up some clients, for recreational fishing.'

'Maybe.'

I steered in silence for a minute, considering that. There was probably a better story, but I was too tired to concoct it just then. The lazy bucking of the boat and the endless grey swells were hypnotic and I had only grabbed a few hours of shut-eye before we'd set out on our misguided endeavour. I stood slumped up against the wheel and at times it felt as if my grip on it was the only thing keeping me on my feet. My head kept slow-dipping, almost like the horse when we'd drugged her, and each time it did I would jerk awake and shake it off.

Jake must have noticed this because he offered to take the wheel.

'I got it,' I said.

'You need rest.'

'What I need is coffee.'

'The horse kicked in your stove. Besides, you can't stay up for two days straight.'

'We sometimes do during season.'

'Good for you, Captain.'

He adjusted the heater, cranking it up. If he'd kept pressing me I would have kept resisting – that's just how it worked with us. But seeing as he'd let up, I started thinking I was only saying no to be contrary.

I said, 'Maybe I'll just rest my eyes for a bit.'

Jake hopped up, as if he'd been waiting for that. He adjusted his bandana and flexed his fingers, all ready to take over. I talked him through the controls – steering, throttle, kill switch – and then showed him the GPS display: a black-and-white LCD screen. The course I'd plotted showed up as a series of dashes leading south in front of the triangle representing our boat.

'You keep us on that course,' I said.

'You got it. It's like a video game.'

'Don't just stare at the display.' I looked out the window, and pointed to a landmass on Vancouver Island – a humped hill bristling with Nordic pines, like a big green hedgehog. 'You can steer just left of that headland. Use that as a marker.'

'I got it – I got it.'

I sat down in the recliner, my body loose and clumsy, just this collection of bones and flesh that sort of collapsed, as if all the controlling strings had been snipped. After a minute I closed my eyes, and as soon as I did the vibrations of the engine changed tone.

'Hey,' I said.

Jake had his hand on the throttle.

'Just opening her up a bit,' he said.

'Wastes gas.'

'We got plenty of gas, you said.'

'We got enough to get us down there, if we conserve it.'

'Okay, okay.' He eased up again. 'I was only testing her out, Aunt Nellie.'

'Just keep her steady, and on course.'

I watched him a while longer, to see if he'd try anything else. When he didn't I closed my eyes and dissolved back into the chair, feeling the ocean roll beneath us like time, ebbing away.

When I awoke, I saw Jake standing at the wheel, silhouetted by a slate-grey sky, striated with rain. It was a hazy and surreal image and at first I thought I might be dreaming. I stood up and pawed at my face, as if I could physically wipe away the fogginess of sleep.

Jake looked back at me.

'Like a baby,' he said.

'What's happening?'

'Everything's fine.'

I remembered the headland, which I couldn't see. Out the starboard window another landmass had appeared: an imposing stretch of granite bluffs, rising from the water like big grey golems.

Off to port side was a boat, maybe ten miles distant. I looked at the GPS. No dashes appeared in front of our position.

'Where are we?'

'Your course finished so I just kept her steady.'

'I said to steer for the headland.'

'We passed the headland an hour ago.'

'Goddammit, Jake.'

I hadn't plotted the whole course yet. I'd needed to check the charts first.

'We were supposed to bear east.'

'What's the big deal?'

'You crossed the border.' I yanked on the throttle, dropping us down to neutral. 'We're in American waters.'

I saw the realization of that register on Jake's face: a slight widening of the eyes and raising of the brow, this theatrically stunned expression that he'd perfected.

'You were the one asleep for two hours,' he said. 'What am I supposed to do, when the captain is asleep on the job?'

'Wake me up.'

'We had to cross over eventually.'

'There's etiquette, man.'

'What are you talking about, etiquette?'

'We're supposed to call in to declare our presence, and raise the Q flag, for one.'

'So raise the Q flag.'

I swore at him and then just began to swear in general and was heading for the door intending to fetch the Q flag from our storage locker when our VHF radio crackled, and a voice came over it: 'Ahoy, *Western Lady*. Do you realize you've passed into American waters?'

We both stared at the radio. Then I looked again out the

window, to that vessel off the port side. It sat long and low in the water, with a squat rectangular deckhouse atop it. Red and white colouring. Not a fishing boat.

The call came again: 'Coast Guard hailing *Western Lady*. Do you copy?'

I made an infuriated sound and shook my bad hand at Jake, in a way that was meant to be threatening. Then I picked up the receiver of the VHF and thumbed the talk button.

'This is the skipper of the *Western Lady*, Timothy Harding. Sorry about the oversight – our navigation system is on the fritz so we weren't aware we'd crossed over the border yet.'

'Not flying your Q flag is a fineable offence, Captain.'

'I'll get that up right now, sir.'

There was a pause, another crackle of static.

'Where are you clearing customs, over?'

'Roche Harbor.'

'What's the purpose of your visit to the US?'

'Just a little recreational fishing, now that herring season has ended. We're with the Westco fleet, out of Vancouver.'

Another pause, and burbling static. I figured they were conferring, and possibly checking up on the vessel.

'All right, Harding. They'll be expecting you. And get that Q flag up.'

'We'll do that now, sir. Thank you, sir.'

They signed off. I put down the receiver and went over to Jake and cuffed him on the back of the head, like I might have done when we were little. A sort of open-palmed slap.

'You told me to follow the course,' he said, resentfully. 'I followed the course.'

I just shook my head and pushed out into the rain, which fell in cold and bitter slivers that pricked my skin and made me even more irked. Jake asked what I was doing and I told him I needed to put up the damned Q flag. When I reached the ladder, I turned and shouted back at him over the wind: 'It's the stupid mistakes that will cost us, Jake!'

It was something that Albert often said. For a while, out there, maybe I thought I was Albert, and I have to admit it was nice: being in charge, bossing Jake around. But I doubt he even heard me say that. I know now it's not true, anyway.

Every mistake costs you. Stupid or otherwise.

Chapter Twenty-One

IT WAS TWO O'CLOCK BY the time we reached Roche Harbor: a collection of white clapboard-and-shingle buildings nestled in a horseshoe-shaped inlet. As we came around the point the wind died down and the waves flattened out. The water looked tarnished and dull, like rumpled tin foil. I'd taken over at the helm, after Jake's little mistake, and by way of penance I'd sent him below deck to board up the broken window. He'd been hammering away down there for the past hour.

When we were about half a mile from dock the hammering stopped and I heard Jake's boots on the upper deck. The door opened and he came in along with a blast of icy wind. He was wearing a yellow slicker and gumboots I'd found for him in the storage locker: a spare pair that Albert kept on hand. For a change Jake didn't look completely out of place on the boat.

'That's all done,' he said, wiping rainwater from his face.

'What's Shenzao up to?'

'Just sitting there, like the Sphinx.'

'Peckish?'

'Her or me?'

'Who do you think?'

'I found some old crackers. We had us a little snack.'

'We'll get food at this stop.'

He hung up his slicker and came to stand with me by the helm. We were both acting as if it was all fine, what we were about to do. The port was creeping closer. We'd be there in maybe a quarter of an hour. I throttled down, slowing our approach.

From what I recalled, the customs office was halfway down the main dock. Further out, there was a particular slip where foreign vessels were supposed to moor, and from there the skipper walked up to the office. Other passengers weren't allowed to disembark.

I explained that to Jake, and then added, 'If they're going to search us, it will happen then. And if they do that, we're done.'

'Will they know the horse is stolen?'

'Won't matter a whit. You can't bring livestock down here on a goddamn boat.'

'I still think we could forget the stop, and sneak on by.'

'Sure – like you snuck us by the Coast Guard.'

'That was plain bad luck.'

'We make our own luck, on this boat.'

That was another one of Albert's sayings.

'All right, Captain. It's your call.'

I told Jake that he could help me dock, and that he could wear that same slicker with the hood up, in case they were observing us from the office. Then, while I went to clear customs, he could fill the water tank and stay with the horse, to keep her from kicking up a ruckus.

He said, 'They'll know there's two of us.'

'That's the idea. Nobody tries to dock a boat this big alone. They'd suspect something for sure.'

'But we don't have two passports. You can't use my passport.'

'I ain't going to use your passport.'

He had a think about that. It didn't take him long.

'Oh,' he said, a little sadly.

As it turned out, the dockside harbour master's office was closed, and so was the customs office next to it. The same building housed both offices: a wooden shack with shuttered windows and a corkboard outside the door, where people displayed notices about boats and marine gear for sale, and local restaurants advertised their fare. A sign tacked to that same board said to check in at the customs office up in the harbour, beside the hotel. I didn't expect that, but it seemed fortuitous: it must have been something they only did during the off-season.

I began the long walk towards shore, my boots drumming the planking. The marina was laid out like a big TV antenna: one main dock with smaller ones branching off. It had about a hundred and fifty moorage slips, some long-term, some overnighters. The time we'd visited before, back in August, every single slip had been full: pleasure cruisers, yachts, tour boats, charter fishing vessels. While Albert barbecued, Tracy and I had sat on deck, sipping soda, just soaking up the sights. It was a carnival atmosphere, during summer. But not in February: most of the overnight slips were empty, and in the long-term slips the boats were battened down to weather the winter. Among the pilings I heard the squeaking of the fenders as they shifted between the hulls and docks. It all felt dead and lifeless and eerie, as if summer had been sealed into a casket.

I crossed the gangway to the landspit, which ended in a set of cobbled steps and some kind of memorial garden. A paved walkway led me between rows of shrubs, their branches bare and grey as bone. Over the walkway arched a wooden canopy, and each cross-beam had been decorated with a famous phrase or quote. One of them stuck with me: *Fare thee well and if for ever, still for ever, fare thee well.* I'd never heard it before, and I didn't particularly get what it meant, but it made me feel melancholy as all hell. On the other side of the garden stood the Hotel de Haro, an old timber-frame classic with wrap-around porches and a colonial feel, and across the street was a more modern brick building that had an American flag jutting straight up from the rooftop. The customs office. I headed in that direction.

Inside, it smelled of window cleaner and wood polish. I'd expected a reception area of some sort but the door actually opened directly into the Customs Agent's office. The desk was opposite the entrance. The man behind it, portly and grizzled and bald, stood up when I entered. He didn't look surprised to see me and he didn't look all that happy about it, either.

'You the guy from the *Western Lady*?' he asked.

'That's right.'

'Coast Guard called ahead. Said some cowboy forgot to fly his Q flag.'

'Stupid mistake, eh?' I said, making a big deal of removing

my jacket. 'The darned Satnav was acting up, and in the mist I lost track of our position on the charts.'

It was peculiar: as soon as we started to speak, I stopped being nervous. I've hardly ever been in trouble in my life, since I've hardly ever done anything wrong, and that showed in my face and my demeanour and how I conducted myself. I lacked all guile and cunning.

'Lucky they didn't sting you with a fine,' he said.

'Oh I know it. They said they'd call ahead.'

I'd brought the boat's registration papers with me, just like Albert had done, and I passed those over to the official. He sat back down to go through them, and copied some of the information into an electronic form he had open on his computer. It was all ready to go, since he'd known to expect us and seen us arrive (the office had a clear view of the harbour) and apparently didn't have much else to do.

'You the owner?' he asked me. 'You Albert Finnegan?'

'No, sir. I'm the first mate. Albert's driving down to meet us in Seattle. Just finished herring season, and we're going on a little rec fishing trip with our families. But his wife, she don't take so well to the open water. So they're driving.'

In some ways, that little lie felt more dishonest than stealing the boat: Evelyn would have had my hide if she'd heard I was making her out to be some weak-bellied landlubber.

'Is that right?' He didn't seem particularly interested in the story. He turned to the next page, scanning the details, and asked, 'You a registered crew member?'

'Yes sir. Timothy Harding. That's me.' I knew it was on the papers, somewhere. 'Me and Albert, we came down here last summer. So you might have a record of that.'

'Let's just see here . . .'

He punched at the keys, using two fingers, and then fiddled around with his mouse.

'The *Western Lady* – August twenty-first.'

'That's the one.'

He seemed pleased that he'd found the record – possibly pleased to show me that they had that information, and that they were way ahead of any trick I might try to pull.

'How many crew members, this time?'

'Just two, until we pick up Albert's family. Just me and my sister Sandra.'

I handed over the passports, both covers marked with gold-embossed maple leaves. I was worried Sandy's looked too new, and unused, but the guy studied them both and added some of our details to his form. He yawned as he did this, and then snapped the passports shut and stood up. He took them and the papers around the side of his desk and walked over to the window. For a second, I thought that was it: he'd decided to come down to check the boat. And quite possibly that's what he was considering. But the bad weather might have helped. And the distance to the dock. It wouldn't have been a particularly pleasant walk.

'Nasty out there,' he said, handing the passports and documents back to me. 'Your friend's wife did good, avoiding the strait in this weather. You know what they call it?'

'Juan de Puke-a,' I said. Albert had told me.

'That's right. Safe journey out there, and good luck.'

'Reckon we'll need it.'

I thanked him and reached for my jacket. I tried to pretend I wasn't in a hurry. Once I had it buttoned up, and the hood pulled over my head, I turned to head for the door and he called out to me.

'One thing,' was what he said.

It felt like that ominous moment: the perfect getaway about to be ruined.

'Yes sir?'

'Your sister's passport is due for renewal, soon.'

'She said something about that.'

'Just letting you know.'

I thanked him for that, probably a little too enthusiastically, and left.

Later, when it all came to light, he got in a mite of trouble, that guy. Americans said: 'What kind of border security do we got, if some yahoos can smuggle a *horse* across, of all things? How hard could it be to do the same with drugs, or people, or a shipment of arms, or what have you?' But the guy, he just said, 'Timothy Harding didn't strike me as the criminal type.'

I appreciated that.

Chapter Twenty-Two

I KNEW WHERE TO FIND the Roche Harbor Company Store, since I'd been before and had walked right by it on the way up: where the dock ended at the memorial garden. I went straight there rather than return to the boat first. I had made a list of things we needed, for us and the horse, and figured it would be best to get it all in one go.

On our previous trip Tracy and I had gone food shopping, and the place looked exactly the same as it had then, and possibly exactly the same as it had a hundred years ago: with oak flooring and wooden shelves and chalkboard signs hanging above the aisles. I got myself a trolley and wheeled that around, grabbing some basic camp food for us: beans and hot dogs and tinned soup and bread and milk. They sold booze, too – like most US grocery stores – and I picked us up a flat of Olympia, for luck, and three bottles of Old Crow.

Shenzao's food was more of a problem. Jake had told me to get carrots as a treat, and oats: the two things a regular store might have that would be okay for a horse's diet. But in the cereals section they only had three bags of rolled porridge oats. I left my cart there and went up to the front.

The girl at the till had her arms folded on the counter, and stood gazing mournfully out the window, glazed over with rainwater. I asked her about the porridge, and if they had any more of it. She straightened and blinked at me blearily. She must have only been about fifteen, and looked as if she was suffering from a hangover, or heartache, or a bit of both.

She said, 'You check the cereal aisle?'

'There's a few bags, but I need more.'

'We might have more in the back.'

She slid away from the till, leaving me there. She shuffle-walked to the door that opened onto the stock room, went on through, and called to me from inside: 'We got a load back here. How much you need?'

'Like a lot. Like ten bags, maybe.'

'I can't carry all that.'

I went to help her. The oats came in boxes of a dozen, so I said we'd take a full box. We hefted that into my trolley, which bowed under the weight. As we pushed it back toward her till, she looked at me like I was loony.

'You really like oats, huh?' she said.

'That's all I eat is oats. I'm crazy about the stuff.'

Something about the way I said it – the outright obviousness of the lie – got us both laughing, and as she scanned my goods we joked about all the different ways I could eat my oats: in sandwiches, with steak, and even sprinkled on ice cream. That went on until I'd paid up and was ready to go: at which point I realized just how much stock I had. I peered at my trolley in utter perplexity, trying to reckon on how I was going to lug all that down to the dock.

It must have showed, since the girl said, 'We got wheelbarrows, if you want.'

They kept them outside, on the porch: big green wheelbarrows. She came to help me transfer my goods into one. It was still drizzling and she had no jacket but didn't pay it any mind. When we were done she squinted through the mist, towards the marina and our boat. Jake stood on deck in his slicker, and it looked as if he'd got the water hose going.

'You need a deckhand?' she said.

'Next season, maybe.'

'One of these days I'm gonna get my own boat.'

'A seiner?'

'Pleasure cruiser. Take the tourists out, catch a few lingcod and salmon.'

'Sounds like a winner.'

She stayed on the porch, leaning against the doorframe, as I hefted the wheelbarrow by the handles and trundled away towards the dock. The front wheel squeaked as it went around, and around, and around.

Down at the *Lady*, things were quiet. As I came up I heard voices in the galley. Or a voice: Jake's. I eased the wheelbarrow down and stood on the dock outside the galley window, my head level with the gunnel. He was talking to the horse in low tones and apologizing for the way we'd treated her. I'm sorry for kidnapping you, was what he said. Then he corrected himself: or horsenapping you. I lingered out there and listened to that, smiling a little. He used to talk to our family dog like that – and after she'd died he had a good long chat with her in the garden, before he and Sandy and I carried her body into the woods across from our house, and buried her. Sandy had said a few words. Not religious words. Just her own.

Eventually I called out, 'Ahoy the ship,' and picked up the wheelbarrow and put it down more loudly, as if I'd just arrived.

Jake poked his head out, and looked at me. I nodded.

'They ain't coming down,' I said. 'And I got supplies.'

He clenched his fist close to his body (a signature gesture, and his way of discreetly expressing triumph) and joined me on deck to help unload my wheelbarrow. I passed up the bag of food, and the box of porridge. When it came to the flat of Olympia he let out a whoop.

'Hell,' he said, 'I didn't think they still brewed this stuff.'

'Seemed like good luck, seeing as we're going there.'

'Luck enough for my taste.'

He cracked one open straight away.

'Hey,' I said. 'This is a dry boat, sailor.'

He paused, the can hovering halfway to his mouth. 'Says who?'

'Albert's rules.'

'Hell – you're the captain now.' He tossed one to me. 'Make your own rules.'

I cracked it and the act was distinctly satisfying. Albert would have been apoplectic. We drank as we finished unloading and when that was all done I checked the water tank. It was halfways full, and while we waited for the levels to rise a bit further we perched on the gunnel, our legs hanging over the side, sipping at our brews. I got out Sandy's passport and opened it to the photo page, holding it as reverently as a psalm book.

'Sandra Jane Harding,' I read.

'Sounds funny, don't it?'

She'd always been Sandy, to us.

'I been carrying it around for so long,' he said.

'Lucky for us you did.'

'Big sis. Still looking after us.'

I tucked it in my pocket. When I looked up, I saw somebody coming down the dock towards us. That girl from the store.

'Damn,' I said.

She waved. She'd seen us, all right. There was no point sending Jake back inside. I'd just have to hope the customs official didn't find out from her that my sister was actually my brother. I hopped down from the gunnel, to intercept her and greet her as she came up.

'Thought I'd spare you running the barrow back,' she said.

'That's real kind of you.'

But she didn't look in any hurry to pick it up. She glanced at our cans of beer, and past me at Jake, and smiled. He smiled back. She put a palm on the hull of the boat, and asked, 'Where are you all going, anyways?'

She said it in a longing way, a real lonesome way. I glanced at the galley, but there was no sign of anything untoward that I could see.

'Ask Cap, here,' Jake said. 'He's the boss.'

'Well,' I said, and stopped. 'South.'

'Long journey?'

'Sure. All the way to Shangri-la.'

We chuckled at that, a little too loudly, and for a little too long.

'Wish I could come with you.'

'We'll pick you up on the way back,' Jake said.

She reached for the handles of the wheelbarrow, hefted it, and that's when Shenzao whinnied. The girl stopped, and lowered the wheelbarrow back down.

'Was that a *horse*?' she said.

I had no answer. I was absolutely dumbstruck, to the point of numbness, by the sudden shift in fortune: from sitting pretty, having made it through, to being caught out by our own stupidity and arrogance. Me and my goddamn Olympia.

Jake said, 'That's right.'

She looked at him. I looked at him.

'Me and my brother,' he said. 'We stole a racehorse. We stole it from some guys who want to kill us, and if we don't get it down to the States, they will. They'll kill us and the horse too. That's why we stole her. To save her from a life of captivity.'

The girl's jaw actually dropped – her mouth agape like a goldfish.

'So now you know,' Jake went on. 'You're the only one who does. Our lives are in your hands. And the horse's life, too. Can you keep it secret? Can you keep it to yourself?'

Her mouth closed. She swallowed.

'I think so,' she said. 'I mean, I will.'

'Good.' Jake stood up, and offered her a can of Olympia. 'Take that for the road. I'm Lefty, and he's Poncho. We're the good guys, okay? You're on our side, now.'

She nodded, real vigorously. And when we got ready to cast off, she ran up and down the dock, untying our lines for us. She tossed them to Jake, and reeled in the water hose. I went up top to fire up the engine. When it roared, the horse roared with it. Jake whooped – *yee-haw* – and the girl, she whooped back. It was the damnedest thing.

And I guess that was how it really started, this whole thing about us being outlaws and activists: in that moment with Jake and the girl. And it just sort of spiralled from there.

Chapter Twenty-Three

LOOKING BACK, I SUPPOSE WE should have been more worried about that girl than we actually were. It was very possible and even likely that she'd renege on her promise. If we'd been thinking in terms of chances, then our chances of getting caught had just risen substantially.

But it didn't feel that way. The sun emerged, setting off little flicker-flares in the waves, and those beers bubbled pleasantly in our brains and we were still on our way to Olympia. Jake had done what he did best: fast-talked his way out of a tight spot. In addition, even if we had wanted to worry about what the girl might say, we had no control over it. All we could do was carry on, so as soon as we left Roche Harbor, I threw the throttle into neutral and hopped down to lower the Q flag, which I replaced with the Stars and Stripes to show we had officially cleared customs. Then we had to feed our girl. We got out Evelyn's big, copper-bottomed pasta pot and dumped in a bag of the oats. Jake added water from the busted tap (it still sprayed like a geyser) and half a cup of vegetable oil, then used a fork to stir that together. Oat mash, Jake called it. Basically a cold porridge, as far as I could tell.

Jake set that down next to her water dish, and she sniffed at it, looking only mildly interested. While she nibbled, Jake pulled two more cans from the flat and held them up.

'Shotgun for the road, Poncho?'

'Let's lay off,' I said.

He went ahead anyway, which I could have foretold. I waited until he took a good long glug and slapped him on the back, unduly hard, making him splutter brew.

'Haul in them bumpers, will you Lefty?'

He coughed and saluted like Popeye. 'Aye-aye, Captain.'

I clambered up to the wheelhouse and leaned hard on the throttle and from there we ploughed south through Haro Strait, down the western coast of San Juan Island. Along the shoreline, shaggy Douglas fir trees formed a solid wall of trunks and greenery. Every few hundred yards the treeline gave way, revealing a waterfront lot and cabin: mostly one-storey bungalows or A-frames. They looked to be summer homes, all empty at this time of year. We didn't see many other vessels, aside from a little aluminium fishing skiff, manned by an old-timer, reeling in crab traps.

The waves picked up, but the current stayed with us and we

made good time, doing about nine knots. From my perch in the wheelhouse I could see Jake sitting on deck in the sun with his back against the seine winch. He'd opened a fresh can of Olympia, and every so often he took a casual sip, as if he was lounging in a sunchair at a Club Med resort. All told, he looked a little too comfortable for my liking. I leaned out the window of the wheelhouse and hollered down to him.

'Go on and stand at the bow,' I told him. 'I need you to check something.'

'What's the bow?' he asked.

'The front, greenhorn.'

He went up there, walking a little shakily on the listing deck. He didn't have his sea-legs yet, and probably never would. When he stabilized, gripping the gunnel with one hand (he was still holding his beer with the other), I steered towards starboard, into the waves. The next big one exploded across the prow like a depth charge, geysering over the foredeck and raining down on Jake – absolutely drenching him. Albert had done the same to me, on my first voyage.

Jake looked back and flipped me the finger, but instead of backing down he took another pull of beer and stayed where he was, ready to ride it out. The next wave came at him and he leaned into the spray, and the next, and after each crash and cymbal-smash he took a slug of his beer and made a circular motion with his hand: one more. The sun caught the spray, making it sparkle and giving it substance, and each time it looked like a cascade of shattered glass raining down on him.

The weather began to change: not all at once, but in the slow and inevitable way it does at times, from fair to foul. We lost the sun again, behind a billowy nimbus cloud, and the wind began to shift. It had been blowing from the north all day, at our backs, but now it slowly swung around to the west, catching us broadside, so that the waves (which had swelled to five-footers) hit the starboard hull, rocking us left and right, back and forth, like babies in a cradle. I adjusted course to accommodate for this and that helped some, but not much.

Jake – who'd been lounging in the recliner, nursing his beer – drained it and said he needed to go downstairs to check on Shenzao. I took that at face value, but when he didn't come back up, I reached for the intercom and hailed him. The boat has a system for talking from the galley to the wheelhouse. I'd shown him how to work it but he'd either not paid attention or forgotten: it took him a minute or two to answer. When he finally did I asked what he was doing. He told me that the horse hadn't eaten that mash he'd whipped up.

'She hasn't eaten *any*?'

'A bite or two.'

I said, 'Maybe you didn't make it right.'

'It ain't rocket science.'

I let the intercom crackle a bit, before thumbing the talk button again.

I said, 'Maybe she don't like oats.'

'Maybe you ought to leave the horse-tending to me.'

There was an edge to his voice that I recognized.

'You drinking down there?'

'I'm just sitting with her.'

'You're sitting and drinking.'

More crackling. An explosion of static, bursting between us.

'What's your beef, Poncho?'

'Just try to stay sober, okay? At least until we cross the strait.'

'I'm sober as a jaybird.'

'Or drunk as a jailbird.'

Neither of us signed off. We just hung up on each other.

The southern tip of San Juan is marked by what they call the Cattle Point Lighthouse. As we approached I could see it winking dimly under the darkened sky. The beacon jutted up from a squat white structure that looked like an old church. Beyond it and to the south loomed the Olympic Mountain range: this impressive mass of snow and granite, half-cloaked in clouds.

About a mile offshore I dropped down into neutral.

Beyond the point, Haro Strait emptied into the Strait of Juan de Fuca. We had to cross over to Port Townsend, on the US mainland, before continuing our journey south. From our position, the crossing would be about twenty nautical miles. The customs guy had joked about the strait being called Juan de Puke-a but it was no joke, that crossing. Every summer you heard about cruisers and sail boats, piloted by novices, that got into trouble out there, capsized by big waves or run aground in the shallows near Smith Island. The strait had fast tidal flows and major shoal areas on the sea bed, making for unpredictable currents. The year Albert and Tracy and I had come down, we'd intended to cross but decided against it when the forecast turned nasty. And Albert wasn't one to shy away from a bit of bad weather.

I turned on the radio and twisted the analogue dial. It whined and crackled until I found the Coast Guard radio. The lady spoke in a low monotone, very calm and soothing. She talked first about Georgia Strait and then Haro Strait and eventually got round to the forecast for Juan de Fuca. The afternoon and early evening were supposed to be fine, but later that night a weather warning would come into effect: westerly winds of twenty knots, rising to thirty around midnight, and continuing through the next day. Rain, too, and a likelihood of thunderstorms. I stood and listened to that, with my ear right near the speaker. Even after she stopped talking about Juan de Fuca I still stood there, listening.

Our intercom crackled. Jake, hailing me from the galley.

'Lefty to Poncho. You up there, Poncho?'

I picked up the mouthpiece. 'Poncho here.'

'Why are we stopped?'

'Just checking the forecast for our crossing. How's our girl?'

'You better come see.'

Normally I wouldn't have left the wheelhouse unattended, but I heard something in his tone. I hustled on down, and when I got to the galley Jake was sitting on the bench seat with his elbows on his knees and a beer can in his hand. The horse lay flat on her side next to the bowl of oats, still untouched. The air in there stank like an outhouse, and she didn't react to my arrival at all.

'She sick?' I asked.

'She ain't well.'

I stood over her for a minute. Her breaths were rapid and shallow and a wet sheen covered her coat. Jake reached down and laid his hand on her neck.

'She feels hot to me. She feel hot to you?'

I touched her skin. It seemed feverish, all right.

'What is it?' I asked.

'She's eaten a bunch of cardboard and a damned cushion. Could be colic.'

'Is that serious?'

'If it's not seen to.'

'Maybe she's just seasick.'

'Either way, the sooner we get her on dry land the better.'

I explained about the forecast: the winds, the rain, the

impending storm. Jake asked me how long it would take to cross, and I had to calculate. I figured it would be four hours, in good weather, going full-bore.

He said, 'We might beat the storm.'

'Or we might get stuck in it.'

Jake took a pull of his beer. 'Better that than stuck here for days, waiting for the weather to turn.'

'I know. Damn.'

I went back outside to stand on deck. I peered into the dusk, studying the strait. On the far side lay a thin strip of land, dotted by twinkling lights. Between it and us, the surface didn't look too choppy. But off to starboard I could see the storm front moving in like a big black wave, an extension of the sea. Long tendrils of rain hung beneath it. A hell of a sight.

Jake stepped out beside me, and I shook my head.

'We can't risk it.'

'We got to,' he said. 'We got to.'

I told him he only felt that way because he was beered up, and he said his drunkenness had nothing to do with it. We argued like that for a minute or two, as we often do.

Jake said, 'I just got this hunch.'

'You and your hunches. I'm the one navigating.'

'I ain't contesting that. But you need some gumption, Cap. You need a little moxie, as sis used to say. You remember that, right?'

'Don't bring her into this.'

'We can't wait it out. Not with our horse in that condition.'

I stood, feeling the deck rock beneath me. Back and forth.

'If we go,' I said, 'we got to go now.'

'What do you need from me?'

I'd already reached for the ladder. As I scaled it I called back to him: 'Batten the hatches, and clear the decks of gear, anything loose – tie-lines, fenders, crab traps, anything. Then fasten the latches on the cupboards and drawers in the galley.' At the top I stopped and pointed at the can in his hand. 'And stop drinking that fucking beer, goddammit Jake!'

He dropped the can. It landed on deck and began to roll, spluttering foam.

Chapter Twenty-Four

NIGHT CREPT ON AS SAN Juan Island and Cattle Point Lighthouse fell away behind us. In the growing dark, for a time, I lost sight of that storm front: it simply blended into the sky, which gave me the false notion that we had made the right decision, and could possibly outrun it. Initially, the waves held steady. We were still near the Saanich Peninsula, on Vancouver Island, which afforded some protection from the open ocean. The wind swung around further and started blowing southwesterly, at a solid fifteen knots. Ahead of us lay a void. Piloting a boat at night, you may as well be blindfolded. I only had about five feet of visibility off the bow, and used the GPS to keep us on course. Due to the ominous weather forecast, no other small crafts were running the strait (it being such a foolhardy idea). Our radar picked up a cruise ship way out to the west, and also an oil tanker coming north out of Puget Sound. Nothing else.

Every so often I checked the readings from the buoy at Hein Bank. Hein Bank is a shoal in the middle of the strait, where the depth drops to thirty feet. The buoy constantly broadcasts weather updates and tidal information and on that night it served its purpose. The readings didn't bode well. In the centre of the strait, conditions had worsened. The storm wasn't catching up to us, but cutting us off, coming in from the west. Over in that direction, I could see roots of lightning sprouting from the clouds.

I used the intercom to hail Jake in the galley.

'How you doing down there?'

'She's getting a bit lively. I had to toss a rope on her, to keep her under control.'

'At least she's on her feet, now.'

'That's for sure.'

'Just wanted to warn you – in half an hour we're gonna hit a bad patch.'

'This isn't the bad patch?'

'This isn't anything.'

'How will I know?'

'You'll know.'

When the storm arrived, it arrived all at once. The wind picked up around us, rising to thirty knots: an actual gale that screeched around the cabin and buffeted the wheelhouse like a colony of rabid bats. And with the wind came the rain, and the waves: big fifteen-footers. During the fisheries, I had run waves of that size before, but these had a peculiar and damnable nature that made them particularly treacherous to navigate.

When running waves upwind, normally what you do is steer sideways into the trough, then turn to face the crest as you go up and break it. I had seen Albert do that, and I had done it myself. But because of the tidal rip and the currents in the strait, the waves didn't come at us from one direction. They seemed to rise up on all sides: these big black phantoms that flung themselves at our boat with fury and purpose, as if trying to claw their way aboard. The crests crashed across the foredeck and the spray blasted right up to the wheelhouse, smearing the windscreen. I felt each impact judder up through the frame of the boat.

But the *Western Lady* could take it. Albert had spoken often about the strength and quality of her carvel hull – those solid oak beams and cedar strakes. He fervently believed wooden boats handled better in the water, and withstood punishment better, than the newer steel or aluminium seiners. No-account tin cans, Albert called them. He'd explained that to me, many times, but I hadn't fully appreciated it until facing that storm without him.

Ten minutes after we'd tumbled into the guts of the storm, Jake hailed me on the intercom. I grabbed the receiver and answered while gripping the wheel one-handed.

'How you holding up?' I asked.

'The horse is making a mess.'

'As in puking?'

'Horses can't puke. I mean the other end.'

'Maybe she's seasick.'

'Or just plain stressed.'

'Can you give her some of that Xylazine?'

'I did. She's too juiced up, though. Hold on.' He signed off for a minute. Then, just when I was beginning to worry, he came back on. 'Well, one of us is puking now.'

'You're seasick too?'

'It's a cesspit down here.'

'Try to ride it out, man. Hopefully we'll push through soon.'

It was an obvious lie, but I didn't know what else to say. After signing off, I tuned in the Coast Guard radio again. The Strait of San Juan now had a small-craft warning in effect: gale-force winds, high seas, torrential rain. Even though we'd already entered the very storm they were warning everybody away from, hearing the voice gave me a kind of comfort. I listened to it and watched the darkness. Every so often distant lightning strikes lit up the seascape, and each time that happened I would catch an eerie glimpse of the waves: an endless series of black peaks stretching into the distance, like a mountain range.

Overcoming those peaks consumed my attention. I didn't even consider the possibility of a lightning strike. That rarely happens, in boats. Instead I worried about the time it might take to cross, seeing as we were only doing about four or five knots, in actual landspeed. I remember trying to calculate that, and not being able to (despite it being a fairly simple calculation) and grasping that such slow-mindedness most likely portended a degree of panic on my part, when the sky around us turned white: the whole windshield flared bright as a cinema screen, and a lance of burning light hit the water thirty feet off the port side. It struck so close I actually saw this bluish crackle, and heard the explosive sound of vaporization, as steam and spray shot back up into the air. It was like witnessing a damned biblical omen, an act of God. The afterglow stained my retinas for five or six seconds. I blinked it back, thinking how incredibly lucky it had been that the lightning had struck so close without being drawn to our flagpole or the top of the wheelhouse.

I grabbed the hailer to call Jake, to ask if he'd seen it. The system didn't come on. I fiddled with the switches, but the whole thing seemed dead. I still didn't quite understand, until I glanced at the GPS display and saw that it, too, had stopped working: the triangular symbol representing our position was no longer moving, and the screen stayed frozen at its last reading. The same applied to the VHF radio: the Coast Guard report I'd been listening to had gone silent. I couldn't even get static.

The lightning had blown out all our electrical equipment.

I stood at the wheel for a time, wrestling with those waves, before deciding, finally, that I had to abandon the wheelhouse. Albert had taught me never to do that while piloting the vessel – let alone in a storm – but I was navigating completely blind, with no landmarks to guide me. I locked the rudder (I hoped it might prevent us from spinning in circles) and pulled on my rain slicker and stepped onto the upper deck.

Until then, I had heard the storm, and seen it, but that was the first time I really *felt* it. The wind ripped into me and the rain flew sideways in cold and stinging flechettes. I held onto the rail and worked my way towards the ladder. Albert had always taught us to have a hold on something with at least one hand, and preferably two, in rough seas. This was all the more important for me, with my bad right hand, which didn't grip well. At the ladder I turned around to descend but halfway down the boat listed sharply and my legs swung off to the left, dangling, before she levelled out. I got a foothold and again scaled down to the aft deck. At the bottom I reached for the galley door – all ready to announce myself and our dire situation – but of course it didn't open, since I'd told Jake to lock the hatch from the inside. With the boat deck rocking like a funhouse floor beneath me, I held onto the ladder and pounded at the door with the underside of my fist and hollered my brother's name.

I only know what happened next from Jake having told me afterwards. He said that he opened the door and saw me standing there, drenched, and that I let go of the ladder and stepped towards him and then got smashed sideways by a wave. At the time, of course, I had no real sense of what had transpired. I felt an impact, which may have been me hitting the gunnel, and I remember inhaling water, and thinking I had been washed overboard. In actuality I lay sprawled on the deck, under the remains of the wave, which drained away towards the stern, dragging me with it. The stern had a drop-down transom, which had sprung open in the storm (Jake hadn't known to lock it, and I hadn't thought to instruct him). I could easily have slipped right off, like a loose piece of cargo. The deck tilted as we crested the next wave and I slid with the water, feet-first, face down. Blinded by brine, I looked up and saw Jake and the horse and the galley door blurrily receding from me, getting smaller.

Then Jake did something valiant and gutsy and, to be honest, completely foolhardy: he took hold of Shenzao's rope and dove headfirst towards me and sort of slithered on his belly and somehow managed to get an arm around my torso without letting go of the rope, using the weight and strength of the horse to anchor us until the greenwater ran off and the boat levelled out. Amid the remaining froth and foam Jake hauled me to my feet and we floundered together towards the galley door, where Shenzao awaited, leaning back on her haunches, providing leverage as we struggled along the rope, so clumsy and so human.

Once we reached the galley door, we had an argument, which

was typical of us: a fight in a storm. My brother and I would fight in hell, given half the chance. And maybe one day we will. Jake tried to drag me inside but I wouldn't let him and kept pulling away, obsessed with going back up the ladder. Later, he would explain that my face was covered in blood from a cut on my forehead (I didn't know this at the time) and that I was babbling and shouting in a deranged way about things that made no sense to him whatsoever. The horse, which had been unaccountably calm and even stoic up until that point, seemed to catch hold of our panic and began to stomp the floor repeatedly with her forehooves, and also to bray wildly, donkey-like, adding to the general sense of chaos.

I shoved Jake towards her, telling him to grab the charts. Apparently I got the point across. As he turned to go, I shouted his name and gripped the ladder and said, 'Two hands! Two hands!' He said that I looked demented, a madman. But somehow I got back up the ladder and into the wheelhouse, where I took the helm. I checked the compass, which still worked (Albert kept a classic magnetic model mounted on the dash), and we seemed to be heading northeast, in the opposite direction we wanted to go. The wind had turned us completely backwards. I worked the wheel, bringing the bow light around to port, so we were facing south again, into the wind. It was goddamn nerve-racking, because to the east lay Smith Island and the surrounding shallows, and somewhere nearby, I knew, a 10,000-ton oil tanker was coming up from Puget Sound. I had a vague idea where it might be, but less with each passing minute.

I'd left the wheelhouse door open and rain lashed in, spattering the floor. Then Jake appeared, cradling a jumbled armload of charts. In a breathless stream of words, I told him that the lightning had knocked out our navigation equipment (I can't imagine how incredible that sounded to him) and we needed the chart, the same chart we'd been looking at earlier. He remembered, or at least understood, and began unscrolling the charts, checking each and tossing it aside, until he found the one we needed.

'Got it,' he said.

'Bring it here.'

He stood by me and held it at arm's length under the light of the wheelhouse. I tried to steer a steady course while reading the map at the same time, which wasn't easy.

'Where's Smith Island?' I asked. 'I can't see Smith Island.'

It took about ten seconds before Jake picked it out. He hadn't brought up the sliderule so I couldn't calculate specifically, but I had our last reading from the GPS, frozen on the display, and assumed we'd drifted a mite north of those coordinates. I compared them with the map and set a course that would take us towards Port Townsend, on the far side of the strait, and made sure to estimate generously to the west, so that we would avoid the tanker and the shallows. I remember feeling very capable and satisfied about that. Albert's belief in being able to navigate by the charts, in case of emergencies just like this, had apparently saved us.

But I'd failed to account for something: the tanker had changed course. It was no longer cruising due north – opposite to us – but had come around, turning west like us, to head out towards the Pacific. If I had thought about it I would have concluded that the open ocean was its most likely destination. But the chaos and the fall and the crack on my skull had addled me, and I perhaps wouldn't have had the foresight to deduce it anyway.

A few minutes later we heard the long, low moan of the tanker's warning blast. It was deafening, even amid the storm. It resounded inside the wheelhouse, inside our heads.

Jake said, 'What in the goddamn hell is that?'

He pointed off the port bow. Out there you could see the darkness moving. The tanker. It looked as if it was right there, practically on top of us, though really it must have been about a hundred yards away, cutting across our course. I'd failed to spot the running lights on account of their height: floating way up in the air, high overhead. And higher still hovered the lights of the cabins and bridge. The ship's vast bulk moved lazily in front of us like a leviathan or kraken – some great sea beast – with those lights its glittering eyes.

The captain lay on his horn again, that low lament, as if to moan, 'What the hell are you yahoos doing?' No doubt he had been trying to hail us for a long time on the radio, not knowing that ours was dead. The big stern passed away and the white, roiling wake flooded towards us, washing over the bow and causing the *Lady* to bob like a toy boat in a bathtub.

Neither Jake nor I said anything. Not then. We were beyond words. All of that, all at once, had been too much. I was still partially concussed and only semi-lucid. And Jake – he had hardly been on a boat before. He held onto the chart, all rolled up. He gripped it like a sword or baseball bat, some kind of weapon he could use to ward off whatever the storm threw at us next. A whale, maybe. Or a giant squid. All the while, the waves rhythmically thumped against the hull, the wind shrieked like a thousand violins, and the rain played percussion on the wheelhouse: the storm had crescendoed to a kind of orchestral peak.

All we could do was keep going. So that was what we did.

Chapter Twenty-Five

BY THE TIME WE REACHED the other side it was past midnight. What should have been a four-hour journey had taken us eight. The storm never really abated but we grew accustomed to its particular brand of tempestuousness. It became more a matter of enduring the onslaught, and riding it out. The horse was sick, and Jake too, but we made it without running aground, capsizing, or sinking. I can't say we reached our destination, as that was hazy from the get-go. I didn't actually know where we had ended up: only that it was on the south side of the strait. I'd been aiming for Port Townsend but Port Townsend is a sizeable settlement and in the bay we entered there looked to be only a few scattered lights on the surrounding hills.

I navigated the *Lady* into the centre of the bay, where we had some shelter from the storm, which continued to rage and thrash behind us. I didn't want to go any further in the dark, since we'd lost the GPS navigator and depth sounder, which increased our chances of running aground or coming up against some rocks. Seeing as we didn't know our specific coordinates, the charts only served as a rough guide.

So we dropped anchor there, and went to check on the horse. In the galley, an inch of seawater covered the floor, having poured in through the broken window during the storm. The water churned sloppily with vomit and manure and (presumably) urine, creating a putrid mess. The tarps floated atop it, soiled and streaked. Shenzao knelt in the middle of all that, her head bowed and eyes half-closed. Her coat was filthy, her mane scraggly, her tail wilted. She looked embarrassed and frightened and humiliated, and shivery from the cold.

I said, 'We're gonna pay for what we've done to this poor horse.'

'I'm already paying for it.'

'You look it.'

'I feel just about as rough as her.'

Jake's face had gone near-white, sickly with sweat. Green around the gills, Albert would have called it.

'Come on,' I said. 'Let's clean this up.'

We did what we could. Jake coaxed her to her feet and I dragged the soiled tarps out on deck. While he mopped the water off the galley floor I shook the tarps overboard, draped them on the seine drum, and hosed them down (Albert had a hose on deck, connected to our freshwater supply, which we used for cleaning the holds). Every few minutes Jake trudged out on deck with a bucketful of foul-smelling liquid, which he dumped over the side. The rain still fell, relentless, rattling across the decking and soaking our slickers, and we both slogged through these chores in a kind of numb aftershock.

When all the muck was cleared out of the galley, it left dirty stains on the linoleum tiles, which had buckled and warped. I went around, trying to stomp down the tiles, but of course that didn't work. They would need replacing, like so much else in the galley. But when I commented on this in passing, Jake shrugged.

'Who cares?' he said.

'Albert sure as hell will.'

'I'm more worried about our horse.'

'I'm not saying I ain't worried about her.'

'What are you saying, then?'

'I don't want to fight.'

'I want a beer. You want a beer?'

'I need a beer.'

While Jake went to fetch the Olympia from the storage locker, I got some old sheets out of the crew's cabin. I spread them on the floor in place of the tarps and backed Shenzao into her usual spot: with her hindquarters near the sink, and her head angled toward the table. She sat on her rump and let her front hooves slide over the sheet, easing herself to the floor, and then rolled and lay flat in the supine position. Her eyes had a glassy, glazed look.

We put water and oats in front of her and sat with her, at the galley table, drinking our beer. The first ones went down easy, and Jake got us two more. As we drank Jake gave me his account of the moment that wave had hit me. Like a big wet palm, he said. Smack.

'You saved my bacon, brother.'

'I couldn't steer this rig without you.'

'I was going overboard, you know.'

'I would have come in after you.'

'Then we both would have drowned.'

'Better that than lose you, too.'

Every so often, we checked on Shenzao. Her temperature seemed to have come down some but that was about all that could be said, by way of improvements. She still looked sickly as hell.

'She has to eat,' Jake said. 'She hasn't eaten hardly anything.'

'And what she did she hurled up.'

'She's probably dehydrated, too.'

He emptied and refilled her water dish, but she just lay there, eyeing it listlessly.

I said, 'We haven't really eaten, either.'

'Go on and get us some of that there food.'

'You get it – I'll cook it.'

He pointed at the busted stove. 'We don't got the means.'

'There's a campstove for emergencies.'

'This sure as hell counts.'

Albert's stove was a classic: a two-burner Coleman that ran off gasoline. By the time I fetched it from the engine room, Jake had laid out a full spread on the table: a loaf of bread and a pack of hot dogs and a tin of beans.

Seeing all that, I said, 'Hey Jake.'

He looked at me.

'I'm so hungry I could eat a horse.'

The stove struck and started, first time. We put a pot of water on to boil, and emptied the tin of beans into a saucepan. While we waited for them to heat up, Jake brought out one of the bottles of Old Crow that I'd bought. We filled up two mugs and sat there cradling them like cups of hot coffee. It tasted damned good. The liquor and the stove warmed us up and we peeled off our jackets and rain gear. As I did I remembered the passport: it had been in my pocket throughout the storm. I pulled it out to check it. The pages were stuck together and the cover felt soft, spongy. I placed it on the table and looked at Jake in apology.

'Ah, hell,' he said.

'I'm sorry. I'd forgot I had it.'

'Well, maybe she looked after you.' He picked it up. He peeled it open so it could stand upright, and then placed it near the stove, and the heat. 'See if we can dry it out.'

When the water boiled we dumped in the hot dogs, and by the time those had cooked we were good and drunk. We turned the heat down low and tore chunks off the bread. We didn't have plates or bowls, so we just sort of scooped up beans with the bread, then laid a hot dog across that. It was messy as hell.

'Damn, this is good,' I said.

'Reminds me of camping.'

'Like that last trip we went on, down Oregon way.'

'I remember.'

It had been six weeks before Sandy was due to fly out to start training in Paris. Jake and I had wanted to take her camping, even though it was winter, as a last trip together as siblings. Maria came too and the four of us piled into the family van, an old grey Previa, rusty but reliable, which we'd had since our dad was alive. We took it on the ferry across to Vancouver Island, and camped at the beach in Tofino.

Jake and I may have organized the trip but we didn't really plan it, or think it through (this was always the case with us). We had no reservation so missed the first ferry, and we hadn't checked the weather forecast. All through the first day it rained and rained and rained: practically a deluge. The tents that Jake and I had brought had no flies or groundsheets and so the four of us ended up huddled in the van, drinking wine from plastic cups and watching the rain and playing poker for pennies. Come nightfall the rain finally thinned to a drizzle and we walked down to the beach, which was completely empty, and completely ours. Sandy had thought to store some firewood in the van, to keep it dry, and we started a bonfire and Jake got out his guitar and while he played the three of us danced around, absurdly, dressed in our jackets and rain gear. That was the last time I saw Sandy dance. Even burdened by all that cumbersome clothing she could not look clumsy, but moved with the same swift certainty she displayed on stage, only in this case she spun and leapt and twirled through the misty dark, kicking up sand, freewheeling amid the elements.

Afterwards we hunkered down around the fire and had a semi-serious talk: the kind of talk you might have, when your older sister goes away. No doubt it was partly triggered by the complete and utter haplessness we had displayed on the trip. She looked at us and asked us what we were going to do without her, and wondered aloud who would take care of us. She asked Maria if she might, but by then Maria was half-cut and – as Jake pointed out – in no condition to take care of anybody, even herself. I remember that Sandy looked to me, and said: 'Maybe it's on you, Tim.' Joking, but also serious. 'You're the next oldest.'

It almost seems too pat, too perfect, that she would say that – though of course that is precisely the reason I remember it. A week later she was dead, and I failed to live up to the task with which she had charged me.

*

That night in the galley Jake and I talked about that memory, and a good many others – so many that each one began to blend into the previous, and the next, since in some ways they were all the same memory, built up over time: an image of our sister that we kept close, held tight, like a picture in a locket. A picture made more radiant by the effects of time, and grief, and whisky: the burning in the throat, the stinging in the eyes, the smouldering in the chest.

'It don't make any sense,' I said, taking a swig from the bottle. We'd moved on from pouring our drinks a long time back. 'No sense at all.'

'Sometimes I still dream she's alive.'

'Sometimes I still *think* she's alive.'

Jake took the bottle from me, and knocked back the dregs. His face was red, glowing.

'I got something to tell you,' he said.

'Tell me.'

'I wish it had been anybody but her.'

'You mean me.'

'Or me. Either of us.'

'She would have looked after the other.'

'She would have made it okay.'

We were both looking at the burner flames, as if into a camp-fire or crystal ball.

I said, 'It's like the sun went down and never came up.'

Jake grinned. I was drunk and being dramatic and you could tell he liked that.

'The sun is down,' he said. 'But it'll come up in a few hours.'

'Ah, to hell with you. Go and get your damned guitar, why don't you?'

'That an order, Captain?'

'It sure as hell is.'

He went up to the wheelhouse, and I sat there with Shenzao. I told her we'd been talking about our sister, and I told her a bunch of other drunken nonsense, which doesn't really bear repeating. But I did have an idea. I dipped a chunk of bread in the hot dog water and mashed it up into a doughy ball and bent down and held that in front of her. She sniffed it once – testing – and licked it, and then folded her lips around it, slurping at my fingers.

'Jake!' I said. 'Jake – come here, quick!'

I heard him drop onto deck (he'd jumped) and he came rushing in, carrying his guitar and the half-empty bottle of Black Velvet he'd brought from Vancouver. 'What?' he said.

'She's eating bread!'

'I thought she might be dead, the way you were hollering.'

'Watch this.'

I repeated the trick, dipping and mashing, and she ate it again. Then she took a few slurps from her water bowl.

'Should I give her more?'

'Let her digest that first.'

'Is bread okay?'

'It's just grain. It's fine.'

Jake settled in with his guitar and I went to work on the Black Velvet. I felt all belly-full and leaden-limbed and foggy-headed. He plucked at the strings for a while, tuning in that pernickety way of his.

'Play the damned song,' I said.

He didn't have to ask what song: the one he'd written for her. He'd been planning to play it at the funeral, but the night before he'd gotten drunk and started a bar fight and broke his thumb. I wouldn't have wanted to listen to it that day, anyway. I'd hardly ever been able to listen to it. But I wanted to listen to it just then. Like all of Jake's songs it sounded raw and wounded, as if the words were being pulled out of his throat on a rusty wire. Something that hurt to get out but would hurt more to keep inside, if that makes sense.

Here's the funny thing: the horse, she sat up to listen. That bread and water had done her good, and she seemed to like the song. She probably hadn't heard much music at the race track, other than what they played over the loudspeaker. That could very well have been the first music she ever heard, and she listened, with her ears pricked up attentively.

When Jake finished, he put the guitar to one side. I lowered my head on the table and stayed like that for a few minutes, as if in supplication, overcome with whisky and grief and stricken to the core. When I finally roused myself I sat back and picked up the passport. The heat of the burner had dried it some, and I opened it and flipped through it.

'How is it?' Jake asked.

'It's done,' I said.

The seawater had warped the pages and drained away the colouring. Sandy's face was faded and stained. It didn't look much like her any more. Or maybe it did and I'd just forgotten. Maybe what she actually looked like was different to what I remembered. I closed it and gazed at Jake, and I didn't have to explain it. I just removed the pot from the stove and held the corner of the passport over the flames. It took a while to catch, on account of the cover being vinyl, but when it burned it burned. The flames licked up hot to my hand and I dropped it in the empty pot. It gave off black smoke and curled up. The cover bubbled and peeled back and I caught a last glimpse of my sister's face, before the flames consumed it.

Chapter Twenty-Six

COME MORNING, I AWOKE TO the heavy, sweet, hot scent of horse breath in my face. After the drunken angst of the previous night, we had collapsed in the bunks: me in mine, and Jake in Big Ben's. One of the holes Shenzao had kicked in the partition wall was right next to my head. Now she had her snout up against it, breathing on me. Her big nostrils, pink and hairy as a hog's, flared at each exhale. I couldn't see the rest of her head: just those nostrils.

'Lefty,' I said.

A grunt. It was like being back at sea during fishing season.

'I think our girl's getting better.'

He rolled over. His hair – which he hadn't washed in days – stuck out in starfish snarls, and patches of stubble peppered his jaw. He looked like a greasy gigolo.

'I knew she would.'

'Lookie here.' I pointed at the nose in the wall.

'What a little pig nose.'

She snorted, as if offended by the comment.

I said, 'Get her some food, will you?'

'I ain't the cook.'

'I'm gonna find out where the hell we are.'

He yawned. 'We are where we are.'

'That's real deep.'

'I'm going back to sleep, Poncho.'

We'd ended up in Discovery Bay, between Diamond Point and Cape George. I deduced that from the nearby landmasses. We had unknowingly moored about five miles to the south of an island that had a distinct boomerang shape. After going over the charts I reasoned that it had to be Protection Island, which (appropriately enough) had provided us with some shelter from the storm. It was a national park and even from a distance I could see big masses of sea lions, sprawled like slugs on the rocks and outcroppings. To the immediate south, Discovery Bay tapered off, leading to a dead-end. To continue our journey, we had to slip around the cape to the east, and down past Port Townsend, into Puget Sound.

Before setting off we made porridge on the campstove, and shared it with Shenzao. She managed to keep it down, along with some water. She looked much improved – though she still stank and her coat was caked in a layer of dried filth. We'd cleaned out the galley but we hadn't cleaned her. Jake wanted to take her on deck and hose her down properly, but I wouldn't allow it. The shores of Discovery Bay were lined with houses, and a number of them looked to be lived in year-round. I figured that it would be better to hold off until we found somewhere more secluded, so as not to draw attention to ourselves.

'I don't want to leave her all dirty like that for too long,' Jake said.

'The south side of Whidbey has a few bays. We'll stop there.'

He thought about that, chewing at his porridge, which was undercooked.

'How far?' he asked.

'Only a few hours.'

'Okay. But no more than that.'

Just before eight, we upped anchor and headed east, under a sky smeared red with wispy mare's tails. The thermometer in the wheelhouse window read two degrees above zero. The strait had stayed stormy: off to port the wind-whipped waves chased each other in rows, but we only skirted the edges of that, and it wasn't nearly so bad as it had been at its peak.

Since Shenzao seemed to be improving, and accustomed to her new abode (she no longer seemed interested in destroying it, anyhow), Jake rode up top with me. He brewed coffee on the Coleman and we drank that in the wheelhouse, with the heater cranked. I had that jittery, partially euphoric feeling you get before the real hangover kicks in. The previous night seemed like a sort of psychotic episode that we had endured and survived, somehow.

We rounded the point at Fort Warden State Park, and Puget Sound opened up before us, smooth and grey as wet clay in the morning light. Villages and refineries appeared along the coastline – that area being significantly more developed than the San Juans – and soon enough Port Townsend came into view. The waterfront had a pleasant, old-time feel, with redbrick buildings lining the shore, and rickety old wharves sticking out into the sound.

We navigated without a GPS map, depth sounder, or radar. This wasn't as difficult or dangerous as it had been at night but it still presented risks. It meant Jake had to act as our navigator. After breakfast I'd shown him the basics of charting and had set him to tracking our progress. By using the compass and sliderule, Jake could mark our position and plot a course. We bickered frequently about the direction to go – as was our way – but for the most part it worked well. Jake spent the morning hunched over the wheel-house table, pencil and ruler in hand, making adjustments.

As Port Townsend retreated behind us, he told me, 'You're off course, to the west.'

'Ferry up ahead.'

It was the Coupeville vessel: a little two-deck affair.

'Well, tell me next time,' he said.

'All right.'

He made an adjustment, muttering about my skills as a helmsman.

'You ever been this way before?' he asked.

'We only made it to the San Juans.'

We were about two thirds of the way to our destination. We didn't have to cross any more open water, but Puget Sound posed a different challenge. The sound is this long, maze-like series of channels, bays, and estuaries, running north–south for at least a hundred miles, past Everett, Seattle, and Tacoma. At the southern-most tip sits Olympia, and the Olympic mountain range. Getting there with functioning navigation equipment would have been fairly straightforward, but navigating by chart required more caution and concentration.

Then of course we faced the problem of docking and unloading the horse once we arrived, and not being seen while we did it. The best way to go about that, and the various options at our disposal, were the cause of much debate and bickering as we journeyed south, but it was a dead-end argument because so much depended on Maria.

'I'll have to phone her,' Jake said.

'You threw away the phone.'

'I threw away the Delaneys' phone. I still got my own phone.'

'And her number, apparently.'

He ignored that, and said, 'I'll tell her to come meet us.'

'She'll be surprised to hear we're on a damned boat.'

'I'll explain.'

'We won't be able to cruise right into Olympia.'

'Their ranch ain't in Olympia. It's outside of town.'

I hadn't thought of that, but of course it made sense. Nobody has a ranch in the middle of a city.

'The thing to do,' I said, 'is find a little isolated wharf or dock, in a secluded bay, that has vehicle access.'

'I hear you. Like the one in Port Moody, where we used to go swimming.'

'We can moor up at night, when we won't be seen. Unless you're aiming to ride the horse down to the ranch, we'll need a trailer to transport her. Will Maria have a trailer?'

'Don't rightly know.'

'Better find out, quick.'

He went down onto the front deck to call her. I kept an eye on him, out there. He held up his phone, searching for signal like a dowser feeling his way towards water. He found it eventually, and must have got hold of her, because he began to pace back and forth, talking and gesturing, in that animated way of his. Behind him the sound looked like a wide grey road, leading us south, and I had what you might call a premonition: I felt very confident we would at least get there, though what might transpire once we did was anybody's guess.

When Jake was done talking he returned to the wheelhouse and pushed open the door and blew on his hands in a jocular manner and made loud, unnecessary comments about how cold it was outside. By that I knew right away that something was amiss, or not right.

'What did she say?' I asked.

'She has a trailer. She'll meet us. We just got to let her know the place.'

'That's all?'

'Pretty much.'

'You had quite the chat.'

He reached for his coffee, and drained it before answering. 'My picture is all over the news, from that gas station.'

I'd actually forgotten. Out there on the boat, we'd been so far removed from all that, and focused entirely on each immediate obstacle that came our way. It's one of the greatest illusions of being at sea: it can make life on land, and all its accompanying ills, seem distant, trivial, and inconsequential. But of course that couldn't last. In a way the feeling I had then was akin to how I felt at the close of every herring season: the isolated world we had created on the boat was coming to an end.

'I guess we reckoned on that,' I said.

'You're not in the shot – in case you're worried about it.'

'I'm worried about you.'

'I'm fine. I'll be fine.'

'What about Maria? She fine, too?'

Jake took a deep breath and exhaled, puffing out his cheeks like a blowfish.

'She's not in a good place.'

'No shit. She's practically a moll.'

'What the hell is that?'

'You know. Like the girlfriend of a gangster. A gun moll.'

'Don't call her that.'

'You gonna defend her honour?'

'I don't know what you have against her. You used to worship her.'

'She ain't the same girl.'

'How do you know? Seen her lately?'

'I ain't seen her for years. Not since you got put away. Same as you. That's when she started hanging out with posers like Delaney, fucking around, really going crazy.'

'Sure – when you were supposed to be looking out for her.'

'I tried, man. But . . .'

I shook my head. My hangover was crawling over me and thinking about those times always made me sick, nauseous, shaky. It had all been such a mess, and he and I'd had the same argument – or versions of it – dozens of times. But Jake wasn't finished. He told me Maria had written him a letter. It had to be a letter, since (according to her) Delaney was a total control freak and kept track of her cellphone – the calls and texts – and wouldn't have liked her contacting Jake.

'Was this before or after they asked you to do the job?'

'What does it matter?'

I was thinking about what he'd revealed, back in Vancouver: about Maria needing help, and that her recommending Jake for the job had maybe been a way of asking for it.

'It might not.'

'It was before, okay?'

He told me that in the letter she'd said she worried about

what she'd got herself into, and also worried about her daughter. The life they led was no life for a little girl. That gave me pause. I'd almost forgotten about Maria's kid. After we'd broken apart, I'd heard about her being pregnant, and having a daughter, but by then I hadn't been in touch with her.

'Whose kid is it? Delaney's?'

'Maria's only been with him a couple years. The kid's older than that.'

'Like how old?'

'I don't know. I guess she'd be seven or eight, now.'

'Maybe it's yours. Maybe it's *your* love-child. Little baby Jake.'

'Fuck you. I was locked up when she got knocked up.'

'I'm only joking.'

'I know what you're doing. And I'm saying fuck you.'

'Fuck you too.' After a beat, I added, 'And the horse you came in on.'

A lot of what I said about Maria – both on the boat and before – I regret now. Of course, the way I was acting at the time (calling her a gangster's moll and making ill-judged jokes about her daughter) was based on the little I knew, and assumptions I had made in that regard. I couldn't be sure if Maria had recommended Jake for the job because he was an obvious patsy, or because – as he seemed to believe – she actually did need his help, and had seen this as an opportunity to get him down there. I suspected the former, and that Jake was deluded. As it turned out, the situation was far more complicated than that, and the same could be said of Maria's motivations. But that's always the case. We hardly ever behave in a manner that might be considered reasonable or rational, especially when love is involved, and family.

Chapter Twenty-Seven

THE SOUTHEAST PART OF WHIDBEY ISLAND (which isn't much of an island, seeing as a two-lane bridge connects it to the mainland) forms a point called Double Bluff, so-called because the peninsula ends in a camel-hump shape. On its southside, it encloses Useless Bay and Double Bluff park. I'd had that in mind as the place to give Shenzao a decent clean.

As we rounded the point, I got out the binoculars to assess the shoreline. The centre of the bay looked to be more developed than I'd expected: it contained a man-made lagoon, including a hotel and holiday resort, neither of which appeared on Albert's charts. But near our position, on this side of the bay, lay a stretch of parkland without any docks or dwellings: just a long swatch of grey beach and the rock face of the cliffs. There were no people in sight and no boats near us. The mid-morning waters were calm and it seemed a good place to stop. I dropped anchor about a hundred yards offshore and Jake went in to untether Shenzao.

We worked together to guide her out, with Jake holding the reins taut and me keeping a grip on her halter. Once we had her on deck she didn't seem skittish or anxious so much as eager and full of beans. She stamped her foot impatiently, and shook out her mane. She'd been cooped up in that filthy galley for thirty-six hours, whereas normally (so Jake said) she was accustomed to a morning warm-up, her daily run, and a cooldown with the hotwalker.

She tried to turn, and Jake held the lead. 'Easy girl,' he said. 'Lively.'

'All those oats.'

We tethered her to the powerblock for the seine handling crane, which seemed safe enough, and ran the hose. The gun nozzle had a dial you could twist to adjust the stream of water, from a steady jet to a soft fan. Jake set it to fan: he'd cleaned horses before and said it was best to start with the hooves, so she could get used to the sensations and the temperature. When the spray hit her there she stood steady and didn't seem bothered at all. He moved up her forelegs slowly. Beneath the water the crusty muck and grime melted away.

I leaned against the seine winch and watched. My brain felt all cotton-balled from the booze of the previous night and I wasn't as sharp as I might have been. The cold sea breeze helped some. I lit one of Jake's Du Mauriers and looked over towards the bay. I was in such a stupor that at first I didn't think much about the horses I saw trotting along the beach in the distance: about half a dozen of them. They cantered along in single file, all mounted by confident riders. Such a calming and pleasant sight, at that hour of morning.

Then, I course, I understood the problem.

I flicked my smoke at the water, and said, 'Jake.'

'What?'

'We got to get her back inside.'

He looked at me in irritation. 'I've barely started yet.'

I pointed. For the time being, the deckhouse shielded Shenzao, but they were riding closer at a good clip and pretty soon she would be in the eyeline of the riders. I assumed they had come from the resort, for a little leisurely ride on the beach.

'Shit,' Jake said.

He got hold of the lead and tried to turn her around. But Shenzao, she liked being on deck just fine. She nickered and leaned back, in that ornery way of hers, as if to say: like hell you're putting me in that cooped-up, dirty, grimy, stinking, no-account galley again.

'Come on, girl,' I said. I put my shoulder to her haunch – my old trick. No luck.

At that point those horses cantered into view along the beach. We panicked and started really hauling on her, trying to force her inside. That might have contributed some to what happened. But also, at that point, one of those horses on the beach just up and neighed. I don't know if it had seen our girl, or if it was simply neighing for the sheer joy of being out and about. But either way Shenzao heard. She raised her head, looking right at them.

You could see it coming.

She swung her body around to face the stern, hauling Jake

clean off his feet. I jumped in and did something typically ineffectual: I grabbed her round the neck in a clumsy bear hug, to
which she didn't take very kindly. She reared. She drew right up
on her hind legs, like you see cowboy horses do in films. Jake
lost his grip on the lead and I got thrown backwards into the
seine winch – cracking my head so hard I saw flashbulbs.

I'm not sure if Shenzao knew what she was doing, or if she
took the water to be a stretch of big blue-green field. Possibly
she recognized it as water and simply didn't give a hoot. She'd
had enough of us and the boat and she saw her kind over there
on the beach and she just reckoned she wanted to go join them.
She took four or five steps towards the stern, her hooves clip-clop-
ping on the teak deck, and leapt right over the gunnel, tucking
in her forelegs like a showhorse clearing a gate. She seemed to
hang above the water, suspended, and for a moment she resembled her namesake: this morning ghost, floating before us.

She landed with a concussive splash and an explosion of water
– so much that it backwashed over the deck – while Jake and I
stood there, just completely aghast.

We rushed to the stern and peered over. Shenzao did not flounder
at all but swam easily and diligently, her legs visible beneath the
surface, bent by refraction, churning away like a paddlewheel.
She'd gone under when she landed and her wet mane stuck flat
to her neck – almost like some kind of skunk-tailed mullet. She
headed towards the spot on shore where the riding party had
slowed to a halt, presumably to gawk at this madness.

Jake swore and cursed in the way you do when you are beyond
the realm of rational thought – just this long line of expletives,
spat out in quick succession. Then he started taking off his rain
slicker.

'What are you doing?'

'Going in after her.'

'Like hell. What will that do?'

'I can follow her to shore.'

It wasn't far. But the temperature had to be near zero.

'You'll freeze your nuts off.'

'Better that than lose her.'

'What am I supposed to do?'

He kept on stripping, right down to his boxers.

'Figure something out,' he said.

Then he let loose with this wild, lunatic cry and leapt headfirst over the gunnel. He came up gasping and sputtering but I've got to give him credit: he broke right into a front crawl and punched his way through the water. Shenzao had a twenty-yard head start. On shore, the riders walked their horses down towards the water, facing us. They could see the whole shebang, all right. One pointed at Jake. Another seemed to be holding up a camera, or a phone.

'Oh, Jesus Christ,' I said.

I started the winch to haul in the anchor, which cranked in laboriously, one chain-link at a time. Before it had even finished I bounded up to the wheelhouse, punched the ignition, leaned on the throttle, and wheeled the boat around. At first the *Lady* chugged real slow – because of all that extra drag – but when the anchor cleared the water she picked up steam.

There looked to be some kind of dock or wharf about halfway down the beach, and I headed in that direction. I couldn't just steer the boat into the shallows, and risk running her aground. I moved away from Jake and the horse at about a forty-five-degree angle, so the three of us formed a triangle. I drew roughly even with Shenzao and, looking over, saw her head rocking as she plodded through the water. Jake followed behind, maybe losing a little ground but powering stubbornly after her. It had become a very ludicrous three-way race.

Before Shenzao reached shore, I reached the dock. Only it wasn't actually a dock. It was a damned log jam: just a bunch of big old fir trees, lashed together, waiting for pick-up by a tug. But it was all I had. So I pulled alongside, cut the engine, and looped a single tie-line to the nearest log. By then, the horse had found her footing in the shallows. Further up the beach, a few riders dismounted. I had sense enough to grab myself a disguise: I took one of Evelyn's tea towels and tied that around my face like a bandana, to hide my identity.

Then I made my way to shore, which proved mighty difficult. The logs wobbled and had a tendency to turn, rotating back and forth, in a way that would have been comical if it wasn't so damn dangerous. Tottering along, I held my arms out like a tightrope walker, and somehow I avoided going under or breaking an ankle. I reached shore, jumped onto the sand, and sprinted pell-mell down the beach.

Up ahead, Shenzao had gone to join the other horses. One of the riders had taken hold of her lead. I hustled up, panting, just as Jake sloshed his way out of the shallows. He did this very casually, as if it was a perfectly normal day at the beach: wading out of the frigid water and right into the wintery air, dressed only in his plaid boxer shorts. He flicked his hair from his eyes and grinned: at me, at the riders, at the situation.

'Thanks for tending to our horse, here,' he said.

Most of the riders had dismounted. There were seven of them: all women dressed in jeans and winter jackets and riding boots, and also – oddly enough – pink tuques with the words 'Kelly's Hen Party' stitched across them. The woman holding Shenzao's lead had red hair and a pug nose and looked like she might be in charge. She looked pretty stern, anyway.

She said, 'Are you okay? What's going on?'

They were both good questions, and Jake considered them seriously.

'I think I'm okay,' he said. 'Just cold. Our horse, see, she jumped overboard.'

I nodded. 'She saw your horses and jumped overboard.'

The woman glanced over at me. I must have been a sight, with that damned tea towel wrapped around my face. The others began whispering and snickering among themselves.

'We didn't mean to disrupt your hen party,' Jake said. 'Are you Kelly?'

The woman blinked, wrongfooted. 'I'm Brenda.'

'Thanks, Brenda,' Jake said. 'We owe you. We can take our girl from here.'

He reached for the lead, and Brenda let it go reluctantly.

'Are you sure everything's all right?' she asked.

'Perfectly under control – as you can see.'

That made them laugh. And, to be honest, I had to laugh too.

'But you've got a horse,' she said, 'on a boat.'

Jake tucked his hands beneath his armpits and looked at me. For all his nonchalance his shoulders were shuddering uncontrollably, from the cold of the water and the wind-chill.

'What do you think, Poncho?' he asked. 'Should we tell them?'

'You told that kid.'

I figured we'd better stick to the same story, for simplicity's sake if nothing else.

'We stole her,' he said. 'We stole her to save her from a life of servitude and cruelty.'

'That's right,' I said. 'We're animal rights activists.'

That was more than a little hypocritical, considering what we'd put Shenzao through. But it was all we had, and in a way I wanted to believe in it myself: that we actually were the good guys, performing a generous and altruistic act.

Jake said, 'Her owners were running her into the ground.'

'We had to get her out, before she got injured.'

'That's amazing!' one of the women cried. She had a feather boa draped around her shoulders, and a bottle of champagne tucked in her saddle bag. She hadn't dismounted. I figured it had to be the bride, Kelly. She leaned towards us, swaying in the saddle. 'You're doing a great thing.'

'Thank you, ma'am,' Jake said. 'We like to think so. Now if you don't mind, we've got to get her back on board.'

Kelly said, 'Can we watch? Nobody will believe this happened at my hen party.'

'Don't see why not. Watch away.'

Jake led Shenzao around, and I went with them. We stood with our backs to the group for a moment.

'What are you doing?' I asked.

'I have no idea. Let's just load her up and get going.'

'That there's a log jam. She'll break a leg if we try to take her on there.'

'So what are you saying?'

'I'm saying we got no way to load her back on the boat.'

Jake lowered his voice. 'Goddammit, Poncho.'

'What do you want me to do?'

'You're the captain.'

I looked down the beach. At the stern of the boat, I could see the crane and seine winch.

'There might be a way,' I said.

*

I left Jake and Shenzao with the hen party and went to fetch the boat. I wobble-walked out across the log jam, cast off, and putt-ered back parallel to shore till I drew level with them. Pivoting around, I threw her in reverse and backed up as close to the beach as I dared without bottoming out. I had one thing working in my favour: the seabed sloped up at a steep angle, which meant the water got deep quickly. I dropped anchor, keeping the chain taut so the boat couldn't drift. Then I went down to the gear locker. The full-size seine net, which we used during the fisheries, would be far too heavy for what I had in mind, but on board Albert kept a smaller beach seine, just for our own purposes and recreational use.

I dragged that to the stern. On shore, the rest of the women had dismounted. They'd brought out some wine glasses, and cracked open Kelly's champagne. Even Jake had a glass. They'd lent him some clothing, too: to go with his boxer shorts, he now had a scarf, a fleece jacket, and one of the pink hen party tuques.

'Hey!' I shouted.

'You ready, Poncho?'

'I need help with this net.'

'Sorry ladies,' Jake said, 'but duty calls.'

He took off the scarf and jacket, but kept the tuque. He waded out to meet me. The water rose up to his neck. When he reached the stern, I unfolded the beach seine and dumped the bulk of it into the water. I told him to spread it out a ways, laying the net flat on the bottom. He took hold of two of the floats on the edge and began to tug. While he did that, I attached the handles of the beach seine to the hook on the single-fall on the boom.

'Is this how you catch herring?' he asked.

'It ain't at all how you catch herring. But it should work.'

'What now?'

'Now go get the horse.'

He went back up. Brenda had been holding his glass, and the horse's lead. He took both from her and knocked back the champagne, then strutted his way down to the surf with Shenzao. She didn't shy from the water. She'd had her taste of freedom and, I suppose, had realized she was very far from home and any place else she knew. Jake led her into position.

'Now back on out of there,' I said.

'I'll stay with her.'

'I don't think that's a good idea.'

'She's been through a lot.'

I threw up my hands, went over to the crane controls, and started the winch. The beach seine slowly tightened as cable fed through the boom. Shenzao grew antsy and restless but Jake held her and stroked her and talked to her. The floats of the beach seine cleared the surface, followed by the edges of the net, rising slowly, dripping water. The sides pressed in on Shenzao and Jake, squeezing them together, and lifted them up in a tangled, sodden mass. Essentially, we had rigged the beach seine into a makeshift cradle, to hoist the horse aboard.

On shore, the women watched this, in awe and hysterics. They all had their cameras and their phones out and we couldn't do anything about that. I just swivelled the crane over the deck, then lowered the load until they touched down. Jake lay squashed right up against Shenzao's shoulder, and one of the horse's legs was sticking out the bottom of the net. I made sure she came down on her side, with Jake atop her. A nifty trick.

'Jesus, Poncho,' he said. 'Get me out of here.'

I shut off the winch and went over there to disentangle them, but ended up having to cut them out with a penknife. I sawed around Jake first, and the two of us coaxed Shenzao to her feet.

A few strands of netting still clung to her back, and she shook herself to clear them. They slithered off and landed on deck, like the final flourish of a magic trick.

The ladies from the hen party applauded and cheered, as if the performance had been for their benefit. When the applause died down, Brenda called out, 'Who are you?'

Jake ran his hand down Shenzao's neck, and patted her shoulder.

'We're Poncho and Lefty, ladies. The notorious desperados.'

Kelly shouted, 'Will you marry me?'

'You wouldn't want to marry me, ma'am. I'm a no-good horse thief.'

'You're heroes!'

By that point Kelly, clearly, was pretty hammered.

'Show us your face!'

'Show us the rest of you!'

They kept joking with us and hollering at us as we led Shenzao into her galley. She seemed surprisingly calm, all things considered. Either she'd gotten that oat-pep out of her system, or found the experience too overwhelming to process. We tethered her to the galley table and returned to deck.

'Now ladies,' Jake called. 'I realize you'll want to put this on social media. But if we get caught, our girl will go back to her owners, where they work her practically to death. Do you mind sitting on that footage for a day or two – to give us a head start – before posting it?'

They murmured and nodded among themselves for a moment.

Brenda said, 'Okay, Lefty. It's a deal.'

Jake asked them if they wanted some Old Crow for their hen party, and they whooped in appreciation. He went to get one of the bottles I'd bought at Roche Harbor, and of course had to dive back in the water and swim it over to them. Once he got there, Kelly insisted on a photograph with him: she got him to kiss her, while all her friends snapped and filmed it.

Shenzao stuck her head out the galley door, and sort of snorted at his antics.

'I know, girl,' I said. 'He's just like that.'

She was gleaming white, and pristine-looking – shining with brine.

'Well,' I said, 'at least we got you clean.'

At that point, we had no idea if those women would keep their word about the footage. But they did. It came out eventually, of course, which partly triggered the final calamity down in Olympia. You can still see it, actually. It's online and easy to find. Once the trial started it went viral and racked up millions of hits. There's Jake, preening for the camera and flirting with the hen party. And in the background you can see me at the stern of the boat, standing nervously with this tea towel tied around my face. As it turned out, that towel didn't matter a whit: the guard at Roche Harbor could attest to the fact that I was aboard the boat, anyway. They were able to prove that, but not that I'd been at the stables, which was crucial. Otherwise I'd be telling this tale from jail.

Chapter Twenty-Eight

ONCE JAKE HAD FINISHED DALLYING with the hen party, we upped anchor and headed south, ploughing through the centre of Puget Sound. A north wind blew at our backs, and we had the currents, too: the narrow channels and estuaries became slow-moving rivers with the flux of the tide. I cranked the throttle and we managed a steady fifteen knots, ground speed. Low, wide swells rolled across the sound, and we loped over them with an easy rocking motion.

At the rate we were going, we'd reach Olympia by evening – but we still didn't yet know where we would dock.

Jake crouched in front of the heater, still wearing boxers and his hen-party tuque and nothing else. I told him he ought to go get changed, and to fetch the charts while he was at it.

'Aye-aye, Captain.'

'I'm gonna miss you calling me that.'

He went down below, leaving me at the helm. South of Whidbey Island the sound opened up, stretching to eleven or twelve miles across. To the west, the Olympic Mountain range loomed over the coastline. We'd had a view of those mountains from afar since setting out but they now dominated the horizon, rising in a daunting wall above the treeline. Snow and glacial ice coated the peaks, aside from the steeper faces, which the wind had scoured clean and black as mica.

When Jake returned he'd pulled on some jeans and a shirt, but was still wearing his hen party tuque. I ribbed him about that, asking if he really thought Kelly and her friends would wait to post their videos.

'They said they would,' he said.

'Better hope they do.'

'You were all covered up.'

'You weren't.'

'Hell, I've already been identified.'

'Nobody knows you're in the States. It'll give the whole game away.'

He waved that off, but I could tell he hadn't taken it into account.

'Well,' he said, 'we better deliver her before that happens.'

'The Delaneys won't be happy.'

'I'll deal with the Delaneys.'

He didn't explain how. He just slapped those charts across my chest. I asked him to take the wheel (the first time I'd allowed that since his little mishap at the border) and laid the charts out across the table. While Jake kept us on course, I hunkered down and studied the terrain near Olympia, a sizeable city situated at the end of a long channel called Budd Inlet. Warehouses, marinas, and industrial complexes lined the surrounding waterfront. It would be too exposed for what we needed to do. But on either side of Budd Inlet two other channels branched off: Henderson to the east, and Eld to the west. Together the three inlets appeared on the map like the tongs of a twisted fork. Both Eld and Henderson looked more secluded and less developed, and Eld seemed to have a public dock with vehicle access.

Jake said, 'Hey – Poncho.'

I looked up. I expected something to be going wrong, since that always seemed to be the case. But thirty feet away, sleek grey shapes were arcing in and out of the water.

'I'll be damned,' I said.

'I haven't ever seen dolphins up close.'

'You still haven't. Those are porpoises. Harbour porpoises.'

'Hand me the binoculars, will you?'

I passed them over and he trained them on the porpoises, scrolling the focus ring with his forefinger. They seemed to have noticed us too, and kept pace off the starboard side in that playful way they have. With each jump they cleared the water in bursts of spray, their dorsal fins cresting, and then nosed back under, real elegantly.

'Are they common or what?' he asked.

'They ain't uncommon.'

'Damned pretty creatures.'

'Almost as pretty as your ladies from the hen party.'

He lowered the binoculars, and grinned his gap-toothed grin.

'Were they lookers? I didn't notice.'

'You and Kelly were getting pretty frisky.'

'All right, all right,' he said, 'I was hamming it up a little. But hell, brother, I had to do something. And I've been at sea for too long. I'm feeling all lustful and libidinous.'

I snorted and started laughing, and pointed out that we'd only been on the boat for a couple of days, whereas typically during fishing season we'd be out for two or three weeks. I told him about the deckhand Albert had caught jerking off in the head, and how he'd dunked the poor kid overboard. We had a good laugh about that.

Then Jake said, 'A few weeks is still nothing compared to a few years in prison.'

That sobered us up, some. Jake hadn't ever really talked about his time in prison. We were both still staring out at those porpoises, riding sidecar with us, and something about that made it easier for me to ask if it was as messed up in prison as they say: with the gangs and the violence and the rape and whatever. Jake shrugged, both nonchalant and uncomfortable.

'It ain't like they make out. I didn't have to deal with too much shit, anyway. But it might have been a lot worse, without the Legion. I do owe the Delaneys that much.' He turned and offered me the binoculars, adding, 'And that was only because of Maria, you know. Why the hell else would they have had my back? She asked them to take me in.'

I accepted the binoculars, and stood for a time holding them and fiddling with the neck strap and not knowing what to do or say.

Jake pointed to the pod and said, 'Have a look.'

I trained the lenses on the porpoises. Jake's eyesight is the same as mine, so I didn't have to adjust the focus ring at all. The animals stood out in stark clarity, as vivid as a close-up in some nature show. I could clearly see their glossy-black eyes and smug little smiles.

I said, 'The two of you ain't no good together.'

'She looked after me. I got to do the same for her.'

'We don't even know if she needs that, or wants it.'

'We'll know soon enough.'

'First it was about the debt, then it was about the money. Now it's all about her.'

'It's a goddamn complicated situation.'

'Maybe you got to make up your mind, little brother.'

'Maybe you got to accept it ain't clear-cut, big brother.'

I let it go. One of those damned porpoises gave off this high-pitched whistle, gleeful and mischievous. I watched them for a minute longer. Each time they breached the surface, the water seemed to roll off their backs, slipping so easily from their rubber-slick skin.

The wind coming down from the north brought an Arctic front with it. The temperature dropped to below zero, and the outside air had that crisp, distinct scent of impending snow.

Jake stayed at the helm. He couldn't stop shivering some from his stint in the water, so I went down below deck to fix us another coffee and check on Shenzao. I wouldn't say she was doing fine, but she was doing better: she'd eaten more oats and drunk all her water and if anything her jaunt overboard seemed to have mellowed her some. While I brewed our coffee I replenished her water and chatted to her, talking her through our ideas for returning to land. She merely snorted, as sceptical as ever about our deluded schemes involving her.

As the day progressed the coastline changed, slowly becoming more built up, more industrial. On the western shore rows of smokestacks pointed at the sky like rifle barrels, leaking gun-smoke pollution, and further along I could see cranes and wharves, and also a refinery yard covered in sulphur, piled up high in yellow pyramids, appearing pure and peculiar as fool's gold. The air took on the stink of chemicals and burning petroleum.

Boat traffic increased, too. Tankers and cargo ships powered north towards Juan de Fuca (the sight of them raising uneasy memories of our close-call) and ferries chugged back and forth from Bremerton, on the mainland, to Bainbridge Island. By midday we'd reached Elliott Bay and Seattle, which lay to the east. We stayed ten miles offshore so only glimpsed the city from afar: a colourful jumble of blocks and oblongs, crammed together along the waterfront. And on the left side rose the distinct tower of the Space Needle, capped by its observation deck, which made it look top-heavy and precarious as all hell, primed to fall.

'Maybe we should roll on into town for lunch,' I said.

'Sure. Tether Shenzao on the dock.'

'You could do some more interviews.'

'Got to please our fans.'

'Poncho and Lefty take Seattle by storm.'

'Animal rights activists and outlaws spotted at Space Needle.'

South, the sound looked even busier. Behind the various vessels you could see the streaks of wake-water, trailing like streamers. Tacoma lay in that direction and a fair amount of boat traffic ran between there and Seattle. Despite Jake's confidence in the hen party's integrity, heading straight on through all that activity didn't seem like the most sensible thing. But to the west a separate channel branched off, between Vashon Island and the mainland. It ran in a straighter line and would cut Tacoma out of our journey entirely, and appeared to be a more discreet route.

I told Jake to steer in that direction while I plotted the course.

The channel (called Vashon Channel) would take us all the way down to Point Defiance National Park, and from there it would only be a few more hours to Olympia. I told Jake about the dock I'd sussed in Eld Inlet. We traded places again and he took a look at the map. He agreed that it seemed all right but said that we ought to check with Maria.

'Sure. Call the boss.'

'She knows the area, wingnut.'

Like before, he went out on deck to talk to her. This time he ducked behind the base of the crane, so I couldn't keep an eye on him, and gauge his body language. I was left in suspense and uncertainty until he clambered back up the ladder, a quarter hour later. By then we had passed Blake Island, and closed in on the entrance to Vashon Channel.

He came in looking worryingly cheerful, with a bounce to his step, and announced that the plan had changed, in a casual way that he damn well knew would irk me.

'Who changed it?'

'Maria said Henderson Inlet is better.'

'Better how?'

'There's an old abandoned pier, there.'

'What about my plan, and Eld?'

'Apparently fishermen use that public dock in Eld.'

'Eld looks less built up on the map.'

'She said it isn't, and she's the one who lives there.'

'Sure. She's in charge.'

'What are you all het up about?'

'We haven't even seen her, and she's already calling the shots, changing our plan.'

'It wasn't much of a plan.'

'It don't matter.'

'I'll call her back, if it means that much to you.'

'Like hell.'

We steamed on, ignoring each other for a time while we entered the mouth of Vashon Channel. On both sides the land rose up sharply from the water: a glacial gorge lined with endless rows of spiky ponderosa pines. It was like steering into a giant iron maiden.

Jake asked, 'How much further?'

'A few hours. But I don't want to dock while it's light.'

'Maria said the sooner the better.'

'And I say dusk. I'm the captain, okay?'

Jake started laughing and – after a moment of trying to act superior – I did too. I was the captain, all right. The captain of a stolen boat, transporting a stolen horse, and an ex-con who had snuck across the border, claiming to be outlaws doing it for noble reasons: and the whole lot of us soon to be wanted by authorities in two countries.

'Tell Maria we'll call when we arrive,' I said.

Chapter Twenty-Nine

MARIA HAD CHOSEN A PLACE called Chapman Bay, five miles down Henderson Inlet on the western side. We arrived at ten past four, just as dusk settled over the water, staining it dark. During the approach I'd slowed down our speed by a few knots to delay our arrival, and if Jake had noticed this deliberate trick he didn't hassle me about it.

In the glassy water you could see the ripples pushed just ahead of our bow. A cold front had settled on southern Washington and brought along with it some dark, lead-bellied snow clouds. A nature reserve surrounded the entire bay, and copses of hemlock and alder stood out all along the shore. The south side of the bay curved out further than the north, and from that point a long wooden pier extended into Henderson Inlet, running northwest, parallel to the mainland. You could see it from miles away. I had no clue what it had been used for but it looked like it might have been a railway bridge at one time. As it turned out, a year after all this happened the US government tore up much of the pier, since it was coated with creosote (a wood preservative that's harmful to waterfowl) and had become toxic as it deteriorated. But at that time, though abandoned and out of use, the pier was still fit for purpose. For our purpose, anyways. I had to grant Maria that.

The landspit from which the pier extended had a small cabin on it. Next to the cabin I thought I could see somebody waiting, but we were still a mile offshore, and in the twilight the figure could have been a stump or a tree or a shadow.

'You better call,' I told Jake.

He got out his cellphone and redialled Maria. This time he didn't step outside to talk to her, so I was actually privy to their conversation for a change.

'We're all ready to dock,' he told her. 'Are you here?'

Apparently she was, since he said, 'Yeah. And bring a light if you got one. We might need it for the horse.'

The pier rested on wooden pilings, which held it a foot or two above the water at the current tide. As we drew near it, I steered alongside the pier and cruised parallel to it, with the throttle low. I saw no need to dock this far out; the charts showed that the bay was deep and docking closer in would save a long walk down the pier with the horse. A few bats circled and flitted low over the water, skimming for bugs, and from one of the pilings I saw the long, elegant shadow of a heron take flight, startled by our presence and the intrusion.

The figure I'd seen by the cabin moved down the beach. It had to be Maria, though from that distance she was still just a shadow in a raincoat. A hundred yards from shore, I cut the throttle and told Jake to put out the fenders. As soon as he had, I used the stern thrusters to push us against the pier. Jake hopped over the gunnel with a line to tie us up (still not doing it like I'd showed him) and when that was secure I cut the engine and the pervasive silence sounded unnerving: it signalled the end of our time at sea, and a return to land.

I joined Jake on the pier and we walked down it together, side-by-side. In places dry rot had eaten away the planks, but those that remained felt solid. Even so I crept along cautious as a cat. My body had adjusted to the rhythms of the water and the pier seemed too stable and unforgiving in comparison. The figure in the raincoat started out from shore to meet us, and something about the walk, the gait, struck me as familiar: it was her, all right. A light came on – she'd brought the flashlight Jake had mentioned, and shone the beam over the pier to light her way. Every so often she'd tilt it up and the glare would catch us full-on, and in those moments I had the impression of a train coming right at us, ready to mow us down.

I didn't get a clear look at her until we met up, halfway down the pier. Her light created a circular pool on the pier at our feet, and lit up our faces from below. I hadn't seen Maria in years – not since Jake's final parole hearing – but in the harsh winter twilight she didn't look all that different. In my ignorance I had expected her life and habits to have taken a toll, and for her to be some hag-like version of her younger self. But she was still Maria, and that was disorientating, and also oddly stirring, heartening. I can't say whether Maria is beautiful by any normal standards. She doesn't have a face that would launch a thousand ships (as the saying goes) but she's always had something else. And it was enough to launch one ship, at least: ours.

She said, 'The notorious Harding Brothers.'

'Poncho and Lefty,' Jake said. 'At your service, ma'am.'

She hugged Jake, folding her arms behind his neck, and after she did the same to me. Beneath her coat she felt as she always had: both strong and fragile, like a glass statue. I'd intended to keep her at arm's length but of course that was impossible. Already, holding her on that dock, I felt my animosity towards her dissipating like wisps of smoke.

'I can't believe he roped you into this,' she said to me.

Jake said, 'He came of his own volition.'

'Is that how you got the boat?'

'We stole the boat,' Jake said.

'We borrowed the boat,' I said.

'You're both crazy.'

'Since we couldn't cross the border, we had to think of something – or we wouldn't have been able to make our delivery.'

She looked at him. It was almost as if she'd forgotten about the horse.

'Where is it?'

'She's in the galley.'

'I've got the trailer hitched to my truck.'

'Well – we better hop to it.'

Jake and I led Shenzao out onto deck, and she came amicably enough. In the evening cold she stood still and alert, her tail twitching, her breath steaming. She looked travel-weary and bedraggled, but as ever the wan glow of her coat had a mesmeric quality, standing out so starkly against the shadows and the dark. Maria coolly scrutinized the horse from the pier, from afar. She made no move to help and didn't look particularly impressed.

'So this is what all the fuss is about,' she said. 'Another horse.'

'She's one of a kind.'

'That's what he said about the last one.'

'The last horse he stole?'

'Normally he buys them. He's got a bunch of them.'

I said, 'I don't get it.'

'It's a fad,' Jake said. 'A gangland fad.'

Maria shone her flashlight across Shenzao, panning the beam from her head to her haunch. She said, 'They breed them and race them and show them off to each other.'

Jake added, 'Or steal them from each other to ransom them back, apparently.'

We led Shenzao towards the ramp, in our now customary way, with Jake holding the lead and me gripping the halter. On first try, she became reluctant and resisted, much to Maria's amusement. Then Jake tried a trick – something he'd seen at the track. Rather than tug and haul and pull, and get engaged in the kind of tug-o-war we'd so often partaken in, he backed the horse up, walked her in a brief circle and then led her towards the ramp at a trot. He stepped up first and Shenzao hot-footed it behind him. Since the gunnel was on a level with the pier, they could simply walk off the other side, and the whole process looked very simple and elegant.

'That's how it's done,' he said.

'Bravo,' Maria told him.

She'd taken a step back to give him and the horse room.

'Maria, meet our girl Shenzao,' he said.

'Me and horses don't get on so well.'

'You live on a damn ranch.'

'I've never been one for animals. You know that.'

'I figured that might have changed.'

Shenzao huffed – as if she sensed a certain lack of hospitality on Maria's part.

Maria said, 'Sam will love her, though.'

'Sam?'

'Samantha. My daughter. She's a regular cowgirl.'

'Sounds like my kind of kid.'

She laughed, and shook her head, and then started walking away down the pier.

'Come on,' she called back. 'I'm freezing my ass off.'

Jake watched her go for a moment.

'How do you like that?' he asked. 'I bring her a goddamned stolen racehorse, on a stolen boat, all the way across the sea, from another country, and this is the thanks I get.'

'So much for your hero's welcome.'

We followed Maria down the pier, walking on either side of the horse to keep her hemmed in. Maria waited for us to catch up to her, then used her light to guide us the rest of the way. Shenzao's hooves resounded on the deck, echoing out across the water, and the old planks creaked and groaned beneath us. We formed this odd procession, with Maria in front like the lantern-bearer. It all felt solemn and ritualistic and significant.

Halfway to shore, something cracked and I stumbled, crying out in terror and surprise. The commotion startled the horse, who cross-stepped sideways and whinnied. Jake struggled to control her. Nobody really knew what had happened, including me.

Once he'd settled Shenzao, Jake said, 'What the hell?'

Maria shone the light on me. A plank had given way beneath

me and my leg had plunged through to the knee. I tried to pull it up, and set off a stinging pain in my calf. I blinked into the light, sheepish and helpless.

'Damned plank gave way,' I said.

And of course instead of sympathy I got only laughter.

'Good old Poncho,' Jake said.

'It hurts like hell.'

'Let me help.'

'No, no,' I said. 'Go on and load her in the trailer first.'

'You sure?'

'She's skittish. You got to hold onto her anyway.'

They turned and continued leading her. I watched the beam of light and Shenzao's shape recede from me, then turned to the task of freeing myself. The splintered plank had folded down, pincering my leg between the broken halves. I pried at the wood, pulling it apart, so I could ease my leg up and out. The back of my calf burned and when I stood up it hurt like a son of a gun. I figured the wood had scraped up the skin some. I hobbled back towards the boat, limping in this lame and lopsided way. I had the notion of cleaning up the galley, before heading over to a local marina to pay for moorage. In addition, I was feeling foolish of course, and preferred to nurse my foolishness in private for a time.

On board I cleared the tarps from the galley and got out the mop and bucket. I didn't fill the bucket, though. I just stood holding the mop like a hockey stick. I could swab the veneer of piss and manure one last time but I couldn't do anything about the buckled linoleum, the splintered cupboards, the holes in the wall, the broken window, the hoof marks on deck. The boat was more than Albert's pride and joy: it was his sanctuary, and what I'd done amounted to a kind of sacrilege. All that hadn't fully registered while we were at sea, and the boat had felt like mine, but of course I'd only been playing at being captain.

I heard footsteps and through the galley window saw the flashlight coming back down the dock. I went outside. Jake directed the light at me and I shielded my eyes from the glare.

'What are you doing?' he asked.

'What I can.'

'We need to get going.'

'I have to moor the boat.'

We'd passed a marina near the mouth of Henderson Inlet, and I told him my plan was to go back there and pay for a few nights' moorage, so the boat would be ready to pick up on my return.

Jake said, 'We don't have time for that. I don't want to hang around here with the horse in the damned trailer.'

I took a step towards him, all worked up and ready to argue, but the flare of pain made me wince and he must have seen that: he directed the light towards my feet.

'You're walking wounded.'

'It's fine.'

'Your jeans are bloody.'

I looked. The back of my pant leg was torn and through that you could see that the skin was torn, too. A three-inch gash showed in the fat of my calf, the skin all blood-slick and gleaming.

'Ah, hell,' I said. 'I'm bleeding like a stuck pig, here.'

Jake hopped aboard and crouched down to take a look.

'That don't look good.'

'I couldn't tell, in the dark.'

'We need to get that seen to.'

'No way. No doctors.'

I said it very dramatically, like I'd been gutshot.

'I just mean disinfect it, zippernuts.'

'After I take care of the boat.'

'You can't moor up and pay fees looking like that.'

'If we leave it here, it'll be found and reported.'

Jake stood still for a time. I couldn't see his face. I guess he was trying to think of a way to say it. 'It don't matter now, man. In a few days those ladies will be posting footage of it, if they haven't already, and it'll be found and reported whether it's docked or left here.'

'Goddamn this to hell.'

'If we had any sense, we'd scupper it.'

'Scuttle it.'

'You know what I mean – then it wouldn't be found. Not for a while at least.'

'That's not going to happen.'

I told him I still had to take it back. I had to take it back to the Westco plant and clean it up properly and get some repairs done, and somehow I had to do all that before Albert and Evelyn and Tracy returned from the cabin next weekend. Jake let me go on like that for a time until I tapered off, sputtering like a candle.

Jake said, 'Even if you did all that, he'd see the difference.'

'I'll be dead to him. He won't ever forgive me.'

'If that's the truth, then he ain't what you thought. He ain't family.'

I took a step, and winced from the snakebite of pain. Seeing that, Jake took my arm and I allowed him to help me up the ramp to the pier. We walked like that, with me leaning on him, as if we were taking part in a three-legged race. He made some joke about my little accident but I didn't laugh. My bitterness was only partly to do with betraying Albert. It was also connected to all that had occurred on the water, and the sense I'd had out there that I had been for a time the kind of older brother Jake wanted, and the kind he'd needed after Sandy's death. But as soon as we stepped off the boat, and joined Maria, I'd reverted to my old ways: clumsy and useless as a landlubber, as Albert would have said.

Chapter Thirty

MARIA HAD A FIRST AID kit in the truck. They set me on the ground in front of the headlights and she used the scissors to cut away my jeans around the wound. The kit included a bottle of iodine and she splashed that over my calf, which stung like a son of a gun and stained the skin ochre-yellow. After patting it dry, she slapped a butterfly bandage on it, wrapped the whole area in gauze, and held it all in place with strips of surgical tape.

'That'll do as a field dressing,' Maria said, standing up.

'You're quite the nurse, these days,' Jake said.

'I've had to patch a few wounds.'

'Guess that comes with the territory, dating a gangster.'

'Don't start, Jake.' To me, she said, 'You need a hand getting in?'

They helped me around the side of the truck: a big GMC Sierra, burgundy red, with a chrome grill and running boards. Attached to the back was a battered aluminium tow-trailer – the kind designed for transporting livestock. Maria and Jake had already loaded Shenzao in there and she seemed to have settled well. She wasn't kicking or bucking or causing a ruckus, at least.

Maria flipped the front seat forward and with Jake's help I crawled sideways into the back. The truck had those small rear seats that face each other across the cab. I pulled myself into a sitting position, and Jake hoisted my bad leg to rest on the seat opposite.

'I'll get blood on the seat,' I said.

'Forget it,' Maria said. She leaned on the doorframe, and winked. 'It's Pat's.'

'He won't care?'

'I hope he does.'

She slid into the driver's seat and turned the key. The engine, stereo, and heater came on all at once, in this bewildering mix of noise. Jake complimented her, sardonically, on her choice of music (it was old-school gangster rap) and in response she twisted the volume dial: first to max, to mess with him, and then all the way to off. We sat without talking while we waited for the windscreen to clear and the silence was not what you would call comfortable.

Maria pulled out a pack of Marlboro and offered one to us.

'You still smoke menthol?' Jake asked.

'Take it or leave it.'

He took one, and so did I. She passed her lighter around and we all lit up. The funny mint-stink of the things filled the cab. On her first exhale, Maria said, 'I'm surprised you remember.'

'I remember a lot of things,' Jake said.

'There are beers under the seat,' Maria said, and put the truck in gear.

'You want a beer, invalid?' Jake asked.

'Pass her back.'

She'd bought us Pabst Blue Ribbon. We'd always drunk Pabst with her, ever since we'd been twelve or thirteen and just getting started. I appreciated the thought, and the first sip tasted metallic and tangy and comfortingly familiar.

We headed out along a gravel access road, beneath a canopy of spruce, skirting the southern estuary of Chapman Bay. Dusk had faded into night and through the trees the water glistened blackly. I looked back through the rear windscreen and caught one last glimpse of the *Lady*, floating abandoned in the dark, before we rounded a bend and she slid from view. We came to a gate, which Jake hopped out to open. At the intersection on the other side we turned right onto a strip of blacktop, which led us away from the nature reserve. Telephone poles appeared at the roadside, and soon enough the trees began to give way to fields and farmhouses. The outskirts of North Olympia.

A few minutes later we reached a two-lane highway and from there headed south.

'How far's the ranch?' Jake asked.

'About eighty miles.'

'An hour and a half or so?'

'More like two. The roads aren't good.'

'Out in the boonies, then.'

'It's his bolthole.'

'For when things get heaty, eh?'

Maria didn't rise to the bait, this time, and Jake let it drop. He turned to ask me, 'How you holding up back there, Poncho?'

'I could use another beer.'

Jake yanked one from the yoke and handed it to me.

'Does it still hurt?' Maria asked.

'I hurt all over. I'm a mess. I wrenched my shoulder getting her out of the stable, got slammed into the gunnel in a storm, and now this.'

She asked, 'What storm?'

'A hell of a storm.'

'I didn't know about that. I've seen the footage in the stable, and at the gas station.'

Jake asked, 'How'd we look?'

'Like a couple of crooks in a *Scooby-Doo* episode.'

'Ah, hell,' I said.

'At least your face was hidden,' she said, ashing her smoke out the window. 'Jake's a wanted man. An ex-con and horse thief and now a smuggler and an illegal alien to boot.'

She said it affectionately, as if he'd done it all for her. And I suppose he had.

He said, 'Wait'll you see the footage from the boat.'

'In the storm?'

'There's no footage of the storm. We were fighting for our lives in the storm. The footage is of when the damned horse jumped overboard to join this hen party yesterday.'

We told her a little about that – exaggerating for effect, though of course it wasn't the kind of story that needed much exaggeration. We got her laughing pretty good: Maria had this full-bellied laugh, which always sounded genuine and not at all put-on or polite. I had missed that laugh. Stirring it up had always been a goal of ours, when hanging around her.

'You're the worst criminals I've ever met,' she said.

The funny thing was, relating our shenanigans in that way made me feel better about all the no-good things we'd done. I suppose that's part of the telling: sharing a story, even a story full of your own stupidity and mistakes and bad decisions, lightens your burden a little.

We circled the outskirts of Olympia and got onto the I5, heading south. From the highway, like so many American highways, you couldn't see much except walls of trees, cedar and alder in this case, and guardrails hemming in those long stretches of blacktop. Every so often, signs advertising gas stations and fast food and rest areas swept by: those blue signs with square logos on them. After one such sign Jake said, 'Man I could use me some grub.'

We hadn't eaten much that day. Just cold soup and bread for lunch on the boat.

'It's only another hour to the ranch,' Maria said.

'I got to take a leak, too.'

'Go in your can.'

'That's cold.'

'I don't want to stop, with the horse in the trailer.'

'She's right,' I said. 'Remember the gas station.'

'Yeah – when you should have been watching Shenzao.'

'I was watching her. I watched her kick the damned doors wide open.'

That exit came and went, but a few minutes later another one appeared. Jake began cajoling Maria again, in that convincing way of his, assuring her we could pull over without taking any risks, and that he would just duck in discreetly.

Maria said, 'Somebody might recognize you.'

'This one ain't even a restaurant. Just a rest stop.'

'No.'

He grabbed the wheel, and started steering us towards the exit.

'Goddammit, Jake,' she said, and elbowed him back.

But she took the turning. The rest stop had a parking lot and a concrete toilet block, and around the other side of the block a serving counter set into the wall – the kind of snack shack you might see at the beach, or a drive-in movie theatre.

'Let me go,' I said. 'Nobody will recognize me.'

'Your leg's covered in blood.'

'Oh, yeah.' I held up my beer, toasting my own absentmindedness. 'I forgot.'

'I'll go,' Maria said. 'You jokers stay here.'

'Forget it,' Jake said. 'I got to take a leak anyway.'

She tried to argue with him but he hopped out of the cab, performing a flamboyant little jig as he started across the parking lot. She shook her head and met my gaze in the rear-view – her eyes narrowing like a cat's.

'Your goddamned brother hasn't changed a bit.'

I was used to that, too. She would get mad at him, through me. Just like Sandy.

'He's putting it on, for you.'

For a minute we waited in silence, with me sitting directly behind her. Over the seat all I could see of her was the swirl of hair on the crown of her scalp, but now that we weren't smoking I thought I could smell her: this citrus perfume that was as familiar as the menthol.

'Does your leg still hurt?' she asked.

'It hurts some.'

'I forgot – there's Tylenol in the kit.' She still had it at her feet. She leaned forward to root around inside it, then sat back up and handed me a pill bottle. I shook out two tabs and washed them down with beer. She asked me if that felt better and I said that it did, as if the painkillers had taken effect immediately.

'How about you?' I asked. 'How are you feeling?'

She asked me what I meant and I said I didn't know. I was getting a bit wobbly by then, and I was thinking of that letter she'd sent to Jake. If she really had sent him a letter.

'I made my bed,' she said, 'and I'm lying in it.'

'That don't sound too positive.'

'I don't mean it to be.'

'What about your daughter?'

'She's a joy. She's sometimes all the joy I got.'

She twisted in her seat so she could see me. She tried to smile but it didn't look right.

'Thank you for coming, Timmy.'

She was the only person who could call me that, without getting on my nerves.

I said, 'Somebody has to look out for him.'

'You've always been the good one.'

'I don't know if there is a good one, when it comes to us.'

Jake came trotting back from the snack bar with a white paper bag in one hand. When he hopped in the front he brought with him the smell of hot grease and fried food. He blew on his hands and said, 'Goddamn, it's cold out there.'

'Anybody see you?' I asked.

'Course they did. SWAT team's on its way.'

'Hope it was worth it,' Maria said.

'Well, they had burritos.'

He sounded childishly happy about that. We ate on the go, with Jake doling out food once Maria had us back on the highway. It could have been any other road trip: the same as the ones we'd taken in our teens and twenties, when the two of them were a couple and I was always along for the ride. The cosiness of the cab, the familiar warmth and menthol smoke, our steam-breath on the windows, the banter and barbs: all that felt the same, and fated.

Chapter Thirty-One

THE BURRITOS AND BEERS AND Tylenol and the dull rocking of the truck lulled me into a doze, and when I woke up the landscape had changed. Low-lying hills spread out around us, and up ahead I could see streetlamps, flat-roofed buildings, and a few gas station signs hovering like flying saucers: a town, of some sort. Jake and Maria were staring straight ahead and talking to each other in terse, intense tones. Arguing under the radar, as it were.

I heard Jake say, 'That's the dumbest thing you ever did.'

'You don't know the whole story.'

'I know what you told me.'

'I haven't told you everything.'

'That's for sure.'

'Lighten up, lovebirds,' I said. I made a big to-do about easing my wounded leg down, and leaned forward between them. Jake had another beer in hand and Maria had one too – in her cupholder. 'The reunion only just got going and you're already bickering.'

'You fell asleep,' Maria said, accusingly.

'Yeah,' Jake said. 'What did you expect?'

That was one of my roles: I'd always been an integral part of their relationship. The tempering influence that allowed them to connect, and made them treat each other decently.

I yawned and asked, 'Where are we?'

'Elma,' Maria said.

'Where the hell is Elma?'

'On the edge of Capitol State Forest.'

'I don't know where that is, either.'

'Southwest of Olympia.'

Just before Elma we turned off and descended a long off-ramp, reaching a junction and underpass opposite a building materials yard. Towards town, road signs advertised hot food and hotels and something called the Summit Pacific Medical Center, but we turned in the opposite direction, beneath the underpass, heading south on a smaller highway – the 12. The town fell away behind us. Freshly laid tarmac rolled out in a long strip between fallow fields on the right and tree-covered hills on the left: the state park that Maria had mentioned.

'We getting close?' I asked.

'Only about fifteen more miles,' Maria said. 'But the last bit is rough going.'

At the next exit we turned off, and our headlights pulled us along a single paved road that wound tortuously through the woods. The ground glittered with frost and old snow lay in dirty clumps at the roadside. Out my window all I could see were the trunks of passing alders, like a rough-hewn palisade, hemming us in and channelling us towards our destination.

We passed a US national parks sign and a few miles on the road dissolved into a dirt track, bumpy as hell and riddled with potholes. Maria kept right on going, riding it out. The rattling hurt my leg and I got worried about the horse. I was about to say something but Jake got to it first.

'Easy on the gas,' he said. 'We got precious cargo back there.'

Maria took a swig of beer and said, 'And I got a nine-year-old at home alone.'

Jake said, 'A nine-year-old?'

'I told you – my daughter. You forget already?'

'I just thought she was younger than that.'

'You lost a lot of years.'

The track had a steady gradient and occasionally doubled back on itself. Maria did ease off a little, for the next ten or fifteen minutes, until we came to the base of a steep hill.

Then she said, 'Hold onto your horses.'

She dropped into first and took a run at it and we rattled up the hill, crested a rise, and levelled out on a kind of mountain plateau, cleared of trees. The driveway – or what served as one – ran a hundred yards further, past a wooden barn and rundown outbuildings. Beyond that loomed the main house, big and dark and abandoned-looking.

'This is it,' Maria said. 'It's a work in progress.'

As we drove closer, our headlights swept across the front: a sprawling ranch-style house with two storeys and a porch out front. The porch sat maybe four feet off the ground, but there was no railing. It looked half-finished. The rest of the house had a similar feel. The wooden siding was painted in a bright orange undercoat, and some of the windows still had that protective plastic sheeting on them that they peel off after the glass is installed.

Maria pulled up in front of the porch and yanked on the handbrake and killed the engine. She took a final swig of beer – tilting the can back to drain it – and tossed the empty out the window.

'Home sweet home,' she said.

We got out. We'd climbed a fair way from sea level and you could tell: the air had a bitter chill to it. Wind sliced right through my jacket and made the surrounding trees shiver.

'I'm going to check on Sam,' Maria said.

'What about the horse?'

She pointed back the way we'd come, towards the outbuildings. 'Stable's that-a-way.'

'Is there a stall for her?'

'Should be. I don't go down there much.'

She gave us her flashlight and told us to come on in when we were done, and then she left us to it.

'You'd think she didn't want us here after all,' Jake said.

'What did you expect?'

'I can't rightly say.'

We went around to the trailer and Jake let down the gate. It served its purpose better than a ramp originally intended for loading furniture. Shenzao had her haunches towards the rear and turned her head sideways to see behind her, trying to suss what was going on. Jake spoke to her and explained what we were about to do. She seemed mighty skittish from the ride and

I couldn't blame her. I felt as if I'd been in a paint shaker for half an hour.

'You're here, girl,' I heard him say. 'No more vans or boats or trailers. We got a nice stable for you to sleep in, and some new friends.'

He untied her and backed her out and together we walked her down. We'd outrun the coastal cloudfront and all across the mountain sky stars glittered like flecks of ice. The dirt in the frozen drive crunched beneath our boots.

The stable turned out to be the barn-like structure we'd passed on the way in. It had board-and-batten siding and a shingled roof, and only one entrance: these big barn doors held in place by a two-by-four. I went to slide that aside and pushed the doors open. It was dark within, and I smelled manure and livestock – a scent to which I was now well-accustomed.

Jake panned the flashlight around the interior. The beam picked up concrete floors and a few bales of hay and the stalls, where the shadows of horses stood in sleepy silence. I could hear the rattling hum of a heater but it wasn't much warmer inside than it was out. Next to the doors was a pull switch and when I tugged that a single bulb flickered on overhead: a tungsten worklamp that they'd strung in on an extension cord and hung from the rafters.

'Well, it ain't exactly the Ritz,' Jake said.

From what I could see, the stable had maybe a dozen stalls and only half of them were occupied. Jake left me holding Shenzao's lead and went to scope out the free stalls. He said the horses seemed to be in decent shape and the stalls looked clean, at least. In one of them we scattered some hay on the floor – to make it more cosy for her – and led her on in. When the gate shut behind Shenzao she manoeuvred around, and appeared startled to see us on the other side rather than in the pen with her. She stretched her head over the gate and nosed at Jake, and he petted her in a manner that seemed both pleased and melancholy.

'Well,' he said, 'we got you here, old girl.'

'Sorry about all we put you through,' I added.

'We're no good as horse handlers.'

'You deserve a hell of a lot better.'

She huffed at us, as if to dismiss our inadequate apology.

'This ain't no place for a horse like this,' Jake said.

'At least he's taking care of them.'

'Sure – he's a real prince.'

'Come on. It ain't worth thinking about.'

We bid goodbye to Shenzao and tried to pretend it was that easy. But when we got to the doors and turned to look back before pulling out the light, she was gazing after us with what I would call a mournful expression, as if she knew we'd abandoned her to a new and uncertain fate, after all we had put her through. Then Jake clicked out the light and she became a white shape in the dark, like a reverse silhouette, and we closed the doors on her.

The interior of the house matched the exterior. Or maybe mismatched is what I mean. The front door looked new, and newly installed, but the frame hadn't been painted or stained. It opened into what was possibly meant to be a hall, but partition walls weren't up yet – just the timber – so you could see right through to the kitchen on the left, and the lounge on the right.

Maria was in the kitchen, leaning on the counter, so we went that way – walking right through where the wall ought to have been. The kitchen was bigger than our mother's entire apartment.

It had granite counter tops and slate floor tiles and a big black refrigerator that looked like a space coffin: all top-of-the-line stuff. But where there should have been a stove, there was just a big gap.

'Don't flip that,' Maria said, pointing to a switch above the gap. 'It trips the power, since it's not connected to anything. It was for the fan over the stove, but Pat sent the stove back. He's very particular like that. So I can't cook properly. Just microwave, but it has a convection oven, at least.'

She sounded lighter, breezier, now that we'd arrived. Maybe that had to do with her daughter, or with the booze. She had a fresh beer in hand. She'd set the table – a big round solid oak number – with paper plates and plastic cutlery. Two more cans of Pabst had been put out for us, alongside a bottle of red wine, uncorked. Left to breathe, as they say.

'Nice and warm in here,' Jake said.

'It's underfloor heating.' She tapped the slate with her heel.

'Drug money's still green, I guess,' Jake said.

'It's not just drugs.'

'No – it's blood, too.'

Maria took a long pull of Pabst, eyeing him over the rim as she did so.

Then she said, 'They're getting out of all that, with the clubs and bars.'

'Going legit, eh?'

She shook her head and muttered something about him being impossible, but at that stage it was just banter: the prodding and needling, baiting and taunting. The tiny torments they could inflict on each other so skilfully.

The microwave pinged and from it Maria withdrew three TV dinners of spaghetti Bolognese. She tore off the plastic wrap and dumped the contents onto our three plates.

'It ain't gourmet,' she said.

'We been eating from pots and pans,' I said, 'so it's a step up from that.'

We sat down at the table. The paper plates and plastic forks and cups made it feel like a play-dinner, and the missing walls gave me the feeling of being inside a big dollhouse. We were the dolls: set up and positioned to act out our old roles.

Maria held up her glass, and we did the same.

'To being back together.'

'To family.'

We drank to that. As we ate, we made clumsy smalltalk about living on the ranch, and what lay in its general vicinity. Maria told us that the nearest town was the one we'd passed on the way in: Elma. A few smaller towns lay to the south, but Elma served as the main shopping hub for groceries and amenities and the like.

'They got a college, too,' she said. 'I'm taking night classes.'

Jake said, 'You weren't one for studying.'

'I'm doing astronomy.'

Jake and I shared a look – raising our eyebrows, as if she'd announced her celibacy.

'What?' she asked.

'You don't mean astrology?' Jake said.

'I know the difference, asshole.'

'I just wanted to make sure we're talking about the same thing, here.'

'I'm trying to keep busy, okay?' She put down her fork. 'And get clean.'

'Hey – I'm sorry.' He held up his hands, nearly knocking over his beer, but catching it just in time. 'I didn't think you had an interest in that kind of thing, is all.'

'I got a lot of interests. You wouldn't know about that. The only interest you ever had was being depressed and making me miserable and singing songs about your sister.'

Jake stabbed deliberately at his spaghetti, twirled a tangle around the tongs of his fork, and stuck the whole bundle in his mouth – as if he needed to block out what he wanted to say.

Maria said, 'I'm sorry, Jake.' Then she added, softer, 'Do you still play?'

Jake shook his head, swallowed. 'Not really.'

'Sure he does,' I said. 'He played on the boat.'

'Why don't you play us something?' Maria asked.

'Guitar's out of tune.'

I said, 'Sounded fine to me.'

'I ain't playing, okay?'

He said it louder than he had to, louder than was normal. In the silence that followed we all focused on our plates, our plastic utensils rasping away like rats' claws on dry straw.

After dinner Maria pulled out this bottle of tequila: clear blue glass, real tall and elegant, with a label all written in Spanish. She poured us each a lowball. It tasted better than any tequila I'd ever had. It didn't even taste like the same drink. She told us Patrick had ordered it from Mexico from a small batch distillery. She said it with a touch of pride and I expected Jake to mock her about that, and I think she did too, but he didn't. He hadn't said much, since she'd made that crack about Sandy.

'What's through there?' I said.

Off the kitchen was another room, all in dark.

'The boys' games room. You want to see?'

'Sure,' Jake said. 'I'm tired of jawing.'

Maria flicked on the light and led us through. They had a

full-sized pool table in there, as well as a crokinole board and a gun rack filled with hunting rifles. But like the rest of the house the room was incomplete: plasterboard lined the ceiling, and loose wires ran between the beams. The overhead light was a bare bulb, without a fixture or shade as yet.

Jake racked up the balls and we took turns potting them without playing an actual game. That went on for ten, fifteen, twenty minutes – just the dull clack of balls and the dead time stretching between. I knew Jake was doing it to get at Maria (for her that kind of silence was unbearable) and it worked. Eventually she broke and went up to the bathroom and when she came down she looked animated and vigorous and angry. She grabbed a stereo remote from the sofa and cranked up some bass-heavy R&B and marched on over to the pool table.

'Whose turn is it anyway?' she asked. 'Mine? Give me that goddamn cue, Jake.'

'It ain't your turn.'

'It is now.'

She cackled and grabbed the cue from him. As she lined up the shot I looked at him, accusingly. Maria sank that shot and kept on going, stalking around to the other side of the table. When she missed she swore and shoved the cue off to me and stood gnawing at her lip, tapping her foot. Her whole body taut, wired up. There were different Marias and this was one of them. Without preamble, she started talking about Delaney and how much she hated him and hated being with him. She said he was a goddamn murderer and so were his friends.

'That's all the visitors I ever have out here. Rapists and murderers.'

'Not much company,' I said.

I didn't know what the hell to say, to be honest.

'You'll see on Thursday. They're supposed to be coming on Thursday, to finish this deal. You'll see how he treats me.'

Jake stood up and held the pool cue sideways across his body, like a hockey stick.

He said, 'Why are you with him, then?'

'I might not be for much longer.'

'I've heard that before.'

'This time I mean it.'

'If it's not him, it'll be some prick like him.'

'Oh, go to hell Jake. Go right to hell and take your brother with you.'

'What did I do?' I said.

'I'm sorry Timmy. You didn't deserve that.'

I took the cue from Jake, and made a pathetic, aimless shot that wandered around the table like a blind mouse. But Maria was rising to it, now.

'Anyways,' she said. 'Me and you had our chance, Jake. It's finished, now.'

'You saw to that.'

'You were gone for years. *Years*, Jake.'

'I was in fucking jail, Maria.'

'And whose fault was that?'

They went back and forth like that, hacking away at each other, trying to get past the scar tissue to where it hurt. And all the while I stood in the middle trying to calm things down and soothe them, saying stuff like, 'Come on, now,' or 'Let's just hold on a second here,' and of course that didn't make a bit of difference. They got more and more worked up, until finally Maria said something about Jake loving Sandy more than her, which was probably true but pretty shocking to hear said aloud all the same.

Instead of answering, Jake took the pool cue from me and

casually snapped it over his knee. The crack of wood was definitive, and in the aftermath the throb of the bass resounded like a massive heartbeat. Then Maria tilted her head, looking up, and reached for the remote to turn the stereo down, while holding a palm out, as if calling for a truce. Footsteps sounded on the floor above. I don't know how she'd heard them over the music. A mother's instincts, I guess. A second later two skinny legs appeared on the landing at the top of the stairs. That was all I could see: these legs in polka-dot pyjama bottoms.

'Mom,' a voice said, 'who's here?'

Maria hurried over, and started up the stairs. 'Just my friends, honey – the ones I told you about. They're good guys. You'll meet them tomorrow. Did we wake you?'

'The music is loud.'

'I've turned it down. We'll go back to the kitchen.'

They moved away from the landing and the voices faded. Jake was still standing there with the pieces of pool cue in hand. He held the half with the tip out to me and said, 'It's your shot.' We actually kept playing like that, sharing half of a broken cue, until Maria came back. When she did she seemed calmer. She looked as if she'd been crying. She wiped at her eyes and without saying anything she walked up to Jake and pulled him into a hug. She told him that she didn't want to fight. She said it was a trying time for all of us and that we each had our demons. I didn't know if she meant then, or now. But she tousled my hair and took us both by the hand and led us back into the kitchen, where we sat down again and had a few more splashes of that tequila.

By then I was feeling pretty gooned, and flagging, and they'd taken to holding hands, which didn't seem at all forced or unnatural. It was what had to happen, I guess. When the chance arose

I asked about where we'd be sleeping and Maria looked at me, startled.

'It's only eleven,' she said.

'I'm about done in.'

'I got something to help with that.'

'Not for me, Maria. Not tonight.'

She mimed a sadly clownish face, but didn't push it. She told me we could sleep in the bunkhouse, where Delaney's guests always slept.

'How do I find the bunkhouse?'

'Down past the stable.'

When I got up, Maria touched Jake's arm and said, 'What about you, Jake? You're not going yet, are you?'

'I could stay for a bit.'

'Let's catch up properly. I haven't seen you for so long.'

She placed her head on his shoulder, and he looked at me, helpless. I just waved it off. It was the final bit of déjà vu from that night. I couldn't count how many nights had ended like that: with the two of them cuddled up and me wandering off on my own. We all have our roles to play in certain situations, and that had always been another one of mine.

I gathered up my bag and got the key from her and stepped out through the new door onto the half-finished porch, now glazed with frost and treacherously slippery. I lingered to light one of Maria's Marlboros and then started down the drive. After a few steps I glanced back, out of instinct. In one of the upstairs windows I could see a figure: slight and small, just the shadow of a girl. The shadow raised a hand to me, and I waved back.

Chapter Thirty-Two

I DREAMED OF WATER AND the taste of salt and when I awoke, in the cold and the dark, I was staring at the underside of a bunk and thought for a moment I was back on the boat, with Albert and Evelyn. I took comfort in that, clinging to it like a blanket, but it slid away from me as I awoke more fully, and sat up.

I was of course no longer on the boat but on land, and in the Delaneys' bunkhouse: a wooden A-frame cabin with two floors. The ground floor – where I had slept – contained a lounge, a single hallway, a shower room, and two dormitory-style rooms with half a dozen bunkbeds in each. The whole set-up looked reasonably new, but had already begun sliding towards disrepair: soiled carpets, holes in the walls, stained bedding. It reminded me of the Woodland – Jake's flophouse back in Vancouver.

I'd stretched out on a bunk in one of the dorms. I hadn't heard Jake come in, but he now lay sprawled on his back in the bunk opposite me, which I hadn't necessarily expected. He'd pulled his bandana down over his eyes to shield them from the morning light, which glowed diffusely through the window (the venetian blinds were bent and broken). His mouth hung half-open and his breathing sounded even and peaceful. His exhales showed in the morning cold and I found it unnerving to glimpse this fragile, intangible evidence of my brother's life, of his being alive.

I rooted through my bag and got out a dirty towel and a bar of soap and went down the hall to the shower room. I hadn't showered since we'd left Vancouver and I had high hopes. But like the rest of the bunkhouse the bathroom had been subjected to mistreatment. The shower door hung loose on its hinges and a starburst crack radiated from the centre of the mirror. When I turned on the water it only ran cold, and due to the temperature it felt like glacial run-off. I braced myself and stood under it anyway, shuddering as water slid over my scalp and neck and the small of my back in a numbing glaze. I only lasted thirty seconds.

I walked back to our room, shivering and shaking, with the towel around my waist. Jake had gotten up, and was fiddling with the gas heater beneath the window.

I said, 'I tried that last night.'

He looked up. A lit cigarette hung from his lips and he squinted at me through the smoke. 'Why the hell can't this rich prick warm his house?'

'Wait'll you try the shower.'

'Busted, too?'

'Colder'n death.'

He stood and kicked the heater without much enthusiasm. It rocked on its stand but didn't tip over. 'Fuck that. Maria must have warm water. I'll shower in the main house.'

'Surprised you didn't sleep there.'

He just looked at me and ashed out on the carpet.

I asked, 'You two have a good time last night?'

'Lay off.'

'Hope it was worth the trip.'

'Don't be jealous, Poncho.'

'Maybe you can have a threesome with Delaney.'

Jake just shook his head and exhaled smoke, in a show of exasperation. I went over to sit on my bunk. I was still wet and half-naked and shuddering from the cold. A bead of water ran down my nose and hung there like an icicle. I wiped it away.

'We've done what we had to,' I said. 'I think we should just go. Before the Delaneys and their crew get here on Thursday.'

'How will I get my money?'

'Our money. They can send it to us.'

'You don't just mail a hundred grand, you dinglehopper.'

'We'll pick it up, then. Later.'

'If we don't get it now, we won't get it.'

'I don't care. I didn't do it for the money, anyway.'

'What the hell did we do it for?'

'I did it for you, bozo. I don't know why you did it. To get laid, apparently.'

'That's a shitty thing to say.'

I stood up. I wanted to say something big and dramatic that would convince him, but I'd forgotten about the towel and it fell off, leaving me standing naked, with my gearstick all shrivelled up from the cold. It was difficult to sound dramatic or convincing in that state.

'Look, man,' I said, 'we leave now and we leave alive, at least.'

'Those jokers owe us a hundred grand.'

'Those jokers also threatened to kill us.'

'That was just a pissing match.'

'You willing to bet your life on it? And mine?'

He stubbed his cigarette out on the windowsill, mashing it far longer than he had to, until the butt was just a mess of soot and tobacco. He stood looking out the window for a time, even though you couldn't see a thing through the glaze of frost.

Then he said, 'I'm gonna go check on the horse.'

'Do that,' I said. 'I'll start packing.'

I said that even though there was nothing really to pack. We hadn't even unpacked.

'Just hold your horses,' he said. 'What about Maria?'

'You two had your dance last night.'

'She might still need us.'

'Or she might be stringing you along.'

He pulled on his jacket and put his hands in his pockets.

He said, 'She might be.'

And he walked out.

I got dressed and put my clothes and towel in my duffel bag and zipped that up. I put it by the door and did the same with Jake's bag. I pulled on my boots and jacket. Ready to go, I sat in a chair beneath the broken TV until Jake came back, about ten minutes later. I expected him to start up with the argument again (I'd already prepared my counter-argument) but the way he looked changed all that. He stood in the doorway and gazed at me for a time, his expression absolutely dumbfounded. He looked as if he'd had a lobotomy. It was so out of character I didn't even ask him what had happened. I just stood up, waiting for the news. He patted at various pockets for his pack of smokes and found them eventually and got one out, only he couldn't light it. His hands were shaking too much, and not from the cold.

He said, 'You better go on down to the stables.'

'What the hell happened?'

'It's better if you just go on down there.'

I actually thought Shenzao had died. It seemed that severe. The journey and travel and our terrible treatment of her had been too much, in the end. And if the stable was half as cold as our bunkhouse she'd probably caught pneumonia in the night. I walked down there with the slow-footed trudge of a mourner at a funeral. I couldn't think of any other explanation.

Overnight a mountain mist had moved in, and the air felt cold and heavy as gauze. Through the haze the morning sun glowed silver, eerie and peculiar, creating what you might call an other-worldly atmosphere. Against that backdrop, or possibly due to what I expected to find, the stable looked hallowed as a church. Jake had left the doors ajar, and from inside pale yellow light beamed out. I approached with trepidation. I had this image in my head of our beautiful horse – she was ours by then, really – lying on her side in the straw, glassy-eyed, the whole scene noble and biblical and tragic.

I stepped inside and looked at Shenzao's stall and saw her standing there, perfectly fine, with her head extended over the stall door. She was nuzzling the palm of a girl, who had her back to me, but I took to be Samantha. She was wearing jeans and a fleece and tuque, and from beneath her tuque her hair hung down, dirty and blonde. I had an inexplicable feeling as I stepped towards her and because of that I tripped on a feed bucket and the bucket clattered and I fell right over it, onto my belly. The girl turned to witness this slapstick display, and as I lay there like a fool I got my first real look at her: lean and sinewy as rawhide, with an angular face – all chin and cheekbones – and a thin mouth, which curled into a sly, scornful smile upon seeing my antics. Her bangs stuck out the front of her tuque and that accentuated the similarity. She looked like Sandy. She looked just like our sister Sandy had, at that age.

And that, of course, changed everything.

She said, 'Who in the hell are you?'

I picked myself up and dusted off my thighs, though they weren't really dusty – they were smeared with horse muck.

'I'm Jake's brother,' I said.

I held out my right hand, which was also now muddied, and of course had only the three fingers, which she must have noticed. But she shook it anyway.

'He called you Poncho,' she said.

'My real name's Tim. Poncho's my nickname.'

She made a face – sticking out her tongue and scrunching up her eyes.

'That's a weird nickname,' she said.

'It's the only one I got.'

'I don't have one at all. Just Sam.'

'We'll come up with a nickname for you.'

'Yeah?'

'Sure.'

I stood gazing at her in a kind of stupefied astonishment.

'What's wrong?' she asked.

'I came to check on the horse.'

'That's what Jake said, too. You're just as weird as him. You both act like a couple of crackers.'

'Isn't cracker slang for a white guy?'

'That's what I mean. You're a pair of goddamn crackers.'

I started laughing. It was the funniest insult I'd ever heard.

I said, 'I'm just hungover is all.'

'I heard you all drinking. Last night.'

'Sorry we woke you up.'

'That was nothing compared to *his* friends.'

It took me a moment to realize she meant Delaney. Shenzao moved to nuzzle Sam again, and she turned her attention back to the horse. In profile she looked even more like Sandy. She had the same sparrowhawk features: sharp cheekbones and a short Roman nose.

She asked, 'Did you really bring her here on a boat?'

'Did Jake tell you that?'

'I didn't get the chance to ask him. My mom told me.'

'We sailed her from Vancouver.'

'How long did that take?'

It struck me as a very practical and sensible question.

'A couple of days.'

'She's gorgeous.' She ran her palm down the bridge of Shenzao's nose, or snout, or whatever you call it on a horse. 'She's like a fairytale horse, or something from a story. The rest of the horses we have are old nags, compared to her.'

The other animals were standing with their heads angled towards us, curious.

'Do you look after them?' I asked.

She kept stroking Shenzao, not looking at me.

'Somebody has to. Patrick's only here once in a while. Mr Jenkins – a farmer – comes out to drop off feed and hay and check the horses over. He's due today, later on.'

'You do the rest?'

'Most of it. Mom doesn't much like animals.'

'She said that.'

She scratched Shenzao behind the ears and the horse started licking her, slobbery and friendly as a dog. Sam laughed and turned her face aside.

I said, 'She seems to have taken to you.'

'Just 'cause I fed her this morning. She was starving.' She looked at the ground and scuffed it with her boot, leaving a mark in the dirt. Then she looked back up, her expression both shy and sly. 'I ride them, too. I'm pretty good. Do you think I could ride her?'

'You asking my permission?'

She nodded, real solemn-like.

'She ain't ours. We only brought her down.'

'For Mr Delaney.'

'I don't really know why, or for who.' She looked so down about it, I just couldn't say no to her. 'Tell you what – she's still ours till we hand her over. So I'd say you can ride her, if your mom will let you.'

'She won't be awake for hours.'

She said this matter of factly. She was already heading towards the wall, to where the bridles and halters hung on wooden pegs. Her whole act – being shy, asking permission – had been put on, and my agreement was taken as a given.

'You're going right now?' I asked.

'I go most mornings.'

'On the trails?'

'In the paddock out front. But I ride the trails, too.'

'Ain't you a bit young?'

'I'm nearly ten years old.'

She said it contemptuously, as if questioning her capability was a real insult.

'Maybe we should come watch you.'

'Sure – you and your cracker brother can watch.'

I laughed again. I had no idea where she'd picked up that word.

Back in the bunkhouse, Jake hadn't moved from where he'd been standing when I left. By that I mean he hadn't moved at all. He'd let his cigarette burn to the butt and all that remained was a curling crescent of ash, dangling there precariously. I stopped in the doorway and we stared at each other. He looked as if he'd just finished crying or was about to start: his eyes wet and red-rimmed.

'You met her?' Jake said.

'I sure did.'

'The timings would work out, if it happened after Sandy, before my trial.' He gripped his head. He looked like he wanted to tear it off his shoulders. 'How could she not tell me?'

'Maybe she didn't know, at first.'

'She must have suspected, even if she was sleeping around.'

'I guess she wants you to know, now. Otherwise we wouldn't be here.'

'What a way to tell me.'

'Maria has her own manner of doing things.'

I went to stand in front of him, mirroring his pose. It was as if we'd both had the wind knocked out of us.

'I had the damnedest shock,' he said.

'Me too.'

'When I first saw her I couldn't even talk.'

'I know. I tripped on a bucket.'

'You tripped on a bucket?'

'A feed bucket. I fell right over.'

Jake started laughing, the kind of relieved, tearful laughter that only seizes you every so often. After a minute I joined in, and once we got going we couldn't stop: something just cracked open in us and nothing but laughter poured out. He put an arm around my neck and tugged me into a hug. It was awkward and weird and oddly tender, for him.

'That's my daughter out there,' he said, wondrously.

'We need a couple of cigars, for this.'

'We need more than that.'

We both looked at the door, where I'd placed our bags and things. We didn't even have to say anything about that. It was clear we weren't leaving, not until we figured it out – until we somehow figured the whole thing out.

Chapter Thirty-Three

JAKE PANICKED WHEN HE HEARD I'd told Sam she could ride the horse. He called me a goddamn fool and claimed I was taking chances with his daughter's life. I had this terrible vision of the horse throwing her and trampling her, and it all being my fault. It didn't matter that I'd been in a state of shock when I'd given her permission, nor that she'd seemed so confident about the whole thing. Letting a little girl ride a racehorse that had been stuck on a boat for two days seemed about the dumbest thing I'd ever done, and after our recent activities that was really saying something.

'Where's she going?' he asked.

'In the paddock out front.'

'Come on.'

The paddock was a big rectangle, about a hundred yards long by fifty across. Sparse grass speckled the ground, hoary with morning frost, and split-rail fencing ran around the perimeter. As we hustled up we saw that we were too late: Sam and Shenzao were already out there. At first, due to the low clouds and morning mist, horse and rider appeared as a ghostly shape, moving across the far side of the enclosure. As they circled towards us they seemed to emerge from the haze, slowly materializing, and the sight reminded me of that day at Castle Meadow, when we'd watched Shenzao train. Sam looked small enough to be a jockey and rode like one, too: leaning low over the pommel, hunched forward in the saddle.

'Try to get her attention,' Jake said.

We stopped at the fence and leaned up against it, waving our arms. At first Sam didn't ride at a gallop, but what you might call a canter. Her upper body stayed completely relaxed and she gave the impression of being part of the horse, like a centaur, rather than separate and detached. As horse and rider floated by together Sam raised one hand in passing – ignoring our desperate and frantic signals – and kept right on going. Shenzao showed no signs of skittishness or nerves and simply looked happy to be let loose, and not cooped up in a trailer or a galley or a stable stall. She was a racehorse, after all, and bred to run.

'What do we do?' I asked.

'Damned if I know.'

Stopping them, clearly, was out of the question. So we lit a couple of smokes and leaned up against the fence, with our arms folded across the top rail, slowly relaxing as it became apparent that no tragic disaster was forthcoming. We watched the pair of them go around and around. We didn't talk much. It felt almost impolite to talk. It reminded me of being at a performance, or recital. Sam rode for about half an hour, never going dangerously fast but occasionally changing the gait, trying out her control of the horse. After a dozen or so laps she slowed Shenzao to a trot and did a cool-down lap. Then she walked the horse up to the fence where we waited. We applauded.

'Where'd you learn to ride like that?' Jake asked, which struck me as funny – more like a line from a dime-store western than something my brother would actually say.

'It's all I do out here.'

She swung a leg out of the stirrup and slid down neatly, without releasing the reins. She had put on riding boots and a helmet at least one size too big, so it bobbed around as she moved.

'How'd she handle?' I asked.

'I didn't have to do a thing. She just wanted some exercise.'

She patted the horse's neck a couple of times and then ran her palm from Shenzao's head to shoulder, just below the mane. The horse was breathing hard – her breath coming out smoky in the cold morning air – and there was a sheen of sweat on her coat. You could smell the sweat, too. A healthy animal smell, different to the sad stink of her being all pent-up in the galley.

'You made it look pretty easy,' Jake said.

'Do either of you ride?' she asked.

'Hell no. I'm a musician and he's a damned fisherman.'

She glanced sidelong at him, looking uncommonly shrewd for a nine-year-old.

'You want to try?' she asked.

Jake probably should have said no, and of course didn't due to his own stubbornness and pride. Instead he clambered over the fence into the paddock, the timbers creaking under his weight. Shenzao eyed him in a way that seemed to me sceptical and suspicious. It was as if she was thinking: not this loser, again.

'Can you hold the reins?' Sam asked me.

I climbed over the fence, too – rolling my substantial bulk awkwardly onto the top rail, since the gouge in my calf was still hurting me something fierce. We hadn't bothered to rebandage it after we arrived and started drinking. I took the reins and stood with Shenzao's head next to mine. Her big eye gleamed that pale, albino blue, piercing and unblinking, as if peering right into my cowardly and no-good heart.

Sam showed Jake how to put his foot in the stirrup and step up and swing his leg over the horse's rump. It took him a few tries but he managed, in his own way, by sprawling himself over the saddle first and then twisting to slide his leg around. It goes without saying that this action lacked any grace or elegance and in that way was almost endearing, seeing as it was Jake – struggling so earnestly to impress her.

'How's that feel?' Sam said.

Jake sat up, gripping the pommel and shifting around in the saddle.

'It feels high. How do I look, Poncho?'

'Mighty fine, Lefty. Like a real outlaw.'

'Shoulda brought my six-shooter.'

Sam talked him through how to sit in the saddle: squeezing the horse with your knees, back straight, head level. She didn't let him have the reins at first. She just told him to hold onto the pommel as she took the reins from me, and led Shenzao around the paddock. It was the funniest damned thing: like seeing those pony rides at the fair, where kids get a short run-around with a trainer guiding the animal. Only here it was the kid in charge, and this grown man sitting awkwardly up there, looking pleased and proud as a schoolboy. When they came back around Jake grinned his gap-toothed grin and pointed an imaginary pistol at me.

'Check it out, Poncho. I'm a goddamn cowboy.'

I shouted back: 'Take the reins, Jake – no training wheels.'

He said something to Sam, and they debated it for a minute. He must have convinced her, or maybe she was just talking him through how to do it. She held onto the bridle while he got ready, raising the reins up and in front of him. He didn't look particularly confident. Sam let go of the bridle and stepped aside and allowed Shenzao to move forward of her own volition.

I suppose what happened next was both predictable and inevitable. Shenzao simply trotted along amicably for a dozen steps and then casually bucked her hindquarters, flicking Jake off as neat as can be. He threw out his hands and clawed the air, like a very clumsy cat trying to spin around to land. Only he didn't come all the way around. He hit the ground hard on his side and lay there, still. Shenzao stopped and looked back disdainfully, as if surprised he'd been undone so easily.

Sam said, 'Holy cow.'

We both ran over there – from different directions – and converged at the spot where he'd landed. Jake was curled up and clutching at his gut and trying to breathe. Sam crouched to check on him but he waved her back, and rolled laboriously over onto his hands and knees. He'd landed in a half-frozen puddle and his face and jacket were streaked with mud. We kept asking him if he was okay, and he grunted out something about being winded. When he had finally caught his breath he looked up and grimaced.

'I guess I deserved that, for all I put her through.'

I helped him to his feet. I asked him if he'd broken anything and he limped in a circle a few times, testing out his limbs and bones and muscles, before declaring that nothing seemed to be seriously damaged.

'I did okay at first.'

'Yeah,' I said, 'for a few feet.'

Sam said, 'I shouldn't have let you.'

'Weren't your fault.'

Shenzao stood off to one side, innocent and obedient. She peeled back her lips and made a funny hee-haw sound – this sort of donkey sound – as if she were laughing at him.

'I know you did that on purpose,' he said, and shook his fist at her.

He was half-joking, but you could tell he was pretty sore at her, too.

'You want to try, Poncho?' he asked me.

'Hell no. She'd do worse to me. Plus my leg is still killing me.'

I could feel the burning sting of the cut every time I moved.

Sam said, 'Maybe tomorrow we can go riding. The other horses are all well-broken.'

'We'll see, kid.'

I heard whistling, and looked at the porch. Maria had come out there, dressed in a ratty pink bathrobe and slippers. She waved at us, beckoning, and shouted, 'Brunch is on.'

Brunch was coffee and cereal. Maria made her coffee black and scalding, bitter as sin. We sat down at the table and drank it from Styrofoam cups and ate cereal out of those tiny travel boxes – the kind that come in packs of six. We did this very civilly: the passing of milk, the pleases and thank yous, slurping and chewing, as if having breakfast together was a natural and frequent occurrence. Sam sat down with us (she had coffee like an adult) and as things dragged on she looked from Jake to Maria, waiting for one of them to explain the oddity of the set-up, and our presence. Tension hummed between them like a filament, but of course neither said anything. It was left to Sam to break the silence. She stirred her Cheerios with her fork and said, 'Jake got thrown into the mud.'

Maria said, 'Who said you could go riding that thing?'

Sam hesitated, looked at me, and said, 'Nobody.'

'I did,' I said. 'But thanks for covering for me.'

Maria said, 'Pat wouldn't want you riding his prize cow.'

'She's a horse, Mom.'

'A spiteful one,' Jake said. He was still covered in mud and looked like a revenant who'd clawed his way out of the grave. 'A spiteful beast with a grudge and a good memory.'

'Did you guys steal her?'

She asked it in the innocuous way kids do – a perfectly natural question. Jake looked to Maria, raising his eyebrows, and she made a helpless, resigned gesture, which struck me as funny. It was as if she was subconsciously telling him, 'Don't ask me: she's *your* daughter.'

Jake, well, he just went and told her the truth, straight up: that we'd stolen the horse to pay back a debt (leaving out the complicated backstory) and that if anybody found out we'd be in a hell of a lot of trouble. Sam put down her fork, and then took hold of it again.

'But that won't happen, right?'

It was a good question. Maria, she just laughed forlornly and reached for her pack of menthols and muttered something about it already having happened, and when Jake started to argue (in his usual adamant and overly convincing way) she reminded him about the footage, which – up until then – had only been a sort of vague and unreal threat to us.

Jake chewed thoughtfully on his cornflakes, and said, 'I got to see this footage.'

Sam asked, 'What footage?'

Maria said it was all online, but that we could watch it on her laptop. She brought that out, and we moved our chairs around to her side of the table to get a better view. Just before she opened the first clip, she hesitated and said, 'Sam – you shouldn't know about this.'

'I'll just look it up myself, after.'

It was hard to argue with that. Maria sucked on her cigarette and sighed smoke and, after a moment, opened the first clip: the CCTV footage from the stables. There we were – scrambling around on screen in black-and-white, wearing bandanas. We looked like a couple of bandits in an old silent film. It even had that same jerky and stilted feel, since the security cameras recorded at a low frame-rate. When it got to the part where I lassoed Shenzao and got yanked off my feet, Jake turned away, trying and failing not to laugh uproariously.

'Real funny,' I said.

'I'm sorry, man.'

'Laugh it up, Jake,' Maria said. 'The next one's funny, too.'

The second clip was part of a newscast, from CityTV in Vancouver. The presenter – a sallow-faced old codger in a charcoal suit – related the details of the crime at the stables in this morbid, ominous tone. Then they cut to surveillance footage taken at the gas station. A guy stood at the till, handing over bills. The high angle and low-resolution partially made his features look different, but I still recognized him, quite readily, as Jake.

'How many hits do these have?' Jake asked.

'Hundreds of thousands, and counting.'

Sam whistled. 'You guys are famous.'

'Jake is,' Maria said.

He shook his head, pointing out that they hadn't identified him yet.

'Maybe they won't,' Sam said, hopefully.

'If they do,' Maria said, 'Pat is going to flip.'

I nodded. 'Somebody could connect us to him – the cops or the Triads.'

Jake yawned, deliberately, just to prove how unshaken he was by the whole thing.

'Well,' he said, 'at least nobody knows where we are.'

I didn't say it, but I was thinking: they sure as hell will when the hen party debacle comes to light.

Maria said, 'Whether they ID you or not, Pat won't be happy about the attention.'

Jake said, 'Who cares what he's happy about?'

'You don't know him.'

'Not as well as you, clearly.'

In the ensuing silence, Sam, who'd been listening alertly, said, 'He's not a nice man.'

She opened a new mini-box of Fruit Loops and dumped them in her bowl. We'd used up all the milk so she had to eat them dry. Me? I went back to chewing my Shreddies, which by that point had gone all soggy and unappetizing, in that way they do.

Jake said, 'I know that, kid. I know that. But we did a job for him and he owes us money so I'm going to make sure we get paid.'

'You're still set on that?' I asked.

'I ain't leaving, if that's what you mean.'

'Jake,' Maria said, closing the lid of the laptop, 'if it goes wrong it could be real bad.'

'Let me handle that. Hell. I just want to talk to him.'

'The last time you talked to him,' I said, 'you threatened to kill him.'

Maria looked at Jake. She sipped her coffee and took a drag of her cigarette and then tapped ash into one of the empty cereal boxes. She looked pale and nervy. Sam had stopped eating to listen.

Maria said, 'You told him that?'

'He threatened Tim.'

He pushed his cereal box aside and got his cigarettes and lit up, too. I almost said something then, about the two of them smoking in front of Sam. What a couple of parents.

'Jesus Jake,' Maria said. 'You got some death wish.'

As if to drive the point home, a horn sounded in the yard – making us all jump. For a second, because of what we'd been talking about, I actually thought the Delaneys had arrived early. But Sam hopped up and said, 'That's Mr Jenkins, with his delivery.'

She ran over and started putting her jacket on. She paused with one arm in the sleeve to look back at me and Jake. 'Do you guys want to help? There's a lot of hay and feed.'

It must have been comical: how we leapt up, scrambling to get our things on, falling over each other to reach the door first, telling her of course we'd help, anything she needed. In his rush, Jake even put his boots on the wrong feet. And in my rush I clipped my hip on the doorframe, adding to my ever-growing list of pains, humiliations, bruises, and injuries.

Chapter Thirty-Four

MR JENKINS HAD PARKED HIS truck down by the stables: a battered Ranger hooked up to a tow-trailer, laden with hay and sacks of feed. He waited next to the trailer with his arms crossed, regarding us as we came up. He struck me as looking very American: a big, beefy old-timer, with a jelly-bowl belly and lanky white hair tucked under his Miller Lite cap.

He smiled at Sam and said, 'You got friends, Samantha.'

'My mom's friends from Vancouver.'

He nodded at us, curtly, but didn't offer to shake or even introduce himself.

'How do you want to run this, boss?' he asked her.

Sam suggested that Jenkins and I toss the bales down, while she and Jake carried them on into the stables. That suited me fine, on account of my bum leg, and I suspected that Sam had done that deliberately: out of consideration for me.

Jenkins climbed on up into the back of his trailer and I followed, with more than a little difficulty. The hay was divided into cube-shaped bales, lashed together by nylon cord. He had a spare pair of leather work gloves that he lent me. Our job was easy enough: just picking the bales up together, shuffling to the edge of the trailer, and tossing them on down. From there Sam helped Jake haul them inside. They weren't heavy so much as awkward.

Between each bale we had a bit of a wait, but at first the old guy didn't seem all that disposed to shooting the breeze with me.

During one such respite, I said, 'Nice of you to help Sam out like this.'

'She don't need my help. She's a competent young lady.'

'I just meant you bringing the supplies and all.'

'Your friend pays me for it.'

'What friend is that?'

'The head honcho.'

'Delaney? He ain't no friend to me, or my brother.'

He peered at me, curious, and looked like he was going to say something, but Jake and Sam were coming back – laughing about some joke he'd made – and old Jenkins and I hefted the next bale down for them. It landed with a whump, sending up a cloud of hay dust.

After they'd carried it away, Jenkins said, 'Just figured you were with them, like all the other yahoos who come through here.'

'We're old friends of Sam's mother – we went to school together.'

'Ah.'

After that he warmed, some. He told me he had a farm on the other side of Elma. He had a few horses himself – just for recreational purposes – and also grew wheat and kept a few dairy cows. He said he came out at least once a week, and more if he was able, not just to make deliveries but to check on Sam.

'Ain't no place for a girl of that age,' he said.

'They're a rough crowd, all right.'

He just shook his head, as if that didn't begin to cover it.

When we finished unloading the hay, we did the same for the feed: big sacks of tiny pellets that you mashed up with water, apparently. The old guy went about our simple task in a slow and deliberate and thorough manner, and his demeanour reminded me of Albert. The thought of him, and Tracy, and the state in which I'd left their boat, caused something in me to shrivel and wilt, to the extent I reacted in a physical way.

'You all right?' Jenkins asked.

'Just hurting some, from an injury I picked up.'

'Take a breather, if you like.'

'No – the work helps.'

He accepted that, even though it didn't make much sense. By the time we finished unloading the feed it was past noon. We lingered around his trailer, jawing a little about the weather (the morning mist had cleared, but snow was predicted for tomorrow) while Sam lounged on the tailgate, swinging her legs. Then Jenkins took a glance at his watch, and said, 'Guess I better mosey.'

This time he shook my hand, and Jake's too.

He said to Sam, 'You gonna take care of these two?'

'I'll keep them out of trouble, Mr Jenkins.'

'Atta girl.'

He clambered into his cab, and looked back out his window at me.

'And you – you gonna take care of her?'

He didn't wait for an answer. He just honked and started away, his trailer rattling over the ruts and potholes in the road.

On the days Mr Jenkins made his delivery, Sam had a set routine that included mucking out the stalls, cleaning the stables, distributing fresh hay, and feeding the animals. So after he left we set right to that. Jake, he knew the drill on account of his job at Castle Meadow, and even though it was all new to me I took to that kind of work from my time on the boat. Sam acted as foreman, assigning us each a series of stalls and guiding us through the steps. First, open the door, making friendly with the occupant. Next, rake the good hay to one side, and shovel out the bottom layer of stinky muck. Lastly, scatter in some fresh hay before spreading it all around. It was pleasantly straightforward, and for me such labours have a meditative quality: the loss of worry and concern as you sink into the physical.

'How's it coming in there, Poncho?' Sam asked me, poking her head above the gate. I'd started on my second stall, scraping spadefuls of manure into a black plastic bucket.

'I'm winning, I think.'

'Throw down a little more hay, will you? It's looking a little scant.'

'You got it boss.'

Across the stable Jake got to work on Shenzao's stall. He'd forgiven her, apparently, for bucking him that morning. He chatted away to her, telling her she probably thought she'd gotten rid of us, but lo and behold – here we were again.

Halfway through the afternoon, Maria brought down a late lunch for us: peanut butter sandwiches and Snickers bars, along with orange juice for Sam, and a couple of Pabst for Jake and me. Maria was still wearing her bathrobe but she'd pulled this big winter coat over it, which was quite the sight. She joined us while we ate, and afterwards lingered by the doors for a time, watching us work.

'What a team,' she said. 'You ought to hire yourselves out.'

'Would go a little faster,' Jake said, 'with one more hand.'

'Like hell,' she said. 'Besides, somebody's got to get dinner ready.'

'What's dinner?'

'Frozen pizza.'

Jake made some joke about that taking a heck of a lot of preparation, but Maria was already shuffling back up to the house. Sam stopped in the middle of sweeping the alleyway, leaning on her broom and breathing heavy as she watched her mother withdraw to the house.

Then she clocked me observing her, and smiled in a way that struck me as too mature for a girl of nine – as if she wanted to let me know she was okay with it, with the way it all was.

She asked, 'You guys are staying another night, right?'

'Sure,' I said, automatically. 'Then heading out tomorrow.'

Jake, who had his head down, grimly shovelling away, said, 'We'll be staying till Thursday, when the Delaneys get here, and we get paid. Don't you worry about that.'

He was still set on that, apparently. I didn't think Jake gave a hoot about the money – the money just served as an excuse – but I'd once seen my brother punch a wall till he broke his hand (and the wall) simply to prove a point to Maria, and that self-same stubbornness had taken hold of him now. He refused to turn-tail and run, and if I wanted to change his mind I only had two days to do it.

By the time we finished cleaning the stables, and feeding all the horses, the sun had dropped behind the mountains and the temperature dropped with it. We came trudging up the drive, wearily satisfied by the simple pleasure of work, and working together. The sky behind the house glowed indigo, and the first few stars pin-pricked the opposite horizon, standing out sharp and bright above the surrounding mountains.

'Man,' Jake said, 'I'm so hungry I could eat a *horse*.'

'Hey,' I said, 'that was my joke.'

'You crackers,' Sam said.

We trotted up to the porch, and I caught a faint whiff of something burning. Behind the windows, the interior of the house looked a little hazy and a column of black smoke was spilling out from the door, which had been left ajar.

'Jake,' I said, and started to hurry.

We barrelled in there. The smoke was coming from the microwave and convection oven – leaking from around the seal – and a cloud of it whirlpooled on the ceiling. The little oven beeped at us repeatedly: either an alarm or a timer. Jake and I flew into a real panic, shouting Maria's name and racing around the kitchen. I grabbed the microwave plug and yanked it out of its socket, and Jake used a tea towel to flip down the door. Smoke whooshed out, making us cough. On the rack inside sat a pizza, black and hard as a hockey puck.

Coming in behind us, Sam looked around, and said irately, 'Aw, hell.'

She propped open the front door, then went to the windows and opened those, too. The smoke trickled out and fresh, wintery air swept in to replace it.

'Where's your mom?' Jake asked.

'In here,' Sam called.

Maria lay on the sofa, snoring. On the table next to her lolled a lowball glass, empty and upended, and a vial of something. As we came in Sam took up the vial and tucked it in her pocket, trying to hide it from us, or protect her mother, or both. That really got to me.

'She's just drunk again,' Sam said blandly, and turned on the TV.

The big flatscreen on the wall jolted to life. Jake and I exchanged a look. Then we went back into the kitchen and tried to clean out the convection oven, but it was a mess – the cheese had melted right into the rotating glass plate, which I'd never seen before. We carried it out onto the porch. It was still smoking and smouldering.

Back inside, we joined Sam on the sofa. Jake sat next to Maria and propped her head up on a cushion. An old musical came on – the one about seven brides, and seven brothers – and we just sat there watching that. Since pizzas, clearly, were out of the question, Sam got us a few bags of tortilla chips and a couple of packs of Mr. Noodle. She showed Jake and I how to eat it raw, sprinkling the spice-mix right inside the bag.

'This is actually pretty good,' I said.

'Told you,' Sam said.

At one point, Maria stirred. She looked up and saw Jake sitting over her.

'I made pizza,' she said, hopefully.

'I know,' he said, putting a hand on her forehead. 'It was great.'

She sighed and turned towards him, angling her head against his belly. 'We need to talk, Jake. We really need to sit down and have a talk, me and you.'

'Mañana,' he said.

On-screen, the brothers were now having some kind of massive brawl, for reasons I couldn't quite figure out. I didn't pay much attention. I paid more attention to Sam, actually, who was watching her mother and Jake. She looked far more shocked by their behaviour, by that turn towards tenderness, than she'd been by the smoke and burning pizza.

I suppose it might be tempting to judge Maria harshly for her conduct, but that would be a mistake. It all has to be viewed in the context of the moment, and part of the reason for our being there at the ranch (I believe now) was so she could show us the nature of her current life, and Sam's situation. So she wasn't putting on a brave face, or trying to hide the cracks and fractures in the façade of her life: if anything she wanted to display them. In addition, even if we were partly there by her design, I can't imagine it was easy for her to cope with the pressures of our presence, and the collision of her past and present, her then and now.

Chapter Thirty-Five

THE NEXT DAY, SAM AND I went into town. Jake got it in his head that he wanted to cook us a 'real meal' (that was the term he used) for dinner that night. Maria pointed out the obvious obstacles to this – we no longer even had a microwave, for one thing – and told him again that it would be best if he and I left today, before the Delaneys arrived tomorrow.

'A barbecue,' Jake said, as if she hadn't spoken. 'What we need is a barbecue. I can cook us up some steaks and potatoes, and whisky-grilled back ribs.'

'That sounds awesome,' Sam said, clapping excitedly.

We had all slept on the sofas, and were still sitting on them – having had coffee and breakfast cereal without really moving.

'Timmy,' Maria said, 'would you tell him, please?'

'We can't stay another night, man,' I said.

'Who wants to make the food run?' Jake asked.

Maria sighed and sat up, fastening her robe around her with the belt at the waist. 'I need to go into town anyway, to get my prescription. I guess I could pick some things up at Everybody's.' She paused, and looked at me significantly. 'Unless someone else wants to?'

It wasn't exactly subtle, but I guess we didn't have time for subtlety.

'I'll go,' I said.

'Are you sure?' she asked.

'Of course,' I said. 'This fool can't go anywhere – he's a wanted man.' Then, as if it had just occurred to me, I added, 'Say – why don't you come with me, Sam? We can pick out the food, take a look around town.'

'Can I, Mom?'

'Tim will take care of you.'

While Sam went to get changed, Maria took me aside and gave me the keys to her truck – or Delaney's truck – and put a piece of paper in my hand. Her prescription slip. She folded my fingers over it and held them.

'You can get it from the medical centre.'

'Will they let me?'

'They know Sam, and I'll call ahead.'

I nodded. 'See if you can talk some sense into him, will you?'

'I'll try,' she said. She kissed me, aiming for my cheek but getting me half on the mouth, which actually made me blush.

*

Sam and I hopped in the truck and set out back along the track. It seemed even more uneven going down and the shocks on the Sierra bounced us around as if we were running choppy waves in a boat. The trees created a tunnel around us and in places the track got so narrow that the branches scraped along the paint-work, making that distinct shrieking sound, like nails on a blackboard.

We turned off it onto the paved road, which was part of the state park, and Sam said, 'Jake and Mom – did they used to date?'

'A long time ago.'

'Back in Vancouver?'

'That's right. The North Shore.'

'I was born there.'

'I know you were.'

She leaned on the door with her elbow, propping up her head, looking right at me. I had my eyes on the road and I was grateful for the excuse.

'But I don't remember much,' she said. 'We moved around a lot – first across town to Killarney, then out to Hope for a while to live with my gran, and then down here.'

She made a face, making it clear what she thought of that.

I asked, 'Do you have citizenship?'

'My mom has both, so she applied for me.'

'I'd forgot she was born in the States.'

'I heard her say it's the only reason Patrick keeps her. He gets a partner visa.'

'Convenient.'

'For him. He needs it for his business.'

She twisted a strand of hair around her finger once, twice, three times, and then let it fall. The gesture jolted me. Again it was like Sandy. So much just seemed to be embedded in her, like an imprint.

'Why'd you really bring that horse down here?' she asked.

'Delaney – Patrick – hired us to.' But she knew that. She hadn't been asking about that. 'And I think it was a way for Jake and your mom to meet up again.'

'Couldn't they have just called each other?'

'People don't always do things the smart way, or the easy way.'

She snorted – a bit like a horse herself. 'People are crazy,' she said.

'We're all crackers, all right.'

We had us a good laugh about that, and I turned out of the park, onto Highway 12, heading north.

The highway led straight back to the overpass at the outskirts of Elma, where we'd turned off the night before. We scooted beneath it, and a little beyond the building supply yard we hung a left on Main Street, cruised past a Chevron station, and came to the Summit Pacific Medical Center. It had a glass-and-metal façade and decorative wooden siding, and looked as if it had been built recently. We were approaching an 'Emergency Entrance' sign at the roadside.

Sam said, 'You can turn in here.'

I'd almost passed it, but I hit the brakes and screeched on in: the place only had the one entrance, apparently. The drive wrapped around the front of the clinic in an oval shape. At the centre of the oval stood a flagpole, flying the Stars and Stripes, flapping all forlorn in the cold. We passed beneath a concrete awning – held up by big supports – and came to the visitors' parking lot. I found a spot and asked Sam if she wanted to come in.

I said, 'I wouldn't want to leave you here in the lot on your own.'

She laughed. 'I'm always on my own.'

'You ain't when you're with me.'

'I better come in anyway. They don't know you.'

We walked to the entrance together. The glass doors swung inwards automatically, opening into a foyer with tile floors and a few chairs and benches. It had that hospital smell: bleach and disinfectant. On our right was a reception desk and Sam led me past that, waving idly at the young woman on duty, and down a hall to the little shop and in-house pharmacy.

Behind the counter stood a middle-aged guy with a goatee and a long, braided ponytail, gone to grey. He greeted Sam by name and seemed friendly enough, but with me he turned distant, stony-faced. For a member of the medical profession he wasn't exactly congenial.

Sam said, 'We're picking up Mom's prescription.'

'Who's this?' he said warily.

'He's Tim.'

'A friend,' I said, holding out the prescription slip. 'Maria said she'd phone ahead.'

'Well, she didn't,' the guy said. He took the slip and studied it. 'But she signed it, at least. And if Sam vouches for you, I guess it's all good.'

He went to get the prescription and came back with a white paper bag, folded down at the top and held in place with a sticky label. He handed it to me without really acknowledging me and told Sam to say hello to her mother.

As we walked back out, I said, 'That fellow didn't seem to cotton to me.'

'He probably assumed you were one of Patrick's friends.'

'Mr Jenkins did, too.'

'At least they're nice to me and Mom. They feel sorry for us, I guess.'

'Funny how they all know about him.'

'He doesn't really try to hide it.'

As we crossed the parking lot, I glanced at the bag in my hand, but the label didn't say anything about the contents. I assumed it would be Valium or some kind of diazepam, which mixes bad with booze, and would explain the way Maria had crashed out. I didn't ask about it, and didn't have to: in the truck I tossed the bag on the seat between us and Sam took it up, holding it at eye level to study, like a scientist checking the results of an experiment.

'Methadone,' she said.

She said it disdainfully, as if to let me know she understood what it meant. I told her Maria had said she was trying to go clean, and that maybe the methadone was part of that.

'She's been trying for a while.'

'Do you pick up your mom's prescriptions a lot?'

'She has a lot to pick up. And this is close to our school.'

I thought of that. Her walking down after school, by herself, to pick up her mom's methadone from Mr Chuckles in there. I actually didn't have a hard time imagining it.

'You're in what? Grade four?'

'Five. My birthday's in August, and September is the cut-off.'

I put the truck in reverse, and looked over my shoulder as I backed us up. 'How much do they dole out at a time? A month's supply?'

'Two weeks.' As I wheeled us out of the medical centre, she added quietly, 'But it won't last that long.'

*

Sam directed me towards Everybody's, the supermarket where they got their groceries. We followed Main Street across town, and turned at Seventh, past a few blocks of bungalows and a squat little credit union. Everybody's could have been Safeway, or Thriftway, or any of the US chain stores: a big beige building with a flat roof, and a red awning jutting out the front.

Inside we got ourselves a trolley and I let Sam push it down the aisles, which she did with reckless zest and abandon, practically power-sliding around the corners. I kept getting the sense that the other shoppers were peering at me slantwise, assuming me to be some no-account thug, but that might have been paranoia on my part.

Maria had given us a list of things to pick up, but the list only had five items on it: milk and cereal and cigarettes and red wine and Tylenol. The essentials, I suppose. We got all that, along with a case of Olympia and a bottle of Lunazul tequila. I also told Sam to grab whatever kind of snacks she wanted and she tossed an assortment into the cart: all-dressed chips and bacon rinds and beef jerky and generic cola. In the homeware aisle she found an entire dinner set, of all things, and dropped that in the trolley, just as casual as can be.

'I'm tired of eating off those stupid paper plates.'

'Okay, cowgirl,' I said. 'Done. Let's see if we can find us a barbecue, now.'

They didn't have any disposable barbecues, seeing as it was February. Only my kid brother would think to hold a barbecue in the middle of winter. In the hardware department, between the edgers and hedgeclippers, they had charcoal barbecues in flat packs. We loaded one onto the bottom of the trolley along with a sack of briquettes and a bottle of lighter fluid.

After that we went to stock up on meat. The meat section

spanned three full aisles, lined with shelves of hamburger chuck and lamb chops and chicken legs and drumsticks and whatnot. They had fresh, they had frozen, they had everything you could imagine. It was a regular abattoir. We wandered through that together, bewildered by all our options.

'Jake wanted steak, and ribs,' I said, to simplify things. 'For his speciality dish.'

'What does whisky-grilled mean anyway?'

'It's a way to do back ribs on the barbecue, with a fancy sauce. It's a pain in the ass to prepare but it tastes damn good.'

It had also been Sandy's favourite, but I didn't say that. On the next shelf we found racks of baby back ribs, sealed in Styrofoam trays. I put two of those in our cart and as we wheeled on, towards the beef, she asked, 'Is Jake as tough as he acts?'

'Nobody's as tough as they act.'

'Are you tough?'

'I ain't tough at all. I leave that to Jake. I'm the good one – a big softy.'

I patted my belly for emphasis, like Santa Claus.

'Is that why Mom trusts you?'

'I don't know if she does.'

'She trusts you with me.'

We stopped again in front of the steaks. They had T-bone and sirloin and ribeye, and a bunch of those cheap frying steaks that taste like liver. Sam picked up a T-bone and studied it, as if checking it for quality. The plastic clung to the meat, vacuum-packed, and you could see the streaks of blood beneath.

'Did Jake really threaten Patrick?' she asked, still staring at the steak.

'They had words.'

'What does that mean? Had words?'

'It means they argued. Sometimes you say things in the middle of an argument.'

'These look good,' she said, and held the T-bone out to me. 'How about these?'

'Sure – get four of those.'

She stacked them in the cart. After she did, she glanced over her shoulder, as if to make sure nobody else could hear us. It was very theatrical, and would have been uncommonly endearing, except for what she said next, in a hushed, solemn voice.

'Patrick kills people, you know.'

'Who told you that?'

'I saw it. I saw him shoot two men.'

'Oh,' I said.

She looked around, by way of changing the subject. 'Hey – can I get an *Archie*?'

She skipped over to the magazine rack, and started rooting through them. I followed, more slowly, digesting what she'd just told me. I didn't doubt the truth of it, and felt more than a little wamble-cropped and sick in my guts. I stood and stared dumbly at the comics as she pulled them out, considering each in turn. She held up a *Betty and Veronica Double Digest*.

'How about this one?'

'Get a couple. Hell, get 'em all.'

'Really?'

'It's your un-birthday, isn't it?'

She giggled, and started piling up comics.

'It's my un-birthday,' she said to a woman coming down the aisle. The woman smiled tolerantly.

We loaded the groceries back in the truck, and since that was what we'd come in for I had no excuse to linger in town with her. I cruised back down the main street, doing thirty, with the heat cranked and the radio on, playing an old Willie Nelson track. Sam had one of her new comics open on her lap. Archie was chasing after Veronica, as usual, with hearts swirling around his head.

'Your mom get you into those?' I asked.

'She used to read them, too.'

'I remember. So did we, back in the day.'

'The old ones are the best.'

'Maybe that's where you got cracker from.'

I was talking in an idle way, while dwelling on what she'd said inside. I didn't know if I ought to bring it up, but I also figured I might not get another chance to talk to her alone.

'The men you saw him shoot,' I said. 'Where was it?'

'At the ranch,' she said nonchalantly, and turned a page. 'Down by the bunkhouse. I saw from my bedroom window. They thought I was asleep. It was, like, midnight.'

I didn't ask anything else. I figured that was enough. But after reading on for a few moments, she said, 'They'd been arguing. I heard the arguing and got up and as I reached the window I saw the flashes and heard the bangs.'

'Does he know you saw?'

'He came up to my room. I sat up and told him I'd heard noises. I thought, if I just lay there and pretended to be asleep, he'd know I was faking.'

'Smart.'

She shrugged, folded her comic shut, and looked out the window. She'd been talking pretty calmly, but her knee was going up and down, trembling, almost imperceptibly.

'You tell anybody else you saw it?' I asked.

'No.'

'Not even your mom?'

'No.'

'Okay.'

I didn't ask why she'd told me. About a mile on, she nodded at a parking lot by the roadside as we passed. She told me that one of the equestrian trails she rode came out there. Hikers and bikers used it, too. She asked me if I still wanted to go riding later.

'That would be swell,' I said.

'Swell.' She smiled at the word. 'You sound like Jughead.'

'I probably read too many of those damn things, when I was your age.'

'Do you still have them?'

'Sure. Most of them were my sister's, so I kept them all.' That seemed a weird way to put it, so I explained, 'Our older sister, she died. She died in a car accident, ten years ago.'

Most people, when I tell them that, tend to get all awkward and strange and not know what to say, or else say something idiotic like, 'I'm sorry to hear that.' But Sam just looked at me in that open and honest way kids have, and said, 'You must miss her so much.'

And then she did the damnedest thing: she reached over and patted my bad hand.

Chapter Thirty-Six

I DIDN'T FIND OUT UNTIL later all that had transpired in our absence, but knowing Jake and Maria I suspected their discussion would have been somewhat lively. Perhaps because of that, upon our return I had the impression of a charged atmosphere hanging about the house, as if some tempest had descended on the place, and only recently abated. As I pulled up I honked the horn to announce our arrival, and Sam and I stomped up the steps carrying our bags of groceries.

Inside, I heard Jake and Maria talking in low voices (the words weren't clear) and that stopped when we pushed open the front door. They were sitting at the big oak dining table, side-by-side, and Maria still hadn't changed out of her tatty bathrobe. It looked as if she'd been crying, and Jake had a split lip. He touched the blood with his tongue, bashfully.

'Hey guys,' I said, as if she wasn't near tears and Jake's lip wasn't bleeding and everything was perfectly normal, just peachy. 'We got the barbecue.'

Maria smiled weakly through a haze of menthol smoke. She looked relieved. She got up and came straight over and grabbed Sam in a hug and held her like that a long time – an unaccountably long time, really – and asked Sam if she'd had fun, if she'd enjoyed herself.

'Mom,' Sam said, wriggling away.

'Did you get my prescription?'

I held out the paper bag. She took it and wiped at her eyes with the heel of her palm (she'd started crying again when she hugged Sam) and told us she needed to freshen up, and have a morning shower. She took the bag upstairs and a second later I heard water running.

I looked at Jake and he just held out his hands, as if to show they were empty – like a poor man asking for alms.

'We got your ribs,' I said.

'And a dinner set,' Sam added.

Jake smiled. For her, he had a smile.

'Wow,' he said, pushing himself up. 'You really went the whole hog.'

He came over to help us unpack the groceries. It gave us something to do, at least. But it didn't take long. When the chips and snacks were away in the cupboards, and the meat and beer in the fridge, we hovered in that space, quiet and uncertain. Sam sat at the table and buried her head in her *Archie* comic, hiding behind it. I tried to catch Jake's eye but he stood and gazed intently at Sam, either avoiding me or struck anew by the wonder of her.

'Do you guys still want to go riding today?' she asked, without looking up from her magazine – as if it didn't really matter to her one way or the other.

'Does a chicken have lips?' Jake said.

'No. I don't think so.'

'Well, it means yes. It's a weird saying that means hell yes.'

A few minutes later, Maria came back downstairs. She'd changed into jeans and a T-shirt and her hair hung down her back in a damp, rumpled curtain. She wiggled her fingers at us and breezed over to the fridge and fished out a beer, an Olympia, and cracked it.

'Mom,' Sam asked. 'Can I take Jake and Tim for a ride?'

'Of course, honey.'

'We'll only be an hour. Otherwise they'll be saddle-sore.'

'You go right ahead.'

Without saying anything else, or looking at any of us, she drifted out of the kitchen, down a half-built hallway. She hummed to herself, quite happy now, and seemed to move as lightly as a ghost, haunting her own house.

Sam would ride Shenzao. That went without saying. In the stable, the reins and saddles and halters hung from pegs fixed to the wall opposite the door. Sam got a saddle, which looked too big and heavy for her, and went into Shenzao's stall and told us to follow her in. She was tall for her age but still had to toss the saddle up to get it over the horse's back. She adjusted it, then did up the cinch beneath Shenzao's belly: it had a buckle and worked like an oversized belt. As Sam worked the horse waited patiently and obediently, as if the two of them had done this a hundred times before. It was the same when Sam fitted the halter and reins.

'There,' she said, patting Shenzao's neck. 'Now let's get you guys saddled up.'

'I want the tamest one,' I said.

She turned to the stall next to Shenzao, and clicked her tongue. A spotted horse hung his big shaggy head over the stall door.

'Old Marley's okay. He just plods along.'

I reached out to touch him, and he tried to bite my hand. My bad hand, no less – as if he wanted one of my three remaining fingers.

'Friendly.'

'He does that.'

She told me to fetch a saddle, which I did, and she helped me fit it. Then she left me with Old Marley. He had wet and rheumy eyes and looked at me dopily. When it became clear we weren't going anywhere soon he lowered his head and nibbled at the straw on the floor of his stall.

Sam had walked down to the last stall, near the wall, where Jake was waiting. He'd picked a big black stallion, its coat sleek and glossy as a grand piano.

'That's Thunder,' Sam said.

'Is he broken in?'

'I've ridden him.'

'I don't want to get thrown again.'

'Well, hold on this time.'

'You're funny.'

Jake wanted to fit his own saddle, so she guided him through it. He listened patiently and obediently and did everything she asked. His expression revealed a juvenile earnestness that, more than anything, seemed to reflect the change that had come over him. And myself, for that matter. We were not so delusional as to believe Sandy had actually come back to us, but something surely had. It felt as if what we'd lost all those years ago wasn't completely gone: it had merely been misplaced for a time, waylaid, waiting to be found.

We rode in a line, with Sam and Shenzao up front, Jake in the middle on Thunder, and me bringing up the rear on Old Marley. I'd only ridden a horse a handful of times in my life – at our uncle's farm. The animal felt too round beneath me, as if I were straddling a beer keg. It was a precarious predicament and I seemed to always be tottering in the opposite direction to the horse's movement, wobbling back and forth atop its back. But Old Marley just plodded along, as Sam had promised, and though not enthusiastic about my presence he seemed at least indifferent to it.

Sam had shown us how to hold the reins: pinched between the thumb and forefinger loosely, with the straps wrapped around the first three fingers (an impossibility for me, with the right hand). We were supposed to keep the reins taut, but not tight, and never jerk on them. You had to steer the horse gently, she said – not tug it around.

She led us across the paddock at a walk. The temperature hadn't risen above zero – it hovered at five below – and you could hear the frosted grass crackling beneath the horses' hooves. At a gate on the far side of the paddock, Sam reined in and slid from her saddle. She raised the latch and opened the gate for us and Jake managed to direct his horse through.

'Come on,' she said to me.

Old Marley had taken to munching the frozen grass. I limply

flicked the reins and heeled him but he ignored me. Sam had to take the reins and click encouragingly and coax Marley along: for her, he came obediently.

'Good work, Poncho,' Jake said. 'Show him who's boss.'

'Yeah, yeah.'

Sam shut the gate. From there we followed a dirt track that meandered through the woods. Sam told us it didn't appear on many maps, and only riders from the ranch used it, for accessing the park trails.

'Does Delaney ride?' Jake asked.

'You're riding his horse.'

'I thought they were all his horses.'

'Well, that's the one he likes to ride.'

Jake petted the horse's neck, looking pleased at that.

'Well, he's mine for now.'

The track linked up with one of the Capitol State Forest trails, which hikers, bikers, and equestrian riders all shared – though we encountered nobody else, it being the dead of winter. The trail ran in a smooth, straight line for a time, up a gentle incline. Sam quickened the pace to a light trot and when Thunder and Old Marley followed suit I had a hell of a time sitting in my saddle. I teetered around like a drunk. On top of that the jolting motion sent little shocks of pain through my calf, where I'd sliced it up on the dock.

The long incline steepened and then wiggled into a series of switchbacks, which we ascended more slowly. Rime prickled the trunks of the trees, and dark clouds, charcoal grey, hung down so low they seemed to rest on the mountaintops. As we climbed higher the snow began to fall: delicate flakes that caught in the manes of the horses like confetti.

At a break in the trees Sam pointed down to the right. Below us the ranch had come back into view, surprisingly small, with its outbuildings and field and enclosure. It looked like a fairytale house: completely encircled by pines, at the end of a valley, with the single drive the only access in or out. As far as boltholes go, the Delaneys had picked a good one.

From there the trail ran level for a time, perpendicular to the slope, before angling upwards again towards the ridge. Patches of old snow dappled the ground, and the air tasted a lot colder and thinner. Sam had given me gloves and a winter jacket (they had a selection of stock at the ranch) but I could still feel the frost seeping into me. I felt it the most in my bad hand: the busted joints and damaged nerves ached something fierce.

At the top of the ridge we reached a plateau and an altitude marker: *Larch Mountain Pass, 1024 feet*. We reined in and sat in our saddles, three abreast, looking out. From there the trail continued back down the other side. Mighty peaceful. A strip of grey highway cut through the pines of the next valley. Sam said that it was the Number 12, which we'd taken that morning. She pointed out the parking lot we had passed on the way back, where the trail ended, and further north the buildings of Elma, partially hidden by the lattice of falling snow.

I shifted about in my saddle, and grimaced.

'How you holding up, Poncho?' Jake asked.

'My ass is sore, my calf is killing me, and my shoulder still aches.'

'Some outlaw you are.'

'We could ride on,' Sam said, 'and right into town, but it's pretty far.'

'And we got dinner to make,' Jake said.

Sam guided Shenzao around and started back the way we'd come.

'Be careful,' she called over her shoulder. 'It can be a bit trickier, going down.'

That proved true. The horses had a tendency to trot, which bounced me around in the saddle and aggravated my leg. I had to lean back to keep myself upright. But at least I didn't need to steer: Old Marley knew the way and all I had to do was hold on and endure it.

When we came out of the switchbacks, the snow had settled on the ground, creating a fine layer that the horses' hooves left prints in. Jake slowed down Thunder, letting me catch up, so he and I were riding side-by-side. Sam was about ten or fifteen yards ahead.

'There's something I got to tell you,' I said.

'Me, too.'

I explained what Sam had said in the grocery store, about the killings.

'You think he knows she saw?' he asked.

'Reckon he suspects.'

'Doesn't surprise me. I heard about other things, worse things.'

'I know you don't like backing down,' I said, 'but I think we got to go, man.'

'Me, too.'

That threw me. I hadn't expected that. I'd been gearing up for another argument.

I said, 'I thought you were all set on some kind of showdown.'

As he rode, he got out a pack of Maria's menthols (he'd used up all his Du Mauriers) and flipped open the lid with one hand and held it up to his mouth, withdrawing a smoke with his teeth. Then he exchanged the pack for a lighter and managed to light it, still just using the one hand. It was a neat trick. He already looked more comfortable in the saddle than me.

'There are other factors involved, now.'

He nodded at Sam, swaying so easy and natural in her saddle just ahead of us.

He said, 'She's going to come with us.'

'What are you talking about? Maria's not going to allow that.'

'It's her idea. I think it's partly why we're here.'

'What the hell are we going to do with a kid?'

'Take her home. What do you think?'

'Vancouver won't be safe – for her or for us.'

'Maria's got family out in Hope. Sam's grandma and aunt.'

'How are we going to get her across?'

Jake blew smoke and looked at me. 'You going to sit there and debate this with me?'

'I'm just talking through the practicalities. They'll arrest you at the border.'

'There's the boat. You've been harping on about taking it back, fixing it up, right? Here's your chance. We'll get Sam home, and after that, if I have to, I'll turn myself in.'

'You'd do that?'

'I stole a horse. I don't know what the charges are for that, but it can't be too bad.'

'Shit, Jake. Let's just hold on, here.'

'You wanted to go, we're going. First thing tomorrow. The Delaneys are coming tomorrow night. We'll be long gone by then – hopefully back in Canadian waters.'

'What about the money?'

'You said it yourself. We didn't do it for the money.'

'What about Maria?'

We rode in silence, the horses' hooves thudding the dirt. Jake exhaled a cloud.

'Right now, Sam's what matters. Maria knows it and I know it and you know it, too.'

'I'm with you.'

'Yeah?'

'It's the only way.'

He reached over, and we sort of gripped each other's forearms, in a strange and awkward handshake – the closest we could get to shaking while riding on horseback.

'What are you crackers talking about?'

We'd fallen further behind, and Sam had pivoted Shenzao to look back at us.

'You, cowgirl,' Jake told her.

She waited for us to come abreast of her, and then jerked her head at the trail and said, 'This is a nice straightaway. If you want to let them run, here's the place to do it.'

She said it like a challenge, and without waiting for a response flicked the reins and took off down the trail, riding low and still as Shenzao stomped the earth beneath her, kicking up bursts of snow and dirt.

'What do you think, Poncho?' Jake asked. 'You want to try it?'

'Ah hell, Lefty. No. You go.'

He heeled his horse, which loped off down the track. I intended to follow at the usual pace, but Old Marley saw the fun they were having and took off in pursuit. I cried out and let go of the reins – which Sam had warned me not to do – and grabbed hold of the pommel and hung on. The falling snow flew towards my face, stinging my eyes, and I jolted along, riding blind. Then I heard Jake yell, 'Yee-haw,' and I did the same and for a few seconds my fear and panic dissipated, blown clean out of me by the wind rushing past and the snowy ground scrolling beneath me and the hoofbeats resounding in my ears.

I wouldn't have been able to stop, but Sam had reined in at

the turn-off and Shenzao stood sideways across the path, effectively blocking us off. Old Marley slowed up of his own accord and as he did I tipped crazily to one side, nearly falling from the saddle, but managed to right myself. Sam sat there smiling, her cheeks all pink with cold. She leaned sideways in her saddle to gather up my reins and handed them back to me.

'Thanks, Calamity,' I said. 'I think that's your nickname, from here on in. Calamity Sam. Like Calamity Jane – the cowgirl.'

She smiled, pleased. 'Poncho and Lefty and Calamity Sam,' she said.

'You're part of our gang, now,' Jake said.

'Like heck,' she said. 'You're part of mine.'

And Shenzao shook herself and struck the ground with a forehoof, as if agreeing.

Chapter Thirty-Seven

WE ARRIVED BACK AT THE ranch full of frosty giddiness, our blood all up and pumping from the ride in the cold. My tailbone ached and my calf had started bleeding again and I couldn't feel my fingers, but it didn't matter. I limped around the house, massaging my bad hand with my good one as warming pain crept back into those mangled digits. Sam put some kind of crazy Cuban music on and started dancing like a dervish. Jake, well, he went on through to the kitchen and shook instant coffee into four of the mugs from Sam's dinner set. Then he splashed a bit of Delaney's whisky, liberally, into one of them.

'You want your coffee Irish, Poncho?'

'May as well.'

'What's Irish?' Sam asked.

'It's Irish if there's liquor in it.'

He added whisky to mine. Then he got out the kettle and plugged it in and reached for the power-switch next to the socket. Something popped and the whole room went dark.

'What the fuck?' I heard Jake say.

Sam laughed and said, 'You blew the power.'

'Maria said not to use that switch.'

Jake swore and admitted he'd forgotten. I heard Sam crossing the room, then a click, and the lights flickered back on. She'd reset the master breaker, on a fuse box beneath the stairs. Jake plugged the kettle into another socket, and made our coffees. Sam asked if she could have hers Irish too, and after a moment's hesitation he gave her a single drop.

'Ah,' she said, tasting it, 'that's good stuff.'

A few minutes later Maria appeared in the kitchen doorway – her hair tousled, her eyes puffy as if she'd been sleeping or passed out – and looked around in bewilderment.

'What happened with the power?' she asked.

'I screwed up.' Jake took one of the grown-up Irish coffees over to her, and held it out. She just looked at it. 'Go on. We're celebrating tonight.'

'What's the occasion?' she asked.

'Things are looking up, aren't they?'

'For some of us.'

She leaned there against the doorframe as if she needed it to hold her up.

'Hey,' Jake told her, touching her elbow, 'we just had fun on the ride, is all. It's going to be okay, now. You'll see.'

He sounded as convincing as ever. Maria took the cup of coffee, and had to straighten up to drink it. She smacked her mouth a little, taste-testing it.

'You want to stiffen this up a little?'

'Take it easy before dinner.'

'Your big feast.'

'Damn right.'

From across the room, Sam called, 'Can I cook with you, Jake?' She was bouncing on the sofa, having a little-kid moment.

'Sure can. But somebody better put together our barbecue before that happens.'

While he prepared his whisky sauce, Sam and I set to building the barbecue. We tore open the box and laid all the parts across the floor of the lounge. It was a basic clamshell set-up: a steel dish, like a giant wok, with a matching lid and three chrome legs that stuck out from the bottom. It came with a cheap tin wrench, tiny and awkward to handle. I showed Sam how to assemble the legs and then started to attach them. They screwed right into the underside of the dish. I did the first two. As we worked, it was hard not to notice my mangled crab-hand. Sam was too polite to mention it, but she eyed it up some.

'I work on the boats,' I said. 'Or I did, until recently.'

It had defined me for so long, I didn't know what I amounted to without it.

'I got careless one day,' I said, 'while we were docking alongside a barge, to get ice for our hold. Crushed it between their hull and our gunnel. Bye-bye fingers.'

I wiggled them, embarrassed, and she nodded. 'That must have hurt.'

'It hurt like a son of a bitch,' I said. 'It still does, most of the time.'

I used my bad fingers to hold the chrome leg in place while I worked the wrench around with my left, snugging up the nut. Oftentimes I found it easier to go southpaw.

I said, 'I don't mind, though. It's a good reminder.'

'Of what?'

'Of how easy it is to lose what matters.'

I finished that leg, and offered her the wrench. I held the third leg in place while she twisted on the nut. Her face was focused and diligent as she did this, taking it very seriously. When we were done we flipped the barbecue over and stood it up.

'Not bad,' I said.

Jake called over to us: 'How's that barbecue coming, Poncho?'

'Just need to fit the lid hinge, Lefty. Me and Calamity got her done.'

'Why Calamity?' Maria asked.

She was stretched out on the sofa, nursing another Irish coffee. She'd put milk and ice in to cool it – an iced Irish latte – and every so often she cracked an ice cube between her teeth.

'It's my nickname,' Sam said. 'Like the cowgirl.'

She said it in that way kids can: like, get with it, Mom.

Maria said, 'Seems everybody has a nickname but me.'

I promised her we'd think of one, but we never got around to it.

When we'd finished fitting the lid, Jake and I carried the barbecue outside. By then the snow was really coming down. A thick layer, three or four centimetres deep, covered the porch, and extended out in a big white sheet that stretched over the drive, the paddock, the stable and bunkhouse. The flakes swirled around us in the blackness, as if we stood at the mouth of a vortex.

As we set down the barbecue, Jake said, 'It's a damned winter wonderland out here.'

'That track ain't going to be very passable, if the snow keeps up.'

'We'll have the truck.'

'Still.'

'I hear you.'

We stood side-by-side and peered into the dusk, as if trying to judge how much snow had fallen, and how much might continue to fall. The forecast was for more snow overnight.

Jake said, 'We could go tonight.'

I nodded. 'I'll stop drinking.'

'How much you had?'

'Just the Irish coffee, and one beer.'

'We'll go after dinner, then.'

'Does Sam know the plan?'

'Some. I think she knows some.'

I stooped to put my beer can down in the snow, and went to fetch the bag of charcoal. We dumped a dozen or so briquettes into the base of the barbecue – rattling around in there like bones – and soaked them in lighter fluid and tossed on a match. They went up with a whoosh before settling into a slower burn. Jake lowered the lid and opened the vent and pleasant-smelling smoke drifted out. It seemed odd, smelling those briquettes in the middle of winter. It was such a summer smell.

Sam poked her head out. 'Are you cooking yet?'

'Need to heat it up first, but you can bring out the ribs, if you like.'

'Just got to get my jacket.'

When she was gone, I said, 'Should I tell Maria?'

'You better.'

Maria was in the kitchen, chopping vegetables for salad. I didn't know how to broach the matter so instead I told her about the tequila we'd bought, and asked if she wanted to help me make some margaritas.

She looked at me funny. 'Sure – if you like.'

There wasn't much to help with, but she stood by me as I went about it. I squeezed the lime juice into a glass, and dumped that into the blender with ice and water. Delaney's designer blender broke up the ice, no problem – whirling it into a smooth slurry paste.

'He's good with her, isn't he?' she said.

She gazed past me, at the big window overlooking the porch. Out there you could see the figures of Jake and Sam, huddled over the barbecue coals, talking and laughing.

'You should have seen him the other day,' I said. 'When he'd first met her.'

'I didn't know how to tell him. I meant to tell you both the night you arrived.'

'Not years ago?'

'I already been through all that with him.' She touched my arm. 'Not you, too.'

'A person ought to know if he's got a daughter.'

'We were all a mess at the time. Just a big disaster.'

'I remember.'

'You do?'

It hung between us, then. I got out four of those plastic cups and poured the margarita slush into them. We both watched it spill out, as if the contents were incredibly valuable and important. When it was done, she said, 'She could be yours too, you know.'

'I know that. I thought of that.'

'Does Jake know?'

'No.'

I felt as if my whole body was humming. It had been during

Jake's trial. We'd both been called as witnesses and on other days we sat in the audience, watching. At night we'd get hammered and get high and on some of those nights things had happened.

I said, 'It's one of the things I feel the worst about.'

She leaned over and kissed me on the cheek.

'We didn't know what the hell we were doing. After your sister died . . .'

'I know about that.'

'Well, I don't regret it, anyway.'

'No regrets, eh?'

'I've done a lot of things I regret, but that's not one of them.'

I didn't know what to say to that. It didn't make me feel less guilty, but it made me feel less something. Less weighted, maybe. Less heavy. I'd been carrying it around for a hell of a long time, even if I'd tried to ignore it. Like a piece of shrapnel I'd picked up.

'Does it matter to you?' she asked. 'Whether she's . . .'

'My niece or daughter?'

'That's what I mean.'

'She's kin. That's what matters.'

'Jake said she looks just like Sandra did, at that age.'

'She's the spitting image.'

I got down one of the bottles of Lunazul, cracked it, and splashed tequila in two of the margaritas. She took one and asked, 'Who's the other virgin for?'

'Me, tonight.'

'You ain't drinking?'

'I may be driving.'

I looked at her fully. I'd been avoiding her gaze without even realizing.

She said, 'Jake said tomorrow.'

'There's the snow.'

Her face crumpled, but only for a split second: it was as if she started crying, and then stopped herself, cutting it off. Just refusing to let that happen or the tears take hold of her.

'I was worried about that.'

'You can come with us. You should.'

She shook her head. 'He'd follow me.'

'He'll come hunting us anyway.'

'That's why I have to stay. I can talk him out of it, make him leave you alone, and let Sam go. You brought the horse. That was the agreement. And you came through. I'm so glad you both did.'

'Maria.'

'I made my bed. I got to lie in it. But my daughter doesn't. She sure as hell doesn't.'

She said it adamantly, almost fervently. I wasn't sure about that, or what it meant. And when I looked at her, she looked away.

'Does Sam know we're related?' I asked.

'I think she does.'

'You told her?'

'Not in so many words. I must have hinted.'

She was knocking back her margarita, gulping it, and she paused, all of a sudden, and palmed her forehead, squinting and wincing. She even cried out. She'd had a little brain-freeze, like you get when eating ice cream. When it passed, she looked at me and blinked back tears. 'Damn,' she said, 'that hurts. It always hurts more than you think it will.'

The door opened, and Sam rushed in. Tinsel-bits of snow clung to her tuque, and dusted her shoulders. Cold air and swirling flakes rushed in after her.

'Jake's teaching me to cook ribs,' she said, as if it was the greatest thing in the world.

When the food was ready we sat down together to have our feast. Sam and I set the table, laying out the dinner plates we'd picked up at the grocery store. It felt more like a proper meal, that way. Maria even lit a few candles, the flames floating around the wicks, the heat rising up from them in thin squiggles.

Along with the steak and ribs Jake had roasted vegetables and potato chunks, wrapped in tin foil and lathered in oil. It had been years since I'd tried his damned whisky-grilled ribs, and they were something else: sweet and agonizingly spicy, smothered in a glaze of hot chillies and liquor. He and Maria were sharing a bottle of wine and Sam's wild salsa music was still playing and the knowledge that we'd be leaving in a little while seemed distant, unimportant.

Jake said, 'Pass the margarita mix, will you Poncho?'

Sam said, 'How'd you get your nicknames, anyway?'

'It's an old country song,' I said. 'The real title is Pancho and Lefty, with an "a". But we always thought they were saying "Poncho" like the ones you wear.'

'I'm left-handed, a lefty,' Jake said, 'and as for Poncho here . . .'

'We don't need to go into that,' I said.

But of course that made Sam want to hear it all the more. So Jake told the story: of how we'd dressed up as banditos for Halloween, and had a firecracker fight. I'd worn an old poncho our father had picked up travelling down in Mexico. But when Jake had tagged me with a Roman candle, the damned poncho had caught fire, and started burning. Jake had to jump on me and help smother it out.

'I could have died,' I said, getting into it.

'Good old Poncho,' he said fondly. 'What would Lefty do without you?'

Maria said, 'Who would have thought you'd become real outlaws, one day?'

'We're not that real.'

After we'd finished the meal we stayed at the table and kept on chewing the fat like that, talking about home and growing up together, and the things the three of us used to do: raising hell in our own small ways. It was mostly for Sam's sake, and really I suppose we were talking around the one thing that needed to be said. But eventually somebody had to say it, and that fell to Maria. She poured herself another glass of red, and sat staring into it, swilling the wine for a time before looking up, her face set.

'Samantha.'

Something about her tone, and the way she'd used Sam's full name like that, got her daughter's attention – and ours too.

'Remember I talked about you going to stay with your grandma.'

Sam sat up a little straighter, as if she'd been pricked with a pin. 'Sure,' she said.

'How would you feel about going back to Canada, with Jake and Timmy?'

She looked around at us anxiously: these three serious-faced adults.

'When?'

'Tonight.'

'Oh.'

'We were going to go tomorrow,' Jake said. 'But don't want to get snowed in.'

Sam picked up her fork (we had real plates but were still using plastic forks) and used it to push a few straggling vegetables around on her plate, herding them into a clump.

She asked, 'What about you, Mom?'

'I'll come later on. I'll come join you in a few weeks.'

Sam shook her head, as if arguing that point in her head, but she didn't say anything about that. She said, 'Do we have to go right now?' She was asking us. Me and Jake.

'Not right now,' I said.

'A little while,' Jake said.

'Give you time to get some things together.'

You could see the uncertainty in her face. But she wasn't scared: she had real pluck. I have to admit I was proud of her, even though I had no right to be. She gripped her fork and bent it back and forth, working the plastic to the point of breaking, but not quite.

She said, 'I hate it here,' and looked up, her face turning fierce. 'I want to leave. But I want you to come with us, Mom.'

Maria reached across the table, and took her daughter's hand. 'We'll see,' she said. 'We'll see.'

I don't know if she was just saying that, if she would have come or not. We sat for a time in silence, with them holding hands, stretched out towards each other, as the snow fell swift and soft outside the window, the sky all dark, and us miles from any place.

Maria said, 'Do something for me, Jake?'

He looked at her.

'Will you play a little for us? I haven't heard you play for so long.'

'Sure,' he said. 'Sure I will.'

He went to get his guitar. While he did, Maria retreated upstairs and I was left with Sam.

'I know it's all a bit crazy,' I said. 'I know you only just met us.'

'It doesn't feel that way.'

'Glad you think so.'

'Is he my dad?'

She just came out and said it, straight up, in the way kids can do: as if she was asking whether or not I liked ice cream.

'You'll have to ask him that,' I said.

Her face folded up into a put-upon frown, and I felt like I'd let her down, somehow.

'But look,' I said. 'We're family, okay? I can assure you of that. We're family, and in our family, we take care of our own. Since you're our family, we'll take care of you.'

It didn't come out very well, or sound as reassuring as I wanted it to, but the gist of it got through to her. She sat quiet and still for a time, staring at a spot on the table, her lips compressed to a line.

Then she said, 'I've never had much family.'

'Hey, hey,' I said, and touched her arm. 'It's okay.'

'I only ever had my mom,' she said. 'And she's . . .'

She didn't finish. She couldn't. She just shook her head.

Jake and Maria came back at almost the same time. She moved her chair around to be closer to Sam and Jake sat down with the guitar across his lap. He strummed and plucked the strings, making his usual adjustments. This time, for a change, he seemed satisfied – though as usual I couldn't tell the difference.

'Finally got you tuned,' he said, as if the guitar could hear.

He struck the first chord, and started singing one of his mournful ballads: about love and loss and most probably about Maria, though it never mentioned her by name. He sang it in this faltering voice, partway falsetto, that sounded wounded: promising to hold her close, to waltz her slow, to be there when she called. Maria sat and listened and even before the first verse finished she was crying. Not sobbing but simply weeping, the tears wet on her cheeks. Sam was still sort of teary-eyed from before and seeing all that got me going. We must have been quite the sight, the three of us: weeping away as the music emptied out of him.

When the song finished, you could hear us snivelling, and Jake laughed hoarsely.

'Well, Jesus,' he said. 'Some goodbye party this is. Here.'

He struck a C major and launched into a more upbeat tune, strumming away. I didn't recognize it until he started singing the first verse: 'Poncho and Lefty', his own version of it.

Maria scrubbed the tears from her face and started clapping along and after a minute she stood up and sashayed over to me. 'Dance with me, Timmy,' she said. She took my hand and drew me up out of the chair: there was no point in resisting. She linked her arms behind my neck and I gripped her waist and we turned around together in a kind of quick-step waltz, her moving smooth and confident and me about as graceful as a tortoise. In my arms she felt light and dreamy, like dancing with an apparition, and I found it hard to meet her eyes. Maria always had a way of looking right at you. She never flinched.

When Jake finished playing he put the stereo back on – to Springsteen – and dragged Sam to her feet to be his dancing partner. He swung and turned her around in the kitchen and at the chorus we broke up our pairings and sang along to 'Atlantic City'. Sam didn't know the words so we had to teach her. Then we kept on dancing, the four of us, whirling around the kitchen in a series of do-si-dos. It went on like that for a time until the track changed and things slowed down and Jake turned naturally to Maria and they sort of fell into each other. Sam and I paired up in a formal waltzing position – our hands clasped high – and tottered back and forth like that. Over the music I could hear

Jake talking to Maria, close to her ear. I thought maybe he was trying to get her to come with us. But when the song ended she put a palm on his chest and pushed him away, tenderly.

'Sam,' she said, 'you better go pack and get some things together.'

'I'll load our stuff into the truck,' I told Jake.

Sam went on up, to do as her mother had asked, and I tugged on a jacket, ready to head down to the bunkhouse. I often think about that moment. If we hadn't lingered for so long – reminiscing and dancing, waltzing down memory lane – then that could have been it: the end, or an ending, of sorts. Jake and Sam and I would have left an hour earlier, and been well on our way to the boat, the border, a new kind of life, maybe.

But thinking like that is about as useful as thinking back to the night Sandy died, and wanting to change it – an inclination that is as inevitable as it is useless. It didn't happen like that, and there's no point in imagining otherwise.

Instead, it happened like this: once I stepped outside, I heard the rumble of an engine. I thought maybe it was a plane. I wanted to believe it was a plane. Until I saw the headlights, flickering in the woods. Two sets. They wavered up and down as the vehicles rattled over the track, and steadied upon reaching the long approach to the house. The beams lit up the falling snow, which circled and whirled in big clouds, like swarming insects. I stepped back inside.

'Somebody's coming,' I said.

'No,' Maria said, rushing to the window. 'Oh, fuck.'

The vehicles were two black SUVs: an Escalade and a Durango. There was no doubt who it could be. They'd had the same idea as us, apparently. The Delaneys had come a day early to avoid the snow.

Chapter Thirty-Eight

SAM MUST HAVE HEARD THE cars. Or maybe she saw them, from her bedroom window: the same window she'd witnessed the murders from. She came running downstairs with a bag of her things and took a few steps into the room.

'You better unpack all that,' Jake told her. 'And stay upstairs for now.'

'Is it them?'

'You too, Maria.'

Maria said, 'He's less likely to do anything if I'm here.'

'Come down in a bit.'

'What does that mean?'

'I just think it's better you not seem to be too friendly with us.'

Through the window, I could see figures getting out of the vehicles, now.

'Go,' Jake said.

Maria looked at us with helpless eyes and led Sam back up the stairs. I heard their footsteps and a door close.

'Jesus, man,' I said.

Jake adjusted his bandana, one-handed, like a soldier checking his helmet before the fray. We peered discreetly through the window, keeping out of their line of sight. Down by the cars they were moving about in the snow and unloading bags and whatnot. I counted four of them. Jake reached up and squeezed the back of my neck, in a strange gesture of brotherly encouragement.

'We're gonna have to talk them down,' he said. 'Get out when we can. Just follow my lead, okay?'

'Okay. Hell.'

'Come on,' he said, heading for the door.

'What are you doing?'

'Going to greet them. It's a success, right? A big fucking success.'

En route he drained his beer and crushed the can, then tugged open the door. The storm had really picked up out there: snow-flakes cycloned around us and the wind surged over the porch in blistering waves. We reached the porch steps just as they came up. Mark Delaney was in the front, and that helped. Jake grabbed his hand and pumped it repeatedly, acting juiced up and energized, asking Mark how the hell it was going, slapping his back with his other hand. He had to talk loudly, over the wind. 'Good to see you,' he said. I stood just behind him with this weird and rigid grin on my face, like some sort of village idiot.

The others appeared behind Mark. In the dark, and the kaleidoscope of snow, it was difficult to make out faces, but Pat Delaney emerged next. Jake went for his hand, too. Pat didn't offer it but Jake seized it all the same, spouting something about what a nice crib they had, just blowing a little smoke up their asses, blowing it everywhere, really. Throwing up this smokescreen of movement, smiles, chatter.

I don't know what they were expecting. Not this. Not to be welcomed at their own ranch by Jake, playing the part of concierge. He waved them all on (two other guys were coming up behind the Delaneys) and pointed towards the door. 'Come on in, boys,' Jake said. 'Damn it's cold out here. You want a hand with anything?'

We backed up a few feet (he'd basically hemmed them in on the steps until then) and they followed us onto the porch. Third in line was that Ukrainian, Novak. He had one hand in his coat pocket, and looked from me to my brother, as if assessing our positions. I thought he might pull out a gun and just shoot us. I figured maybe that's what they'd talked about, in the car. Doing to us what they'd done to those other guys. On the porch. Bam. And maybe they had intended that. But Jake had made the right play. He was walking alongside Mark, his shoulders hunched against the cold, asking him about the ride down, driving in the snow.

I reached the door first. I opened it just as they got there and held it wide, polite as a doorman. The funny part was that they all accepted this; nobody considered it odd or even looked at me, really. I was simply this nonentity. Mark and Jake passed by, followed by Pat Delaney and Novak, and at the rear came a heavy-set guy laden with a lot of luggage, moving more slowly. The mule. He was dressed in a loose pinstripe suit and the falling snow stuck to the shoulders like flakes of dandruff.

Once they were all inside, I stepped in there, too.

Jake was already walking around, blowing on his hands to warm them. The table had a few beers on it, but we'd turned off the music and cleared the remains of the meal, at least.

'What a fucking night,' Jake said. 'The snow is what, half a foot deep now?'

'At least,' Mark said. He'd gone to stand by the table, leaning on the back of a chair. 'It got pretty hairy on the track coming up.'

'No shit?' Jake said. 'You got four-wheel drive on those things, though?'

'We got four-wheel drive.'

'Good thing you came down early, though. We were worried you'd get snowed out. We got lots to talk about. Fuck. Hey,' he said, as if it had just occurred to him. 'You guys want a beer? Tim got beer. What'd you get, Tim?'

'Olympia. It's good stuff.'

Novak said, 'Horse piss.'

'Sure – but *good* horse piss.'

Mark laughed. Not Novak. He lurked in the corner, watching, his face flat and expressionless as a shovel.

'You want some horse piss?' Jake asked Mark.

He held out a can to Mark, who took it without opening it. Jake tossed one to me and I did something weird. I cracked it and handed it to the heavy-set guy, who had tan skin and might have been Hispanic. He shrugged and took a big swig, but Pat looked at him, hard. So he stopped and put it to one side, on the windowsill, like a kid caught eating candy. This whole time Pat hadn't said anything. He was prowling around the place. He checked in the lounge, in the games room at the pool table, and padded into the kitchen. Sensing something amiss. Even when he was silent he was a big presence. You could tell the other guys were waiting on him. Novak still had his hand in his pocket.

'Where the fuck is my microwave?' Delaney asked.

'On the porch,' Jake said. 'Maria broke it.'

Mark giggled, and looked out the window. 'It's there all right,' he said.

'And where the fuck is she, then?'

'I think she's upstairs. I heard them up there a while ago,' Jake said.

'What are you two jokers doing in the house?'

Jake held out his hands. 'Hey – it's cold, man. Your bunkhouse is like a fridge. The goddamn heater doesn't work. So we came up to have a few drinks.'

'It is pretty cold down there,' Mark said, agreeably.

'So you just come in here, eating my food, drinking my beer?'

'We bought the beer,' Jake said.

'Shut up about the fucking beer.'

Novak moved from his place in the corner and stood in front of the door, deliberately blocking it. For a few seconds it was extremely quiet.

Then Delaney said, 'You punk.'

He was talking to Jake. Like I said, I was incidental. I was just a tagalong.

Jake held up his hands. 'I didn't mean to infringe or whatever the fuck. Me and my brother just wanted to warm up. No disrespect, all right? Your house is your house.'

'That's not what I'm talking about.'

'Wait a minute,' Jake said, and laughed. 'You're not still mad about that phone call, are you? Hey – I'll be the first to admit, we said some heated things. I was under duress, man. But look. It's all good. The horse is here. Okay? The horse is here. We did it.'

'You did it, all right. And your face is all over the news.'

'But not my name, yet.'

'That's true,' Mark said.

'How the fuck long will it take them to ID you?'

'My face, my problem.'

Delaney shook his head, this violent jerk, and said no, no – this was *his* problem. Because people knew there was a connection, so people would know who was behind it.

'What connection?' Jake said. 'I'm nobody. I'm just some bum.'

'People talk.'

'People talk shit all the time.'

At the door, Novak shifted and said, 'What do you want me to do with these guys?'

'Hey,' Jake said, looking at Mark. 'Hey.'

We heard footsteps on the stairs, and a voice: 'Patrick?'

From the shadow of the stairwell, Maria appeared. Her hair was all mussed up and she looked puffy-cheeked, vacant-eyed. I thought she'd gone and done more methadone, but then I understood it was an act, put on for us. She smiled at Pat, at Mark, at all of them.

'It's good to see you boys,' she said.

She went to Pat and gave him a kiss and casually picked up one of the cans of beer and cracked it and took a sip. She was acting as if everything was normal, which made it hard to act as if everything wasn't.

'Where have you been?' he asked.

'Putting Sam to bed. When d'you get here?'

'Just now.'

'Have you seen the horse?'

'Not yet,' Pat said.

'It's in the stable,' I said, hopefully.

'We were just talking,' Pat said, to Maria. 'Me and your friend Jake.'

He was trying to tell her to leave, but she pretended not to understand.

'You should go see it,' she said. 'It's really something.'

'Since when are you interested in horses?'

'This one is different.'

Pat stood, tense and bristling, for another few seconds. Then he said, 'So let's go and see the fucking horse, then.' He pointed at Jake. 'Just me and you. Just the two of us.'

They got their boots on, and stepped back outside. I had to watch through the window as Jake hiked down there with him, veiled by the snow and dark. At that point I didn't know what the hell was going to happen. I had to trust that Jake could talk his way out of it, and I believed that he could. When he needed to – for example, when his life depended on it – my brother could be uncommonly charming and congenial.

'You boys want some food?' Maria asked. 'We barbecued ribs and steaks.'

Mark made an appreciative sound, and patted his belly.

'What about you, Ricky?'

Apparently that was the heavy-set guy. 'Hell, yeah,' he said. 'We didn't stop to eat.'

He sat down at the table, and Mark joined him – placing the beer I'd given him aside, still without opening it. I went, too. I went and sat with them, trying to act nonchalant about it all: about us having leftovers while the fate of my brother and I was being decided. Maria brought out the ribs and steaks and the remains of the potatoes we'd had. She put a plate in front of me as well but was very careful not to treat me any differently to the others. Mark and Ricky helped themselves and tore into the whisky-grilled ribs appreciatively, chewing loudly and making smacking noises with their lips. I listened to that and every so often looked at the window, where Novak was stationed, peering out, attentive as a terrier.

'This is fucking good,' Mark said.

His mouth was full, and the cold had given his voice an odd rasp, as if he'd had asthma as a kid.

Ricky nodded and said, 'Tastes like my mother's.'

Mark said, 'You taste your mother?'

Then he wheezed, and slapped me. 'This fucking guy tastes his mother!'

I smiled, politely, but maybe didn't laugh as hard as he would have liked.

'What's up?' Mark asked.

'Your brother seems pissed.'

'It was a long ride. He'll get over it.'

They gnawed at their ribs, Novak stood watch, and I waited. About ten minutes later, footsteps sounded on the porch. Jake and Pat were back, coming towards the door. I didn't know if that was good or bad, but when they stepped inside Pat was smiling. He saw the food and came over and picked up a rib – holding it like a drumstick – and ripped a chunk of meat off with his teeth. Then, after tossing the bone down, he jerked a thumb at Jake and said, 'You know these jokers brought that horse down on a boat?'

Mark spat out a mouthful of potato. 'A *fucking* boat?'

'A fishing boat.'

'My brother's boat,' Jake said.

'That's genius.'

Pat sat down by his brother, and started helping himself to the food. He didn't comment on it. He just accepted the food was there, and his, like everything else in that house. 'You know what's genius?' he said. 'We could shift a lot of product that way.'

Mark said, 'I heard the Triads are doing that.'

'Beats the hippy hikers, or fucking air drops.'

Ricky said, 'The Angels run the docks.'

Jake pulled up a chair and turned it around, straddling it. 'Talk to my bro,' he said, nodding at me. 'He's on the boats. And he's a hell of a captain. Piloted us through a bitch of a storm on the strait. What fucking strait was it again, Tim?'

They all looked at me, as if noticing me for the first time.

'Juan de Fuca,' I said. 'But they call it Juan de Puke-a.'

'It had me puking, all right. And the horse shitting herself.'

Mark giggled. He had a smear of whisky sauce on his chin. 'I can't believe you put a horse on a *boat*.'

He wanted to know the details and practicalities, so we told them about turning around at the border, and thinking maybe we'd take the horse back, except the cops had already been there at the stables. So we ended up at the docks, with no place left to go.

'Hey,' Mark said. 'We're sorry about that. Our guy at the border wet the bed.'

Pat grunted. 'He's a dead man, that guy. Dead.'

'Well, we found a way.'

We told them about loading the horse, and clearing customs, and when we got to the bit about Shenzao going overboard, and us catching her in the seine net, they were laughing. Even Novak. That bastard still wanted to shoot us – clearly – but he couldn't help laughing. We didn't mention the hen party, and all the footage they had of us, for obvious reasons.

'You clowns,' Pat said, shaking his head. 'You fucking clowns.'

Mark finally cracked the beer that was in front of him. It was like a signal. Ricky and Pat started drinking, too. Pat took a long pull and burped and attacked another rib.

He said to Maria, 'Where the hell did you get this meat?'

'Jake cooked it,' she said.

'Yeah?'

He looked at Jake, appraisingly.

Then he said, 'You're a good fucking cook.' He slapped Jake on the back, hard, and laughed, and all the other guys laughed, too. As they did, Jake and I made eye contact across the table. Just a look. Just enough to say, 'Okay – so what the hell happens next?'

Chapter Thirty-Nine

WHAT HAPPENED NEXT, AS IT turned out, was crokinole. The board they kept down there was the same make as the one in Vancouver: a high-end mahogany model with a smoothly lacquered veneer. Pat had brought his personal set of shooting discs from home. He began to lay those out reverently on the table where they kept the board. He even had this special wax powder that you sprinkle on the playing surface to ensure the discs slide smoothly.

On the wall above the table hung a chalkboard for tallying up snooker scores and Pat used it to create a grid for a round robin tournament, with each of our names on it. He didn't ask us if we wanted to play. That was simply a given. It was like being in the presence of a very demanding and very dangerous child: a tyrant prince.

We had to do what he wanted, or else.

'Who the fuck wants a shot of Jack Daniel's?' he said, brandishing a twenty-sixer.

We said that we did, except Maria (she had withdrawn into the kitchen) and Novak, who simply sat in a chair and didn't drink anything and observed – patient and careful as a sentinel – as we each took a turn swigging from the twixer.

'What are the stakes?' Mark said, wiping his mouth.

'The usual.'

'Two C-notes to buy-in.'

Jake and I looked at each other.

'We don't got that kind of money on us,' Jake said.

Mark giggled. 'Ricky don't neither.'

'I got an eight ball,' Ricky said.

'Forget it,' Pat told Jake. 'You can take it from what we owe you.'

He said it in a sly, insincere way, and looked at his guys – as if to say, these losers still think we're actually going to pay them.

'Sure,' Jake said.

Pat turned to me. 'What about you? Three fingers enough to play with?'

'Enough to jerk off with,' Ricky said.

He'd been waiting to burn somebody, ever since Mark's comment about his mother. But he said it in a kind of friendly way. I mimed tugging at my crotch with my bad hand.

'I ain't good,' I said, 'but I can still give it a go.'

Mark laughed and shook the discs from the bag (nobody else

was allowed to use Pat's discs) and they clattered out onto the table. We began to sort them, separating the light wood pieces from the dark. While this went on, Pat changed the music and cranked up some drum and bass – boom boom boom – and on the table next to the board he and Ricky started cutting up Ricky's eight ball: creating long fat lines of coke, like albino banana slugs. They snorted one each before the game started. After pawing at his nose, Pat made this weird hiccupping, gagging sound in the back of his throat.

'Hell yeah,' he said, cracking his knuckles. 'I'm gonna school you tools!'

We settled down around the table. Crokinole isn't complicated: you just have to flick the discs towards a hole in the centre of the board. The closer you get, the higher your score. But the other guy can knock your discs off, so in that way it's a lot like table-top curling.

'Twenty-shot to see who starts,' Mark said.

Ricky's disc was closer, so he got first shot. He used it to nestle up behind one of the peg-guards. Jake was rusty and sent his own disc careening off the peg into the gutter. But by his second shot he had settled and managed a double-clear. Pat snapped in appreciation.

'Look at this fucking southpaw,' he said.

They went back and forth, shot-for-shot, clearing each other's discs pretty cleanly. As the game continued, I looked around for Maria. She was hovering in the kitchen, watching. She caught my eye and beckoned. I announced I was going to get myself a drink, but nobody paid me much mind: they were engrossed in the game. I sidled on through. Maria greeted me in an overly polite way, and said she was making vodka sodas and asked if I might like one.

'Why, sure,' I said, just as formally. 'I appreciate that, ma'am.'

As she mixed the drinks, Maria spoke without looking at me: just talking low and hurriedly under her breath.

'You got to get out,' she said.

'I know it.'

'Here.'

She laid something on the counter, behind the toaster. The keys to the truck.

'What about Sam?' I asked.

'I'll tell her.'

'You still want us to take her?'

'If nothing else, just get her away from here.'

I heard footsteps on the hardwood. Novak had come into the kitchen. He crossed to the sink and filled up his glass with water. He turned and stared at us and drank it, slowly.

'You want a beer, man?' I asked.

He didn't even say no, or shake his head. It was like I hadn't spoken. When he'd finished the water he filled the glass up again and walked back out. The guy was unsettling as all hell.

'I'll tell Jake,' I said to Maria.

I slid the keys across the counter and casually put them in my pocket. I wanted to reassure her but thought Novak might still be keeping tabs on us, so I just met her eyes one last time and took the drink she'd made me back out to the crokinole table. Jake was on his last shot. He cleared Ricky off the board and left himself in the centre circle, sealing the win.

'Jake owned you, Rick!' Mark said, sounding unnaturally excited.

'Ricky-dicky,' Pat said. 'You gave that shit away.'

Rick stood up, swearing about luck, and took a swig of Jack. Mark and I were up next, and it wasn't much of a game. I'd learned to do a lot of things with my left hand, but playing crokinole wasn't one of them. Mark went to town, creating a cluster of discs in the fifteen circle and bagging himself a twenty-in-the-hole.

'Take it easy on my brother,' Jake said.

'Yeah,' Pat said, 'he's fucking handicapped.'

When it was done – sixty to zero, for Mark – Pat chalked it up. He was due to play Ricky next. We made way for them and Pat brought out his special set of discs. The rest of us sat back, watching. I tried to look as if I cared about their game and sipped my vodka without really drinking much. What I needed was some kind of excuse to talk to Jake, alone. I patted at my pockets, as if looking for something, then asked him if he had his cigarettes.

'Sure,' he said.

He seemed to get the idea. He brought out his Marlboros and tapped two smokes from the pack, offering one to me. Pat looked at us in irritation, distracted from his game.

'Nobody smokes in here. Take that shit outside.'

It had played out perfectly, but we moaned a little about the cold and shrugged on our coats and went out there together. Jake stood directly in front of the bay window and grinned at me and said, 'Just talk and look happy – like we're shooting the shit, okay?'

'Okay,' I said, and grinned weirdly back at him.

'You hear him joke about the money?'

'It didn't sound good.'

'He don't intend to pay us, and never did.'

'You reckon they intend to kill us?'

'If they feel like it.'

I told him Maria had given me the keys to the truck. He took a long drag, and nodded, still with this deliberately cheerful expression on his face. We looked down at the vehicles. The Delaneys had parked behind Maria's truck, which looked pretty hemmed in. We might not get around their SUVs, and even if we did there was the possibility we'd get stuck in the snow. But it was the only way out, as far as I could tell.

I said, 'They ain't gonna let us just drive off.'

'We need to be ready. In case this turns sour.'

'And then what?'

'Make a break for it. Unless you got a better idea.'

I shook my head. 'We'll need our passports, for the border.'

He took a drag, and laughed good-naturedly – and it took me a moment to realize he was still play-acting: pretending we were shooting the shit, rather than planning our escape.

'How do you reckon we'll manage that?' he asked.

'I'll slip down there, stash them in the truck.'

'We got one bottle of Old Crow left. That's an excuse.'

The door to the house opened behind us. I figured it was going to be Novak, checking up on us in his creepy way, but it turned out to be Mark. He had a beer in one hand and gave us the thumbs up with the other.

'Jake – you're up! You and me.'

Jake flicked his smoke into the snow, where it landed lightly, still smouldering.

'Fucking ace,' he said, looking significantly at me. 'Let's do this.'

Chapter Forty

JAKE AND MARK SETTLED INTO their match. I took my seat and poured myself a substantial highball of Jack Daniel's, then shared the whisky around, splashing it liberally into the other glasses. For our ploy to work, I needed that bottle to be finished. I hadn't been intending to drink much but it would look suspicious to abstain, so as they traded rocks I knocked mine back, feeling that molten burn. And to be honest, I needed it for what I was about to do.

When my glass was empty, I put it down loudly.

'Hey Jake,' I said, 'do we still got that Old Crow?'

'Down in the bunkhouse,' he said, without looking up from his shot – nice and smooth. 'Go grab it, will you?'

'Fuck yeah,' Pat said.

That part was easy: they had no reason to suspect anything.

I let myself out, passing Novak at the door, and trudged down the drive. The wind had dwindled to a whisper and the snow had let up, at least for the time being. But over a foot of it blanketed the ground: a soft dry powder that compressed beneath my boots and made this unsettling squeaking sound, as if I were stomping on mice.

As I passed the vehicles I took a closer look. The two SUVs had us really boxed in. We could potentially squeeze past in the truck, but the edge of the drive sloped up in a steep bank, and that was covered in snow. Manoeuvring around that would be touch-and-go.

'Goddammit,' I said, under my breath. 'Goddammit to hell.'

At the bunkhouse I went into our room. I didn't take everything. There was no point. I just got our Ninja Turtle backpack and stuffed our passports and wallets in it and the last of the cash we had: a few hundred bucks. The extra clothes I left, along with the random crap we'd brought from Jake's apartment. I was so rattled I almost forgot to grab the Old Crow.

As I stepped outside, I noticed that the stable doors were ajar, and the lights on inside. I figured Jake and Delaney had left it like that, when they'd come to have a look at Shenzao. But it would do no good for the animals, letting the cold in. I moseyed on over there, and as I drew nearer I thought I heard movement within. I pushed the doors open wider. The horses were standing quietly, dozing. The heater rattled away, but that was the only sound. I didn't see anybody.

'Hello?' I said.

I heard shuffling from the end stall, which was unoccupied. Or should have been. A head poked up from within, chipmunk-like, peering over the gate at me. Sam.

'I didn't know who it was,' she said, stepping out.

'I thought you were upstairs.'

'I snuck out the back door.'

'What are you doing?'

She came towards me, and we met near Shenzao's stall. I still had the bottle of Crow in my hand. Sam looked at it, and scuffed her hiking boot on the ground, scattering straw.

'I just come down, sometimes, when Mr Delaney and his friends are over.'

She didn't look at me as she said it. She looked at the horse. As we stood there, I got my first real sense of what it must have been like for her, living in that place: the atmosphere poisonous and plagued, a big playhouse overseen by a maniac, with all these terrible bastards passing through. Cokeheads like Ricky and killers like Novak.

'Is that so?' I said softly.

She held out her hand and started petting Shenzao. I watched her with the horse for a moment. Her face remained stoic, expressionless. I touched her shoulder, and she jumped.

'Hey,' I said.

'Sorry.'

'We're going to get you out of here.'

'Tonight?'

'If we can. The damned cars are blocking us in.'

Shenzao snorted, and took a step towards Sam. She only meant to encourage Sam to keep petting her, but it drew my attention to the animal. Shenzao eyeballed me right back, in what seemed to me a challenging and insolent way. That was what gave me the idea. It was crazy, all right – even crazier than transporting her on the boat.

I asked Sam, 'You ever ridden in the snow before?'

'Sure.'

'You think you could follow that trail you took us on today, at night?'

She looked at me. She didn't ask what I meant.

'I could,' she said.

I looked around. The riding gear and saddles were right there. It actually made more sense than anything else, or than any of our other options, which were basically non-existent.

'Tell you what,' I said. 'You saddle three horses up. The same ones we rode earlier. If me and Jake can get away, we're just going to go, all right? We're just going to ride out.'

She crossed her arms and nodded, looking stern rather than nervous. That, more than anything, made me believe it was possible. We would ride out. It was as simple as that.

'I'll wait down here,' Sam said.

'Here's our things.'

I handed her our bag. I lingered awkwardly for a moment, appreciating the security of Sam's little hideaway. But I had to go. I turned towards the door, then checked myself and glanced back.

'When the time comes,' I said, 'we might be in a hurry. If you get me.'

She said that she did.

On the way back up, I could see somebody standing on the porch, smoking. It was just a shadow, backlit by the porch light, but I could tell it was Novak. He had a thin and sinewy body and he always looked poised to strike, like a snake. I had to assume he was watching me. I meandered up the drive with my hands in my pockets, my head down against the cold, acting as if I hadn't noticed him yet. I uncapped the bottle of Old Crow and faked taking big, extravagant swigs – slopping a little over the snow in the process.

At the porch stairs I looked up, as if spotting him for the first time. He was right there at the top of the stairs, and again I had the sensation that there wasn't much keeping him from pulling his gun from his pocket (I was convinced he had a gun) and simply pointing it at me and pulling the trigger. I clambered up the steps and nodded at him, and then stopped to look back – as if to see what he was staring at. In truth, I wanted to know if he could have seen me coming from the stable. But it was dark down there, the buildings a jumble of shapes. You couldn't make much out.

'You want some whisky?' I asked.

He didn't bother to answer me, as I'd come to expect from him.

'Ain't you cold?' I said. 'Fucking cold out here.'

He just stood there in his grey hoody and tracksuit bottoms. He was also wearing running shoes. He looked ready to go for a casual jog. Or ready for something, anyway.

'Are you truly so stupid as you act?' he said.

'I ain't stupid.'

He peered at me, as if honestly trying to unpuzzle me.

'Look man,' I said, 'I just want to party. I just want to have a good time. Everybody wants to but you. What is it with you?'

He blew a thin stream of smoke at me. Right in my face.

He said, 'I do not like your brother.'

'You don't know my brother at all.'

'You will both be lucky if Pat does not tell me to shoot you tonight.'

'We're harder to shoot than you think.'

I said it like a little kid. I turned to go, feeling adrenaline-sick and all a-tremble with fear, halfway expecting him to hit me in the base of the skull or grab me in a chokehold or drygulch me like a fucking bastard in the back. But none of that happened. I reached the door okay and looked behind me and saw him watching, waiting, a shadow in the dark.

I stepped inside. The game between Jake and Mark was still going on, and Pat Delaney was still sitting at the table with them, and Maria was still in the kitchen. The only change was Ricky: he'd moved into the lounge. He had his legs up on the sofa and was watching videos – porn, of some kind – on his laptop.

As I came in, Jake glanced up and shouted, 'You got the Crow, Poncho!'

'The fuck took so long?' Pat asked.

'Had to take a dump,' I said.

Ricky cackled, 'A steamer, eh?'

'A big one.'

Pat said, 'I don't want to hear about your shit.'

I planted the Old Crow on the table. Pat reached for it and poured himself a highball – splashing it on top of whatever dregs were in his glass – without looking at me. I pulled up a chair and sat a bit back from the table. They were on their final few shots. Jake was down on the board but had a twenty in the hole. They both traded clears and then Mark had last shot. Jake had left a disc nestled behind a peg in the ten circle. A tricky clear.

'You got to shoot the alley,' Pat said, coaching his brother.

'I could take it from the side.'

'The line's not there.'

Mark shifted back and forth in his seat, testing out different angles, trying to find a bead. He finally settled on his brother's alley shot, and flicked the stone, which ricocheted off the peg-guard and into the gutter.

'Ah, shit,' Mark said. 'You always screw me. You and your advice.'

'That was the smart play. You just fucked it up.'

'What do you know about smart play?'

'I'm the smart one. I'm the brains of the outfit.'

'Like hell. You're the muscle. I'm the brains. I made us.'

They were kind of joking, and kind of not. Mark's face was red – from the booze and excitement – and when he stood up he did it so fast his chair fell over backwards, banging on the floor. He muttered something about the furniture being bullshit and picked it back up.

Jake stretched and yawned. 'Who's next?'

'Me and you,' Pat said.

'I need a piss break.'

'No pissing between games.'

'That's not a rule,' Mark said. He was still choked about losing. 'Go take a piss. Don't listen to head honcho, here. Brains, my ass.'

Jake shook his head and got up and went down the hall. I was about to follow him – to pitch my new crazy plan – but I had no real excuse to give, and Mark sat beside me and railed a line and started talking, loudly and too quickly, in this coked-up way, about why he should have tried the angle he wanted. He said this to me while looking at his brother, who was carefully cleaning each of his discs with a soft cloth.

'Look at this guy,' Mark said. 'Thinks he's some kind of pro.'

Mark giggled, and slapped me on the back. Pat didn't laugh.

'Just watch how it's done, little brother,' he said.

'Jake's gonna own you,' Mark said. 'His finger's golden tonight.'

I nodded sagely, even though I knew Jake was an average player at best, and that night his shots had all been pretty standard. But of course I didn't say that. I just sat tight as Mark went on about the skill of Jake's game.

'Against a guy like that, you got to play defensive. That was my mistake.'

'Your mistake,' Pat said, 'was getting too drunk and too high – like Ricky.'

Ricky looked around from his laptop. He'd switched from porn to news feeds.

'Who's high?' he said dopily.

Jake came back and took his seat and they shot for first disc. Pat took that – with a clean twenty – and then the game started in earnest. At first they played cautiously: just trading discs, clearing each other. It's a funny thing, watching two people play crokinole seriously, since it's such a simple and juvenile game. But their faces were as focused and intense as two guys playing high-stakes poker. When Pat sent a disc into the gutter, and Jake sunk a twenty of his own, Mark started needling his brother about wetting the bed. You could tell the mockery irked Delaney, as did the possibility of losing to Jake.

As he lined up his next shot he said to Jake, 'You haven't asked for your money yet.'

'I figured we'd get to that.'

'You haven't forgotten, then.'

'I wouldn't forget a hundred grand.'

'Was that the deal?'

'That was the deal. The horse delivered, and a hundred grand.'

'That was the deal, Patty,' Mark said. 'I was there.'

'You shut up, you fucking amateur.'

Maria, who had been listening to the exchange, stood up from the kitchen table and wandered in to join us. She looked fairly dazed and airy-headed, and by that point I didn't know how much of it was an act put on to help us, and how much actually due to the booze.

'Are you boys okay in here?'

'Your friend was just telling me I owe him a hundred grand.'

'I said that was the deal.'

'What if I said I want to renegotiate the terms?'

'How about we finish our game, and negotiate after?'

'Ignore him, Jake,' Mark said, 'he's just trying to throw you off your game.'

Looking broody as a spoiled child, Pat finally took his next shot. The attitude didn't help his game, any. He missed that shot, and Jake countered by sliding a disc neatly into the fifteen circle. I don't think Jake was even trying (winning clearly wasn't going to do him any favours) but Pat was making it hard for him to lose. Pat's follow-up shot went wild: clipping a peg and flipping right off the board. The disc landed in my lap like a dead beetle.

Pat glared at me. 'That retard moved as I shot. He threw me off.'

'Whoa man,' I said. 'No way.'

'I saw it. You did it on purpose.'

'Pat,' Mark said. 'You're wigging out. I'm sitting right here and I didn't see it. Did you see it, Ricky?'

'I don't fucking know anything,' Ricky said, without looking over from his laptop.

'It must have been an accident, Patrick,' Maria said soothingly.

Pat was still staring me down. 'Don't sit there,' he said.

'Shit man. Okay. Calm down. I'll move over here.'

I shuffled my chair around. I had this sick, feeble feeling I get in situations like that.

'If you need to blame my brother for losing,' Jake said, 'that's pretty weak.'

'You're fucking weak.'

'Boys,' Maria said. 'Just play your game. I'll mix you all some drinks.'

She drifted into the kitchen, swaying a little as she went. I heard her opening and closing the fridge, and the glug of liquid. Then the ice cracking. As that went on Jake began lining up his next shot. His upper body was still. He looked calm. But under the table his right knee was twitching up and down. As we sat like that, with the game nearing last shot and everybody on tenterhooks, Ricky leaned forward and said, 'Holy fucking shit.'

We all looked. I could see the laptop screen from my position at the table. What I saw was video footage of a boat, and a horse, dangling in a seine net. There were two guys on deck and you could hear women giggling and catcalling to them. I looked at Jake and he looked at me.

'Well,' he said to me, 'we did only ask them to wait a couple of days.'

Pat Delaney hopped up. 'What the fuck?' he said, pointing.

'It's just something that happened,' Jake said.

'On the way down,' I added, helpfully.

Mark was giggling. Maria was standing in the doorway, her mouth open in awe and alarm, clutching two drinks. She held them out and asked, 'Anybody want a whisky sour?'

'Fuck the drinks,' Pat said. 'Put that shit on the flatscreen.'

While Rick plugged in his laptop, the rest of us gathered in front of the television. Jake yawned – as if it was all no big deal – and casually picked up his guitar from where he'd left it leaning against the wall. He perched on the arm of the sofa and twiddled with the tuning pegs, not even looking up when the footage appeared on the big screen. It was an extract of a newscast, off CBC. We'd become national news, by then. At first we couldn't hear so Ricky tapped up the audio. A severe-looking news anchor with a picket-fence hairline was talking about Shenzao, and behind him garish graphics flashed: *Stolen Racehorse*. He said that one of the thieves had been identified and that the horse had been spotted in transit, on a boat, headed for Washington State.

'The bandits claim,' he said, 'that they are doing it for altruistic reasons.'

They cut to the clip of Jake, spouting that nonsense about animal welfare and saving Shenzao from a lifetime of cruelty. He was talking right to the cameras, hamming it up, and you could tell it was him, all right. After that there were a few interviews with Kelly and her bridesmaids, who said that we were real gentlemen and called us 'charming and generous'.

The news anchor chuckled as they cut back to him. He said that one of the gentleman outlaws was thought to be Jake Harding, a known associate of the Legion gang, and anybody with information regarding the horse's whereabouts should call in (a hotline number started scrolling across the bottom of the screen). The clip ended frozen on an image of Shenzao.

In the house, it went completely quiet. Pat Delaney clutched his head and said, 'What the fuck is this shit?' He just actually couldn't believe it. His mind was completely blown. It looked as if he was trying to hold his brain inside his skull.

'We told you,' Jake said, and plucked a guitar string. 'The horse jumped overboard.'

'And we had to fish it out.'

'A hen party just happened to be there.'

'And you didn't fucking tell us?' Delaney shouted.

Jake shrugged, focused on the tuning. 'Well', he said, 'we knew you'd be pissed.'

Mark was still giggling, but it sounded slightly hysterical, now. Ricky said that the clip already had over a million hits. Novak drifted over from the door, taking up position to the left of Delaney. He had his hand in his coat pocket again. Ready for his orders.

'This screws up everything,' Pat said. 'They know who you are, and they've linked you to us. How long before they come to the ranch?'

We could all agree on that, at least: not very long at all. Maria, seeing the turn things were taking, made a last play on our behalf. She went to Pat and put one of her whisky sours in his hand and told him he needed to take it easy.

'Just calm down and have a drink, honey,' she said.

Pat, he just threw the drink at the wall, where it exploded in a burst of glass and ice.

'Would you fucking shut up about your drinks and get out of here?'

Maria scurried back to the kitchen, mouse-like, and I figured that was it.

'We're going to have to get rid of the horse. Ditch it or fucking kill it.' Pat started pacing back and forth, partially muttering, blinking and just looking completely strung out. 'We could shoot it and bury it, maybe. Out back in the woods.'

Jake stood up with his guitar. 'You're not going to kill the horse, Pat. Get real.'

Pat spun around, as if he couldn't believe Jake had spoken. He stomped over there and shoved Jake in the chest and started shouting at him: 'Get real? Fucking get real? I'm going to kill it and you and your fucking retard brother. How real is that, huh?'

Jake didn't answer. He just jabbed the headstock of the guitar into Pat's face, hard, catching him off-guard. Pat jerked back, and Jake switched his grip on the guitar and swung it, using the whole thing like a bat, smashing it over Pat's head. The wood splintered and some strings snapped and it was all awkward and messy and things just sort of snowballed from there: Mark running over, trying to get between them, and Ricky shouting coked-up gangster shit, but what really terrified me was the sight of Novak moving in, quick and predatorial, a pistol in his hand.

Nobody was paying much attention to me, and so I just ran straight at him. I don't know the first thing about fighting, but I wasn't trying to fight: I simply body-checked him from behind, totally blindsiding him, hitting him with the full force of my two hundred and ten pounds. We slammed together into the crokinole table and bounced back onto the floor and beer glasses shattered all over us and the gun skittered away across the room. It was insane. Delaney was screaming something about murdering us both and around then, in the middle of all that chaos, the lights went out.

Chapter Forty-One

MARIA HAD DONE IT. WHEN things started to turn sour she had gone straight to the switch in the kitchen and just reached up and tripped the power. It was a desperate and ingenious thing to do. Out at the ranch, there were no streetlamps or other sources of artificial light: only the houselights, and when they went out the whole place was thrown into darkness. The shouting and screaming didn't stop – it got louder and more intense. I knew Novak was somewhere in front of me and when I got up and tripped over something soft I kicked at it a few times, as hard as I could. I heard grunting, a cry of pain. Then I bumped into a different person and felt something smash into my face. A fist, I think.

'Tim!' Jake was shouting. 'Tim!'

'Jake!'

'Mark!'

'Pat!'

All us brothers were calling to each other, in our confusion and our need. Somebody – Ricky I think – started shouting about getting a flashlight or a phone or something, anything. I floundered around, fell over the sofa, cracked my head on a chair. Picking myself up, I saw the faint outline of the window, the starry night outside. I knew the door was beside that.

'Poncho!' Jake called, from near it.

I headed that way, banging my knee brutally, and en route came up against somebody. I raised my dukes, ready to throw, before Jake said my name and I knew it was him.

'We got to get out of here,' he said. 'Come on.'

The other guys kept on yelling and floundering around. You could hear Novak or Pat or one of them moaning in pain. While all that carried on Jake eased open the door and we slipped outside, where we could actually see a little better. The storm clouds had parted and a gibbous moon glowed in the sky, lighting up the porch and vehicles and, further on down, the bunkhouse and stable. We ran to the edge of the porch and jumped off together, landing hard in the snow, and got up and started sprinting.

'You got the keys to the truck?' Jake said.

'Forget the truck. There's no room. We're taking the horses.'

'The *horses*?'

'Sam's got them ready. It's all good.'

'This is fucking crazy.'

We sprinted down there in the snow, full-tilt, not dressed for the cold at all: we weren't even wearing jackets. I looked back once but so far nobody had followed us. The house was still completely dark. Amid the chaos, they possibly hadn't even figured out that we'd snuck away yet. We burned past the bunkhouse and hurtled towards the barn, panting heavily and breathing big plumes of frost-breath. My socks and the cuffs of my jeans were covered in little balls of snow, like white bobbles, and I could feel the wet cold leaching in.

At the barn we flung open the doors, and they swung wide to reveal Sam: standing there in her riding outfit – boots, jacket, tuque, gloves – and holding three sets of reins, with our horses waiting obediently behind her. All of them saddled up and ready to ride.

'Are we going?' she asked.

'You bet we're going,' I said.

'Right now,' Jake said.

She looked at us. 'What about your jackets and boots and clothes?'

'No time,' I said. 'They're coming.'

Jake was already scrambling to get on Thunder. I tried to follow suit but had some trouble mounting Old Marley. Somehow, with Sam's help, I floundered my way into the saddle. Sam handed Jake his reins, and asked him what had happened. He explained in a nutshell: 'They want to kill us and maybe the horse too, so we got to get the hell going.'

Sam didn't argue or debate that logic. She just put a foot into the stirrup and hopped up onto Shenzao, and as soon as she was sitting in that saddle she looked calm and ready.

'Okay,' Jake said, giving her the go-ahead to lead us out.

Sam turned Shenzao and trotted out through the stable door.

We crossed the drive to the paddock gate, which was already open (Sam had thought to do that ahead of time) and entered the field beyond. As we did I heard shouting, and I looked back. I could see shadows moving around out front of the bunkhouse. That's where they'd gone looking for us. They had no reason to think we'd go to the stable, or that we'd be riding out on horseback. The craziness of our plan helped some: it was so outrageous we took them completely by surprise.

'Stop!' somebody shouted. Mark, maybe. 'What the fuck are you doing?'

One of the shapes started running down towards the paddock. 'Let's give it some gas,' I said.

Sam heeled Shenzao, who loped across the field, kicking up big bursts of powder. In the moonlight it was surprisingly bright, surprisingly clear. You could see the shadows of the horses in the snow and you could see beyond the fence to the trees. Jake followed just behind Sam, hunched forward in his saddle, and I brought up the rear. Every so often I checked over my shoulder. They couldn't catch us – not on foot. By the time they got to the paddock we'd already reached the gate on the far side. Sam slid from the saddle to open it, and once we were through we could see that they'd stopped chasing after us. They'd given up.

The first fifty yards made for tough going. That part of the trail was uneven and narrow, and the trees on either side stood so close together that their branches created a canopy, blotting out the moonlight. We couldn't see as much and the dark made the horses nervy, but Sam knew the way and knew how to handle them. We just had to follow her. And once we came out onto the parks trail – the wider section that had been better maintained – we could see the way more clearly, the moon lighting up the strip of snow like a bar of ivory. From there the trail carried on in the direction we'd ridden that afternoon.

Sam held up at the junction. 'Do we keep going?'

'We got to go over the top, make it to town.'

Jake was referring to the pass we'd reached earlier. Sam looked that way, tilting her head back, gauging the challenge. The peaks up there were now laden with snow.

'I've ridden it in the snow before, but not at night.'

'Do you think we can make it?'

'Don't see why not.'

'Okay, Calamity,' he said. 'Lead the way.'

'What do we do in town?' I asked.

'Go by car, or cab – any vehicle that will get us to the boat.'

She twitched the reins and said, 'Go on,' and Shenzao shook her mane and started off up the track. Through the snow Sam set a careful but efficient pace: moving along at a steady canter. I had a strange sense of déjà vu, since we were retracing our own steps, but it was as if we'd entered an alternate world, a twilight version of where we'd been earlier that day – and it was hard to believe it had only been that day. The trees now all seemed to have shrivelled in on themselves, the branches snow-boughed and bent towards the ground. I could see the shapes of the horses and riders in front of me but the covering of snow muffled the sounds of the horses' hooves in a way it hadn't done earlier.

Within twenty minutes we'd reached the beginning of the incline up the valley, and shortly after came the series of switchbacks as the slope steepened. Beneath me Old Marley worked diligently and we made good progress. The cold, however, presented a problem. It was actually a reasonably mild night – maybe six or seven below – but it felt a lot worse, the way the two of us were attired. I at least had a hoody, but Jake didn't even have that: he only had a long-sleeved T-shirt. He huddled up in the saddle, trying to retain body heat.

'You're gonna freeze, man,' I called ahead.

Sam held up, turning Shenzao to look back.

'There's riding blankets in my saddle pack,' Sam said.

'Can you get those out, Calamity?' he asked.

She had two of them. Jake wrapped one around himself, and I got the other. We had to drape them over our shoulders, like cloaks or capes. They were woven from coarse wool, but not particularly thick. It wasn't much, considering the conditions, but it was something. Sitting there, as we waited for Sam to remount, Jake looked across at me and grinned.

'They're like ponchos, Poncho,' he said.

'You heard the news, Lefty. We're real outlaws, now.'

'What news?' Sam asked, gathering her reins.

As we rode, we explained to Sam about what had happened at the house. Talking helped. We needed the distraction. The cold got worse the higher we went, partly on account of the altitude, and partly because we were more exposed to the wind, which had real bite to it. A frosty numbness crept into my bad hand, and I had a hard time keeping a hold of the reins. I took to sort of wrapping the edges of the blanket around my palms.

We reached the point on the trail where we could see down to the ranch. The lights were back on now. But I could only make out one vehicle: the truck. Not either of the SUVs.

'They're looking for us,' I called ahead.

Jake turned in his saddle to see. 'Guess that's to be expected.'

'What do we do?'

'Hope they don't find us.'

We were safe, so long as we were in the mountains. Higher up, the snow got deeper and that slowed us down. On the final stretch leading up to the pass the snow reached the horses' knees and they had to really struggle through it. Old Marley's breathing grew ragged. That section took us twice as long as it had earlier in the day. My watch said quarter past midnight, and I figured we'd been riding for about an hour. My ass was saddle-sore and my toes stung by cold and my fingers had curled into claws. I thought they might be frostbit, and that worried me. I damn sure didn't want to lose any more digits.

Jake and I fell a little behind. Sam had to wait for us at Larch Mountain Pass, the spot we'd reached earlier in the day. From up there you could make out the lights of Elma, sparkling like a spider web stretched across the terrain to the north.

'How you holding up, Poncho?' Jake asked me.

'I'm cold, Lefty. I can't feel my hands.'

'Here,' Sam said. 'Have my gloves.'

'No way, darling.'

'I got liners. I'm fine. You're not dressed at all.'

It was true. We'd really messed that part up. Jake was visibly shuddering and his teeth were chattering and the skin of his face was white as the surrounding snow.

'Is there only the one way down?' Jake asked.

Sam shook her head. 'Three ways.' She pointed. 'One heads south, to a little town called Porter. That's maybe only forty minutes. The other drops down to the highway, and a parking lot near Elma, which me and Tim passed today. That's about an hour. The third way heads north along this ridge. It winds towards a recreation area, and comes out east of Elma.'

'How far's that?'

'That's like four hours.'

Jake shook his head. 'No way. We got to get down before we freeze.'

'What if they're waiting?' I said.

'Will they know these trails?' Jake asked her.

'Pat and Mark will.'

He looked at me. 'Elma or Porter?' I asked.

'They might expect us to go for the closest one. So Elma.'

'If we can make it without you getting hypothermia.'

'I'm okay,' he said.

'Here, Jake,' Sam said, and handed him her tuque. He accepted it, and I could tell by that just how cold he was. He fit it on his head, over his bandana, and it looked mighty odd on him: this bobble-head tuque with rainbow stripes.

'Go on, Sam,' Jake said. 'Get us to Elma.'

The route down wasn't as hard going as the route up. Instead of sharp switchbacks the trail wound back and forth more gently down the slope. The path was wide, about six feet across, and the ground was relatively even. I came up with a solution for my hands that seemed to help: I would hold the reins in one hand while tucking the other in my opposing armpit, and when the exposed hand became clumsy and useless I would switch. I also moved the blanket up over my head, instead of just draping it around my shoulders, since I remembered reading somewhere about losing all your heat through your scalp. That seemed to help, some.

'Jake,' I called.

He looked back.

'Put your blanket over your head, man. Over your head.'

It took him a few seconds to figure out what the hell I was talking about, but once he did he imitated me, so that the pair of us must have looked like poor travelling pilgrims.

From then on, we simply had to endure the cold, which was

scathing and merciless and, when the wind picked up, sliced through the flimsy defence of my blanket. In time the numb sensation in my hands spread – to my toes, my nose, my tailbone – and I no longer felt discomfort so much as a kind of dull resignation. I knew that was probably bad, but it didn't seem to matter. I'd settled into the hypnotic rhythms of the ride, and the tranquillity of the setting, so lifeless and still.

To keep from drifting off, I concentrated on Sam and Shenzao. The white of the horse against the white of the snowscape was a mesmerizing sight. My awareness of everything else faded out, and I held onto that image, that vision. Every so often Sam looked back at us and it seemed to me, the longer we went on, that each time she looked back she appeared more and more like Sandy. I think I even imagined at times that I was following Sandy. That I'd crossed over to some other place, some higher plane, and that our sister had returned on that ghost of a horse to guide us safely through, away from all our sorrows and to a better life.

The winding section of trail flattened out and became a road – one of the park's access roads, maybe – and we floated down that, moving softly and steadily over the snow. Cedar and spruce trees, feathered with hoar frost, rose up on either side like frozen angels. Every so often Sam said encouraging things like, 'Almost there,' or 'Just a little further.' She had been speaking like that for a long time so I didn't put much stock in it, and in fact had stopped listening to the specific words while still appreciating the warm sound of her voice. But then we came to a single chain stretched between two steel posts, marking the end of the trail. We had reached that parking lot she and I had seen from the highway. We were only about a mile, or less, from Elma.

I suppose, if we'd been smart (or in a state that allowed us to make smart decisions) we might have tethered the horses and crept into the trees and worked our way around, or at least scoped out the situation. But Jake and I were both on the verge of hypothermia and Sam was just happy to have led us there, to have completed the task we'd charged her with. She guided Shenzao around the obstruction and we followed obediently, as we'd been doing the entire time, and in single file our three horses stepped out into the parking lot.

We didn't see the SUV until the headlights came on.

Chapter Forty-Two

IT WAS BLOCKING THE ENTRANCE to the parking lot, but its position didn't matter. We were in no condition to turn around and flee on horseback. We could barely sit our saddles. I heard the car doors shutting and, through the glare of the headlights, I could see two shadows walking towards us like phantoms.

Jake turned to Sam.

'This is for me and Tim to deal with. If anything happens to us, and they take you back, you wait until you get the chance and just get out of there and go to the police and tell them everything you know, everything you can.'

'What's going to happen?' she asked.

'I don't know.'

He slid from his saddle, and I did the same.

'Jake,' Sam said.

He reached up and squeezed her hand, and held it. We didn't go to meet them. We waited and shuddered in the cold. Jake said, 'Can you run, Poncho?'

'I ain't going anywhere without you.'

'I'll try to do something. When I do, run.'

'Don't be stupid.'

'One of us has to make it, to take care of Sam.'

I didn't know what to say to that. I couldn't imagine them shooting us here, in the parking lot, in front of Sam. But I guess most people feel like that, before they get shot. And if it didn't happen here, it would happen back at the ranch. At the prospect of that, I didn't feel dread or terror, but more a furious frustration that we'd only just met Sam and were now being cheated of our time with her.

Jake said, 'Here we go, Poncho.'

As the figures came closer I could make them out a little better in the headlights. If it had been Mark, who was far more congenial towards us, it might have turned out differently. But it was Pat, and he had Novak with him. Both of them seemed to be walking wounded. Pat was hobbling, hunched over, as if he'd bruised or busted some ribs, and Novak was favouring his left leg. Pat held a paper towel pressed to his nose, which drizzled blood into the snow.

They stopped about five feet from us. From his coat pocket Novak pulled out his gun – a sleek black pistol – and pointed it at us. Little cuts criss-crossed his face, like razor nicks, presumably from rolling in the broken glass after I'd body-checked him.

They didn't speak right away. Their expressions were vindicated and satisfied and, quite clearly, murderous.

Pat looked from Jake, to me, and then up to where Sam sat on her horse.

'Samantha,' he said. 'Get in the car.'

'No,' she said.

'Go on, Sam,' Jake said.

Sam hesitated, then slid from the saddle reluctantly. She stood there holding the reins. Shenzao scraped the ground with a fore-hoof, anxious. The other horses seemed skittish, too. Maybe they could smell the blood, or sense the threat.

'Samantha,' Delaney said. 'You don't want to see this.'

'What are you going to do?' she asked.

Her voice broke a little as she said it. She was trying not to cry.

'You can't kill them,' she said. 'I'll tell people. I'll tell every-body. If you kill them I'll tell everybody and I'll tell them how you shot those men by the bunkhouse and you'll go to prison for a long time.'

'Shut up,' Pat said.

He grabbed her by the wrist and jerked her forward, hard, nearly pulling her off her feet. Jake made as if to go for him but Novak held the gun higher, pointing it right at Jake's face – nearly touching the tip of his nose – and so we stood as Delaney hauled and dragged Sam towards the SUV. She was screaming and crying and calling Jake's name and my name and telling Pat she hated him and begging for him to let us live, please let them live.

In reaction, Shenzao whinnied, increasingly on edge and – in her animal way – understanding that we'd landed in a dire situation. Her reins lay loose in the snow. She stomped a hind leg and pivoted around, settling into a tense, defensive pose. I don't know if Jake saw that and sensed the opportunity, or if he just thought we had a better chance with Pat over by the car.

He looked at Novak and said, 'Look at this piece of work. Him and his gun. Going to shoot us in front of a little girl, is that it? Going to kill me and my brother.'

Novak simply looked bored, and impatient. He'd been waiting for this for a while. The door to the SUV slammed and Pat started stomping back towards us and Novak asked, quite casually, 'Can I shoot them now?'

Then three things happened so rapidly that it almost seemed simultaneous: Jake leapt for the gun, the gun went off, and Shenzao kicked Novak in the head.

I say all that as if I understood what was going on, but I didn't. I heard the bang and then I saw this blur of motion, and Novak flew up and backwards, as if he'd been jerked by an invisible rope. He landed in the snow about five feet away. Jake went down, too – first to a knee, then tipping over onto his side. The gun had landed at my feet so I picked it up. I picked it up and waved it around and pointed it at Pat, who'd stopped about ten feet away.

'Come on,' I said. 'Come closer.'

He looked at me holding the gun, and looked at Novak lying there, and then just turned around and ran back towards the vehicle. Halfway to it, he passed Sam coming in the opposite direction and didn't try to stop her. He threw himself into the driver's seat and started the SUV and peeled out of the lot, churning snow. The sound of the engine dwindled to a buzz, leaving us in the quiet and the cold.

I looked at Novak once and that was enough. The side of his skull had caved inwards and his face was all swollen, the skin bulbous and puffy as a water bladder. He was dead or dying very fast. Shenzao, having performed this execution, stood calmly and patiently next to me. The other two horses had taken fright and scattered to opposite corners of the lot.

Sam ran to where Jake had fallen and sat and cradled his head. I knelt down there with her. Jake's eyes were open and he seemed lucid, but underneath him a patch of red was spreading slowly through the snow.

'Are you guys all right?' he said to me. 'Is Sam all right?'

'You saved us, brother. It's going to be okay.'

'Where's Novak?'

'Shenzao killed that bastard.'

'Good girl.'

All the while I was checking him over, trying to find the wound. It seemed to be in his stomach, right in his guts. I pulled up his shirt, which was soaked through, and saw the hole and the blood bubbling out. I covered it with my hands automatically. The blood felt so hot, almost scalding, and there was so much of it. Where it had run down into the snow, the snow had melted from the warmth, turning to pink slush.

'He shot you,' I said dully, still not quite believing it.

'I'm all fucking numb.'

'You're just cold,' Sam said. 'You'll be fine. He'll be fine, right?'

She was asking me, and I said that he would be (even though I had no idea) and I did several strange things in quick succession, most of which were only vague notions that I no doubt had picked up from films or television. First I grabbed desperate fistfuls of loose snow and packed that all over his belly. I thought the cold might help. Then I took Jake's bandana off, bunched it into a ball, and stuffed that right in the bullet hole, which made Jake scream. Lastly I removed my belt, strapped that around his midriff, and cinched it tight. He cried out again and his eyes rolled back and I thought he might be on the verge of passing out.

'Tim,' he said remotely, 'am I fucking dying? Is that what this is?'

'You're not dying.'

'You're going to live,' Sam said.

'That's right. You're going to live.'

She and I said that over and over, like a prayer we could make true through repetition, as I stooped down and got an arm beneath his neck and another beneath his knees, and then I lifted my little brother up from the blood-covered snow. He writhed and screamed from the pain, which was a horrible thing to hear.

'Sam,' I said. 'Get on the horse. Get on Shenzao.'

She didn't ask why. She just did it, fast. I hoisted Jake and eased him over the saddle – so he was draped in front of her, between her knees and the pommel.

'Now listen,' I said to her. 'You're only a mile from that medical centre. The one where your mom gets her methadone. You ride there now, down the highway, as fast as you can – as fast as you've ever done. Just don't stop and keep going. Do you understand?'

'I get it, I get it,' she said impatiently. 'Just step back. Get out of my way.'

And I let go of my brother and stepped back. I think he was unconscious by then. Sam heeled Shenzao and shouted, 'Ha!' and together the three of them just flew, across the parking lot and out onto the highway, moving dreamily, the hoofbeats muted by the snow.

'That's your dad,' I called after her. 'That's your dad!'

In the darkness the horse stood out longest, floating away into the night, while I was left beside a dead man and a puddle of my brother's cooling blood.

Chapter Forty-Three

WHEN I ARRIVED AT THE medical centre, lumbering along on Old Marley with Thunder in tow, I saw Shenzao standing out front, beneath the awning. Sam had tethered her to the bike rack, using it like a hitching post. I did the same thing with the other two horses. As I slid down from the saddle the doors opened and somebody rushed out: a short and stocky woman, dressed in a pale blue uniform. An orderly or nurse of some sort.

'What is this?' she said. 'Are you part of the same incident?'

'Not an incident,' I said, struggling with the words. 'A shooting.'

'That's what I meant.'

I nodded, still huddled up in my blanket.

'Come on in,' she said, leading me towards the doors. 'You're freezing.'

As soon as I hit the warmth of the foyer I started shaking uncontrollably. The man at the front desk sat upright and stared at me in alarm. The orderly tried to guide me towards a chair but I wouldn't sit: I demanded to know where they'd taken Jake, the person who'd been shot. The desk clerk wanted ID, wanted to know who I was, and I just started babbling that I was his brother and I needed to be with him, and the girl who'd come with him.

The orderly directed me to the emergency ward. I shuffled in that direction, with her following me warily. My joints felt stiff and my feet were clunky as clogs, still half-frozen. In my hands I had no feeling at all. We went down one corridor and under a sign and turned left, through a set of swinging double doors. On the other side of the doors was Sam. She had blood all over her hands and jacket and I suppose I must have been covered in it too. She looked completely stunned, frightened as a doe. Seeing that, I thought it was done: Jake was gone. But Sam told me that they were operating on him – they were trying to save him. She pointed to a room with blinded windows and I understood it was all happening in there.

I stood and stared dully at the door to the room, reeling, still half-frozen and feeling partially separated from my body. The smells, the scene, the late-night eeriness: I'd been there before, but it was reversed. Jake had taken Sandy's place, and I was waiting out here with her. It was what he'd always wanted. Anybody but her, he'd said. Me, him, anybody.

Sam must have seen the utter dread in my face, the horror at the thought of it, because she broke down and started sobbing and trying to tell me something. She fell against me and I held her for a long time before I made out what she was saying: 'I rode as fast as I could. I got here as fast as I could.' I had put all that on her. I had put his life in her hands, which had been a terrible and no-good thing to do, but I hadn't had a choice. Or so I told myself.

We stood together with the weight of that knowledge between us for thirty minutes. Then the door to that room – the operating room – opened and a doctor came out: a stooped, older woman with dark curly hair. She asked us to confirm our relationship to Jake and I said that we were his family, and she instructed us to sit down and once we had she told us what we needed to know.

Later we were allowed to see him. He lay in the bed, peaceful and pale and still, like one of those marble sculptures you see on tombs. The machines around him hummed with electronic life and the whole atmosphere felt subaquatic, and that, too, stirred up my memories of Sandy and the night we'd lost her.

I walked over to the side of the bed and Sam circled around to the other. My fingers had started stinging as the circulation came back into them, and I felt this most of all in my bad hand, which I placed clumsily over Jake's open palm. He was breathing very shallowly – almost imperceptibly – but he was breathing. At my touch his eyes flickered open.

'Poncho,' he said.

He managed to roll his head. Sam pawed away tears, and smiled hopefully.

'And Calamity.'

'We're both here.'

'Did they tell you?' he asked.

'Your legs.'

'Well, half dead is better than all dead.'

He sighed, settled, and closed his eyes. We stood with him for a time. Then, when I stepped back, I tripped over his damned heart monitor and pulled the wiring off him and the machine started flatlining, and for a second I actually thought I'd killed him until the orderly ran in and affixed those little suckers to his stomach again and assured me he was still alive.

'But maybe you should sit down,' she said.

'I think I better.'

'I'll get you some soup, warm you up.'

As she went off, Sam and I sat in the chairs next to Jake. From our position we could see out the window to the entrance, where we'd tethered the horses. Old Marley and Thunder were on either side of Shenzao. They were all three standing quietly. It had started snowing again – lightly sprinkling flakes, like angel dust. It swept through the ochre glow of the lamp in the clinic's drive. The whole scene looked as peaceful as the backdrop in a snow globe.

Chapter Forty-Four

I TURNED INTO THE MOBILE home park, which they called Ridgeview, seeing as it perches on a hillside outside of Hope, overlooking the town. It's a decent enough place, and each trailer has its own patch of artificial turf. Most of the community are older folk, just past retirement age, and decorate their plots with assorted lawn ornaments: gnomes and windmills and bird baths and whatnot.

It was eight in the morning but the day was already looking to be a scorcher: hazy blue skies, temperature in the mid-twenties and climbing, and that sea-heavy humidity you only get near the coast. I parked Jake's truck in front of their place – a sizeable double-wide – and the door banged open and Sam came sprinting out. She's a few inches taller, now, and only has one more year before she starts high school. Whether that will be out in Hope, or in the city, now that things are safer, is something that hasn't quite been decided.

'Poncho!' she yelled. 'You're late, you goddamn cracker!'

Her grandma came to the door to see her off. Maria's mother is round and soft as a big old pierogi, and she wagged a plump finger after her granddaughter, chastising her.

'Language, Samantha! Some young lady you are.'

Sam didn't apologize, so I did for her, as if that was all my fault. And maybe it was – the no-good Harding blood she had in her. I waved and Maria's mother waved back. She and I, we get along just fine. I promised her I'd have Sam home for bedtime, as usual.

As I backed out of the drive, Sam asked, 'What's the plan, Poncho?'

Sam's window was down and she rested her elbow on the sill, peering at the world through her shades: an oversize pair of Ray-Bans Jake had bought for her birthday.

I said, 'You look like a narc in those glasses.'

She grinned and mimed pointing a gun at me. 'Tell me the plan, or you're busted.'

I laid it all out for her: two of our usual stops, and then a surprise.

'What surprise?' she said.

'You'll see.'

She tried threatening me with her fake gun again, but I wasn't having any of it.

'A surprise is a surprise,' I said.

To make it out there to pick up Sam by eight, I've got to be on the go by six, since it's about an hour and a half from Vancouver to Hope, if you put the pedal down. But I rise at that hour most days, and our Sunday road trip (that's what she calls it) is the highlight of my week. I know that pretty soon Sam will most likely grow tired of spending time with me, in the way that teenagers do. She'll have parties to go to, or friends to see, or homework to do. I'll be consigned to another part of her life, a less important part. But for now, this is what we've got, and we have the damnedest time, trucking back together towards Vancouver.

On the way in, to reach the North Shore, we usually take the Trans-Canada straight to the Second Narrows Bridge. That day I had a pick-up to make for work, so we took a detour along Main, and ended up at the waterfront before swinging east. The route led us past the Westco plant, and it pained me something fierce to see the old place. I looked for the *Western Lady* in her berth, but the boat wasn't moored up. It being August, and salmon season, I presumed they were already out at sea, waiting for the fisheries window to open.

'That's where you used to work, right?' Sam asked.

She gestured to the cluster of docks, zigzagging across the placid waters of the boatyard. A few gulls floated above the plant, and I could smell the fish-stink from afar.

'Yes ma'am,' I said.

That's all it is, now: a place I used to work. I haven't been asked back, and I won't be. Albert might have forgiven me for jumping ship, with time and coaxing from Tracy, but he wouldn't ever forgive what I'd done to his boat – no way, no how. During the trial, he lied and said he'd agreed to let me use it, not knowing my intention to help my brother transport an animal with it, and I suppose I ought to be grateful for that: it spared me jail time (along with Jake's testimony that I hadn't been his accomplice at the stables) but still it grieves me to think of the wrong I've done them, for which Albert will allow no amends. I mailed him a cheque to help with the repairs, but it was never cashed, never used.

I talked to Tracy a few times, and even met up with her, but we didn't get back to where we had been. I guess she figured it wasn't worth crossing her old man for, and I'm prone to agree. The hard-hearted stance hurt me at first, until I realized it simply meant Jake was right: I wasn't quite family, to them. At least not in the way I am to Jake. And Sam, now.

As she and I headed west on Powell, the plant and boatyard fell away out of sight. And when we reached the Second Narrows Bridge, with that view of the North Shore mountains – some of them still capped with snow, even in summer – I felt a lightening, as if we were lifting off, the two of us, and taking flight.

When Ma opened the door, her face lit up with this beatific expression: pure and unbridled blissfulness. She didn't have her shower cap on, though she was wearing a pair of large and obviously mismatched earrings: one a golden hoop, the other a carved wooden cross, in the Celtic style. It's a new habit she's developed of late. Sam predicts it could become a trend.

Ma beamed at us and said, 'Kids – come on in.'

She ushered Sam and I down the hall to the kitchen. On the table sat a box of Tim Hortons' doughnuts, next to a steaming pot of coffee and three mugs: she had remembered we were coming. Her memory, well, it ain't half bad these days. She has her good spells and bad spells, but there are more good than bad, and the people at her care company believe she's had a turn for the better (that was the phrase they used).

'Sit, sit, sit,' she urged us. 'We have so much to talk about.'

She doled out the doughnuts, poured the coffee, tapped a cigarette from her pack, and lit it with shaky fingers. I'd hazard that wasn't from the nicotine need, so much as the elation.

'How are you two? How *are* you?'

'We're great, Ma.'

'We sure are,' Sam said. 'We're on our way to see Jake.'

'Poor Jake,' she said.

'He's doing okay, in there.'

I can't quite tell if Ma knows he has gone back to jail, or if she thinks he's in there for the first time, all over again. But she's lucid enough to grasp that's where he is, and on some days I even take her over for a visit.

'And how's *your* work, Timmy?'

'It's good, Ma. It's fine. It's a job.'

I'm working cutting lawns, and doing landscaping – at least for the summer. What my long-term plans are is anybody's guess. But it keeps me afloat, and helps pay her bills.

'That's wonderful, Tim,' said Ma.

But really her interest in my lawn-cutting career was a courtesy. She took a sip of coffee and placed it deliberately on the table and turned her full attention to Sam.

'Now Samantha,' she said, 'tell me how my favourite grand-child is.'

'I'm your only grandchild, Grandma.'

'Don't you think I know that?'

And she sat back and let Sam regale her with every detail of her life: how her hockey team was doing, the movie she'd seen on Tuesday, whether she intended to come down to the city for high school, and heck, even what she'd eaten for breakfast. And Sam, as ever, was happy to oblige.

The first time I brought Sam out, I thought Ma might have a

heart attack, out of shock or joy or what have you. And she damn near did. But the jolt seemed to rejig some part of her brain – the part that got wiped out after Sandy died. And since that one occasion, she's never again mistaken Sam for her daughter. She still doesn't talk about Sandy much, but she's no longer living in some fantasy realm, where her only daughter is still alive.

'And what about the fighting?' Ma said. 'Is that settling down?'

There'd been a few incidents, upon Sam transferring to Hope. We were infamous by then and Sam, she didn't take kindly to people making snide remarks about her family.

'A bit,' Sam said. 'One girl called Jake a cripple, so I hit her.'

'Good. I hope you knocked her block off.'

'Jesus, Ma,' I said.

'Well,' she said stoutly, 'that is a nasty thing to say about your brother.'

It was getting near on time to go, and I broke it to Ma as gently as I could.

'Oh,' she said. 'So soon?'

'We'll be back, Grandma.'

Then Ma perked up and said, 'Wait! I almost forgot.'

She pushed herself up and shuffled out of the room, into the kitchen. I heard the microwave in there, and couldn't figure out what the hell she was doing – until she came back in, holding a microwaveable burrito, steaming in its plastic wrapping.

'Take this for the road,' she said, grandly.

Sam ate the burrito on our way to the Fraser Regional Correctional Centre, the place out in Maple Ridge where they're keeping Jake. He was arrested in America but due to the main charge – the theft – having taken place in Canada they allowed him to be extradited and tried back home. The only crime he'd committed in the States was a smuggling one, and despite the bizarre nature of the offence, smuggling an animal isn't nearly as serious as drugs, or even alcohol or cigarettes: such are the ways of the law. For his crimes, he was given four and a half years, but with good behaviour there's the chance he'll only serve three.

They put him in the minimum security wing on account of his disability. At first that was crucial, since it kept him separated from the actual criminals, including the Legion and the Delaneys' boys, but that's not as much of an issue now. Shortly before the trials, another drive-by occurred in front of the Delaney house on Upper Lonsdale. Pat Delaney was getting out of his SUV – that big Durango – and was shot and killed. He'd been wearing his bullet-proof vest but that didn't save him. Whether the other gangs had simply had enough of his antics, or whether the kidnapping of the horse had been the last straw, I can't rightly say. It meant that Jake could claim Pat had been his accomplice all along, and the one who'd stolen the horse with him – since Pat wasn't around to say otherwise I'd merely been coerced into the transportation of it.

A few months later, Mark was arrested and is currently awaiting trial for drugs trafficking. What with that, and the death of Novak, the Legion is in freefall, and it doesn't look as if there will be any repercussions for Jake's own role in the kidnapping of Shenzao.

All the same, Jake's glad to be where he is.

I wheeled into the visitors' entrance, parked up, and Sam and I hopped out together. In the sun, on a bright summer day, the place didn't look like a prison, lacking as it did any guard towers or gun turrets or barbed wire. It consisted of one long central block and a series of outbuildings, all built from beige brick and lined with tidy turquoise trim. It looked more like a further education college or community centre.

'Ready for your surprise?' I asked Sam.

'I thought the surprise came after the usual stops.'

'It does. But it starts here.'

We were accustomed to going through the visitors' entrance, checking in at reception, and walking down a long corridor to a room where Jake could meet us – and either chat to us there, or join us in the yard.

But that day, as we entered, he was sitting in his chair just inside the doors.

'Jake!' Sam said, and ran to him.

He hugged her and held her, leaning forward to do so.

'They gave me a day pass,' he said. 'I get to fly the coop.'

He looked past her, to me, and I went up and crouched down and gave him a big hug, too. I still ain't gotten used to it – seeing him in that chair – and I don't reckon I ever will. He himself rarely mentions it, and when he does it is without bitterness or regret, but more with a sense of stoicism, as you might refer to an unavoidable accident, or natural disaster.

'You ready to ride, partners?'

'Hell yeah,' Sam said. 'You want a push?'

'I got it.'

He wheeled himself towards the door, with us on either side.

'Tim tell you we got a surprise for you?'

'I thought this *was* the surprise.'

'This ain't the half of it, Calamity.'

Then, as we came out the doors and he rolled into the sunshine, he stopped himself and tilted his head back, closing his eyes, just soaking up all that warmth and freedom.

Sam must have begun to suspect, when we drove her out to Castle Meadow, but Jake – he played it pretty cool. He's a damned good liar and always has been (I should know) and he told her we just intended to spend an afternoon out there, watching the horses train, having lunch and enjoying some time together.

'Oh,' she said, cautiously. 'Okay.'

But when I parked up, instead of heading towards the clubhouse, we took her on over to the stables. Jake said he wanted to show her where he used to work, and how we'd stolen Shenzao. He distracted her with the story of that night as we passed between the stalls, with Sam steering his wheelchair left and right to avoid piles of manure. In the daylight the place looked cheerfully rundown, and it's hard now to imagine Shenzao being kept there: she's gone on to the real races, at Hastings Park, and wins more often than not. Which means we win too, since we always bet on her.

In the middle of the stables, and his story, Jake got Sam to stop in front of the stall we'd chosen, and with a big gesture of his hand he told her, 'And this here is the very stall.'

Sam looked. Inside stood a brown gelding, with a splash of white on its forehead. It regarded her bashfully, and she looked from it to us, puzzled.

'The stall you stole Shenzao from?' she asked.

'And the one you'll keep your horse in,' he said.

'That horse there, as a matter of fact,' I added.

I expected her to maybe shriek, or squeal, or do any of the kinds of things that a young girl is prone to do. But Sam, she just up and shouted, at the top of her lungs, so it echoed throughout the stables: 'Are you fucking *kidding* me?'

Then she whooped and tried to hug us both at the same time, and nearly tipped over Jake's wheelchair.

It goes without saying that we never saw a cent of the hundred grand we'd been promised by the Delaneys, but in the end we came into some money by other means. Those video clips of us online shot up in popularity during Jake's trial, and the ladies from the hen party started turning a tidy profit through ad revenue. It wasn't a fortune but it wasn't peanuts, either, and the gals were kind enough to cut us in on it. Some of it went towards Sam's horse, and some to getting Jake a laptop and microphone to record his music. They let him do that, inside.

'You laying down any new material?' I asked him.

We were sitting on the clubhouse patio, looking out at the training paddock, nursing a couple of cold Molsons. Sam had stayed in the stable, to get her horse saddled up.

'Some,' he said.

'You should put together an album.'

'I got a bunch of tracks, but they need shaping.'

'The ones I heard sound ready to go.'

'You're tone-deaf.'

'Don't wait too long. You got to cash in on your popularity.'

What with the trial, and being shot, Jake's got something of a cult following, due in part to a website set up by that girl – the shop clerk we met in Roche Harbor. She's even started a campaign to grant Jake early parole, which is as hopeless as it is endearing.

'I need you to break big,' I said. 'I can't cut lawns forever.'

'You want your vegetable farm.'

'Damn straight. The fat of the land, remember?'

A horse came trotting out of the stables, and we both leaned forward, but it wasn't Sam. As we settled back, Jake asked about Maria, and if I'd seen her lately. I told him I'd seen her in passing a few times, out at Sam's grandma's. She's moved back to Vancouver, and has a new boyfriend: an accountant she met online, who has a stutter, a Ferrari, and an apartment in Yaletown. Sam thinks he's square (another of her *Archie* comic insults) but

I get on with him all right. It's a step up, I suppose, and he's been good for Maria.

'The last time,' I said, 'she said she'd been thinking of checking into a clinic.'

'You reckon she's serious?'

'I hope so.'

'Ah well,' Jake said.

'She come to visit you?'

'No,' he said. 'She hasn't yet.'

'She'll get around to it.'

'If she does it'll be just that: a visit.'

'If it makes you feel any better, Tracy's dropped me, too.'

'So we're both lonely losers who didn't get the girl.'

'We got the one that mattered, I guess.'

'Or she got us.'

'Hey,' I said, leaning forward, 'that's her there.'

A brown gelding was coming around the enclosure. I could tell from a distance the rider was Sam: she had that confident poise, a sense of dauntlessness, just like her aunt. And of course, on her first lap she was already going hell bent for leather, and far faster than was safe. Jake hollered out, telling her to slow down, but she tore right past us in a low crouch.

'Jesus Christ,' Jake said, and gulped his beer, 'she's crazier than me.'

'She takes after her dad, all right.'

It sounded right, calling him that. The other possibility, well, it's just never come up. It's clear enough whose daughter Sam is, and whose she needs to be. We watched her hurtle away from us, down to the far end of the paddock, and then circle back, overtaking a slower rider. Both Jake and I stood up to watch, anxious and fretful and worrisome in a way that's already becoming far too familiar around her, and will no doubt only worsen with the years. And as we watched her go around and around, faster than a carousel, I gripped my bad hand with my good, telling myself over and over that I had to let her grow, that I had to let her live.

Acknowledgements

Many thanks to all the people who have contributed to the development of this story: Annie, Becky, Fraser, Hannah, Holly, Jonny, Naomi, Malachy, Marilyn, Mike, Rhian, and Richard.

Thanks as well to Mr Bruce Springsteen for the permission to quote from 'Highway Patrolman', Golden Castle Riding Stables for teaching a tenderfoot how to saddle up, and Stiwdio Maelor for providing a quiet place to work on the manuscript.

About the Author

TYLER KEEVIL GREW UP IN Vancouver and in his mid-twenties moved to Wales. He is the author of three previous books and has received a number of awards for his writing, including the *Missouri Review*'s Jeffrey E. Smith Editors' Prize, the Wales Book of the Year People's Prize and The Writers' Trust of Canada/McClelland & Stewart Journey Prize. He lectures in Creative Writing at Cardiff University.